frozen

frozen

Richard Burke

ORION

First published in Great Britain in 2003 by Orion Books
an imprint of The Orion Publishing Group
Orion House, 5 Upper St Martin's Lane, London WC2H 9EA

A CIP catalogue record for this book is
available from the British Library

ISBN (hardback) 0 75284 767 3
ISBN (trade paperback) 0 75285 768 1

Typeset by Deltatype Ltd,
Birkenhead, Merseyside

Printed and bound in Great Britain by
Clays Ltd. St Ives plc.

This book is for Valerie, who believed.

My thanks to Wayne Brookes, Christine Gilder, Hanegraaf, Victoria Hipps, and George Lawson for their comments on earlier drafts of this book. Without their encouragement, it would never have reached publication. The insights of my editor, Kate Mills, have been invaluable; she has the uncanny knack of seeing more in what I have written than I thought was there. Two of my school teachers, Stephen Sleigh and Simon Taylor, inspired me to explore the power of words: it's good to be able to thank them at last. My thanks also to Euan Thorneycroft, for putting the deal together. Finally, and most importantly, I would like to thank Valerie and Daniel for their support, their patience and their love.

verity

Sometimes they come, sometimes they spin it. When the hoop spins, the pictures move –
   – and I am alive again.

Spin it and –
   – yes. There, yes.
   – a girl in the sunlight, a leap, a joyous scream. And later – later, screams again: yes, screaming, pressing in, and the darkness –
   – and it stops.

Wall.
   Window.
   Wall.
   They come again, it spins again –
   – and, oh, but the summer was endless, and swifts screamed, and the chest-high grass, and the warm boards of the treehouse under me, and the games, and the waiting—

Window.
   Wall.
   Shadows moving. Voices.
   It spins—
   It spins and –
   – and later he will come to me, and we will lie together, and the moon will turn the clouds to quicksilver, and the leaves will stir and whisper to each other –
   – and we will kiss.

I

And then I will slap him, and run home in the moonlight, laughing.

harry

Begin at the beginning, if you want to. But, frankly, it would make as much sense to start anywhere. Perhaps it makes no sense wherever you start.

Why did Verity end up drooling at the walls in a hospital, with the nurses occasionally spinning her beloved zoetrope, and she herself blank and saying nothing? Why did I lose her all those years ago, and why have I lost her again now? Perhaps the answer is, that's who she always was, just as I am simply me. We can't help it. Call it destiny, call it justice, call it life: does it really matter? It all happened and I can't unmake it. The same questions go round and round for me: cause, effect, cause – and I'm back where I started. So begin where you want to.

You could even say that it began with those photographs, with an impossible, wild idea that Verity, being Verity, made happen – and I couldn't prove you wrong. She realised that if you took lots of photographs, all of the same thing, all at the same time, all from different angles, then the shots would make up a three-dimensional picture. You would see a single moment of time, but from every perspective. It was brilliant. It was mad. It was wonderful – and it worked. In many ways, I wish it had remained a fantasy – but then I wouldn't be here, would I? Verity would still be Verity, and I'd be someone else entirely.

It all connects, you see. It was just a piece of fun, but it has haunted us ever since. I could have said no, we all could have, but the madness of it swept us along – and so the wheel began to turn.

That was only one of many beginnings – and, anyway, it's done.

3

And here we all are – well, some of us. And you must be wondering who I am and what I'm on about. I'll tell you.

My name is Harry and, if it's all the same to you, I'll begin my story at another beginning, another of the moments scattered through my life when, for me, it all started.

I'll begin with Verity's fall.

one

I wasn't there.

I heard about it the next day, and by then it was far too late. But, as I said, perhaps the idea that we can change things is only a comforting illusion, perhaps I couldn't have stopped it even if I'd been there or even if she'd told me what was going on beforehand.

I wasn't there when she fell two hundred and twenty feet through the air from the cliffs near England's most famous suicide spot – she hadn't even made it to Beachy Head, just to a lower spot nearby. I didn't see her crack her shoulder and the side of her face on a chalky outcrop half-way down. I wasn't on the stony beach another fifty feet below to see her crunch into the loose flint with little more sound than a footstep. I didn't wait with her as she lay misshapen and unconscious on the shingle, her body cooling and her life ebbing with the retreating tide. (If the tide had been coming in, the sea would have taken her; sometimes I wish it had.) It wasn't me who found her half an hour after her fall; it wasn't me who called the police. I didn't witness the rescue: not the helicopter that picked her up from the rocks, its blades sweeping perilously close to the cliffs; not the frantic rush of the gurney across the helipad; not the clipped, urgent voices of the men and women who struggled to save her – and succeeded. It seems unfair that these ghosts haunt me, because they are not my own. But perhaps that's why they do: Verity needed me, and I wasn't there.

I was eighty miles away, sitting in Jim's in London, wondering where the hell she had got to.

Jim's is a pub, hidden in a narrow side-street a few blocks off the unfashionable (and therefore, in Verity's perverse reasoning, trendy) end of Battersea. It's not actually called Jim's, it's the Dog and Duck, but it's in one of those areas that prides itself on having a village atmosphere: everyone is supposed to know everyone else. The Dog and Duck's landlord is Jim, so Jim's it is.

The area is comfortably middle class but has retained a suggestion of grime and roughness, which Verity loved. The streets smelt of the leather interiors of open-topped cars, of perfume and the expensive cigarettes of the chattering classes, but Verity detected an old, faint whiff of the gutter in the mix. She liked to say that the thrill of living there was the feeling that anything might happen to you if you walked up the wrong street. Alongside the successful thirty-year-olds who were something in the City or insurance or the media, there were garage mechanics made good and older men and women who were well-off from letting out houses they had bought thirty years before for a few grand. Now, the original natives served to add a little spice and the odd scandal to the newcomers' too-tame lives. Verity adored it all. She always said that the common touch was essential in her job. She needed real people about her, an antidote to the pseudery of the fashion world. Jim's quickly became the centre of her life – and therefore of mine.

I always felt a little out of place there, but she never noticed and I never told her. We met there every second week on Wednesdays (Thursdays, Fridays and the weekends were 'hot nights' when Verity might get lucky: she didn't want me anywhere near her). Seven thirty on the dot, with her always twenty minutes late, table in the corner by the fireplace under the mounted shove-ha'penny board; first one there (always me) to line up the drinks, a pint of Kronenbourg for me and a tequila for Verity with a Pils chaser (it was a dead rough area, honest); last person to need a piss chose the restaurant. But the twenty minutes before she arrived were always uncomfortable. The place would be quiet, only four or five people in there, a couple playing pool, the others hunched over the bar exchanging silences. Every time I stood at the bar and ordered the drinks, Jim would stare through me for an uncomfortable moment, and the silence of the other drinkers suddenly seemed less companionable.

I might have been imagining it. I have never been entirely at ease with myself. I think of myself as clumsy, affable, mildly inept, likeable, in an amusing way, but charming, confident, magnetic, these things I am not. If I had been, then perhaps I wouldn't have waited for two hours and four pints (plus one tequila and a Pils lined up and waiting) before I finally decided I'd been stood up.

I'd phoned her every half an hour or so, ringing off just before I had to leave a message, because it was embarrassing in an otherwise silent pub. No reply. Eventually my battery gave out. So I'd made excuses for her. She was on her way. She'd been late from the studio but she'd lost her mobile so she couldn't ring. She was caught in traffic. By my third call, the excuses were getting strained. She was still at the studio, but stuck on the phone, sourcing fabric she could only get from Brazil perhaps. She'd lost my mobile number, she didn't have Jim's, she couldn't ring.

That night, as during all twenty-plus of the years I'd known her, there was a small whisper inside me that I very much did not want to hear. She'd forgotten me, she didn't want to see me. She never had. Not ever. She hadn't noticed that she was supposed to be with me, she was off with someone else, having *fun*.

The police say she fell at eight thirty, give or take half an hour. Alone.

I sat drinking and trying to look at ease, as though it was the most normal thing in the world for me to be there – which, on alternate Wednesdays, it was. I started on fantasies of what would happen when she arrived. Righteous and sarcastic anger was top of the list, along the lines of 'Oh, never mind me, I mean how could I *possibly* be upset? Sitting in a strange pub being stared at for hours on end is what I *like* to do with my evenings.' But I never could stay angry with Verity. She knew I'd forgive her and I knew it too. So I moved on quickly to reconciliation. She'd rush in, she'd be so concerned. 'Harry, sweets, what can I say? Nightmare at work.' Down goes the tequila and a slug of the Pils. 'Mmm. Lifesaver. Look, I'll make it up to you. Let's go back to mine, have a takeaway. More relaxing, yes? Only promise me, you're not angry, are you? Forgive?' She widens her wounded eyes, looks so fearful and expectant. I laugh masterfully and reach for the remains of my pint. She puts a dainty palm over the top of my glass and presses it back on to the table. 'Let's go now,' she whispers. Then she links arms with me and chatters gaily, without stopping, all the way to her flat. What happens later in this particular scenario I'll leave to your imagination, and to mine. It kept me going for most of a pint, but then reality crept back to sit at my table. My glass was empty and there was no point in getting another: she wasn't coming. I dumped it on the counter, muttered a thank-you to Jim and left, imagining that behind me the joyless place would immediately burst into life.

I couldn't believe that she had stood me up. I was hardly blind to her faults, but I also knew *her*. She was generous (sometimes), thoughtful (likewise), energetic and enthusiastic, half mad, inspirational. Loyal. There were people she would drop without a moment's notice, but not me. We were part of each other's lives. She'd have rung at the very least. Surely. She was my friend. Of course, that line of reasoning didn't stop me brooding. It takes more than reasoning to banish self-doubt – a truth Verity frequently had to remind me of.

'*I* love you, Harry,' she'd say. 'I do. You *know* I do. Lots of people love you.' She would lean forward to reach my hand and the soft darkness of her cleavage would tug at my eyes. '*I* love you. And you'll find someone, you'll see.'

Of course I couldn't ever tell her the truth. Instead, I would stare into her face, narrow with large brown eyes that could drip sincerity or glow with mischief in a blink. Her complexion was olive-pale, her skin flawless. Her mouth was a little too large for her face, so generous. Her lips were full, wide and parted; her teeth were fine and delicate, and the front two were broad and flat enough to give the impression that she was caressing them with her lower lip. And her hand, absently stroking mine where it lay unresisting on the tablecloth, carelessly familiar, told me as always that what she meant was not what I secretly hoped, not at all. In the low, late light of whichever restaurant we'd chosen that week she would let her eyes melt and crease slightly with friendship and naughtiness, and she would say it again: '*I* love you Harry.'

And love me she did, in her own dizzy way – she *did* love me, and she would never have stood me up, not ever.

I rang her from a phone box opposite the pub. It smelt of stale breath, piss and failure. There was no reply from her mobile. After two rings on her home number, a machine kicked in. 'Hi-i-i-i-i, this is Verity.' Her voice was a rushed drawl, the words fast but relaxed, the syllables drawn out breathily. 'Hi . . . Look, I'm not answering

8

the phone. Obviously, so . . . Leave a li'l message and I'll get back. G'bye, y'all.' Her giggle was cut short by a high beep.

They were the last words I heard her say.

'Where were you?' I mumbled sulkily. I paused for a moment, thinking what else to add, then I put the phone down, feeling helpless and rather silly. I wanted her to know that I hurt. I wanted her to feel remorse. If she didn't feel guilty – *she didn't care, she hadn't even tried to ring* – then I had just made a fool of myself. Poor little Harry, clinging to Verity's coat-tails. Sad, hopeful, dependent, dependable Harry. Well, alcohol does that to you. So does rejection.

But however much I hurt, her injuries were worse. She couldn't feel them because she was unconscious. She was on her way to hospital, a tube pumping air down her throat, her crumpled skull gripped tight against a head-brace, her hair leaving fine blood-smears on the orange plastic.

And I wasn't there.

two

'You all right, Harry?' Adam glanced over at me, frowning, then turned his gaze back to the motorway. It was the fifth time he had asked me. But it's hard making conversation with someone in shock, and I was grateful for his attempts, however clumsy.

'Not really, Ads,' I mumbled. 'Thanks for being here.'

'Anything. You know that.'

Thank goodness for friends.

I had rung Adam at seven thirty that morning. There was no reply from his home, but I caught him on his mobile. He was in Manchester, part-way through a complex, high-profile court case of the sort he normally killed for. Within five minutes of my call he had cancelled several meetings and had passed over his entire court brief to one of his juniors. He promised he would be with me before noon, and he was as good as his word. This was important: I should explain that Adam was ambitious, both as a barrister and as a politician – a day off work was a big sacrifice. He was even doing all the driving, although that might not have been charity, perhaps more to do with his preference for his huge BMW over my beaten-up Renault 5.

We were on our way to Eastbourne General Hospital, where Verity lay unconscious in intensive care.

Adam glanced over at me and smiled gently. He set his shoulders firmly, his hands square on the wheel, as though his grip could squeeze an extra few minutes from our journey.

I was numb. Horror takes time to sink in.

I was nervous too: I didn't know what to expect. It's not an experience I can easily describe. There was only one thing I could think of, but I knew nothing about it so I couldn't really think, and my mind spun, round and round. I picked out strange rhythms in the ticks of the air-conditioning and the sighs of passing cars: *let it be over, let it not be, let it be over, let it not be . . .*

The telephone had woken me at seven thirty. I had taken my time answering, because I knew who it was: Verity, ringing to apologise. The last person I had expected was Gabriel, her father. We only ever spoke when I went up to Oxford to see Mum, which was rare, these days. He'd never phoned me before, which meant it could only be bad news. Adrenaline lurched in the pit of my chest. I'm not sure I was shocked when he told me, though: not then. These things never seem to hit in one overwhelming blow. The information dribbles in, one tiny ripple at a time. It is only later that you realise you are lost and struggling. I had already known something was wrong: I had known the night before when Verity wasn't at Jim's. By the time he rang, all that remained were the details – and you know most of those already.

On Wednesday evening, between the hours of eight and nine, Verity Patience Charlotte Hadley fell two hundred and twenty-four feet from the clifftops near Beachy Head in Sussex, striking the cliffs once during her descent. She was discovered at nine fifteen by David Curzon, an unmarried fifty-two-year-old sculptor, who was out scouring the shingle beach for driftwood. He telephoned the police from the nearest phone box and had nothing further to do with it. Verity was airlifted to Eastbourne General, where her head and body injuries were assessed and she underwent emergency surgery, which she survived. At this point, the police rang Gabriel. They had found an organ donor card with him neatly marked as her next-of-kin. There had been no answer, so the local police were sent to wait for him. When he arrived home, at eleven at night, one of the policemen – in an amazingly kind gesture – had offered to drive him down to Eastbourne. They had arrived at three in the morning, and Gabriel had waited until a more civilised hour before ringing me. After all, he thought, why rush? What could *Harry* do?

I hadn't been there.

I was brisk, competent, efficient – and scared. Said I'd be there. Rang Adam. And here he was, and here I was.

Now the world whirled about me, unreal. The miles bled indistinctly past. Occasionally I let out a little groan, aimed at no one in particular. Mostly, though, the journey passed in silence, and the cars whined past us, each following its own obscure purpose, in transit, faceless.

The door to the Intensive Treatment Unit had a window. I peered through it.

Gabriel was in the reception area. He was standing in the corridor, staring blankly at a row of prints on the wall. The lighting in the corridor was subdued; beyond him, it faded completely and there was darkness until the nurses' station, which was lit in pools by Anglepoise lamps.

The door opened with a suck of air and a muffled click. He looked up, but stayed where he was. We stopped just inside, unsure what came next – and the door clicked closed behind us. Adam put his hands on both my shoulders and pushed me forwards with a squeeze. 'Go,' he said. I walked towards Gabriel, alone in a lake of watery bleak light. He shook my hand, and his deep-sunk eyes locked on mine, puzzled and a little desperate.

Gabriel. He was six foot three – or he had been: at seventy he was beginning to stoop. He did not seem quite to fill his clothes; they hung limply from him as though they were outsized. He had a great curling milk-and-steel shock of hair, all at strange and unruly angles. Beneath it, his face was thin and deeply creased. He had high cheekbones that stretched the skin beneath his eyes and made it seem as pale and weak as yellowed paper. His mouth was pulled into a wistful smile, or perhaps into a reflection of some profound inner sadness, you could never tell. His mouth and eyes gave you the feeling you were looking at a man in the throes of the deepest emotion. Generally, he said little, and now was no exception. He took my hand briefly, bloodless and damp. He nodded, and turned away without words, shuffling ahead of me towards the nurse, who was waiting for us by lamplight.

The sister in charge ushered us into a waiting room and insisted that we see a doctor before we went in to Verity. He arrived quickly. He swept into the room and scanned us impassively. He was a young man, younger than me, with the brisk but slightly dazed manner that junior hospital doctors always seem to have. I wondered how many hours he had been working without sleep: twenty, thirty?

'Mr . . .' he glanced down at a clipboard '. . . Hadley?' He looked up expectantly. Gabriel rose wearily from his plastic bucket seat. 'Excellent. Good, good,' said the doctor, leaning steeply forward to shake his hand. He was already looking at me before their hands had touched. 'And you are Mr . . .?'

'Harry Waddell. Family friend,' I mumbled. He shook my hand too, so lightly that I was hardly sure it had happened.

'Excellent,' he said again. 'I'm Mr Balasubmaranian.' (That's what he said, honest.) 'I'm the senior house officer on duty for ITU and Neuro on Mr Oxley's team.'

That last bit slipped straight past me, partly because he was speaking incredibly fast – he'd obviously said the same thing to hundreds of people on hundreds of occasions – but mostly because I was gobsmacked by his name. Let's be honest, it's not a name your average white middle-class Londoner comes across all that often. He had a faintly northern nasal accent, which I couldn't quite place, Lancashire maybe; there was no trace of Indian, Tamil, Malaysian or whatever. I'm sure I have his name right, though, because I spent the rest of our brief chat trying to read it from the little badge on his lapel (well, quite a big badge, in his case). I learned it by heart. It was definitely Balasubmaranian. And he was definitely a reassuring, thoughtful and exhausted man. I liked him. That was why I wanted to learn his name, so I could thank him by name when we were done. Hospitals always make me behave oddly. I feel as though I have to work that much harder at being human. Whatever: the name was so striking that it has stayed with me ever since.

What mattered, though, was what he told us. There had been minimal internal bleeding, which they had easily contained, he said. By some miracle, none of the fractures had punctured anything vital. Many of her organs were bruised and her whole body was in shock, but those symptoms would rapidly disappear. She had lost very little blood. The broken bones would heal with time, none of them were serious. With luck, none of these injuries would kill her.

But her skull had been partially crushed. There was damage to

13

her brain, and brain damage, Balasubmaranian told us, can often kill for no reason that anyone understood. She might die, she might survive. They might switch off her life-support and find she could breathe for herself, that her heart kept pumping, that bags of liquid food alone were enough to keep her alive – or they might not. He didn't know, he couldn't say, it would be inappropriate to speculate . . . But he did tell us one thing: it was unlikely that she would ever recover consciousness, and even if she did, she would never again be the Verity we had known. In effect, he said, if she didn't die, she would either be unconscious with her eyes closed or with her eyes open. She would sit there, immobile, staring, blank. This was her future.

'Verity's tough,' I said. 'She'll fight it. You'll see.'

Almost immediately I felt stupid. I don't know what I was thinking. That somehow she'd overcome the limits of her own shattered brain, I suppose. That sheer force of will could transform her prognosis. Not that she'd ever had much will-power.

I saw a film once where that happened – I don't remember its name. Come to think of it, films are full of it: people come back from the brink of death, or recover the use of their limbs. In movieland, miracles happen every day: people triumph over impossible adversity. But, then, maybe films about people who suffer appalling accidents and then just survive, comatose, for years don't have quite as much Hollywood appeal.

And there's another lie in the movies too: that there is always hope, that we are in control, that we can make things better if we only believe we can.

'She may regain some function over time, Mr Waddell, but really her injuries are very severe,' Balasubmaranian said carefully. 'I wouldn't hold out too much hope. More than likely she'll need round-the-clock nursing for the rest of her life. I'm sorry.'

And I suddenly felt like I needed to justify myself to him, to explain why I'd said something so idiotic. 'Well, it's just—' I stopped, because I became conscious of Gabriel next to me. Why do I always shut up when it's just too late?

'I am sorry, Mr Hadley, Mr Waddell,' Balasubmaranian said gently. 'There really is nothing we can do. It was a very big fall. Most people don't survive it.'

Most people. I wondered how many people fell from the cliffs here each year, perhaps each week. Verity was just another among hundreds, nothing special – except that she had reached the hospital alive.

Gabriel let out a heavy breath and sat down, staring at nothing. The doctor looked at him for a moment, then nodded briefly, muttered, 'If you need me . . .' and left, white coat-tails cracking and flapping in his wake. I never did get the chance to show off my mastery of his name.

I sat down next to Gabriel and stared at the same nothing as him. Perhaps it was the future we were looking at. Whatever it was, it was blank and uninviting. 'Gone,' he said flatly. His voice was weak and breathy. There was no room for emotion, just horror. So I sat wordlessly with him, wondering which memories of her were haunting him, what he might be hiding behind those fierce, unblinking eyes. Eventually he slapped his knees softly, and stood. 'Well, then. Best get it over with,' he muttered.

In a darkened room beyond a glass wall, shrouded in linen and pale white light, Verity was motionless and silent except for the slow sighs of the machines holding vigil at her side, waiting for us.

three

'Are you our new neighbour?' A head was poking through the hedge near the bottom of the garden.

I didn't know how long she'd been watching, but it didn't really matter. All I'd been doing for the past half an hour was try to hook my old half-inflated football high enough for it to catch in a three-pronged niche in the upper reaches of the apple tree.

I was bored and lethargic, not wanting to settle to anything. I had nobody to play with, and I knew that what my mother kept telling me was true: that it was my own fault. The village was full of children. I knew several of them from school. If I wanted company, all I had to do was go out to the front of the house and kick the ball around there. Sooner or later someone would come along. I didn't want that. I felt awkward. The prospect of making the effort to have friends and be sociable made me uncomfortable. I preferred solitude.

(These days, I'm not at all bad with people. Most people think I'm charming and confident – at least that's what Mum says, and Verity, of course; but when you're thirteen the world's a more complicated place. I had only lived in the village for a few months, two school terms. Settling in had not been an easy process. Neither had my parents' almost immediate separation. Just being a thirteen-year-old wasn't much fun either. I didn't know quite who I was supposed to be, or to whom. So I played out roles in my head, notions of who I might be. This particular day, the character I'd chosen for myself was First Victim. It wasn't much of a speaking part.)

'Huh,' I said.

16

It was disturbing to know that this girl had been watching *me*, just blank-minded me, kicking a ball in a high arc towards an apple tree over and over and over again, saying nothing, thinking nothing. She must have thought I was more than a little strange.

'Depends who you are,' I added, and hooked my toe under the deflated ball. I hoisted it up, hoping that this would be the time it stuck. Instead, it hit the trunk about three feet too low, and fell with a soft smack. Not a good start, when you thought about it: surly replies and a display of inept footwork. And she obviously *was* my neighbour. After all, she was poking her head through the fence from next-door's back garden. And in any case I'd watched them move in the day before, a tall gaunt man and a young girl. I had hung around at the window hoping for another sight of the girl, and the more glimpses I caught the more I thought that for once something good had happened to me. Now, in person, she was as pretty as I'd hoped, with big brown eyes and a face like an elf who's about to get into trouble and is looking forward to it. All in all, not the best time to start behaving like a prat. Mercifully, she giggled.

'Oh, I'm your neighbour,' she said merrily. 'No doubt about it. Only I was asking if *you* were *my* neighbour.'

I sniggered at the joke despite myself. I hoicked the ball up again, and once again missed. That made her laugh too. She slipped through a narrow gap between two spindly trunks in the threadbare hedge, and stood next to me. I swaggered off to collect the ball.

'It would work if you used a sling,' she said. Neither of us looked at each other, only at the ball and the tree: rules of engagement. 'I don't think you can control it well enough with your feet.' I snorted a sarcastic thanks. 'I don't mean like that.' She giggled. 'I mean you're never doing it the same twice, so you don't get any better. You're just starting again.'

Which was true enough. I hadn't been thinking of it that way because, of course, perfecting the result wasn't the point. I was just passing time. I hadn't yet succeeded with the ball that day – in fact, I could remember only ever having done it once. I ambled back with the ball.

'What do you mean, a sling?'

'Like the Romans used in sieges.' She waved her delicate hands about airily. 'A catapult. A lever with the ball on one end, and a weight on the other. Or a spring in the middle, doesn't really matter. And you'd need some kind of release thing so you wound it up to the same tension every time. Otherwise it'd go all over the place.'

I kicked the ball twice more in silence. She stood with her hands behind her back twirling idly from side to side. Her yellow print skirt was slightly translucent because the light was behind her. Her shadowy legs were long and lean, and where they appeared from under her skirt her knees bulged slightly. Her thin brown calves had a haze of transparent hairs. Her sandalled pigeon toes scuffed at the tussocky grass with every sway. She kept her head still as she swung her shoulders back and forth, and the yellow light reflected from her dress cupped her chin, first on one side then the other. She was almost as tall as me – but, then, I was short and stocky. I was lumpen and graceless, my growth spurt had all been sideways while everyone else went up. She was long and supple as a willow. She didn't seem to notice the contrast. Mostly she seemed to be eyeing up the tree. The thin fabric pulled gently at the two small bumps on her chest with every twist of her scrawny arms. I decided I liked her. Sort of.

'Won't work,' I said surlily.

'Rubbish.' She pouted. 'Anyway, why not?'

'Well, have *you* got a spring and a ratchet and a lever and all that other stuff?' I asked petulantly. ''Cos I haven't.' I kicked at the over-long grass around the football (did I mention that it was my job to mow the lawn?). I kicked the heads off a couple of dandelions. Then I said, 'Look, I've got to go for tea and stuff. See you around.' And I slouched away, feeling her gaze on me and knowing my ears were going red. I wasn't trying to push her away, but that was exactly how it sounded, and I knew it.

''Bye, then,' she called softly. I pretended I hadn't heard. I didn't turn round. A moment or two later I heard the leaves rustling as she pushed back through the hedge.

When I was inside I buried my head in my hands. I was stuck inside for the rest of the afternoon now. Tea wasn't for two hours and I couldn't go out again before then without looking utterly stupid. I congratulated myself on having blown it on the first day.

I spent most of the afternoon at the window, but I didn't see her again.

The next morning it was eleven o'clock before I went out into the garden. It was a bright day, already hot, with a few small clouds moving so slowly that they could form or evaporate in the time it took them to pass behind the tree. The sky was full of unhurried birdsong and the eager screams of swifts. The smell of grass and summer tightened my chest; each breath was slow and heavy.

I had woken late. Mum had already gone to work but she had left me breakfast. I ate, then dumped my plate and bowl in the sink. She always hated it if I left stuff hanging around: it was one of the things that was guaranteed to get me shouted at. She was more uptight than ever now Dad wasn't around.

But who cared? It was a Friday.

I hated Fridays. Not every Friday, just every other Friday, and this was one of them. After tea I'd have to go upstairs, get my things packed, then sit around waiting until Dad turned up after work some time. Generally when he arrived Mum would kick me out into the garden for half an hour while she and Dad screamed at each other, as though I couldn't hear, as though the neighbours couldn't, or the whole village, come to that. Then Mum would come bustling outside, all sniffles and sharp words, and tell me to hurry up because I was going now – '*now*, Harry, chop-chop.' And while I struggled with one too many bags in the hall, Dad would snarl, 'For goodness' sake,' from the car. Then we'd drive off, too fast, saying not a thing. It was all right once we got there: it was just that I didn't look forward to it. Fridays were spoiled in advance.

On this particular Friday, though, things were different. Spread neatly on a patch of flattened grass in the garden were some lengths of old wood, a much-repaired bicycle inner tube, and a seaside spade with a long shank, a slotted plastic T for a handle and a metal blade with red paint peeling from it. I'd never seen any of the objects before.

The undergrowth crackled and swished, and I heard a voice.

'You got up, then.' She grinned at me. Her slim hips swung subtly as she walked. She was wearing yesterday's dress (now a little rumpled), but today her feet were bare and already grass-stained. She dropped an armful of assorted ironmongery on to the ground, then stood back and dusted off her arms. She frowned at the pile in front of us, hands on hips, her forehead creased into delicate bumps. 'Tools,' she said decisively. 'Saw, hammer, nails.

Then we're ready.' She turned to look at me, then stepped a pace closer. 'I don't know where my dad's tools are. We haven't unpacked yet. Does yours have any?' She was standing so close that she had to look up at me. She seemed so innocent and trusting suddenly, as though I was the only one in the world who could help her, as though she was lost and she needed me more than anything.

Luckily for me, Dad hadn't yet collected his tools. They were all still in his shed, where he had spent so much of his time in the few months we had been together here before Mum sent him packing. Me and Mum had never been allowed in the shed. That had always puzzled me, because it was really dull in there, nothing thrilling, no secrets. I knew, because of course I'd broken Dad's rule the first time I had the chance. But, dull or not, there *was* a saw, a hammer, there would be nails. When I came back bearing them, she clapped her hands, and her large eyes glowed with excitement, as though I had just slain a mammoth single-handed and dragged it to our cave. For a moment I preened, and then she turned to the pile and started muttering directions. Which I followed.

The Great Sling took shape.

We went straight through lunch and didn't miss it. Mum was still at work, and I assumed her dad was too. The first I really noticed of time passing was when Mum called me in for tea at six and yelled down the garden – had I packed yet? She didn't come to find me, just poked her head out and shouted, and she didn't talk to the girl, even though she was squatting next to me. I called that I'd be in in a minute, and turned back to the sling.

We had been trying to decide how many twists to put in the inner tube, which stretched across the middle of the frame. It was doubled over so that the lever (the spade) could be pushed between the two strands. When you 'wound up' the spade, the doubled inner tube would twist. It was a good idea – hers, of course – but we were having problems getting the tension right, and we couldn't afford·to nail on the inner tube too many times at the wrong strength because the rubber would rip.

Two minutes later Mum came back out and screamed down the garden, 'Harry! Tea. *Now!*' She waved a fishwifely arm at us. 'And you, young lady, scram!'

We both stood and looked at each other. I could see my own

excitement reflected back in her sharp face, all angled bones and warm plump lips. Her teeth were white and broad.

'You're called Harry, then. Finish it later, Harry?'

'Can't. Got to go to Dad's for the weekend. Split up. Yours?' I heard Mum's shrill voice – 'Harry!' – a million miles away.

'Mum's dead,' the girl said idly; not as though it mattered, just as though it was true.

'Oh. Right,' I mumbled, suddenly my old familiar clumsy self. She shrugged. 'When d'you get back?'

'Sunday. Late, though. After dark.'

'Finish it Monday, then, Harry?'

'Yeah. All right.' I knew I sounded unenthusiastic, but I felt my heart speed up and the blood rush dizzily about my head. ''Bye, then.' I turned and headed towards the house.

'Don't you want to know who *I* am, Harry?' she called after me. I twisted back to look at her. The light was behind her again: her teeth and the big round whites of her eyes glowed in the shadow beneath her sunlit hair. I said nothing, and she giggled. 'Verity,' she said, with a little mock-curtsy. 'My name's Verity.'

She whirled and vanished through the gap in the hedge, leaving the long grass nodding and confused, and a half-finished tangle of wood, rubber and metal lying incongruously beneath the apple tree.

Somehow the journey to Dad's didn't seem to take as long as normal.

four

Most of her injuries were hidden. Bandages covered all of her hair and one side of her face. The visible side was purple with bruising, the eye puffed shut, her perfect skin tight and shiny over the swollen flesh. A clear plastic ventilator tube plunged into her throat, gaggingly deep, and a thinner tube disappeared into her nostril. A huge plastic collar hugged her neck and thrust her mottled chin up at a proud angle. Her arms were outside the covers, one in plaster, the other bare, bloated and blackening. A needle sank through thick wads of tape into her elbow. I couldn't help thinking that it must all hurt terribly. Her name-tag was on her wrist: Verity Hadley, and a number.

After a while, Gabriel mumbled something incoherent, and left me on my own with her.

A few feet away in both directions, caught in their own sharp downlights, other figures were stranded somewhere between life and death, ghost-pure within their machines, their white gowns and sheets a kind of shroud.

I'm sorry, I'm being self-indulgent, aren't I? But the place affected me. I'd seen ITUs in countless films but until you've actually been in one you cannot possibly know. The only sounds of life come from the machines, softly breathing, pumping, trickling. Even the nurses sit at their station in respectful silence. No one is alive, it's just that no one is quite dead either. Each of the unconscious people in that room had had a life until recently. Each had once had someone who looked at them and saw them smiling or crying or running – husbands, lovers, children, teachers and friends. They saw them joking, talking, just with their eyes open.

Verity had never really given up her childhood. She was still innocent and wicked. She still loved and disliked for no reason other than the love or dislike of things. For all her disfigurement, now she looked the part: she looked like a sleeping child. It must have been even worse for Gabriel than it was for me. No wonder he'd left me to it.

I bent and kissed her forehead. 'I'm sorry, Verity,' I whispered. So sorry.

Adam was chatting with a young nurse. When he saw me emerge, he hurried over. The nurse brushed past me with a small warm smile. There was a waft of perfume, cool and fresh.

Adam looked at me earnestly. 'Bad?'

I nodded mutely.

His face softened. 'I'm sorry, Harry. Truly.'

I breathed out sharply, hoping to clear the fog from my thoughts. 'It's OK,' I muttered. 'What did that nurse say?'

'I was just asking her about Verity ...' Adam frowned and glanced around. Beyond the glass, machines rose and fell in pools of disinfected light.

'And?'

He shrugged. 'You already know. She's in a coma. It's bad.'

I might have known it, but Balasubmaranian had not put it quite as starkly. 'How bad?' I asked sharply. 'Is she going to die?' I was on the edge of panic. I desperately needed at least the illusion of hope.

As gently as he could, Adam shattered it for me. 'Not die, no ...' He scanned an empty distance, his lips pressed tight. When he spoke again, his voice was hoarse. 'Harry, I don't know what's worse. For you, I mean.'

Adam's hand on my shoulder stopped me shaking. I had not even realised that I was. He coaxed me round to look at him. His eyes, magnified by his glasses, were large and anxious, full of care. He said nothing, just peered into mine sorrowfully. Then he muttered, 'Come,' and pulled me into a brief, fierce hug, before propping me upright again. It felt oddly uncomfortable. 'Take your time,' he said. I nodded, not sure I could talk without cracking.

A nurse drifted behind the bed next to Verity's, bent over the patient's head doing something with a plastic tube. The quiet was overwhelming. From where we stood, Verity was indistinct, one part of a jumble of sharp white lines and edges, machines, bandages, bedclothes. No cards, no flowers. Against the wall was a small locker for her personal effects, set back neatly from the bed so that it would not be in the nurse's way as she tended her motionless patients.

My panic gradually faded. Emptiness remained. And anger.

'There's people to see you,' Adam said, after a while. He nodded towards the visitors' room. I looked at him enquiringly. He shrugged. I trudged towards the room.

The police. Gabriel was already with them, standing at the room's far end, staring out of a grimy window into the concrete courtyard below. There were two of them, a man and a woman, both in shirtsleeves and each weighed down with a beltful of their own personal selection of hardware: CS spray and a couple of obscure black leather boxes for the woman, handcuffs and a baton for the man. (*Handcuffs?* In an ITU, for God's sake! Who was going to escape?) And, for a moment, I could almost have smiled. I could imagine Verity sighing and rolling her eyes. This was a fashion disaster: just look what those belts did to the line of their uniforms. Even I could see that she'd have a point. The walkie-talkies clipped to their epaulettes looked silly, their drip-dry shirts fitted badly, and those nylon trousers ... The gear on their belts made them walk with a swagger.

After the formalities, they settled down to asking us about Verity. The man was clearly senior, but he let the woman do all the questioning. The conversation was unreal. It was like they were talking about a different person. To stand there with two strangers trying to formulate reasons why she might have done something that I simply couldn't imagine her doing ... It was madness, a dream.

The man stood still while the woman talked, but he managed at the same time to give the impression that he was prowling. He craned his neck occasionally, he stared about proprietorially, as though she was a young cub having her first playful stab at being an adult. If I'd been the woman (PC Jefferies? Jefferson? Honestly, I don't remember. She was kind, she was brunette, and I liked her), I'd have hit him. Instead she just seemed to get a little softer and sweeter every time he leaned over to check what she was writing in her notebook, or finished her sentences for her, the patronising bastard. She was quite pretty, actually, in a bland sort of way. Perhaps that was her problem: he'd cast her in the role of dumb blonde before she even opened her mouth. And before he'd bothered to notice that her scraped-back hair was dark. She was good, too, sensitive but not indulgent. She kept her voice neutral and efficient.

'This is really just a formality,' she said. ('Formality,' echoed PC Bastard. She glanced at him, then pointedly turned her gaze back to Gabriel.) 'There are no suspicious circumstances, so we just need to complete an Incident Report.' ('Report,' he said.)

She asked us for Verity's personal details, and Gabriel and I alternated answers as if conforming to an unspoken system. Age, thirty-three; job, freelance fashion designer; residence, Gladstone Terrace, Battersea; single, no children; next-of-kin, Gabriel; there was no one else to notify. Yes, we could confirm it was her. We could be contacted at the following addresses and numbers. Yes, she had our names down right. PC Brunette made it as easy as she could. All the same, it was a depressing process.

'Thank you,' she said. She carefully folded her notebook into her breast pocket. 'I know how difficult this is.'

No. She didn't.

PC Bastard harrumphed in a haven't-you-forgotten-something way. She blinked slowly, gathering patience. 'Do you have any idea why she might have done it?' she asked.

Gabriel looked half hypnotised. He had shrunk even further into his clothes, and was scuffing his fingers back and forth across his threadbare jacket. He said nothing, so I spoke for us both. 'No . . .' I said doubtfully. 'No idea at all. I thought she was happy.'

But happy people don't jump off cliffs, do they?

'I see . . .' She sighed in a never-mind kind of way. For her the reason really did not matter, it was enough that it had happened. She could complete her paperwork. 'Well, that's pretty much all we can do for now. Our report will record this as attempted suicide. Unless either of you have reason to think otherwise?' We shook our heads meekly. She continued sympathetically, 'Well, we didn't find a note in her car. Perhaps there's something in her flat. If you do find anything, please let us know. We'll keep the file open.' She smiled warmly at us both, and handed us each a card with contact details.

'Car,' PC Bastard said suddenly. She frowned at him, then nodded. We must have looked blank.

'Ms Hadley's car,' she explained. 'We found it in the car park at Beachy Head. It's in the pound. But I'm afraid we really can't keep it there.'

I looked at Gabriel, who shook his head, not returning my gaze. 'Don't drive,' he muttered hoarsely.

Down to me, then. 'Where do I go?'

'It's all on the card,' she said. 'Eight thirty to twelve thirty, and two to four thirty.'

I nodded. They nodded. They left.

Gabriel and I sat and stared at the floor. Eventually Adam came in and stood waiting for us to notice him.

Gabriel glanced listlessly up at him, and I roused myself enough to make the introductions, 'Gabriel, you remember Adam.' It must have been at least fifteen years since they had seen each other. Gabriel cast an apathetic eye in his direction. Adam grimaced his sympathy and murmured, 'If there's anything I can do ...' Gabriel's gaze returned to the floor, his face expressionless.

'Harry?' Adam sounded as though he was talking to someone else, someone far distant. '*Harry?*' I looked up tiredly. His face was etched with concern. 'What next?' It came out like a conspiratorial whisper: he did not want to disturb Gabriel.

'Car,' Gabriel croaked.

I had forgotten about that already. Reminded, I groaned. It seemed so cruel to have things to *do*. I was so weary. All I wanted was silence, and a featureless piece of floor to stare at. 'Car,' I echoed. Adam waited while I gathered myself, showing none of the exasperation I am sure I would have felt in his position. Finally I explained that we had to collect Verity's car from the pound.

'OK. I'll drive you down there, Gabriel.'

'Gabriel can't drive,' I muttered sullenly.

'Well, I'll drive it, then, and you can take the BMW. We'll go in convoy. Where am I taking it?'

I looked to Gabriel for an answer, but he was lost somewhere. I sighed again. 'Best get it to London. Deal with it later.'

Gabriel showed no reaction at all.

A new awareness pressed down on me: I was going to have to do everything. Gabriel was all but paralysed; and if he wasn't capable of sorting out Verity's life, then who else was going to do it but me? He was her family, all of it, and although she had countless friends, not many were truly close: most were more like partners in fun, and not one had known her anywhere near as long as I had. And the practicalities: the rent to be settled, her tenancy cancelled; bills and contracts to be dealt with, services to be cut off; her possessions, what to do with her possessions? The burden was inevitably mine, just as the horror was, and the grief that I knew would eventually come.

Adam came across and sat next to me, surveyed the patch of floor I was staring at, put a hand on my shoulder. 'I'll do it,' he said quietly.

'It's not just the car, Ads—' My voice cracked.

He squeezed my shoulder. 'I didn't *mean* just the car, Harry.' There was nothing to say. Instead, I concentrated on not crying. He sensed my difficulty, slapped my shoulder and stood briskly. 'I hate to say it, though, but the car does still need fetching.' He was right, of course. Time to be responsible. I stood, heavily, and drew myself up as tall as I felt able.

Adam smiled at me, then grimaced and gestured at Gabriel with his eyes. It took me a moment to understand what he meant. Gabriel was the real problem. He was still staring at the floor. His lips were working, as though he was trying to find words to whisper to himself.

'Gabriel?' I said. He didn't look up. 'Gabriel? Will you be all right?'

He blinked hard and looked up at me. His expression seemed carved into his skin: soulful, wise, careworn. His deep-set eyes held no clue to his thoughts. 'You're a good man, Harry,' he said. 'Verity was fond of you.' He stared at me for a moment, then drifted away again. Adam spread his arms helplessly.

'Gabriel?' I urged. 'Go home for a few days. The hospital will let you know what's going on. *I* will, I'll call you. You need some rest. There's nothing you can do.'

'Harry's right, Gabriel,' Adam said.

'I'll give you money for the train,' I added. 'Will you go back to Oxford? Go and get a few nights' sleep. You need it.'

Suddenly, he stood. Then, painfully, he straightened himself. His gaze glittered. 'Don't patronise me, Harry.' His voice was cold, and addressed solely to me. His eyes glowed darkly, and his face tightened; I could see the blood pulsing in his neck and jaw. 'I'm no use here. I'll go. I don't need money.' Verity had told me that he had a fierce temper, but I had never seen it before. It was a little scary. His posture relaxed slightly, and he smiled thinly. 'I don't need charity,' he said, more gently. 'But thank you, Harry. I could do with a lift to the station.'

We dropped him at the station and saw him to the platform. As we left, he seemed to shrink back into himself, until he was small and grey against the desolate stretches of concrete and iron.

As we looked for the police station, I started brooding again, this time about Verity's car. Adam's offer to drive it home, and for me to take the BMW, was kind. He loved his car, he had never let anyone else so much as touch it. To let me drive it was a humbling token of how much he cared for my well-being. But I realised that I could not possibly accept his gesture. I *wanted* to take care of Verity's affairs. What else did I have of her? These scraps of her life were my only remaining connection to her. To have allowed someone else to rummage around in them would have been unbearable. I told him. He was uncertain and unconvinced, but finally agreed.

When we arrived at the police pound, Adam went to retrieve Verity's car while I wrestled with a pointless mass of forms and releases: insurance waivers, liability disclaimers, declarations of proxy. It took me fifteen minutes, and when I emerged into daylight the car was already outside the office. Adam's backside was high in the air, facing me, his head buried somewhere in the driver's footwell.

'Hey, there,' I said flatly.

'Hey, Harry,' he answered, his head still buried in the car. 'You took your time.' He withdrew himself carefully ruefully rubbing his back. In his other hand, he held a bundle of bits and pieces, which he waved at me. 'Thought I'd have a poke around, see if I could find anything useful.'

'And?'

He passed me the items one by one. 'Filofax. Could be handy.

Some kind of bum-bag – make-up, I think. Keys.' I recognised the keys: they were for her flat. Adam went on, 'This postcard, from Spain, it looks like, from . . .' he held it close and screwed up his eyes '. . . I dunno. "S", whoever that is.'

I took it and flipped it over: the Sagrada Familia cathedral. Stamped in Barcelona, postmarked two weeks ago. Generous handwriting, big and expansive, looping blue ink: 'Wow!!!!! Barcelona!!!! The clothes . . . The boys . . . The buildings . . . The boys . . .' Then a gap, then, 'Paris, Babes, slay 'em or die!!! (By the way, did I mention the boys? Hot hot hot!!!!). Love 'n' hugs, S' and a heart. The echo of a past life.

'Sam,' I said. 'Verity's business partner. Sam Mandovini.'

When I looked up, the concern I saw in Adam's face was almost too much for me. He spotted my distress immediately, and pretended to have noticed something fascinating on the far side of the pound. It was at least a minute before I was confident of my voice again. 'Thanks, Adam. For everything. I mean it.'

He peered sideways at me, and grinned shyly. 'Friends. What they're for.' He patted me on the shoulder and frowned at me. 'Look, I'm not sure you should take her car, Harry. You're still pretty upset and it's only going to remind you. Why not take the BMW? I'll pick it up when I drop this one at your place.'

'Honestly, Adam, I'm fine. Truth be told, I *want* to drive it. And I'd probably smash yours, anyway, and then you'd never forgive me.' Her car would smell of her. It would have her things in it. The mirrors would be adjusted for her eyes. The seat would be moulded to her shape.

'But . . .' Adam must have seen something in my face. He shut up.

I gave him a lift to his BMW, a few hundred yards down the road. When I pulled up next to it, he opened his door but did not get out. He just looked at me, worry for me written clearly on his face.

'She was happy,' I muttered, at last. 'She *told* me. Last time I saw her. She told me she really felt on top of everything, she felt she was getting somewhere at last.'

A van ripped along the street. It thumped past Adam's half-open door, rocking the car and leaving me reeling from the sudden implied violence. I was filled for a moment with a terrifying awareness of all those near misses that we bury and forget, the endless parade of moments when our lives could have changed irrevocably and, through chance, had not.

'Thanks again, Adam,' I said softly.

He shook his head mournfully. 'No more thanks, Harry. Beer. This evening. You need it. So do I.' I nodded, reluctantly.

Adam hopped out and strode across the road towards the BMW. He waved briefly, pulled out and roared away. I stayed behind the wheel, gazing blankly at the road ahead of me.

Verity, bruised and bloated, crippled beyond recovery. She had chosen to die alone. She had not come to ask my blessing. She had not come to say goodbye.

Perhaps I never knew her at all.

five

Adam plonked two pints on the table – bitter for him, lager for me – and settled opposite me astride a stool. His knee nudged the table and he grabbed his pint hastily to prevent a disaster. He swept a patch clear of puddles with the edge of a beer mat, planted his elbows, and frowned at me. 'Harry, you look terrible.'

There was not much I could say. In fact, there was not even much I wanted to say. I was lethargic and numb. I really did not want to be there.

Adam raised his glass and took a hefty swig. 'Drink up. Dr Yates knows best.'

Possibly he did know best. I certainly did not. I just wanted everything to go away. I wanted to wake up and find that none of it was real. There was relief in having someone else take charge. So I took a gulp. It was gassy and cold, and left me completely uninterested. The low table between us was crazed with circular stains; I brushed my hand over them absently. It did not help bring the world into focus. The real world around me was miles away. 'That's the way,' Adam said. 'It'll come.'

The trouble was, I didn't want it to.

We were at a designer pub near the town hall – you know the kind of place: huge, lots of bare wood, classy beers and overpriced food, part of a chain with themed names, the Slug, the Rat, the Pitcher and the Pickled Ferret in a Boat. Or something. Verity would have hated it. Someone edged past my chair with an armful of drinks, tripped, and I narrowly missed having my shirt sluiced with an obscure Czech lager.

'Another.' Adam meant another swig. He peered at me over his glasses.

'Adam, I really don't—'

He reached over and put his hand on my forearm. 'Harry, you need this, trust me. You're in shock, I know, but you're going to have to face it, else you'll be walking round like a zombie. It *happened*.' He waited until I met his eyes, then leaned back and gestured at our drinks. 'So the plan is to have a few of these, loosen up a little. Not much of a plan, I'll grant you, but the best I could come up with.' He jerked his head expectantly at my pint. 'Go on.'

Another swig. Sharp and unsatisfying, but perhaps it warmed that empty place in my chest. Maybe drinking would help, maybe not. Either way, it was better than staying at home staring at the wall. And Adam was all I had left. I had other friends, of course, but I was only ever really close to Adam. And Verity.

'It doesn't make sense,' I mumbled.

'What? Getting drunk?' He raised his eyebrows, surprised. 'Well, that's the beauty of it. You—'

'Not that. Verity.' But I almost laughed, a little. Then I hated myself for it. Adam gazed at me, his pupils large and deep through the lenses. 'Oh, forget it,' I muttered, and sank my face into my beer.

'You didn't see this coming at all, did you?' His voice was gentle enough that it did not sound obtuse and insensitive: it was just an invitation to talk.

'Look, Ads—'

'OK, OK, I know.' He drained his pint and pointed to mine. 'Seconds away, time for another round.' I knocked back what was left of my first. It sat heavily inside me. I was not sure if my light-headedness was an unexpectedly early reaction to the alcohol or just part of my general confusion. I did not care. At least I could feel it. Adam scooped up both empties and headed for the bar, leaving me to brood. Which was bad. Because when he came back and prompted me, 'So you were saying that it doesn't make sense . . .' it was the last thing I wanted.

'Can we just leave it, Adam?'

He raised his hands in surrender. 'Point taken. Drinks, not talk. Understood. I just thought – oh, forget it, I'll shut up.'

So now I felt guilty as well. I tried to drown the feeling in beer.

Adam gazed at a huge TV screen at the far end of the pub – grainy pictures of footballers running around, coloured boxes filled with indecipherable statistics – and my thoughts drifted slowly away from my annoyance and guilt towards Adam, and spiralled down towards one inevitable truth.

Gone. Verity, gone.

Time passed. More drink.

'It *doesn't* make sense, Ads . . . She was happy. She was.'

'And now you're wondering if she was keeping something from you.' Adam's tone was matter-of-fact.

'She wouldn't. Never.' But I was not as sure as I sounded.

He looked at me again, another long, contemplative gaze. 'So tell me,' he said.

My head was floating somewhere, spinning in furious circles, analysing, finding no sense, frantically ordering shards of thoughts and watching them dissolve into chaos. Colourlessly, I told Adam about Verity standing me up, about leaving the message for her and going to bed angry with her; about discovering what had happened from Gabriel the next morning. I told him I was worried about what would happen in the future: who would look after Verity, and how? But most of all I told him how I felt: that I couldn't help believing that what she'd done was somehow my failure.

Adam listened. He prompted me when I could find nothing to say. When I was near to tears, he reached out and squeezed my arm. When I was embarrassed he told me to sod the rest of the pub, I should cry if I wanted. Mostly he just listened. He hunched broadly over our table, his shirtsleeved forearms resting unnoticed in a sweaty sheen of spilt beer and condensation. His eyes were wise and steady. His high forehead was creased with concern. When I finished my third pint he raised a finger for me to pause, downed his own drink and drifted through the throng to the bar, managing again to get served almost immediately. He slid back with two fresh beers, and settled attentively. To be honest, I don't have much idea what I said, only what I felt. There was gratitude to Adam, for listening without question. There was relief that I was not alone. It was grief, of a preliminary sort: another beginning, perhaps.

And when I'd done, he said, 'Drink,' again, very firmly, and

33

ghosted through the crowd to fetch yet another round – our fifth, heaven help us. It felt good. We sat in silence for a long time, a vacuum Adam would normally hurry to fill with words and laughter.

After a while I took pity on him. 'Thank you, Adam,' I said. 'I needed that. Badly.'

His face split into a boyish grin, and he raised his glass to me in a silent toast. Then he asked, 'So, do you want to hear about *my* day now?'

And I actually laughed.

Adam . . . He was all that stood between me and despair in the days after Verity's fall.

He was big and broad, and getting badly out of shape. He referred to the swelling mound of fat on his stomach as his 'turtle': imagine one clamped to your belly, all four flippers wrapped around you – as you walk, it jiggles up and down, an embarrassing hump. His hair was dark, his complexion pale and a little blotchy. Behind his thin-rim designer glasses, his eyes alternated between wisdom and hawkishness, shyness and laughter. His face had always been plump, even at school, and his mouth was a little too broad for it. When he smiled, which was often, it seemed to take over his whole face, and his brilliant white teeth formed a ragged line. His grin was diffident, but full of lopsided mischief.

We first met when I was thirteen, shortly after Verity moved into the village, although I had seen him at school before then. He was in the year above me. He had been an isolated boy, often sitting alone, occasionally hovering at the edges of the group of larger boys who used to dominate the playground. But our friendship had nothing to do with school. It developed in the evenings and at weekends. Throughout our teenage years, we would sit and share silences, watching the river slide past, or the clouds drift, or the stream of car headlights on the distant Oxford ring-road. I think it was isolation that kept us together. It was something we both understood: we held ourselves a little apart from the world. In many ways we were both solitary types during our youth, trapped into being who we were by chance events, by the pressures of life in a small community, and by our families: his, large and uncaring and

34

occasionally violent; mine, a single scared woman, lonely, confused and haunted by regrets. In our silences, Adam and I found comfort.

As adults, we changed and remained the same. After university, Adam took pupillage with a large barristers' chambers in London. I spent a year finishing my arts course at Oxford Polytechnic, then moved to London also, hoping to establish myself as a photographer but earning most of my cash as a less-than-average interior decorator. Perhaps we were both compensating for our backgrounds. Whatever the reason, I lived in a garret and struggled to make ends meet, while Adam became a paid-up member of the establishment. We remained close, but our social circles were so far apart that we rarely saw each other's friends.

Adam was ambitious, socially and professionally. He was not aggressive or pushy but, in his own thoughtful, methodical way, he gradually 'arrived'. By thirty he was a successful barrister, working in corporate arbitration. By thirty-five he was a QC, and had branched into politics, working three days a week at the Bar, and the rest of the time serving as a councillor for Wandsworth. His aim was to move full-time into national politics, with legal consultancy as a sideline. He looked set to achieve it: word had it he was a hot favourite for selection as a candidate at the next general election. Needless to say, his political colours were far from red.

Adam married the same year he took silk (that's becoming a QC to you and me), making a grand entry to both the social and professional stages simultaneously. Sarah McKyle was pretty but not attractive, charming but not warm. She was nervous, a bit scatty, but kind in that brusque way that the children of moneyed families so often are. She was bossy but insecure, thoughtful but distracted. I felt neutral about her. I couldn't see what Adam saw in her – but, then, I didn't have to because I wasn't the one marrying her. And she had many good qualities. She was generous and thoughtful. There was always a present at Christmas and on my birthday, wrapped in conservative paper, all the edges impossibly neat. It was always a silk tie or a scarf, or handkerchiefs. But Adam loved her, and that was what counted. With Sarah on his arm, at last he *belonged* ... Sort of ...

But between ourselves, I was simply Harry, and he was simply Adam. And we sat and watched the world, these days, from the pine tables of designer pubs and restaurants. We shared silences and stupid stories, and left our real lives at the door. I would not have had it any other way.

After a few pints, and a couple of hours, though, my friendship with *Adam* was hardly at the front of my mind.

'Why'd she do it, Ads?'

'Hmm?'

'Doesn't make sense.'

It must have been the tenth time that evening I'd said that. I couldn't help chewing at what had happened, with the doggedness that only truly drunk people can muster. There was a mystery there somewhere, there had to be. For the last couple of months she had been so positive, so full of purpose. She had been more intense than I had seen her for years. She was vibrant. She had attacked every element of her life with a kind of happy rage. If she had wanted to kill herself, I would have known. It made no sense, no sense at all.

Adam shook his head, slowly and sadly. 'Of course it doesn't make sense. It's not a rational thing to do.'

The bar was getting more and more packed, he had had to shout above the din. It was reassuring: it made me feel as though we were having a normal conversation, just one of hundreds happening all around us. As though we were discussing football-team selection or a scientific discovery, not the reduction of a person's life to machines and stark white sheets. Adam must have seen the frustration in my face, because he gestured resignation. 'I hate to say it, Harry. I know you're not ready yet, but eventually you're just going to have to accept it. And you'll probably never know the reason, because people don't work that way. It just happened.'

It was around half past nine, and still light outside. I swilled my remaining beer around in its glass, held it up to the window and squinted through it. The streets, distorted by the glass and the thin foam drying round its rim, were grey and luminous and quiet. People drifted along the pavement, strangers, all ignoring each other, but simultaneously reading each other's movements and imperceptibly adjusting their step, brushing past each other gracefully without a word exchanged.

Adam pressed: 'And, besides, from what you've said, she was pretty unpredictable at the best of times.'

'Oh, come on, Adam!' I snapped. 'There's a difference between being a bit unpredictable and jumping off a bloody cliff.'

What did Adam know about anything, anyway? It was the beer that was making me brood, of course – that and the fact that I had just lost Verity for ever. He had not even seen Verity for fifteen years or more. They only had me in common. Over the years, I had suggested several times that the three of us should get together, but it had never happened. I had realised that there was nothing to be gained by pressing the issue: they were such different people. Had they met, I was pretty sure they would have hated each other. What right did Adam have to judge Verity now?

'Get real, Adam,' I muttered. 'You don't know what the fuck you're talking about.' I buried myself in my drink.

He gazed at me mildly. 'True, Harry. I don't. I just meant that suicide – attempted suicide, whatever – is *never* going to make sense. But I shouldn't have said it. It's the last thing you want to hear. Sorry.'

'You should be,' I grumbled – well, slurred.

Adam let that sit between us for a minute before he answered, his tone cautious. 'I'd like to help, Harry. Seriously. We'll find out what happened, why she did it.'

'That's not what you said a moment ago.'

'But—'

'You said there wasn't anything to find out.'

'I did. But—'

'So you can't help, then, can you? What are you going to do? Are you going to keep telling me to face it, she's gone and that's that? Is that your idea of help?' I was being nasty, and I knew it. I can only plead drunkenness and distress. I wasn't really angry with Adam – I wasn't even angry. I was . . . It didn't have a name. But whatever it was, I needed to get it out, and Adam was the closest target. I glowered at him, waiting for more apologies, more fuel for this gathering rage.

He looked small and fragile and alone. He held himself very still. He spread his arms. 'Harry, you've just lost Verity. I don't want to lose you.'

The fury went, and left me on the edge of tears.

'Finish your pint,' Adam urged quietly. 'Time we were gone.'

As we walked unsteadily towards the main road, in search of taxis home, he said, 'I meant it, Harry. About helping.'

'I know.'

'Still friends?'

I sniffed back some tears. 'Yeah. Course.'

'Whoah – taxi, hang on!' Adam leaped out into the road and waved frantically at a cab that was passing on the opposite side of the street. It did a U-turn in the light traffic, and headed towards us.

'You take it, Ads. I'm going to walk for a while.'

He peered at me suspiciously. 'Sure?'

'Sure. I'll be fine.'

He clapped me on the back. 'I'll call you tomorrow.'

I watched the taxi go, then meandered slowly towards home in the twilight.

Without Adam, I think I would have fallen apart that day, within hours of hearing of Verity's fall. Without him, I would have been so ... severed. But he was there.

And I felt more alone than I could ever have imagined.

six

Sam Mandovini's over-bright clothes did nothing for my hangover – and she wouldn't stop talking, her voice low and monotonous, which didn't help either.

'I just can't believe it,' she mumbled. 'I spoke to her on Wednesday morning. On the phone. She was working from home.' She was distracted, picking at the tasselled hem of her crop-top, looking at the ground, the street, the sky – anywhere but at me. I stood on the pavement, because she had not yet thought to invite me in. The London fumes were making me feel sick.

I had woken late, with the sun shining directly into my eyes. Dizziness and nausea had struck the moment I tried to lift my head. This wasn't just a headache, this was the kind of hangover that convinces you you're genuinely ill. Grilled some bacon for a sandwich, nearly threw it up. Ran a hot bath, couldn't face it. Switched on the telly and lay on my bed, not really watching, and wondered whether the black coffee I was cradling was such a good idea after all. But being alone with my thoughts didn't suit me either, and in any case I had a job on later in the day. Time to get going. I went to the corner shop, bought a newspaper, which I couldn't face reading. Eventually I admitted to myself that my first duty of the day was to deal with Verity's Filofax.

It was sitting on the table in the living room, with the keys and the postcard next to it – *Paris, Babes, slay 'em or die* – and I had decided that maybe I *could* delay the Filofax by going to see Sam. Perhaps she would help with it. I flicked through it, trying to gauge the scale of the task. Names and addresses, some I knew, many I had never heard of, diary dates heavily circled or with exclamation marks next to them – dates she had never mentioned. There was even an entry for the day she had fallen: '3.30', ringed, with 'B. Gap Hotel, thatched bar' next to it, and below that, 'A259 => Eastbourne. R turn – BIRLING GAP'. Three thirty: five hours before she fell. What had she done with those hours? Who had she spent them with? I looked at a map. Birling Gap was between Brighton and Eastbourne, on the coast near Beachy Head. Whatever she had been doing there, I couldn't see how it could have kept her more than a couple of hours. If she had been there at three thirty, she would have had time to get back to Jim's by half past seven for her date with good old Harry – Harry who, it seemed, knew next to nothing about the life of his closest friend. I folded the Filofax back together, and trudged to the tube station.

And now, with my hangover ripening nicely, I was facing Sam and wondering if she would be any help at all.

'I mean, it's just dreadful.' Her voice was flat and dull. She studied the button holes of her tiny fuzzy pink cardigan. Sail cloth trousers and black platform shoes completed her outfit. 'It's just . . .' Her gaze flicked to me and then away, to follow a bus as it growled past. 'She . . . I can't believe she . . .' Finally her eyes locked with mine, and widened in surprise. 'Oh . . . I'm sorry, Harry. I'm just . . . Come in. You look dreadful.'

It's always nice to start the day with a compliment.

She led the way. A piece of paper had been stuck to the wall with masking tape, falling away where it had pulled at the flaking pale green paint, 'Verity Hadley, Sam Mandovini, Fashion Services,' and an arrow pointing up. Another beginning, I suppose. The day I began to look for the truth about Verity.

The studio was three storeys up, right at the top of a mouldering building in the no man's land that fringes Soho to the north. You entered through an anonymous door squeezed between a shop selling old vinyl records – singles in a tottering wooden tray outside, LPs in a chaos of piles and racks inside – and a boutique with a tiny mullioned window and a minimalist display: two lava lamps and a cigarette lighter shaped like a penis. Each storey of the building was separated by four narrow flights of stairs. The boards were worn and grey, with green paint at the edges. The turns between each flight were so tight you had to edge your way round.

Verity and Sam had the usual Soho collection of neighbours. The first floor was a knocking shop ('As in knock twice and ask for Rosie,' Verity used to say). The second floor was a flat: an old and completely silent man lived there, with a wild look in his eyes, a drooping fleshy nose, and a torn once-white vest. When anyone came or went, he would open his door a slit and watch them pass. He never spoke. Verity and Sam had decided unilaterally that they would call him Norman. Verity swore she'd seen young women traipsing in and out, and that he held regular orgies, but he was seventy-five if he was a day, and the flat stank – you could smell it even when the door was closed.

'Poor Verity,' Sam muttered, as she climbed up past Rosie's knocking shop. She glanced back over her shoulder to check I was following. 'And there's Paris in two weeks. This is a nightmare.' The old man's door was closed, but she yelled cheerfully, 'Mornin', Norman,' and paused briefly on the landing for a reply. Something rattled woodenly behind the door. Sam wrinkled her nose, and resumed climbing. 'I mean, why now? Paris was going to be dynamite. Her collection's brilliant, really it is. She was so happy.' The stairs ended with a blank door, flat and painted a deep, flaking blue. There was a Yale lock set into a flat metal plate. Sam prodded at it with a key. 'Why didn't she tell me?' She pushed into the studio without looking back.

It was a long, low room with floor-to-ceiling windows along the length of one wall. Ancient cast-iron radiators stood in front of them; the marbled lino had curled up round them, and buckled seams stretched in parallel lines across the floor. Rolls and swatches of fabric were jumbled on trestles, making the room almost impassable and filling the air with the sharp, solvent smell of new cloth.

A young man was just visible in a far corner, half buried under a mound of gaudy material. He was bent over a sewing-machine, his wet-look hair almost touching it. As he worked, his head wove slowly back and forward as though he was trying to puzzle the meaning of what he was creating. In fact, he was so close to the gauzy orange fabric that I was half convinced his nose-stud would catch on it and rip it. Or the spike in his eyebrow. Or the one just above his chin. Nearer the window, another boy was fussing around a clothes dummy, also pierced in unlikely places – him, not the dummy. He was scrawny, dressed in army fatigues and a vermilion-sequined waistcoat. He had a mouthful of pins and a haggard look. 'You remember Jean-Marie and Nathan, don't you, Harry?' Sam said.

I didn't. The boy at the machine glanced up for a moment but said nothing. The other looked over and said, 'Mmm-mm-mmmm,' through his mouthful of pins.

'Nathan, Nathan, *looser*, love-bun. *Pleeease!*' Sam dashed over to the dummy and primped at a seam near the waistline. To me the dummy looked as though it (He? She? Impossible to tell) was wearing a patchwork of discarded plastic bags – but then, I was far too unhip for the fashion business, as Verity never stopped pointing out. Even Nathan's studs unnerved me. Sam looked back at me, still fiddling with whatever the dummy was wearing. 'Made from supermarket bags,' she called, in my direction. 'Part of Verity's collection. Brilliant, isn't it?' Her hands fluttered uselessly for a moment, then she collected herself and walked back to me, suddenly matter-of-fact and bleak. '"Damaged Goods", she called it.' She moved her finger along an imaginary banner and gazed at me expectantly. 'The name of her collection. "Damaged Goods". Had a slogan too: "Damaged clothes for damaged people in a damaged world". Brilliant.'

And there was me, thinking fashion had something to do with dress sense.

Sam nodded for me to turn and lead the way to the office area. I did, skirting another trestle, which threatened to topple several tons of samples on top of me. Two facing design desks were partitioned from the rest of the room by another dummy, with a note pinned to its heart reading, 'Abandon hope, all ye . . .' One of Sam's. She gestured for me to sit on Verity's stool, then leaned against the edge of the desk and pointed at the scraps and drawings in front of me. 'This was the big one,' she said calmly. 'I really think she'd cracked it. Paris was just going to be amazing.'

Verity had always been cagey about her designs. She always told me to wait and see. On the occasions when I met her at the studio, if one of her creations was on the mannequin, she'd always screamed shrilly at me not to look. I'd never been allowed near her desk. Perhaps she thought I wouldn't understand, and perhaps she was right. In front of me was a series of sketches of waifs and thugs.

Their clothes were ripped and unshaped, partial garments held together by outsize zigzag stitching that looked more like the scars of Frankenstein's surgeon than the work of a seamstress. Gashed leather flapped around their toes – when they had shoes at all. Vivid streaks of filth patterned their bare skin, and there was lots of that. The models all had cuts, or trickles of blood, or swollen bruises that puffed their eyes shut. Some, of both sexes, looked impassive; others were drawn as if they were in pain. On some, the clothes seemed ripped away. Breasts and genitals were half covered by inadequate arms and hands. Beneath uneven punky hair, their faces were wide with horror or thrill – and what shocked me was that I couldn't tell the difference.

'The ultimate fashion victims,' Sam breathed. '*Real* victims. Says it all.'

I had always felt excluded from Verity's work, shut out because I was inadequate and could not share her visions. Now I was glad she hadn't shown it to me because I don't know what I could possibly have said that wouldn't have widened the gap between us. And for the first time it occurred to me that maybe she hadn't wanted *me* to judge her because, on the surface of it, Verity's collection was just another ridiculous piece of fashion madness. But looking at it, and thinking of her, looking at all the agonisingly fragile people she had conjured, I felt a tiny shock of guilt and grief. 'Damaged Goods': well, Verity certainly was that, now.

'I never knew,' I said.

'Yes. Well,' Sam answered brusquely. She pulled up a sheet of paper that had been flopped over the back of the desk. It floated down over the pictures, covering them all. In a way it was a relief, but it did seem horribly final.

'Look, I know this is daft, Sam,' I said, 'but I really thought she was happy. I know she's always up and down, but I never thought the downs were so bad that she'd – you know . . . I thought she was on a bit of a high.'

Sam shrugged. 'Me, too,' she said simply. 'Paris was it. We were both going to make it big. *Big.*' For a moment she looked utterly lost.

There was a yell and a crinkly thud from Nathan's direction. The mannequin had fallen on him. Flailing limbs and shreds of plastic were everywhere. Jean-Marie strolled casually over to help him, and I worried all over again about whether the studs would catch on anything. Sam sighed. My hangover thumped. 'What am I going to do, Harry?' she said bleakly. 'I'll have to move to a smaller studio, lose one of the boys, heaven knows which. Or both. Maybe go and work for one of the big houses again.'

I rubbed my throbbing forehead and tried to keep calm.

The charitable way to put it is that Sam was an enigma to me. I could never tell what she was thinking. She and Verity had met at art school. They'd got on, but they weren't particularly close. They'd been flatmates for a while, and then they'd gone their separate ways. Their friendship had grown stronger when they were in their late twenties. They had both decided to set up their own studio, and to keep costs down they had decided to share office space and apprentices-cum-dogsbodies (Verity called them rent-boys, but not to their faces). Sitting together all day, sharing the dramas and traumas of fashion life, they had grown closer. Sam quickly became Verity's best girlfriend. It was about then that Verity started trying to match-make – 'Sam's gorgeous, and she's just desperate for a hunk like you. And she really likes you, she told me . . .' But the truth was that I hardly knew her, and I did not have eyes for her at all. She *was* gorgeous, but I found her more striking than beautiful. She could have been a model. Tall, high-boned, gaunt, with astonishingly sleek almost-white hair. Her powerful pale eyes, to me, expressed almost nothing. I couldn't read her. She made me uneasy.

'Nathan?' she called anxiously, distracted again by muffled sounds of plastic being crimped and pleated. She half got up, craning her neck. He squinted at her, his mouth still full of pins, then bent back to his plastic bags. Sam settled again, looking uneasy.

'Look, I've been going through her Filofax,' I said.

'Nathan!' Sam leaped off her stool and bustled over to him. 'Not the red, the *blue*. Blue, blue, blue.' She fished around in the heaped plastic bags around the base of the dummy's stand, and pulled up a thick navy bag with white lettering. 'Blue for the patches, red for the lining.' She shoved the bag at him. 'For goodness' sake!' She picked her way back towards me. 'Listen, Harry, I really can't think about it with all this going on, it's just too much.'

I sighed. 'OK. Look, can you spare me a few minutes some time when you're not so busy?' I slipped past her to get my coat, which was on a hook behind Verity's desk.

Sam hovered round me, uncomfortably close. My head thumped harder. 'It really is just a nightmare at the moment,' she twittered. 'There's Paris coming up, and now I've got to do it all on my own, and –'

– and I gave up.

'Sam? *Fuck* Paris.' She looked at me like a startled doe. I pushed briskly past her, and slammed the door as I left – unnecessary, but I couldn't help myself. Perhaps there's a bit of the drama queen in all of us.

I clattered down three flights, and had almost reached the next floor down when the door above creaked open. I heard her boots on the bare boards.

'Harry?' Sam called. She sounded anxious.

I stopped and listened. There was a longish silence, which I suppose I could have broken – 'Yes' would have done the trick nicely – but I didn't. After a while, I heard the door scrape shut again. I continued down, more slowly. The door to Norman's was open a slit. A wild and watery blue eye stared at me. I snarled at him and feinted a lunge. The door clicked sharply shut. That cheered me a little, and I rattled down the last stairs and out on to the street.

I had work to do.

It was a family portrait. The Carlisles: a simple enough job, but time-consuming – and most definitely not what I would have chosen to do that afternoon. I had rung to ask if they would consider rescheduling, but they refused. Mr and Mrs had both taken the afternoon off work, they had given the nanny a half-day, the elder child had been brought home early from nursery. I can't say I blame them, but I could have done without the lecture Mrs Carlisle gave me on the phone.

'Mr Waddell,' – this despite my pleas to call me Harry; everything about the way she spoke was designed to put me in my place, – 'I'm sure we're all terribly sorry about your friend, but I really don't think you understand. It's all very well for *you* to change your plans at short notice but some of us have other commitments. It cost a great deal of time and money to arrange this

45

afternoon. I've had to cancel two very important meetings. Goodness knows how my husband managed to get the time off. We're paying for the nanny even though we're not using her, and we've already paid you – quite handsomely, I might add. We've had several far better quotes since we talked to you, but we'd already booked you and *I* always stand by my agreements . . .' She went on, but I shut it out. I know when I'm beaten. Her voice had a nervous edge, as though she was just barely keeping control of a chaotic and impossibly busy life. Her substitute for control, I thought, was an insistence on formality. The effect was of a woman so brittle that if you shook her hand it would probably shatter.

'That's fine, Mrs Carlisle.' I tried not to snap. Perhaps she was just having a bad day. 'I do understand. We'll stick to the original plan. I'll be with you at one thirty.'

'Well, good. Oh, *stop* it, Giles!' A small child's howl was building in the background. I hastily confirmed their address and rang off.

The conversation was still fresh in my memory when I pressed their doorbell. I'd had plenty of time to think about it because I'd arrived three-quarters of an hour early. I bought a sandwich, and parked round the corner from their house, eating to kill time, and listening to the news on the radio.

For me, severe hangovers bring with them a kind of self-hatred, and now, with nothing else to occupy me, it crept over me. I was still smarting from my conversation with Adam the night before. I had been angry. I had repaid his effort and concern with irritation at every question he asked, every point he made. I needed Adam, now more than ever, but I'd done my best to push him away. Fresh from that, I had sworn at Sam. Replaying the incident now, her behaviour seemed more like distress than disinterest. And with Sam thoroughly alienated, the crowning glory was that I had now also managed to piss off Mrs Carlisle, a woman with whom I was going to spend the next several hours, being paid to make her and her family look good.

I groaned aloud.

On the news: some crucial negotiation or other had failed, violence was expected; stories of children lost or excluded or starving; riots, murders, arms and executions. The old, relentless suffering, inflicted in the name of what someone somewhere believed was right.

I was ten minutes late ringing the doorbell, and my eyes were red. And, bless her, Mrs Carlisle was kind to me. 'Harry? Hi. Emma Carlisle. Thanks so much for coming. I'm so sorry we couldn't rearrange. You must have thought I was a real dragon on the phone ...' She was charming. She kept talking without stop until she had ushered me in, taken my coat, and led me through the house to a kitchen at the rear. Coffee and two children were produced: a baby, and a toddler who hid behind her legs and refused to talk to me. The husband thumped heavily downstairs and introduced himself – Tom. We chatted for a few minutes, then Emma suggested we get on with it, briskly, but pleasantly enough.

Their garden had crumbling red-brick walls, softened by flowers and climbing plants. It must have been about seventy feet long. There were a couple of small trees, plentiful shrubs, trellises of jasmine and roses. The house itself was four storeys and double-fronted. This was a smart area of Fulham: the Carlisles weren't short of a few pennies. For my purposes, the garden was perfect. The early-afternoon sun was slightly hazed, blunting the sharp edges of the shadows while keeping the colour and definition of the gardenscape.

I put the family in the almost-shade of one of the denser trellises, three-quarters back-lit, with a deep view behind them along one wall towards the house. I chatted with the parents as I settled them on a picnic rug, with the children half on them, half between. I clowned a bit for the children, pretending to be surprised by an elephant that I kept popping up behind the camera. I gave the toddler, Giles, an elephant exactly like my own, and told him he had to make it say hello every time mine appeared. He forgot his earlier shyness and joined in with the game, if anything over-enthusiastically. Then I let the parents gradually take over their children, and began to shoot as the four played together, their smiles became slowly less forced, until they had all but forgotten I was there. Occasionally I asked Emma or Tom to move slightly, or to move one of the youngsters, and once or twice I had to make the elephant perform a few tricks. I murmured to them from time to time, keeping them just aware enough of the camera that they would look at it – but I became uninvolved, an observer. I was on the inside of their lives, but just as a shadow.

The trick with photography is to keep shooting. In an average one-hour shoot I might use four or five rolls of film – a hundred and forty-four exposures – and expect to get five or ten good pictures. But you are reading your subjects all the time, anticipating them. You come to know them. When she smiles, the toddler will sink on to her lap a little further and pout; when he makes a joke, she smiles. When the toddler tickles the baby, the husband's shoulders relax and the frown lines soften. It's a kind of trance. Your own reflexes become attuned to theirs, you release the shutter by instinct, again, again, again. And with each moment you capture you see a little more of them, and for each of those moments you feel wise beyond all words. I can't describe it. If I could, perhaps words alone would be enough and I would never feel the need to make pictures. But I cannot resist the lure of catching those instants when other people are truly themselves – at least, as much as any of us ever are. For an hour, almost without talking, certainly without listening, I sank into the Carlisles' lives.

And I found that they were in love, all of them with each other.

There were stresses, of course: Emma and Tom both had worry lines. They looked a little tired, there was tension in their necks and weariness in their movements. From time to time one of them would do something the other clearly did not fully approve of. But there was patience and affection, and a kind of stillness – tranquillity is far too grand a word for it. They were happy. I knew that, when I developed the pictures, it would be there on every frame: four happy people, together on a sunlit day, together always.

And in another part of my thoughts different images played themselves out, a counter-rhythm to every shot. 'Damaged Goods' ... Battered people in a hostile world, the news on the radio. Verity running on the beach, caught in mid-stride. Or again, with her eyes wide and brown, lips half parted, always so serious and so alone. Verity in stiff white sheets, bloated, bruised and broken.

It was intolerable, impossible to believe, a savage rip in the pattern of my oh-so-normal world. Something was so badly wrong. How could I just ... *accept* it? And how could I *not*? After all, it was real, it wasn't about to change. Reality was not obliged to take my feelings into consideration.

Get used to it, Harry.

The trouble was that in order to get used to it, I knew I was going to have to understand it. And I wasn't at all sure I could face that much truth.

When I got home my message light was flashing. I ignored it and sat staring at a wall as the sun slid quietly round the room. The shadows shifted restlessly. I had shot five rolls. The dark room waited.

I ignored my work, though, and went to see Adam.

I waited in Rita, his secretary's room while he finished off his day's work. It was eight o'clock by the time I arrived at Wandsworth town hall, and Rita was long gone. I poked my head round the door to let him know I'd arrived. He looked surprised, then waved breezily, mouthed, 'Just a minute,' and turned back to the phone.

'Yes, yes, I do understand the problem, Gavin. We all understand. We all know it's a problem. But the problem is that it's not *our* problem, it's yours. And I'd like you to make the problem go away.' Adam waved me away and frowned at the phone. I withdrew, closed the door gently and sat on an uncomfortable red nylon sofa to wait, profoundly glad that I had no interest in local politics.

The room was large, cheap and ill-proportioned, with an ungenerous window behind the secretary's desk, cut in half by the recently added partition which had created Adam's office. On the wall there were large cork message boards, several with advice leaflets about citizens' rights, health and the like, and one with Adam's electioneering material from last year. Pamphlets, rosettes, newspaper clippings, shots of Adam with half-famous politicians, strip-banners in blue – 'Adam Yates, *the* choice for Wandsworth' writ large. All this paraphernalia was pinned round the edges of a campaign photograph, which was so unflattering that I'd always been astonished he was re-elected. Like the banners, it was trimmed in blue. His name was printed in blocky blue letters beneath it, with another blue strap-line below that. Everything was designed to frame and enhance a two-foot-high photograph of him. The simple bold design was clearly intended to make a powerful statement about the force of the personality of the person in the picture. 'Here is Adam Yates,' it seemed to suggest. 'Adam Yates is all you ever need to know. Life is that simple. Adam Yates.' Strong stuff.

Except, of course, that the picture was crap. It was black and white, it gave the impression of being slightly out of focus because it had been printed so cheaply, and it had been shot against a blank wall. If you'd put a number round his neck you could have put up Wanted posters for him in police stations. The photo had lost everything that made him who he was: there was no generosity, no laughter, no charm. He looked like a badly drawn cartoon. I'd told him all this: he'd mumbled something about how it was always done this way, and the need to understand the common man. It sounded like standard reactionary bollocks to me, so I shut up. And, to be fair, the opposition's posters were just as bad so I suppose it made no difference.

'Harry, sorry.' Adam burst out of his office. He dumped paperwork and a dictation tape on his secretary's desk. 'Thursday's always the day from hell, God knows why. The judge was already pissed at ten this morning and we never got past lunch. So I had all afternoon here, which should have been easily enough to get everything done except I've just had Gavin Tosspot on the phone for an hour, the fuckwit who runs Finance, telling me my own office – this one – doesn't exist.' Adam frowned. 'Would he deign to come up and see for himself? Would he hell. And that was before he got on to whingeing about some subcontractor who's defaulted. All his problem, all his fault, except the subcontractor's appointment was political, so now it's my problem.'

Adam paused in his rant long enough to look at me closely. He frowned and chewed his lower lip. 'Harry, you look terrible. Has it been rough?'

'Yes. No. Sort of. Hangover.'

Adam, true to form, was showing no sign of suffering: he could drink a distillery dry and bounce out of bed the next morning as though he hadn't touched a drop. He winced in sympathy. 'And here's me rabbiting on about some arsehole in Finance. What an idiot.' I tried to shake my head, which turned out not be a good idea. 'That bad, huh?' Adam tutted. 'Come on, let's get you out of here.' He strode out of the office, waited for me to emerge, then locked up and marched off. He paused when he spotted that I was having trouble keeping up. My head was beating with every step. I reached him, and he set off again, more slowly.

'Adam, don't say you're an idiot,' I said. 'If anyone's an idiot, it's me. Actually, I came to apologise.'

'Hmm?' Adam spotted someone he knew and waved at them. 'What on earth for?'

'Last night. I was pissed off. When you kept saying the whole thing was just normal. I mean, I know that's what the police thought, but I didn't want to hear it from you. I was upset. I never even thanked you for taking the day off to go down there with me.'

Adam stopped again and looked at me silently. He chuckled. 'Harry, you're too polite, that's your problem. I'm a politician, remember? My hide is the envy of rhinos everywhere.' He was lying, of course, but I knew from past experience that there was no point in pressing it. He steered me down the halls of regional government towards the world outside.

'It should be me apologising,' he said. 'A day like that, and there's me trying to get you to think about her as though she was a complete stranger. You'd've had every right to give me a bloody nose.' He pointed towards a flight of stairs, and we clattered down them towards the marbled lobby. 'Isn't that true, Malcolm?' he called to the security man in the lobby. 'Politicians. Insensitive. Talk too much, never pay attention.'

The man looked up and grinned as his name was mentioned. By then we were past him and on our way out of the building. 'Whatever you say, Mr Yates,' he called back. 'Night-night.' He raised a hand. Adam had the knack of being popular with everyone. I'd long ago given up being jealous.

He waited for me again on the pavement. We leaned against the wall. 'So . . . would another beer do you good?' he asked dubiously. 'Hair of the dog?'

I laughed, as gently as I could, to avoid jolting my throbbing head.

'Hmph . . . Shame. Ah, well,' he said. There was sympathetic laughter in his eyes. He thought for a moment. 'OK. In that case, listen.' He took a deep breath, and stared across the street while he spoke. 'You're my friend. You know that. So whatever you say or do, just remember, even when I'm being pompous or insensitive, I care, OK? You're unhappy, and until you're sorted I'm here for you. Whatever it takes, I'll help. Scream and shout at me, fine. Need a chauffeur, fine. Anything. I'll freely admit, I'm not entirely convinced there's a mystery anywhere in this – but I'll help you check it out anyway. Because it's not me who's hurting, and it's not me who needs convincing.'

'Ads—'

He held up a hand. 'Friends. Like I said before. It's what they're for. You'd do the same.' He grinned shyly. 'At least, after all these years, I bloody well *hope* you would.'

He knew I would – and I knew he would, too. In any other circumstances I wouldn't have needed his reassurances that he cared, but until the day before, I'd have sworn Verity would come to me if anything was troubling her. Today was different. Today I was vulnerable. Today was a good day to be reminded that I was not alone.

'Sure about that beer?' Adam urged. 'Do you good.'

'Best go home,' I muttered. 'But thanks. Seriously, Ads.'

He smiled. And, for that brief moment, I could almost have believed in the future. Almost.

seven

'Ah, come on, Verity.'

She lowered her head and looked sideways at me through her fringe. 'I'm not coming, no.'

I was excited to be off. I was scampering about in the alley down the side of the house, restlessly tapping the wall with my foot, swivelling and tapping the fence, pacing back to tap the wall. It had taken me less than a week to decide I would show her the treehouse, but I did not want to tell her where I was taking her, I wanted it to be a surprise.

'You'll love it,' I said hopefully.

'Why should I trust you?' She was pouting.

What did *trust* have to do with it? What did she think I was going to do? I was hardly going to jump on her the moment we were out of sight of the village although ... I was thirteen, she had just turned twelve and, to me, she was ravishing. I had dreams about her, and I enjoyed them. Part of it was that she was unattainable. She was coquettish, wild, she played hard (impossible) to get. But the idea that she might not trust me was baffling – I hardly even dared let our arms brush. The treehouse was just a great place to muck around.

'Ah, go on, Verity ...'

The summer had changed for me. I was having fun. I had stopped being aware of my self-imposed misery or the sluggish tick of passing days. Each morning she would be waiting in my garden, head cocked sideways, her thin knees hugged up under her dress; if she wasn't, I would sneak through the hedge and wait for her. Hot days slid by.

The Great Sling worked brilliantly. It didn't once get the ball into the crook of the tree because the ball never lodged even when it was on target. But who cared? We graduated quickly from targeting the tree to competing for distance and height, launching the ball from one garden to the other. Our targets were clumps of flowers, wheelbarrows and the like. Aiming blind over the hedge was part of the fun.

'Come on, Verity, it's brilliant, this place, you'll see.'

'Daddy won't let me.'

'Don't tell him.' I shrugged.

She said nothing, but she bit her lip. 'I had an idea for the sling,' she said eventually.

'It's a treehouse,' I blurted. 'It's just a treehouse. In Whiteham Woods.'

'But you're not allowed in there.' Verity looked at me sharply. That had caught her interest.

'That's why it's secret. I haven't told anyone else about it, not ever.' I added, bolshily, 'It was going to be a surprise.'

'What sort of a treehouse?'

'You'll see.'

She looked at me suspiciously. But she kicked the wall in time to my lazy rhythm, then the fence, then the wall. I grinned at her, and her eyes creased and her cheeks dimpled.

We went on our bikes. The shadows had left her face even before the village was behind us. When we got to the hill down to the woods, she stuck out both legs sideways and rattled ever faster down the rutted track. Her hair bounced in the wind, shot sparks of sunlight, and she screamed with happy abandon.

The treehouse was about fifteen feet up in the arms of an immense hornbeam. Great branches, three or four feet thick, swept outwards from the vast trunk, ancient and rimed with mossy green. They spread twelve or more feet horizontally, before reaching ponderously upwards. Thinner branches drooped still further out, and down again towards the ground. The tree stood alone: no younger trees had grown in its shade. Its crown was unreachable, out of sight high above the wood's canopy. The tree was old and wise, and I liked to think it was glad of our company.

You could climb onto the lower limbs by shinning up one of the smaller branches that stooped towards the ground. Getting round on to the big branch while dangling fifteen feet above the ground was a challenge, but not impossible. And only once you were up there could you see it.

It was almost invisible from the ground. It rested on the second layer of branches, which were as thick as the ones immediately below, and offset, so that they filled the gaps between them, so that if you looked up from the bole of the tree, you saw a dense mass of radiating branches and very little of what was above them. That was why the treehouse was so hard to spot. You might glimpse it if you knew to look – but why would anyone look? This was private property. It belonged to Oxford University, and was strictly off-limits to all but a select handful of university officials. The people who came to the woods weren't the types to build treehouses – or to seek them out. A groundsman patrolled the area occasionally, but he was looking for poachers, not concealed wooden platforms. I had only found it myself because I climbed the tree for the hell of it – again, something neither distinguished academics nor game wardens were famous for.

Who made it? I have no idea. The boards were already powdered green when I found it, although the wood had not yet rotted. I never did discover whose dream we had taken over, but even today I am grateful to them. It was a simple platform jutting perhaps two or three feet out from the trunk, and forming a semicircle. It ran a little more than half-way round the trunk. From where we had climbed up, it curved away to the right.

Verity climbed up first. 'Wow,' she breathed, and I could imagine her large eyes, wide and sparkling, her mouth open just a little, her delicate teeth. She was standing on the branch without holding on, knees grazed and greened and her blue dress stained by the climb. She had taken off her shoes and socks, and she held them idly in one hand. I could imagine the rough feel of the bark beneath her bony feet. 'Oh . . . This is brilliant, Harry.' It took me a moment or two to respond. I was below her, and transfixed by the fact that I could see up her skirt.

'Told you you'd like it.' I wriggled round the branch to stand behind her.

'Yeah,' she said, in a long sigh. 'Wow . . .'

I took off my own shoes, carefully gripping the branch with my spare hand. She almost skipped along it. 'Oh, *wow*.' She clambered up on to the platform. I followed, and set my shoes down next to hers. We walked round the semicircle to where the boards appeared to sink into the flank of a vast branch. When she turned to me there was wonder in her eyes. We sat side by side with our backs against the gnarled bark, feet stretched out towards the edge, and looked out into a dizzying cage of leaf-light. Tremendous spars of wood leaped out to buttress the green wall that sealed our universe from the world outside. I remember the comfort of being there, knowing that we need say nothing. For a small while we held hands, then we released them – let it mean whatever it meant. The air was full of the scent of dry wood, and the chatter of the leaves. This was the place that would make the summer magical.

It wasn't long before Verity took over. Not content with the treehouse as it was, she wanted to improve it. Within a week she had made the place thoroughly hers.

First, there was her insistence that no treehouse was complete without a swing. She scavenged a good length of hemp rope from old John Taylor, who repaired cars in a mire of greasy filth he called a yard – and who also owned the best orchard for miles around, which Verity and I regularly plundered. Goodness knows how she got the rope out of him, she wouldn't tell: he was a mean old sod, I can't imagine him ever doing anything out of the kindness of his dark and oily heart. But Verity had a way with her – her determination and innocence were hard to resist.

Then it turned out she had a flair for three-dimensional thinking because she found an anchor spot that let us use the swing in countless ways. She spotted a cleft in a branch about ten feet up and out from the platform's far end. To my eyes, it didn't look promising, but she insisted. To attach the rope she had to stand on my shoulders and pull herself up on to a branch way above head height, then crawl out along it until she was hanging perilously perhaps twenty-five feet above the ground with nothing to break her fall, wrestling with a thick and uncooperative mass of hemp.

'You should let me do it,' I called anxiously. She had just lost her grip for the fifth or sixth time, and was swinging beneath the branch by her knees. She stopped trying to get back up and hung upside-down, staring at me intently. Her dress had fallen away. Its hem brushed her chin, and she swung gently, coils of rope looping around her. I tried hard not to look at her legs and knickers.

'Harry,' she said, after a pause. Her face was reddening and bulging, clotting her voice.

'Yes, Verity?'

'Shut up.' So I did. I watched.

Eventually, the swing was hung, and a small spar knotted into it for a seat. I stood on the platform holding it, feeling stupid. 'Go on,' she urged. She looked enchanted, her eyes dreamy and unblinking, her stillness the only sign of her excitement. I leaped upwards and plunged from the treehouse. '*Yeeee-hah!*' A sudden perilous drop – the breath rushed out of me – and I arced upwards, then out towards the shimmering curtain of leaves. I had to stretch almost to my limit to grab the platform's edge as I swung back. I pulled myself on board.

'That was brilliant! You can almost touch the leaves! I bet you could if you jumped high enough first.'

Verity's eyes glittered darkly. 'If you hold it lower down and run along the edge before you swing, you'll reach that branch.' She pointed to one of the large horizontal limbs, which jutted outwards further round the tree, beyond the end of the treehouse. She made no move to take the rope.

The angles looked all wrong to me, but I tried it. I swung out and round, and my fingertips brushed bark before my momentum carried me past and smashed me into the main trunk. I rebounded outwards, spinning and a little dazed. On my second return, she caught my arm, and hoisted me back to safety.

'Got – got to – run a little faster,' I gasped, my chest in agony.

'Second time lucky!' She giggled and clapped her hands. 'Gimme!' She flew outwards, screaming happily, not caring about the knocks.

For Verity, the swing was only the start. She announced that a treehouse was not a treehouse without a roof, so we built one over part of the platform. It was flat, and doubled as a second level: by using it as another starting point, the swing had even more permutations. Next we knocked up a ramshackle shelf. We kept biscuits and pilfered apples, and bottles of Coke, which were always warm and flat by the time we were finishing them.

I secretly relished the implied intimacy of my lips touching the bottle where hers had been: it sealed our companionship, acknowledged our oneness – I had a lot of romantic notions when I was thirteen. We shared everything, food, drinks, games, trivial flirtatious secrets. Some days she would be distant and uneasy, though, and even the most spectacular stunts on the rope would not bring her back. I learned to give her time.

We improvised a rope-ladder, which we hid on the platform and pulled down with a stick when we needed it. We kept the stick hidden in long grass against the fence just where we slipped through into the woods. From the ground, despite all our modifications, the treehouse was still all but undetectable. Of course, it probably stood out like a sore thumb in winter with no leaves to shield it, but I never gave that a thought. The gamekeeper never found us – or if he did, he left us alone.

Someone found us, though.

And it changed everything.

We didn't go to Whiteham Woods every day. Occasionally we'd get out the sling and play target practice instead, or cycle to Port Meadow and swim in the Isis, or rummage out our roller-skates and sweep down the hill into Wolvercote at lethal speed in the middle of the road. We broke into the grounds of the local private school, St Edward's, and swam in its huge outdoor pool. We spent lazy days on the swing-bridges across the canal, and exploring the old cement works. It was summer: there were endless days, endless ways to spend them.

But one morning when we arrived at the treehouse, the rope-ladder was hanging down. Someone had been there in the two days since we'd been. They'd even taken our biscuits. I thought Verity was going to cry. Her hands waved about, apparently uncontrolled. She began to stammer. She looked around constantly, her gaze flitting fearfully from place to place.

'They can't,' she whispered sadly. (I'm leaving out the stammer. It seems unfair to her.) 'Not here, no one can come *here*.' She sat on the platform hugging her knees, rocking, her eyes large and soft and seeing nothing, the way she waited for me some mornings. 'Ours. This is ours.' She stiffened, and turned to look at me. 'We have to catch him.' From the first moment, she was always sure it was a boy – but, then, I suppose I was too. It never occurred to me that it might be a girl.

We spent a few days staking out the treehouse, waiting to see if the interloper would make another appearance. But he was cleverer than that: if he came, he spotted us first and slipped away. We spent four uncomfortable days in prickly undergrowth, and saw no one.

Verity suggested traps. It quickly became a game, and the strangeness of that first moment of discovery vanished, replaced by exaggerated fantasies – concealed pits filled with spikes, specially weakened boards that only we would know about. We even considered deploying the sling in anger: it would fire a projectile – rotting fruit or ink or, (my favourite), spiked steel balls – when the intruder triggered a trip-wire. Ink was the best idea because then we could track down the intruder later, hold an identification parade, have him incarcerated for trespassing (as, of course, were we). The experiments with the sling were promising, but ink and steel balls were out: whatever method we used had to be private and non-lethal. We settled for milk cartons filled with water. They worked perfectly. It was not enough for Verity, though. She announced that whether or not the sling worked as a deterrent, we still had to find out who the invader was.

'What we need is cameras,' she said, and she gave me a certain look: that questions were not allowed. She frowned intently for about a minute, then her teeth flashed as she giggled. She ran down my garden and through the hedge. For a few paces, I swear I saw her skipping.

I knew what that meant. She had a plan.

Verity had a little 16-millimetre Instamatic. Mum didn't have a camera, but I knew Dad had left one behind when he went, an old Olympus he'd always said he should throw away.

I climbed up into the loft. It was intolerably hot, airless, with no wind to ruffle the layers of dust. The camera was in a packing-case full of things Dad hadn't bothered to take, underneath a few shabby items of clothing he'd used for working round the house. It was in its own box, frayed brown leather with two clasps, set in sparkling grey foam along with a flash, a trigger-wire and a couple of spare lenses.

I set it on one side and continued to delve. I don't know what I was searching for – clues, perhaps, to the muffled yells and shouts that had kept me awake night after night for months before Dad left. I felt guilty that I was peering into his private, unhappy world. I stopped at the slightest sound, fearful that Mum would discover me, because Dad's Old Things were a no-go area. I found nothing. I heard Mum coming upstairs, and hurriedly tidied everything away. I hunted for a tripod, but there wasn't one, so I swung myself out, pulled down the camera case, and closed up. Mum was in her bedroom, so I slipped downstairs and dodged quickly out of the kitchen before she could ask what I'd been up to, then hurried down the garden with my trophies. There was still time to get to the woods and set up.

As well as her own camera, Verity also had a professional-looking machine, which she held as though it was infinitely precious – I know now it was an SLR, a single-lens reflex, very posh. She wouldn't tell me where it came from: she just said it had been hard to get, and looked distantly at the nearest wall. So that made three cameras – and she insisted we take the sling, plus a supply of empty milk cartons to fill from the stream. I couldn't see the need for three cameras – but, as usual, she was ahead of me.

'Insurance,' she said brightly.

She began to construct a simple hide of twigs and leaves around the first camera. She squatted with her knees high. She moved quickly and easily.

'When we get him ...' she grunted as she yanked a branch towards her '... we need three photos of him. If we only use one camera, he might be facing the wrong way.' She hid all three, with logs balanced precariously above their shutter buttons, hooked up to strings that trailed away from them to where the trip-wire was to be set. The idea was that when the intruder triggered the wire, the logs would fall and set off the cameras.

Verity sat with her legs half curled under her. Her big serious eyes seemed almost emerald in the shade. There was a green-brown scuff mark on one cheek. 'And another thing,' she said firmly, 'he might realise we've taken his photo. If we're lucky, the milk cartons will distract him – but even if he does spot a camera, he won't spot *three*, will he?'

'Devious,' I growled.

'Mean,' I added.

'Underhand,' I suggested.

'I like it.' I grinned.

Verity smiled, as if all was suddenly well with the world. She twitched her eyebrows up and down to show how cunning she was. When she set back to work, she hummed absentmindedly. If I had recognised the tune, I would have joined her. Instead, I smiled at her – and her eyes shone back.

Unbelievably, it worked – all of it.

We set the trap, left it there for a day – and when we came back, the wires had been tripped and the sling had fired. Most amazingly, though, all three cameras went off. The falling logs had knocked them over, they looked a little beaten, but they'd taken the shots. We fired off the remaining exposures, and took the films to the nearest chemist in North Oxford. A few days later, the prints were ready.

There was the intruder, frozen from three angles, his arms up to ward off the flying milk cartons, water already looping from them. One carton was clearly going to hit him.

We crowed. We hugged each other excitedly. Triumph was sweet. Her fine hair tickled my nose as she pressed against me, and I bent over her to get my first glimpse of our villain. The first shot showed his back, his arm half raised, the cartons motionless in mid-air flying straight towards the camera. In the second shot, he was smaller – the Instamatic had been further away from the action and (I now realise) had a wider-angle lens. His face was indistinct and too small to recognise. The third shot was from my Olympus (and why shouldn't it be mine if Dad didn't want it and Mum had left it in the loft for so long?) and it was the clincher: a three-quarters profile with the spray from the cartons hanging out of focus in the foreground, the face recognisable. Not bad for my first-ever photo. Verity spread out two shots and handed the third to me. Our hands touched as we arranged them in a neat row.

Adam Yates. A boy at school. He was a year above me, but I knew who he was. A big boy, but often picked on. He was always the one whose gym shoes got peed in; smaller children threw things at him because he never fought back. I had teased him myself, from the safety of a sniggering group. I knew him without knowing him.

I opened my mouth to tell Verity, but she was already thinking about something else.

She was frowning at the photographs. She set her two prints at an angle to each other so that all three together made up three sides of an open square. Then she took back the one I'd been holding and squatted on the pavement. As I crouched next to her I could hear she was humming again, faint familiar snatches. Carefully, she propped the photos upright, as though she were building a house of cards: the prints all touched at their top corners, each became one side of a triangular box. She shuffled round them in a circle, nudging me out of the way. As she passed, I smelt a hint of woodscent.

'We need more cameras,' she said finally.

'What are you talking about? It's Adam Yates. From school.' I was getting a little exasperated.

'Yes, yes.' She waved her hands about impatiently. 'But we need more cameras.'

'Wha—'

'Look,' she said firmly, and grabbed my wrist. She dragged me round the tiny construction of photos. 'Here. The same moment – here – here – here. One, two, three. You've got the milk cartons, Whatshisface Yates, the tree, all from different angles, *all at the same moment*! We need more cameras!' She clapped excitedly, and bounced to her feet. She shuffled the photos into a pile, and gave them to me.

I was perplexed, unable to keep up with her quicksilver thoughts. She stopped hopping around and frowned at me, then spoke slowly in case she lost me again. 'Take a bunch of cameras, loads of them, twenty or something ... Put them in a big circle, all pointing in towards the middle ... Then set them all off at exactly the same time! Wham!' She threw her hands dramatically into the air. I still didn't get it. She rolled her eyes. 'OK, stay completely still ...' She mimed taking a picture of me and said, 'Click.' Then she jumped round so she was sideways on to me – 'Click.' Another jump, nearly behind me now – 'Click' – and so on, until she was in front of me again. 'Three-D photos,' she said simply. 'Each picture's the same thing, at the same time, but from a different angle. Then if you hold them in your hand and flick through them like a book, it'll feel like you're flying around whatever's in the picture.' She rushed off

62

towards her bike. 'But we need more cameras,' she shouted over her shoulder.

I had to pedal hard to catch her. We rode home in silence, with houses and then fields flickering by. Some time after we reached open countryside, I plucked up courage. 'What about Adam Yates?'

'Cameras,' she said, ignoring my question. 'We need more cameras, Harry.'

She grinned and leaned her bike towards me until our shoulders bumped, and we both swung away, wildly trying to regain our balance. She giggled.

We cycled on in silence, and her eyes were alight, and the wind whispered for our ears alone.

eight

The phone woke me. It took me about five rings to reach it. By then the answering-machine had kicked in. I had to fight my own recorded voice while I fumbled for the off-switch.

'Hello?'

'*—ry Waddell. Sorry I can't get t—*'

'Hello, hold on. Wait a second, I'll switch it off.'

I heard Adam's voice at the other end. Couldn't understand what he said, though.

'*—bout a job you can call me on—*'

As I groped for the switch, I knocked the machine off the table. '*Fuck!* Oh. Sorry.' The machine gave one protesting beep when it hit the floor, and stopped. I looked at it, confused, trying to gather my thoughts. It was half on the floor, half suspended in a snarl of cables. Amazingly, the message light was still flashing. I stared at the machine. Probably broken. Great.

'Hi . . . Adam?'

'You all right, Harry?'

'Yeah. Half asleep. Woke me up. What time is it?'

'I didn't mean to, I thought you'd be up. Ten to eight. I wanted to check how you were, what you were up to.'

'Yeah. Thanks.'

In my dream, there had been clouds, a huge cool storm that filled the sky but never arrived. Hungry faces, big wise eyes staring.

'Harry?'

I rubbed my face fiercely.

'I'm here, just trying to wake up.'

'You up to listening?'

'Yeah. Sorry, Ads.'

'Don't go there, just listen. I'm taking today off. That's why I rang early. Fridays are almost as bad as Thursdays anyway. Court's closed because judge fancied a long weekend and I'm not going anywhere near the town hall – Appropriation Committee, Policy Steering Group, all garbage. So I'm devoting today to the newly created, officially sanctioned Harry Waddell Outreach Programme, HWOP for short. Catchy, don't you think?'

'I don't deserve you, Adam.'

'Shut up and tell me what we're doing.'

'Seriously.' I smiled into the phone. Grinned, actually.

'And when we're doing it.'

'OK, OK.'

I'd been planning to go to Eastbourne. I wanted Verity to have a few of her own things, even if she was in a coma and couldn't appreciate them: you never knew. Then I was going to follow her footsteps, find the place in her diary, Birling Gap. She'd had an appointment there at three thirty on the day she fell. 'I'd like it if you could come,' I said. 'I mean, if you're serious.'

'Deadly serious,' he said. 'We'll take the BMW.'

'Pick me up at Verity's, then. Give me an hour to get there, maybe half an hour to sort out some things for her.' I glanced at a clock. Just past eight. 'An hour and a half,' I said. 'Make it half nine.'

'See you there, then – and don't say thank you again, Harry, or I might have to shoot you.' He hung up before I could think of a reply.

I set the answering-machine straight, and wandered into the bathroom to prepare for the day. When I looked in the mirror, the face I saw smiled back broadly.

I was dreading going to Verity's flat, and at the same time I was desperate to be there. Of course, if I wanted to collect things to take down to Eastbourne for her – a decent nightie, ornaments for her bedside cabinet – I had no choice. I was far from sure that such things were allowed in ITU, but I wanted to try – and behind that, of course, was the real motive: I wanted to see her again. I couldn't admit it to myself, because I already knew the horror I was letting myself in for – the stark white light, the damaged body, the blank face, the silence. Even so, the truth was that I wanted to see her.

Verity's flat also seemed the right place to go through her Filofax and ring everyone who needed to know what had happened to her. I had neatly asterisked the names of her friends, the ones whose names I knew. Most were just names I had heard; in many ways, I had always been on the fringes of her life, comfortably isolated from the neurotic world of fashion.

There were fewer people than I had expected: the address pages bulged and threatened to push open the Filofax's clasps, but most of the entries had been crossed out, some with a single neat line, others violently scrubbed. Not many were current. There were a few old and constant names – me, Sam, Gabriel, a couple of others from college days – but most were fairly new. There weren't as many calls for me to make as I had imagined. Probably I should have been grateful that I was not part of her social circle: if I had been, doubtless my name would have been vigorously scratched out years ago.

Verity had a way of reinventing herself. She had a regular cycle: it began with enthusiasm, then there was a slow slide into aimlessness and dissatisfaction, then depression, then resurrection. Her friends changed with each cycle: she would move to a new flat in a new area, her ideals would change, she would announce a new creative vision to all who would listen (so, mostly to me). And, of course, she would still be exactly the same old Verity, brilliant, scatty, emotionally disorganised, and always on the rebound from some disastrous fling. Then the slide would start again, as the complexity and compromises of bank managers and men and fashion politics smothered her sense of self. It usually took about two years.

What was strange was that she had just come through her latest bad patch. She had been full of sap and enthusiasm, she was creative and alive. When I had seen her at Jim's two weeks before, her eyes had been clear and purposeful, lined with laughter. She had teased me all evening, told me I wasn't irresponsible enough, that whatever was bothering me (work, I think, or perhaps that no one really loved me) mattered not at all. It had been Verity on top, mad form, full of big ideas and philosophies, so sure of herself. So happy.

And I think that perhaps that was the real reason I wanted to go to her flat. To get inside her head. To touch the same things, look at the same walls. Find the connection between the Verity I thought I had known and the new, real Verity, mashed and stitched, in a bright pool of hospital light.

I certainly did not expect to find the flat occupied.

He was tall and pale, with rough stubble on a narrow chin. His eyes were dull, his nose sharp and straight. His thin lips twitched sometimes at the corners. He smoked endlessly, pinched little roll-ups, preparing the next one as he puffed, his eyelids fluttering in the smoke. His booted feet were on Verity's white calico sofa, and grey ash flecked the cushions. He was using a saucer as an ashtray. Verity didn't smoke, and couldn't abide anyone smoking near her – unless it was one of her bits of rough, and this guy fitted the bill perfectly. He didn't look surprised when I walked in. He glanced at me casually, then bent back to the cigarette he was rolling, twitching his head sideways to avoid the fumes of the dog-end in his mouth.

The television was on in the corner, a bland quiz.

'She out.' His accent was Slavic, his voice deep and blurred. He leaned forward to stub out his cigarette, and a thin line of ash dribbled onto the sofa, the floor, the table. The saucer overflowed as he prodded the butt around in it. He lit up again, and leaned back to watch the quiz again – as though I wasn't there, as though Verity's flat was public property. I sized him up. Distinguishing features: (1) he was a bastard, clearly; (2) long legs in rancid-looking jeans, a ripped, over-tight T-shirt, groomed over-shiny hair; (3) probably a model; (4) probably unemployed; (5) probably Verity's type, damn him. She had probably pulled him at some two-bit fashion show.

I crossed the room, and switched off the TV. 'You're going to tell me who the fuck you are,' I spat, 'and then you're going to fuck off.'

He jerked upright and pinched the roll-up from his mouth. 'Shit, man, relax, baby.' I wasn't sure if it was his weak English or if he was on drugs. He seemed to understand me well enough, though. 'Hey, I say same for you. Who are you? What you do here?'

I hadn't expected him to challenge me, and it punctured my indignation temporarily. I told him who I was, and he shrugged. I

67

told him about Verity's fall, and he shrugged. He didn't seem to care, although he obviously knew her, because here he was. Then he put the cigarette in his mouth and put his feet back on the sofa. After a deep drag, he introduced himself. 'Karel,' he said lazily. 'Verity and me, lovers. You know. I give her good time. She like me.'

'Well, stop smoking, then,' I snapped. 'She hates it.' And I hated him.

He ignored me. He sat forward and started working on his next roll-up. When he was finished, he looked up at me appraisingly. 'Is Harry, yes?' I said nothing. 'Harry, there is things for you to learn. A girl like Verity, you know, you got to show her who the boss. She not like smoke, no problem – *I* like smoke.' He tapped his chest and scowled. 'So smoke, no problem. She complain, I go. She not want this.'

A better man (meaning one with more guts) would have hit him. Instead I barked, 'You've got thirty seconds to get out of this flat or I'm calling the police.'

He snorted. 'And say what? Is burglar?' He fished in his pocket and dangled a set of keys in front of me, exact copies of the ones I was still holding. I took a step towards him. He shook his head soulfully and raised a finger to stop me. 'Is all right, Harry, man. You stay cool. I go. This place is no point now.' His English was ridiculous, limited to hackneyed slang and compressed self-importance, but somehow it made his arrogance impossible to puncture. There was no way to hurt him. I stood firm, balled my fists and took a heavy breath.

He rose, relaxed and lanky. He flicked his roll-up on to the table, and left it to burn there. Then he walked – strutted – lazily towards Verity's bedroom. 'Hey!' I yelped. He waved a hand dismissively without looking back. I followed and watched from the doorway. A few clothes were scattered on the floor. Three pairs of her shoes were jumbled on an armchair in the corner. The bed was unmade. He ignored this, and went to a battered chest-of-drawers on the side wall. He opened one of the top drawers and fished at the back of it, emerging with a small key. He unlocked the other top drawer and peered in. He tutted.

'Not much,' he drawled. He pulled out a wad of money and flicked through it. He pursed his lips. 'Fifty? Eighty, maybe.

Usually is more.' He walked back towards me, and waved the money at me. 'I make her feel good. Is worth more than this, but, hey ...'

He grinned nastily and pushed past me. I was paralysed by his contempt. I couldn't quite believe it. He turned when he reached the door, with Verity's keys hung casually from his finger.

'Hey, Harry, man,' he called, much more loudly than he needed to. 'You know something? Your girlfriend, man, she frigid. She is worst fuck I ever do. Maybe she fancy girls, yeah?'

His boots jangled on the steps, then the pavement, and his laughter drifted through the open windows as he walked away.

I started by clearing up the ash. I even took off the cushion covers to put them in the washing-machine. I couldn't wash the sofa cover because it wasn't loose. Instead I hoovered it. Then I cast about for other traces of Karel. The work surfaces in the kitchen were a mess – crumbs and dried red stains from a tin of beans. The plate and saucepan would need to soak, as would the ash-encrusted saucer. I filled the sink, then went into the bathroom – nothing there – and then the bedroom, the only other room in the flat.

It smelt of smoke. The snarled-up bedlinen and the confused piles of her clothes forced me to imagine them together here. How had it been? *She not like, no problem – I like* ... I put her room in order. I smoothed and folded her clothes and set them in piles on the shelves in her tattered wardrobe. I pulled away the sheet, pillow-cases and duvet cover, and put them aside to wash. I dressed the bed in clean white linen, straightening, patting, tugging at the corners. I threw open all the windows and let in clean air. I did all the comforting things for her that she could no longer do. I spent the next hour cleaning. I emptied the washing-machine, reloaded it, hung everything out to dry. Then I made myself a coffee and sat on a hard chair near the windows in the sitting room – I couldn't bear to sit on the sofa – and I cried.

Who the hell was he, this man? She had never mentioned him, but he had the keys to her flat – which she'd never given me, because, she said, she cared too much about me: she didn't want me to catch her unprepared, it might put me off her. This man had walked casually over my feelings, in pipe-thin jeans and cowboy boots: what would he have done if he had seen her in hospital?

69

Tapped ash on the white sheets, perhaps? Blown smoke at the ventilator, to prove his superiority? But, no, he didn't care enough for that. He hadn't even asked about her or the accident. *No point in staying*, that was all he thought about it. He'd just stolen from her, and walked away. From his perspective she was all used up; time to move on. I was terrified that I would find she had loved him, that her growing happiness and certainty were because of him. The thought was intolerable. And if she had loved him – *please, no* – how would she have felt if he had rejected her?

I shook myself. Get practical. Adam was coming.

I went through her post. There were four letters. The first was a mammoth phone bill: I was glad it wasn't mine, the listed calls ran to twelve pages. Next was a letter from the bank, informing her that her overdraft now exceeded £1,500, which was the limit she had agreed two weeks before. They had bounced her last two cheques – both to fabric suppliers by the look of it – and unless her finances were set in order immediately (underlined, in bold) the bank would be forced to demand the return of her cards and cheque book, and would warn all credit agencies of her unreliability. The third was junk mail, telling her that she had been exclusively selected for a platinum credit card with an automatic £20,000 limit. That made me smile – then I stopped. Poor Verity, what a nightmare. The last was a credit-card bill, spent up to its £8,000 limit and beyond. I'd known she was broke, she always was, but I hadn't known it was this bad.

Was it bad enough for her to kill herself? It wasn't a thought I wanted to pursue. I set the bills on one side, and moved on.

There were three messages on the answering-machine. One would be from me, of course, my petulant message from Wednesday. I assumed the other two were from that bastard Karel – he'd probably tried to call before coming over. I couldn't face the prospect of hearing him again, so I left the machine alone. Its flashing light followed me as I moved around the flat, a blinking, reproachful eye.

Verity was all around me. The hot yellow walls, the thin muslin instead of curtains; the mad tangle of ironwork that served as a candlestick on the dining-table, the calico sofa she loved. And everywhere the kitsch touches that had changed almost every time I visited. An irregular clump of unmatched tassels hung from the

70

main lightshade. A furry pink boa framed the doorway to the kitchen, and clashed boisterously with the walls. A voluptuous nude in Perspex stood next to the candelabrum, its base lit up in acid green, a flex trailing to a wall socket. There was a second telephone, not plugged in, shaped like a randy frog.

Verity loved to laugh.

And alongside the always-changing parade of frivolities, her other things, the things that were always with her. The shabby old furniture salvaged from a nurses' hostel, the oval oak table Gabriel had given her for her twenty-first. Two of my photos were mounted on stands on a bookshelf: one of her holding a rude-looking lollipop, on a day at the seaside we'd had years ago; the other of a row of schoolchildren, all with their tongues out, except one urchin on the end with a gap-toothed grin.

And the zoetrope.

I'd made it for Verity long before I knew what its proper name was. I eventually found the name 'zoetrope' in a book about the history of cinema at a friend's. When I got home I looked the word up: 'An optical toy ... A cylinder with a series of pictures on the inner surface which give an impression of continuous motion when seen through slits with the cylinder rotating.'

Yes. Well. Whatever. The one I made for Verity was hardly posh. It was a broad hoop of card, with a series of photos spaced around the inside. Between each photo, I had cut a narrow vertical slot: on the opposite side of the hoop from each slot, there was a photograph, so if you peeped through each slot, you saw a different shot. There was a spindle sticking up in the middle, and the hoop had cross-pieces that rested on top of it so the whole hoop could spin freely. You put your eye against the first slot, spun the hoop, and image after image flickered in front of you, like a primitive movie projector.

Each picture was of the same thing: a girl, frozen in mid-leap and mid-happy-yell. Her arms were thrown out, her hair lifting, her slim legs kicked up behind her. A great hornbeam arched overhead, a brilliant green shell. Some pictures were larger or smaller, some were a different colour, but they were all of the same moment. In each shot you saw the moment from a different angle. When the hoop was spinning, you had the feeling that you were flying jerkily around her.

I spun it – and there she was, free and happy, for one mad instant long ago. Verity, frozen for ever in the middle of the air.

A horn sounded in a staccato burst on the street below. I looked out, and saw Adam peering up at me through the windscreen of his BMW. Startled, I checked my watch: ten forty. He was late. I had been in the flat almost two hours, and I still hadn't accomplished what I came here for. I waved at Adam, then hurried into the bedroom and rummaged for nightclothes.

I found a large old shirt that she could only have slept in; she certainly never wore it out. I felt very uneasy going through her drawers: her bras and knickers brought out thoughts in me that I would rather have kept buried, and which, in any case, were more than a little inappropriate when the woman you were thinking of was in a coma. I found a dressing-gown folded away in a corner of the wardrobe, some warm socks in a drawer, loose calf-length trousers and a sweatshirt. I grabbed a toothbrush, a hairbrush. There was a leather case on top of the wardrobe, and I jammed everything in. I closed the windows, grabbed the zoetrope, and carried the bag down to the car, double-locking the front door behind me.

'So this guy Whatshisname—'

'Karel.'

'Karel. He's got a key.'

'Yes.' I was weary. 'I'll have to get someone in to change the locks tomorrow.' I didn't really want to talk about it, but Adam was doing his best to be supportive and I didn't want to seem ungrateful.

Verity's suitcase was on the back seat. Next to it, in two halves, was the zoetrope. It looked impossibly fragile. The paper hoop was so light that it bounced off the seat with every bump. The base was solid enough, but the thin wire spindle jiggled subtly in time to the vibrations of the engine. I hadn't designed it with travel in mind. I had made it for her birthday, inspired by a drunken evening of reminiscence. When I gave it to her, she had hugged me. She laughed and she cried. And when she spun it and looked through the slits at the tiny world frozen inside, her eyes were as large and glossy as they had been all those years ago. To her it was ancient history, but once I had reminded her she had been swept up in the

72

idea all over again. We'd sat in silence, both staring into a long-gone past, me staring at her, she through the open window into the dark, gazing at somewhere far away.

'And he nicked the money right in front of you?' Adam shook his head. 'Amazing.'

We rode in silence for a while.

'Sounds like she has some rough friends,' he said reflectively.

'She has pretty bad taste in men,' I admitted.

He glanced sideways at me. 'Yourself excluded, Harry.' He laughed. I snorted back, to show I appreciated it. Sort of. Adam peered at me again. I had a feeling he was about to say something I wasn't going to like – again.

'She did care about you, you know, Harry.'

I snorted again. 'How would *you* know?'

'Point,' Adam conceded. 'I can't claim I *know*. But you only have to think about it. She spent an evening with you once every two weeks, minimum. And there's all the things you've told me – she listens to you, she doesn't care if you're up or down, she still wants to see you. You always said she was there for you, no matter what. She cared, trust me.'

I really didn't want to hear this. I tried to concentrate on the road, the ceaseless loom and whip-past of trees, bollards, signposts ... And failed.

'Trouble is,' Adam went on, 'there's caring and then there's *caring*.'

I said nothing. Tried to think nothing. He was only trying to help. But I wished he would stop, until later. I knew that one day I was going to have to face all this – but for now, even a glimpse of the truth was unbearable.

'Hey,' he said. 'You think Whatshisname's the reason she jumped?'

'Karel, he was called.' I could see what Adam was thinking, but I couldn't bring myself to accept that Verity had ever really ... *cared* for such a bastard. It was a horrible idea, and I didn't want to think about it. 'Listen, Adam—'

He held up a hand to forestall me. 'Didn't mean to open wounds, Harry. Sorry. How about some music?' He rummaged with his free hand among a chaotic assortment of cassettes in the well by the gearstick.

Before I could answer, he slapped in a cassette. The Eurythmics, 'Sweet Dreams', at top volume. It was a blast from the old days, the words and tune familiar, the delivery so confident, the comfort of another old friend. Adam's fingers drummed the wheel in time to the beat. I looked ahead. The road blurred towards and underneath us, and Eastbourne drifted ever closer, while behind me the zoetrope tapped restlessly against the seat.

nine

'But I haven't *got* a camera,' Adam said miserably.
'That's *your* problem,' Verity said self-righteously.
'Four cameras or you don't go anywhere near the treehouse again, not ever.'

He stood with his back to a rotten oak tree on the outskirts of the village, at bay after a quarter of an hour of yelling and poking by us both. We had his confession, we had his apology and we had him pinned; and Verity had surprised me by not following through. I had thought the idea was to warn him off – after all, the treehouse was our private domain and it had been Verity who wanted to keep it that way – but here she was, telling him he could be part of the treehouse gang (she'd made up the 'gang' there and then, I'd had no say in it) on condition that he could get us four cameras. I can't say I was happy about it. And to make matters worse, through a mixture of threats and will-power, it was looking like she'd won.

Secretly, I think I understood why Adam wanted so much to be allowed to use the treehouse. I can't say I was happy about it, but the sympathy was real whether I liked it or not. When I looked at Adam, I saw a boy a little like myself. Adam was lonely. He craved solitude, but he was also desperate for friendship. He wanted to be alone and he wanted to belong. Verity's 'gang' was perfect for him. And although I hated the prospect of his intrusion, I also felt sorry for him – and for that, I loathed him.

I wanted a private world that only Verity and I inhabited, a world of secrets and intimacy and mad fun. I was happy and I hadn't been for ages, and what had changed was that Verity was there and that she liked me and I liked her. She was half a friend and half an object of hopeless desire, and I wanted nothing to stand between me and either. But she had made up her mind and I couldn't stop her any more than Adam could.

Adam never stood a chance. At first he had denied that he had been anywhere near the treehouse. The photos had soon put paid to that. Then he admitted he had been there and told us that it was none of our business. Verity told him the treehouse was ours and ours alone. He said it wasn't, because it had obviously been there for ever and we couldn't have built it. Adam was big, but that didn't stop Verity. She screamed and pummelled him with her tiny fists. He had no idea how to deal with it. That was when he'd started the slow stagger backwards that finally put his back against the rotten oak. At that point, Verity stopped hammering him and the stand-off began. She told him that the treehouse was now booby-trapped with far more lethal weapons than milk cartons full of water; she said her dad had a pistol and it was set up to shoot anyone going near the treehouse; she said there were big wooden spikes that would impale him if he crossed a trigger wire. And he believed her – or, rather, he didn't have the spirit to question her.

And then Verity had dropped her bombshell about the cameras. I don't know who was more startled, Adam or me.

'I can't,' Adam whimpered.

'No treehouse, then,' Verity said. 'Come on, Harry, let's go.' She yanked at me with a nod and we turned to go, both of us scuffing at the field's long grass, the tips of the stalks tapping tartly at our shoes. There was a dusting of pollen on her thin gold shins, evidence of the hairs there too fine and short for me to see. As we turned she looked up at me: her eyes were wise, her face was solemn and full of thought. And suddenly I was powerful again, because Adam was banished, it was just me and her and we'd triumphed.

Then Adam yelled, 'Wait! Wait. *Please!*' And she smiled to herself and turned back, and suddenly I felt as low as before I had been high. I had lost, after all.

'Four cameras,' Verity said firmly. Adam nodded. He looked terrified. Verity clapped her hands and laughed. She hugged my arm and held herself close to me, a small comfort. Through the thin material of her dress, a small breast was pressed against my bare arm. I tried to stay as still as I could, desperate not to break the connection. 'When we see the cameras,' she said, 'we'll let you join.' I stared woodenly at Adam. He stared woodenly at her.

The next day, he had a camera.

Verity and I were in the garden at my place. We had reclaimed the sling from the treehouse and were experimenting with firing nails and marbles, which we planned to smash first to sharpen the edges. We weren't actually serious, but it was delicious to be so analytically gruesome, working out the most effective way possible of causing grievous bodily harm. Mum called that someone was here, and ushered a nervous-looking Adam into the garden. He was clutching a school satchel, the straps ripped and loose. He came hesitantly, the bag clamped defensively against his chest, and stopped a good ten feet away. He flashed a glance at the pile of rusting nails and the sling, and licked his lips before he spoke.

'I got one,' he said nervously. He rummaged in the satchel and pulled out a scuffed brown leather camera case. The poppers were open and I could see brushed chrome and black dials inside. He held it out in one hand, leaning as far forward as he could, as though he was afraid to come closer. Verity made no move to take it.

'One?' she said caustically.

Adam nodded. 'It's my sister's. She'll kill me if she finds out.' He cleared his throat as unobtrusively as he could.

'No treehouse, then,' Verity said briskly, and turned back to the sling. 'Harry, if we added an extra bit of inner tube, d'you think it would be too lethal?'

I squatted beside her, and glanced appraisingly at Adam. 'We want to maim him, not kill him,' I agreed.

'Three! I can get three!' Adam blurted. He was nearly crying. His eyes were shiny and unclear, his eyebrows raised imploringly. His podgy lips were trembling. 'I can't do four,' he said. 'Honest. I *can't*.' He slumped in the long grass with his grubby knees up near his shoulders, and wept. I felt immediately guilty. All I sensed from Verity, though, was excitement. Adam still had the camera in one drooping hand. She took it.

'Three? You swear? Before Friday?'

Adam nodded, without lifting his head. 'I'll try.' His voice was muffled because his head was still buried.

'All right,' she said flatly. And my world changed.

She plonked the camera back down in front of Adam and headed for the gap in the hedge calling, 'C'mon, Harry,' over her shoulder. As I wriggled through the spiky gap behind her, I heard her whisper, 'Yessss!' Behind us, I heard Adam sniffle, collect his single camera, and trudge back down our garden towards the street.

That afternoon I went to the library in Summertown and took out three books on photography and studied them whenever I could. I had competition.

When we had eleven cameras, Verity announced that it was enough.

Long after the event, it dawned on me that this was extremely odd – how did three children manage to get hold of eleven cameras? So, as an adult, I did some research. The answer was even odder than the puzzle. Almost every grown-up appeared to own at least one unused but fully working camera – and no one could say why. Camera manufacturers must wet themselves with glee. It was our gain as well as the manufacturers', though, because without other people's surplus cameras Verity's plan would have foundered. The line-up went something like this:

Verity – 2 from Gabriel, one old, one new
        – 1 she'd conned Gabriel into buying, and she wasn't
           saying how
Harry   – 1 from Mum's loft
        – 1 from Dad, broken but he agreed to fix it
        – 1 from Dad, which he'd bought when the other one
           broke
        – 1 from Mum
        – 1 from Mum's oldest friend, Mrs Scobie, an elderly and
           slightly scary woman, on condition I visited her once a
           week for the rest of the holidays – a painful sacrifice,
           but needs must . . .
Adam   – 1 pilfered from his sister
        – 2 others, origin obscure

I once asked him where the other cameras came from. He just stared at me and said, 'I got them for you, didn't I?' I could understand his bitterness. He had only provided them under duress.

The project began, under Verity's direction.

She rushed around in an excited daze, aware only of the camera set-up she had in mind, and not at all of me or of Adam. She ordered us about with total confidence – and with total submission, for our separate reasons, we did as she said.

She was brilliant. She was sharp and intense and astonishing. She had a vision of what she was trying to achieve and she had no doubts that it would succeed. She flitted between her own work and ours, hopping excitedly; her words were so hurried that she never seemed to complete a thought before the next ran over it. It thrilled me every time she squatted next to me, her knee touching mine as she leaned in towards me, so close that I could smell the warmth of her skin.

Occasionally we stopped and played for a while, swinging out into that wonderful green space, crashing back into the tree's warty trunk. A favourite trick was to sneak away while someone was wrestling with twigs and string, clamber aloft, and dive-bomb them from the rope. The aim was to get as close as you could without hitting. Often one of us would cut it too fine, but the bruises never seemed to hurt. Sometimes Verity would join in, and other times she would snap at us to stop mucking around, her eyes sparkling with that strange mixture of excitement, anger and urgency I remember so well. And we would stop, of course – for a few minutes.

Once he was sure that he was allowed to join in, Adam turned out to be fun to have around. He was shy but he told good jokes; and whenever we stopped work and fooled around, he was vigorous and creative. I enjoyed having someone my own size to wrestle with and compete against – and if he ever got too competitive, there was always the unspoken threat of banishment. He wanted to belong, and Verity had allowed him to; conditionally, to be sure, but nevertheless he was in. It wasn't the treehouse Adam cared about: it was us.

I liked him, but I was also jealous of him. With Adam on the scene, I had far less time alone with Verity. There were occasional days when he had to stay at home – because his relatives were visiting, or because some family outing had been arranged. On those days I did everything I could to remind Verity of how it had been with just the two of us. I brought biscuits and bottles of Coke,

I'd sit and reminisce about building the sling, or how she had not wanted to come here at first, or how we'd hated it when we found out there'd been an intruder . . . Sometimes she would come and sit beside me, so close that her dress would brush my arm, and I would think that perhaps . . . But her eyes were always on the cameras in the clearing below, and after a few minutes she would shin down the rope and get back to work.

And, of course, for every day that Adam was away, there was another day when I was. There were weekends at Dad's, there were pub lunches where Mum dragged me along to meet people she hoped might turn into friends – lunches where I would spend hours in the pub garden, rocking disconsolately on a rickety swing, and when we got home, Mum would bustle and fuss and be busy over the washing-up, the laundry, the cleaning, and then cry. I would comfort her, but only half-heartedly, because all the time I was gazing out of the window towards Whiteham Woods, and Verity – and Adam. Those days were torture.

Worse, even when we were all together, Verity flirted with him. I knew that she was only using him – he was with us because of the cameras, that was all – but it was obvious that she liked him, too. She liked his devotion to her, his eagerness to please. She liked his roughness when we played: I was always hesitant to touch her, scared of the intimacy, what it might betray, what would happen if she hated me for it. Adam had no such inhibitions: if the game was physical, he was physical. So I reassured myself that she was only flirting with him because it made her feel good. Much to my relief, Adam didn't respond in kind. If anything, her play-acting seemed to annoy him. I think he understood that she joked with him because he was not a threat: it reinforced her control. I was only half aware of it, but those rare moments meant a lot to me. They meant that, in the way that mattered most, I still had Verity to myself.

But the truth is, we were mostly too busy for these subtleties. We were simply glad to be there, each in our own way. We allowed Verity to sweep us along. She was doing what she wanted to do – and that made her happy.

Verity, happy. I do not know if I can describe to you what that was like. She glowed. Her skin was like rough gold. She squealed as she laughed. When she worked on the cameras her whole being bent to the task, and her face was still and calm as a picture. Her skinny body was graceful as a deer's. And her knees touched mine when we squatted as we worked. Her clean breath mingled with mine. Verity was beautiful when she was happy. I think we would both have done anything for her.

One day it was ready.

It was late afternoon, six thirty or so. The sun was gold and low. The wood was full of birdsong and strange rustles. The air was thick and it moved in warm, drowsy currents. We stood together, Verity leaning against a drooping branch, me next to her, Adam on the far side. We looked at our work.

The contraption – I can't think of anything else to call it – was eleven cameras in a circle, all primed to fire at the pull of a string. They were each perched on their own small mound of earth or rock or wood, carefully arranged in a ring nearly twenty feet across. Each camera pointed in towards the centre of the clearing beneath the tree, and each had a cable release wedged to precisely the right position, so that the plunger itself pointed upwards and outwards. Carefully lined up above each plunger was a weight – logs or stones – held up by the lightest twig possible. The plan was that strings would yank away the twigs, and the weights would fall on to the plungers: all eleven cameras would fire at once. The strings were to be pulled from behind the tree, where someone could crouch without appearing in any of the shots. Two mounds flanked the hornbeam's broad bole.

'So, who goes first?' Adam asked. Verity tutted impatiently.

'Verity,' I said piously. 'It's her idea.'

Verity squealed, held my arm and jumped up and down. Then she gave Adam a contemptuous glance and handed the strings to me. I had to give one bunch back for her to pass to me round the other side of the tree trunk. It was a tricky operation because the strings had to be held almost taut, ready to be triggered. I crouched against the bark, and gestured with my head for Adam to stand behind me. He did so, stepping over the strings, then leaned out to peer at Verity. He seemed as excited as she was, focused and tight.

'OK.' Her voice came from the clearing. I could not see her. She giggled. 'I'm going to count down from five, you fire on zero. This is brilliant!' Then she yelled at the top of her voice, 'BRILLIANT!'

and whooped. It was so loud I half expected an echo – but woods don't do that. All that came back was a nervous, insistent 'Ssssh!' from Adam and me.

'Ready?' She was still talking loudly, but at least she had stopped shouting. I tensioned all the strings.

'Ready,' I whispered. 'Verity, *sssssh*!'

'OK.' She was still loud. 'Here goes ... Five, four, three, two, one, *go*! YAH-WHEEEE!!!'

I tugged as sharply as I could. There was a sort of crackling-crumpling sound as (I hoped) all the twigs flew away, the weights fell, the plungers sank home, the camera shutters opened. The noise seemed to go on for ever – a second, at least. I hoped it was just the sound of twigs and strings settling, not the cameras firing too late, or tipping over before the shot was taken. If it had gone wrong, the pictures might be seconds apart. There was no way to know until we developed the films.

Adam and I rushed round the trunk. Verity was collapsed, giggling in a tangle of skinny limbs. She bounced upright.

'That was brilliant!' she said. 'They all went! It worked, I know it!' And she threw her arms round me and pressed her cheek against my neck. Hesitantly I put my arms round her, afraid she would move away. Instead I felt her take a deep breath, then sigh it out happily. Adam hunched a few paces away with his arms folded, trying hard not to look. I nuzzled Verity's hair. I could feel my groin stirring – and panicked in case she pulled away. She squeezed closer. Her cheek rubbed against my skin where my shirt was open, and her hair smelt of woodbark and grass.

And hope.

We took photos until the light failed, and then we sat on the edge of the treehouse, legs dangling, Verity sandwiched between us clutching eleven rolls of film. We shared the silence and the birdsong.

'Where'd they come from, then, Adam?' Verity said, after a while.

'What?'

'The cameras. You nicked one from your sister—'

'Not nicked. I'll put it back.' His tone was pleading.

'Yeah,' she said simply. 'But what about the others?'

Adam drew his knees up and hugged them. His face tightened.

'They're your dad's, aren't they?'

'Shut up! Just shut the fuck up!'

He swung himself down off the platform, hanging by his arms and then dropping to the ground. I thought he was going to leave – and I felt guilty and excited at the same time, because if he left it would mean I was alone with Verity, and I remembered that embrace – but instead he crouched against the tree trunk, out of sight because he was immediately below us, but still there. You could glimpse him through the cracks in the boards.

We sat in our own private worlds as the dusk thickened around us. A gust sighed through the leaves, then faded.

'What would he do if he found out?' Verity called quietly. 'Does he hit you?' There was no answer. 'Scare you, then?'

I heard him sniff away tears and shuffle himself into a new position.

'Mine does. Sometimes,' Verity offered.

I looked sharply at her, but she didn't seem aware that I was there. Her legs kicked back and forth in a slow rhythm, and she whistled absently, a sound like the wind. The silence was something between the two of them.

'My dad took his belt to me once,' I said. They both ignored me. The silence persisted.

I tried to imagine Gabriel beating her: a belt, or a slipper maybe, his wise eyes full of fury, his thick brow knotted. The image didn't fit. I decided she must be lying: she was doing it to get something out of Adam. It was another hook. She was wielding her power. I felt inadequate; I think I came as close to hating her as I ever could. I didn't hate Adam for it, he was as much a victim as I was. And, of course, I didn't hate her either, not really. But I felt bitter and defeated. Today, of all days, with the labour we had put into her crazy camera plan, the reward for success should not be rejection.

Mind you, she did have a point about Adam's dad. He was a man with a reputation. I had never actually met him, but even seeing him from a distance you were aware that there was something wild about him. Perhaps it was in how he moved or stood. You had the sense that he was unpredictable and unrestrained, that anger was never far away. He was talked about: his womenfolk (village gossip had it that there were three, none married to him), his three children, Adam, his sister, and an older brother in prison, the farm labourers who worked for him occasionally – all were the subject of the village's collective sympathy. I was scared of him, just like everyone else. So was Adam. He avoided talking about his father whenever he could.

It was obvious that neither Verity nor Adam was going to say another word. It was getting dark, and I sensed a lightening of the silence: enough time had passed for their strange mood to dissolve.

'Better get home,' I said.

They both stirred, and in the half-dark I could see Verity next to me blink hard and become alert again.

'What's the time, then?' Adam mumbled, from below.

'Dunno,' I said. 'Late.'

Verity stood up and headed for the rope-ladder. I swung down the same way Adam had. We collected the cameras, and picked our way through the woods towards our bikes, and home.

The next day, whatever had passed between them was gone. We needed money to develop the films, and to get it, Verity was prepared to use every weapon she had.

'Ten quid, or I tell your dad about the cameras,' she said contentedly. She already knew she had won.

'I can't,' Adam whispered. 'He'll kill me. He will.'

'Best not let him find out, then.' She shrugged unhelpfully.

I felt sorry for him; but the extortion seemed justifiable. She and I had dredged up ten pounds each; surely, it was only right that Adam should do the same. The truth is, though, that we were bullying him – and I knew it. I hung back, guiltily letting Verity twist the knife. It was doubly unfair, because we had only let Adam stand in on the seventh set of photos, and by then it had been so dark you could hardly make out his face: we knew the shots wouldn't come out. I knew Verity was being cruel, but I did nothing to stop it, and that made me part of it.

'I don't have a tenner,' Adam whined. 'Where am I going to get a tenner?' He looked scared, as though he had shrunk.

'Don't care,' Verity said idly.

'You wouldn't tell Dad, though, would you? Not really?'

She picked up a pebble and examined it, disinterested.

'Please, Verity. He'll kill me.'

'You owe us a tenner, Adam.' Absently, she threw away the

stone. He stared at the ground and chewed his lip, arms crossed, hugging himself. 'Suit yourself,' she said. 'Come on, Harry.' She walked away. I mumbled something apologetic to him, about needing to check the treehouse and, sheepishly, I followed her.

'Harry?' Adam called feebly. 'Please, Harry. He'll kill me!' I didn't dare look back. The nape of my neck burned as I carried on walking, as helpless in my own way as he was.

We had the money the next day – and the photos the day after.

Some of them were quite good. The first three or four sets were fine. After that the sun had been low enough to white-out some shots and sink others into irretrievable gloom. The last five attempts were useless, and the last two utterly black. One by one, we put each set of pictures in a line and crouched over them.

We were in Verity's garden. She and Adam were squatting side by side, and I was opposite, looking at the pictures upside-down and trying hard not to look up Verity's skirt. She leaned against Adam. As she looked at the shots in front of him, she seemed to nuzzle her head in towards his chest. He stayed very still, his eyes soft and nervous. I sidled round to the same side as them and crammed myself next to Verity, but she stayed closer to Adam, even when she was looking at the pictures at my end of the line of eleven. Perhaps she sensed that he needed reassurance. I hoped so.

The pictures were magical. The first three sets were of Verity. In the first and second, we had caught her in mid-air. In the first, she had only just left the ground; she was stretching upwards, toes dangling, her mouth contorted by a yell. But the second set was perfect, and the third was almost as good. In both, we had caught her in mid-leap. Her legs were kicked up under her, her arms thrown out. In the second set her mouth was wide open in delight; in the third her expression had begun to collapse into neutrality as she started to fall. The fourth set was of me. I hadn't known quite what to do with myself and the end result was hopeless. In any case, only about half of the shots had come out at all well: by then the sun had been too low. The fifth and sixth sets, of me and Verity together were indistinct and clouded. The rest, including Adam's set, were useless.

I'm in love with those pictures now, and with the memory of them, but at the time I think we were more excited than fascinated.

These days, my copies live in a brown envelope, worn soft at the edges, in a tea-chest in Mum's loft. When I made the zoetrope for Verity, I fished them out to copy them, but although it's important to me to know that they are there, I hardly ever look at them. Memories can be painful.

Adam leaned across Verity to look at the photos, and she stood up sharply, still staring at them on the ground in front of her. We both stood too, and spread out, embarrassed.

'Your turn first next time, Adam,' Verity said, with a bright smile. He grinned back. I felt a bitter little lurch.

Verity twirled from side to side, her short blue skirt kicking up with each swing. In its shadow, her legs were shaded green by the grass. She was smiling to herself. When she turned to look at me, I grinned back oafishly. She didn't seem to notice. She gazed through me, at what I could not imagine.

That was when the yelling started.

A door crashed inside somewhere, in her house. Then indistinct roars began, one man bellowing, and another – Gabriel – talking rapidly.

'Oh, shit,' Adam whimpered. 'Oh, shit.' Suddenly he was crying. He was hugging himself tight, doubled over, rocking. A moan slipped out of him.

The back door smashed open. The man's voice exploded out at us.

'– don't fuckin' care, you slimy git, 'e's comin' away! *Now!* Got that, 'ave ya?' Adam's father was blocking the door, glaring back at Gabriel who was still inside. I heard Gabriel say something mild. The man raised a finger and scowled. 'Try it, mate! Go on, fuckin' try it!' He yanked his shoulders back sharply, then sneered at Gabriel's reaction. '*Yaaah*. Wanker! Fuck off!' He swaggered towards us. He was wiry and wide. His arms bowed outwards, thin but knotted with muscle. His hair was crew-cut, his face contorted.

Adam was crouching, still whimpering, clutching frantically at himself, shoulders, knees, chest, shifting and twitching, curled into the tightest ball he could manage. A trickle of piss was running down his leg, a damp stain was spreading across his sock. A thin whine came out of him, punctuated by sobs.

His father kicked him savagely in the chest. It knocked him on to his side. After a moment, the moan started again and a sticky thread of vomit slid from his open mouth.

'*UP!*' Adam's father screamed. Adam hunched round his own chest, his head thrown back, retching.

'Dad?' Verity ran to Gabriel, who was standing helpless by the back door. 'Dad, call the police! Dad? Dad!' Gabriel was watching, paralysed.

Adam's father glared at Gabriel, his finger raised again. 'I'll fuckin' 'ave you!' he snarled.

'*Dad!*' Verity hit Gabriel with both fists. Gabriel bit his lip. He turned and hurried into the house, grabbing her as he went. Adam's father howled after them inarticulately. He turned his attention back to his son. He crouched calmly down by his head.

'*My* – fuckin' – *money!*' His voice was soft. His teeth were clenched. '*Mine.* Understand?' He grabbed the back of Adam's shirt and hauled him partly upright. Then he buried his fist in his solar plexus. Adam collapsed, his mouth a rigid O, his eyes bulging. His father heaved another half-hearted kick at his back. 'Nick my fuckin' dosh – *would ya*? Ya little fuckin' *shit!*' Adam still hadn't managed to pull in a breath. His whole body convulsed. His dad ripped his belt out of its loops, wrapped the buckle end round his hand, and slashed the other across Adam's back, bending savagely into each stroke – no pause, relentlessly, each blow crisp and moist, snap, snap, snap, snap.

'Stop it!' I yelled.

Trust me, I didn't mean to. The words ripped out of me before I could prevent it. I stood there, clenched and trembling, ready to run. He stopped beating Adam, and scowled at me blankly. 'Who the fuck are you? Fuck off!'

I stayed – quaking, but I stayed. He hefted the belt and straightened to face me. At the same time, Adam gulped his first breath, a huge inwards groan, and the man turned his attention back to his son. He had forgotten the belt; instead, he grabbed a handful of Adam's hair and pulled him to his feet. He bent until his stubbly cheek was next to Adam's face.

'*My* money, boy. *Mine.* That was very, very bad. *My – fuckin' – dosh.*' He straightened, glared at me, then yanked Adam by the hair and dragged him towards the house. Adam staggered forwards. After a few steps, his father snarled in frustration at Adam's slow pace, let go of his hair, and jerked his knee hard into Adam's stomach. Adam collapsed again, and lay twitching spastically in the grass, the muscles in his jaw and neck roped and rigid as he strained for air.

His eyes caught mine, and stayed locked there despite his body's convulsions. His face was smeared with tears and snot and puke. And there was something in his look – something that had nothing to with fear or pain, something that had to do with the fact that I was *there*: terrified, but there. I shot him a panicked look that, I hope, showed him that I had done what I could, and that I hoped . . . But, of course, there was not much hope for Adam just then. So all I hoped was that it would be over soon. And in between the twitches and gasps and spasms, with his eyes still fixed on mine, I saw him try to nod – and almost succeed.

Then his father's hand was in his hair again, hauling him upright. I watched him drag my friend away, still moaning and retching. What else could I do?

I went into the house. Gabriel was in the living room, slumped in a shabby armchair, looking vaguely at the window. His face was slack, his eyes blank.

The police never came. They only come if someone calls them.

I found Verity at the treehouse.

I clambered up a drooping branch, and along the tree's broad limb. I walked around boards, and sat next to her without a word.

She was hugging her knees, resting her chin on them, rocking back and forth. Eleven pictures ran in a row along the powder-green boards, all from different angles, all of the same moment. Verity in mid-leap, screaming.

'These are the only ones that're any good,' she said.

The leaves whispered in the twilight, the sky reddened. Overhead the clouds were a luminous grey. I waited.

'I didn't want it to happen,' she said.

I nudged a photo, neatening the line.

She picked it up, frowned at it, put it back. 'It was just for fun. It was supposed to be fun. I didn't mean it. I didn't.'

We sat.

'Going to Dad's this weekend,' I mumbled. 'Still got to pack.

Going to be late. You?' I was dreading her answer. She shrugged and picked at a splinter on one of the boards.

'See Adam. Maybe swim. Do photos. It's his turn.'

A sigh rippled the hornbeam's outer branches.

'I'd rather be here,' I said. 'With you. Specially 'cos . . .'

She glanced at me sideways, and kept picking. Then she unclasped her knees and sat cross-legged. Her bare knee touched mine, resting on it. I sat motionless, terrified to move.

'Yeah,' she whispered softly. She peeled a sliver of wood away from the board, and threw it over the edge. It spun slowly as it fell.

She leaned over to adjust a photo, putting her hand on my thigh to support herself. Her hips rose slightly, and her T-shirt pulled away from the back of her neck. I saw fine hairs, the jagged bumps of her spine. A gap opened between her shirt and her skirt at the back, a finger's width – not enough to see, but enough to imagine. My hands were rooted to the rough wood behind me. She pushed herself upright using my leg. Her hand stayed a beat, then she let it slide gently off. Our hips were touching, just, and our thighs were pressed together. Her leg was cool and smooth. Something without a scent came from her skin, something I still cannot name. I breathed it in and held it.

'Specially what?' She traced a circle on my knee.

'What?' I spoke clumsily, but her finger still drifted over my knee.

'You said you wanted to be here specially 'cos of something.'

'Adam,' I blurted.

She stopped. Thoughtfully she took away her hand and rested it back on her own bare leg. We were still touching, but now she looked out towards the shimmering wall of leaves, which hid us from the world outside.

'Not the – not his dad,' I babbled. 'Just – *him*. He likes you.'

'So?' Her voice was remote.

'Just *because*.'

I was defeated.

We sat again in silence. I found a splinter of my own and picked at it fitfully. She watched the leaves shiver in the light. Then, still looking outwards, she leaned against me, and her head settled against my shoulder. I nuzzled her, and she turned her face to meet me.

We kissed.

When our muscles spasmed with the effort of staying upright, we lay back, our mouths pressed together. I was lost in her. The creamy sharp taste of her teeth, the scent of her cheek, the strange bumps and curves of her body against mine. I inched my hand towards her breasts, and she wriggled to bring them closer with a little grunt of approval, sliding her tongue over mine. I groped the closest one clumsily, unsure what I was doing. Encouraged, I slid my hand down over her belly, towards where my leg was wedged between hers. She rose towards me at first, then she grunted – meaning no, this time. I pretended not to notice. She shook her head, grunted again; but her mouth still pushed hotly against mine, and I felt the soft skin at her waist, and my fingertips were just slipping under the band of her skirt—

'Harr*yyyy*!'

She shoved me away roughly, and slapped my cheek. Hard.

I rolled off her and hunched sulkily, facing away. I could hear her straightening herself; clothes being tugged, legs and skirt dusted off.

'Harry?'

I didn't turn, but we both knew it was only a matter of time. When I looked, she was standing at the edge of the treehouse, where the long branch led out and down. I could see her breathing, light and rapid, I could see her waist where her shirt hung loose, air against her skin, her long bare legs. She was holding her shoes. She bit her lower lip, and her eyes creased. Her cheeks were warm, her eyes alive. 'See you soon, Harry,' she said quietly.

And she ran away along the branch.

I waited as long as I dared before leaving. Already, I could see the moon. When I got home, I would be late and Mum would scream at me, and I would have to pack, and Dad would bark at me for making him wait. It didn't matter. *We kissed.* I could still taste her, a coolness on the roof of my mouth.

I hugged myself, and let myself shiver with the thrill of it. *We kissed.* And on Monday I would see her again.

And as she ran off through the woods, I had heard her happy laughter.

ten

Adam waited by the hospital lifts, and I went in alone.

Somehow I'd been expecting her to have changed. She hadn't. I had forgotten what she really looked like. I had been chewing away at the *idea* of her fall: I remembered the starch and the whiteness, I remembered her immobility, and the machines, patiently pumping a thin substitute for life. I had developed an image of clinical perfection, of Verity in unblemished repose. The reality, of course, was ... messy. The bruises had spread a little; flowers of purple and brown blossomed on her skin. I found the thought horrifying, a sci-fi nightmare, she was being slowly consumed by some cold alien thing: too much pulp fiction when I was young, perhaps, but it was unnerving none the less. She was terribly swollen, more so than before. Her skin was puffed and shiny, warm under the hot lights. She was ugly and broken, and the tube into her throat must hurt, and those bruises ... Brownish liquid seeped through her bandages and stained the sheets.

I had been thinking of things to say. I wanted words to whisper in her ear, to bring hope, perhaps to bring her back. My first glimpse of her ripped away that fantasy. There was the stench of disinfectant, there were encrusted bandages, the jerks of the machine that gave her breath. *Damaged goods.*

I bent and kissed her forehead, barely touching her for fear of pressing on her swollen skin. I imagined the heat of her injuries radiating on to my face. I whispered to her: 'It's all right, Verity. It's all OK. Sssh.'

Yeah, Harry. Right.

I left her bag and the zoetrope with the nurses, and went to find

Adam, my lips and face still hot. He led me wordlessly to the car, and we set off.

'A259 => Eastbourne,' Verity's Filofax said. 'R turn – BIRLING GAP, B Gap Hotel, thatched bar, 3.30.' We were coming the other way, from Eastbourne rather than towards it, but Birling Gap was easy enough to find on the map. The hospital was on the outskirts of Eastbourne, so we headed through the town to the coast, then turned right along the seafront.

It was like a seedier version of the promenades of the French Riviera. I had visited Cannes and Nice on a cycling holiday as a student: they, too, had a pink pavement lined with palm trees; they, too, had a parade of grand hotels with sea views; they even offered the same glimpses down the side-roads of eateries, and stalls stacked high with inflatable beach toys, T-shirts and postcards. But here it was fish and chips, the postcards were gaudy and saucy, and the palm trees were tired and stunted. There was a pier on stilts with a wood and glass pavilion perched on top. There were ice-cream vans, and queues of children hopping barefoot on the hot pavement. Beyond the balustrade, the sea was chalk-green and restless.

The town ended where the road met rising ground. We looped upwards through a series of switchbacks, in the shade of the dense woodland that covered the hillside; then, suddenly, we broke out on to the high rolling grassland of the Sussex Downs.

It was bright and bleak. The low hills and shallow valleys were rounded smooth and grassy, unrelieved by trees or hedges. The grass rippled ceaselessly, and when I glimpsed a solitary man walking a dog, I could see that a savage wind was ripping at him. Inside the car's safe shell, I felt nothing.

Half a mile later, there was a pub by the road – Beachy Head was written over the door in large gold lettering, with a pebble-dash exterior, and a huge car park was packed to overflowing. As we ghosted past, my eyes caught a phone kiosk by the roadside, with a green sign next to it –

THE SAMARITANS
Always there day or night

– and a number to ring.

I wondered if Adam was right, that I should have waited before coming here. Verity had been here. Had she seen that sign? *Verity, you should have called them. Or me.*

Further on there was a lay-by, and a path rising to a lighthouse on a hilltop. Metal letters on a gate near the road declared it as the Belle Toute Lighthouse. It had vanished from sight round a curve before I made the connection: the police had told me that her car had been found there, this was where she fell.

Another mile, and the land sank again towards the sea. At the road's lowest point, a row of grey cottages hunched against the wind along one side of a large gravel car park. Three cars were parked in it; it could have held three hundred. Opposite the cottages, a low building sprawled along the car park's edge. Beyond, there was an assortment of wooden shacks and barns. A discreet sign announced this as the Birling Gap Hotel. We parked between the cottages and the hotel, at the edge of a low cliff: beyond was the sea, a wide expanse, foamed and heaving, flanked by rising headlands in both directions.

Tucked away round a corner from the hotel's main entrance was a doorway signed the 'Thatched Bar, and Oak Room Family Restaurant.' I truly did not want to go in there, so I stared out to sea instead.

Although he wisely said nothing, I was aware of Adam studying me. I ignored him. But I knew what he wanted to say – and I couldn't stand there for ever in any case – so eventually I answered his implied question. 'Yes, Ads, I'm still sure,' I muttered. 'Come on, then.' He gestured for me to go first. I pulled open the door.

The Thatched Bar was so called because the bar had a straw awning above it. The room was low-ceilinged, with dark beams and rough-rendered walls. It had been decorated throughout with an assortment of nineteenth-century farm implements – ploughs, harrows, and, obscurely, some disturbing-looking tongs. There was a hearth with a wood-burning stove – mercifully not lit – and near the door the inevitable fruit machine flickered incessantly in the corner of my eye. Only two of the fifteen or so tables were occupied: at one, a family of four, looking sunburnt and disillusioned, and in a far corner a couple sitting opposite each other, uncomfortably examining their drinks, glancing up and then back

down, as though summoning the courage to talk to each other –
divorce, I thought, or the first day of an affair. I assumed the pub
was aimed at the holiday trade, but it was two o'clock, in high
season, and there were just six people in there, eight if you included
Adam and me, and two were under age.

'Sorry, love, no food.' The girl behind the bar peered at us
through the gloom. She pointed unhelpfully to a sign – *Food Served
Until Two Thirty* – and then to a clock behind the bar. It was nearly
three. She seemed pleased by her announcement.

I didn't want food, I wanted answers, but Adam had other plans.
'So, how do we persuade you?' He grinned at her.

'What did you have in mind, darling?' She dimpled back at him,
and swept her hair behind her ear. She was young, probably not yet
twenty, and plump. Her green gingham pinafore was stained.

'Ah . . .' Adam frowned seriously. 'Well, I'm married, so I'm
afraid our options are a bit limited . . . I could offer you the price of
a sandwich?' She giggled and twirled her hair again. 'Any old
thing'll do,' he urged, sounding earnest and cheerful at the same
time. 'We're starving. Been on the go for hours.'

'Oh, go on, then.' She twinkled at him. 'Cheese sandwich, do
you? Chef's gone.'

Adam grinned. Her cheeks dimpled again, and she headed for the
kitchen, hips swaying.

I don't know how Adam does it. I know I can't, though: if I had
tried to persuade her, she would have dug her heels in. Then I'd
have got ratty with her, she would have insisted that rules were
rules . . . Adam had no such trouble.

'And some drinks, please, love,' he called after her. 'One bitter,
one lager.' She came back, pulled the pints, then bustled off. Adam
chuckled.

We sat with our pints, comfortably silent. I thought about the
promised cheese sandwich, and realised that I was very hungry
indeed. It must have been at lunchtime the day before that I'd last
eaten, waiting outside the Carlisles' house. The trouble was, every
time I thought of Verity a cold nausea swept through me, and my
appetite vanished. I tried to picture Verity walking in, but couldn't.
This dingy pub seemed such an inappropriate place for her. It had
been only hours before the fall: what had she been thinking,
feeling?

'Cheer up, love, it might never happen.' The girl dumped our sandwiches on to the table. 'Here you go.'

I bolted down a mouthful. Grated cheese and raw onion on pre-sliced white bread: I was so hungry it tasted almost good. I shook my head vigorously. 'Already has happened.'

'Ooh, love, I *am* sorry,' she said, as though she knew exactly what I meant and fully understood. She widened her eyes into a cliché of attentive sympathy. Then, without pause: 'Hey, you're not going to jump, are you?'

Adam sniggered, then looked solemn. I stared at her. She looked surprised.

'No,' I said carefully. 'Thanks, but no. I'm not jumping.'

'Good, 'cos I hate that. They all come here, you know – well, some of them. It's only five minutes' drive, did you know that?' I frowned. She gave an impatient grimace. 'Beachy Head,' she explained. 'The drop. People jump off it. Top themselves.' She scooped up my empty glass with a neat, satisfied movement. She looked expectantly at Adam. He knocked down the rest of his beer and asked for two more. 'Had one in the other day, as it goes,' she said cheerfully, and flounced off. I glanced at Adam, who raised an eyebrow speculatively. We grabbed our sandwiches and shuffled after her.

'Um, excuse me?' I called. 'Did you say you had one in? It wasn't on Wednesday, by any chance?'

She set down our empty glasses, and leaned on the bar conspiratorially. 'A woman,' she said. 'Not your usual type. Mostly it's men of a certain age, know what I mean?' She laughed merrily – at Adam, I noticed: she wasn't really talking to me at all.

'This woman,' I pressed. 'Was she in her thirties? Big brown eyes, about this tall, dark hair?'

'Could be.' The girl shrugged. 'Did you know her, then?'

'She's a friend. Was. Is. We're . . . we were close.'

But not close enough for her to call.

She winced. 'Well, it *has* already happened, then, hasn't it? Sorry I asked.' She turned to go, embarrassed perhaps.

'No. Wait,' I called hastily. 'She was here, wasn't she? I mean, you saw her?'

She picked up a glass and started to polish it, looking at me appraisingly. Adam came to the rescue. 'Same again, please, love,' he reminded her.

He gave her his best smile. 'And how about something for you?' He grinned warmly, and waved a twenty-pound note.

She looked at it like a bird eyeing a scrap of bread. 'Ooh, ta, love, I'll have a Bacardi.'

Courtship ritual completed, she talked as she prepared the drinks. 'She came in about three. Dressed all scruffy with a big black bag. Had a vodka on the rocks, a double. I thought, Aye-aye, we've got one here – 'cos that's a big drink for a Wednesday afternoon and she was on her own. They do that, you know.'

She enjoyed this, I realised. It made her interesting, in her own eyes at least. I hated her for it. She made the poor people who came here sound more like commodities than individuals with shattered lives and an intolerable burden of pain.

The people on the other side of the pub left. The father called out a cheery 'Thank you,' which she ignored. The other family members looked grim.

'Anyway,' the girl continued. 'She just sits there listening to one of them walkman thingies. Winding and rewinding. She's staring straight ahead and playing this tape. So I goes over and strikes up a bit of chat. Got to get them talking, see?' She tucked her chin against her neck, as though the story was a little too rich even for her. 'And she's really sniffy. Says to mind my own business. Straight out. Says she's fine.' She sounded indignant. 'She wasn't, though, was she?'

'A tape-player?' Adam said, puzzled.

'Mine,' I said. Verity had given it to me for my thirtieth. She had asked to borrow it a couple of months ago. Apparently she wanted to make some recordings of 'real life' for her next show: she needed a tape-recorder small enough to go unnoticed. I hadn't had the heart to ask her to return it. Too late now.

Adam frowned. 'What was she playing?'

'Well, *I* don't know, do I?' She gaped at Adam as though he was an idiot. 'She'd got those earplugs, hadn't she?'

'Of course. But was it music? Classical, pop?'

Adam knew more about human nature than I did – I'd have taken her denial at face value – but she answered him. 'I told you, I don't know, do I?' She rolled her eyes impatiently. 'Not music, though. Speaking. Someone talking.'

I was baffled. Verity had said she wanted to record the sounds of the city, traffic and sirens and pigeons and tube trains; I couldn't imagine why she'd need the sound of someone talking for her show, particularly given the theme. 'Damaged Goods'. Verity, here, waiting out her last hours, alone in this abandoned place, listening to . . . what?

'So, when did she come in?' Adam's question jolted me back to the girl.

'Must've been after three, 'cos I'd just closed the bar. Had to open up again.'

She shrugged unhelpfully.

'Did she stay long?'

'Only three bloody hours, and just the one drink all that time. Cheap, if you ask me.'

Neither of us *had* asked her, and I was getting irritated. This girl might be glad of the attention, but Verity deserved better than gossip. We had learned everything we could. Verity had come into the pub, she'd sat with a single drink for three hours. She had listened to a tape. She had left. I looked at Adam. He was clearly thinking the same thing.

'Thanks, love, you're a star.' He racked his grin a notch wider.

We wolfed down the remains of our sandwiches, and headed back to the car.

'Where the hell is it, then?'

'Hmm? Where's what?' Adam seemed absorbed in thoughts of his own.

'My Walkman. It wasn't in her car.'

'Maybe she had it with her when she fell.'

'It wasn't with her things at the hospital, though.'

'I didn't look.' Adam spread his arms in exasperation. 'It's on the beach somewhere. Or at the top of the cliff. Or someone nicked it from her car. Or it's there and you missed it. How would I know? After a fall like that' – he gestured towards the sharp cliffs rising in both directions – 'it's amazing they found anything at all.'

I looked back at the Birling Gap Hotel. Under other circumstances it would have been a pleasant enough place, inoffensive, if uninspired, but to me the building squatted on the landscape like a lumpen spider, its windows blank and beady, a row of unforgiving eyes. I could feel its gaze on my back as I crossed the huge empty car park, my footsteps inaudible against the endless moan of the sea.

We reached the car. Adam leaned on the roof. 'Where to?' I took a last look round. Verity had been here, she had moved through this space. But there was nothing of her left.

'The Head,' I said. 'I want to see where she fell.'

We parked in the lay-by below the Belle Toute Lighthouse. The land rose gently away from us for a hundred feet, then ended abruptly. Adam perched on the bonnet of his BMW. 'Go on, then. I'll wait here.'

I headed for the edge. You could smell the sea below, you could smell how the sun had warmed the grass. The air was strong and cool, the wind bruising and refreshing by turns. I breathed deeply. The headlands rolled along the coast like a vast smooth swell, a vivid green sliced through by chalk cliffs, which fell sheer to a gravel beach and the sea. The drop had to be at least two or three hundred feet. To my right, the land rose towards the lighthouse; to the left the rise was steeper, and the cliffs fell five hundred feet or more, sheer to the tumbled boulders at their feet. There was another lighthouse at the base of the cliffs, neatly striped in red and white, dwarfed by the huge promontory above. Beachy Head: had Verity walked any further that way, she certainly would not have survived.

The cliffs were brilliant white in the sharp sunlight, the sea was soft green. The wind brought a warm salt tang, more a taste than a smell. The coastline had a monumental beauty that was breathtaking. It was tranquil, impassive. It swept me up.

She had walked here too. My body was passing through the same volume of space as hers had, my head was where hers had been. Perhaps our feet were in step, separated only by time. Of course it was a silly notion. I was a good four inches taller than her: there was no way our stride lengths would ever have been the same, or our heads level; but the illusion helped me. I wanted to get inside her head, see what she had seen, think her thoughts. I wanted to be close to her. I didn't want her gone.

There was no way I could tell precisely where she had jumped, but somewhere along this stretch she had chosen her spot. Possibly I walked past it, or did not go far enough, there was no way to tell. The cliffs were featureless. I sat and watched the sea, its roughness flattened by my high perspective. Its surface glittered with warm yellow light. A supertanker stood in the middle distance, its colours bleached to grey by the sea's haze, its oily wake smearing the sea flat. Perhaps this was where she had sat in the two hours after she left the pub, just taking it in, emptying her thoughts, reflecting. The sea dazed me. It became a meaningless tangle of sparkles, crossed by gulls, warm blurs sliding across the sky. It wasn't a bad spot to die. Despite the battering of the wind, it was peaceful here.

Did you even think of me, Verity? You could have called. You could have. You know that – don't you?

Miss you, Verity.

Beachy Head was beautiful. The clichés didn't do it justice. I had imagined it would be rather tacky. I mean, it was such a hackneyed idea, such a popular conception of Where To Do It. I'd half expected a souvenir hut selling candy-floss and badges saying something tasteless – *Beachy Head, Worth a Look Before You Leap*, that kind of thing. Let's face it, the Sussex coast – Brighton, Eastbourne, Hastings – has an image problem, and I confess that I'd bought the stereotype. But, being there, it was dramatically obvious that my preconceptions were wrong. Beachy Head was stunning. It's a place that, normally, I'd have been glad to see – and I'd never have bothered to come if it weren't for Verity. I wished I could have shared it with her.

And that's when I realised . . .

The fact that Beachy Head was beautiful changed everything.

Adam was pacing, mobile clamped to his ear, his other hand chopping at the air. 'I don't care if it's difficult, just fucking do it.' He swivelled to start back in the other direction and caught sight of me. He stopped walking and scowled blankly at me, listening to whatever was being said at the other end. He waved me over. 'OK, I'm going to interrupt you there,' he said briskly, into his phone. 'Yes, I know it's difficult. Yes, there are problems. You're paid to solve them. Do so. Now. Understood?' He didn't wait for the other person to respond, he just carried straight on. 'Ring me when you've got a result.' He folded his phone and rolled his eyes. 'Lord save us . . . Sorry, Harry. Feeling better?'

'Much.'

I meant it. For the first time since Verity's fall, there was something I was sure of. Something I absolutely knew. She had not come here to kill herself. She would never have chosen this spot – and the reason was that she had the same prejudice about this stretch of coast as I had. She'd thought she knew what it was like here. She thought it was all sticks of rock, sunburnt children weeing in the sand, knotted handkerchiefs for sunhats. It didn't matter that she was wrong, that Beachy Head was beautiful, because her preconceptions would have prevented her coming here and finding out.

Adam squinted at me, perhaps puzzled by my expression. I grinned back.

And if Verity had not come here to kill herself, then perhaps after all I knew her as well as I'd thought. Because if she hadn't come to kill herself, then she wasn't suicidal – so why bother calling me? She was going to see me later that evening anyway.

A new vision of Verity took hold in my mind. She was waiting for someone at the pub – not desperate, not suicidal, just waiting. The place had been chosen by whoever she was waiting for, because she would never have thought of it, or even have known it existed. She waited, her friend failed to arrive, and she left. Before driving back to London (for her hot date with me that evening), she decided to enjoy the scenery for a while – scenery she'd never imagined might exist among the weeing kids and the fish-and-chip stalls. She parked the car, walked along the cliff-edge, as I had . . .

. . . and then what? She slipped. Or the wind took her. Or she looked down and got vertigo and—

Whatever. She didn't mean to kill herself.

'Harry, has something happened to you?' Adam asked. 'You look completely different.'

I smiled and shook my head.

I wasn't going to tell him, not yet anyhow. He wouldn't see it. We'd argue again, and I didn't want that. He had taken two days off work for me, and already I had put an enormous strain on him. He cared, and I needed that. I needed his support and his generosity – and the price of keeping those was that I couldn't tell him. I couldn't prove it, he wouldn't believe me – but I knew, I *knew*.

I waved my hands about. 'It's beautiful,' I said simply. The truth, but avoiding the point. Adam looked puzzled, then gazed around him. I had the impression he hadn't even noticed where he was.

Another gust sent ripples rolling through the grass.

'Yes. I suppose it is. Stunning.' He took a deep breath, sighed out. 'Good for the soul, eh? More than I can say for that dickhead in Accounts I was talking to. Did I ever tell you about him?'

I laughed. 'Only ten or twenty times, Ads – but one more won't hurt. Tell me on the way home.' He grinned back, and unlocked the car.

When we reached the motorway, we settled into a comfortable cruise. Adam put the radio on, light classical music, Mozart or something. 'It's good to have you back, Harry,' he said. 'Thought I'd lost you for a while there.' He raised a warning finger. 'Don't bother with the health warning. I know we've still got a way to go, the value of friendships can go down as well as up, all that stuff. But seriously, Harry, seeing that little spark of the old you, that makes it all worth it.' He beamed at the road ahead.

'There's still stuff I need to do, Ads,' I said.

'I know. I'll help.'

So maybe it wouldn't end in confrontation after all, maybe he'd come to accept what I now knew. I settled back into the car's soft seat, and smiled to myself. He'd find out in time.

As the car purred towards London, I closed my eyes and pictured her: her heels kicked back, her hair spreading, dappled by sunlit leaves, screaming happily in the air. And I promised her that I wouldn't rest until I knew the truth.

Adam dropped me at the end of my road. He brushed off my thanks, as usual. I watched his car purr away, then strode purposefully towards home. I noticed someone was waiting when I was twenty yards away. At eighteen yards, I recognised her – and my elation vanished.

Sam Mandovini sat with her knees together and her feet spread, squinting through the last of the sunlight at the traffic. She didn't notice me until I was next to her. I said a guarded hello. She started, then unfolded herself, dusting off her jeans. 'I've come to apologise,' she said, in a rush, 'to see if I can help.'

Her eyes wouldn't quite meet mine. I was uneasy, but I couldn't really say no so I unlocked the door and gestured for her to go in.

I offered her a chair, and fiddled in the kitchen while the kettle boiled. As I worked, I tried to recapture the energy and clarity I had felt at Beachy Head. I failed, and irritation settled in. What the hell did she think she was doing? Not content with her performance yesterday, she was now ruining the remains of my week. I felt pressured and put-upon. I knew it was unfair to blame all of that on her, but she was there, and she was reminding me just how unpleasant my reality was at the moment. Whatever the reason for Verity's fall, she *had* fallen. She was gone for good.

'Black and strong,' I said gruffly. I dumped her mug by her elbow, and plonked myself opposite her ungraciously. She gave me a short smile. I didn't trust myself to talk, so I waited. Eventually she blew out heavily. 'Look, I came round to say sorry, not to get the third degree. I know I was a louse at the studio. I didn't mean to be. It's just—'

'Paris,' I said flatly.

'Yes, Paris. But after you went I felt terrible. Just awful. I mean, Verity's had this horrid accident and all I could think about was a bloody fashion show. You must think I'm such a self-centred cow.'

Again I said nothing. After an uneasy moment, I heard her suck her teeth. 'OK, I probably deserved that. Look, Harry, I want to help. I mean, if you'll talk to me. There are things Verity and I talked about, which might help. About how she was feeling and stuff.' She paused briefly, and when she continued her voice was a little softer. 'Harry, I'd really like to talk. I loved her too, you know. I don't know what the hell got into me. Please.'

'I'm amazed you've got the time to come and see me, with Paris just round the corner,' I said, then winced. I'd been aiming for a jokey tone, but it came out savagely.

Sam's voice hardened. 'Yeah, Harry. Good one. Whatever.' She stood.

I breathed in sharply. 'Oh ... Sam, I'm sorry. Really. I didn't mean that. I'm just a bit ...' *Start again, Harry.* 'Yes, let's talk. Fine. Please. And thanks for apologising.' She smiled weakly and the silence stretched again. 'Look, Sam?' I continued, when it got awkward, 'That Paris thing. How's it going?'

'Finished,' Sam said tonelessly. She sat again. 'Cancelled.' She laughed without looking up from her cup. She swirled the coffee, then set it on the table, watching the whirlpool slow and come to rest.

'You cancelled it?'

She bit her lower lip and nodded. My surprise lasted only a moment. Then the guilt set in.

'Um, look, I hope it wasn't because of—'

Sam looked up at me, her eyes wide. 'Oh! How sweet! No, Harry, it wasn't because of you.' She cupped her hands round the mug of coffee and hunched over it. 'But you were right, who cares about Paris? Well, *I* did,' she smiled, 'but I got home that night, and I started thinking . . . About Verity, about what had happened. I'd had this daft idea that somehow doing Paris was the best thing to do for *her* . . .' She shrugged in a doesn't-really-matter kind of way. I said nothing. 'Look, Harry, there's something you've got to understand. I didn't mean to be a bitch yesterday, but I was completely freaked. And there's this fashion-luvvie thing I do. Normally it's me and Verity, we do it for a laugh. In our business you *have* to, you've got to keep up with the competition. And then the work and the fun get mixed up, and you find yourself doing it all the time, particularly when you're stressed. And with Verity gone, and then the whole Paris thing, I was pretty uptight. I shouldn't have let you come to the studio.'

She looked fragile and strong at the same time, defiant but vulnerable. She could almost have been a different woman. She wore black jeans, black ankle boots, and a white shirt hanging loose at the waist; her hands were half lost under the unbuttoned cuffs. She wore no makeup, and it suited her. It softened her features. Her eyes seemed cool and thoughtful instead of the cold blue they had been at the studio; I wondered if she had been wearing tinted contacts. Her skin was clear, pale but not unhealthily so; her eyes creased when she talked, her hair was reassuringly less than perfect.

'What will you do?' I asked.

'No idea,' she murmured. It suddenly hit me that she was every bit as adrift as I was. 'Nathan and Jean-Marie will have to go. No point now. I couldn't afford them, not on my own.'

'I'm sorry.'

'It happens. Nothing compared to Verity, is it?'

There was no arguing with that.

Sam took a swig of coffee and grimaced. 'God, Harry, this is awful.'

I bridled. She looked at me and then laughed. 'Can I make another?' She got up and busied herself at the sink, pouring out the old, rummaging for the coffee jar, refilling the kettle. 'So, anyway, I cancelled Paris,' she called, as though it was a piece of idle chat.

'But you really wanted it, didn't you? Wasn't Paris going to be the big one?'

She leaned back against the kitchen units. She had a nice figure, I thought distractedly. 'Not without Verity,' she said. 'It was for her, really. *My* collection wasn't going to make any waves.'

'Well, maybe next time . . .'

The corners of her eyes tightened into a hint of a smile. 'Yeah,' she said. 'Maybe.'

The noise of the kettle built gradually to a roar, and we waited without talking. She made a fresh mug of coffee, but stayed leaning against the sink, cupping it against her chest.

'Oh. I nearly forgot . . .' She put down the mug and went back into the living room. She fished in her bag, and slid a key across the table towards me. I picked up her coffee and came over. The key was small, less than an inch long, with a hollow centre and a simple pattern of pegs, the kind of key you find in wardrobe or drawer locks. 'I found it with her things at the office,' Sam explained. 'It doesn't fit anything there. I thought it might be something at her place.' She looked at it thoughtfully.

'She didn't do it, Sam. None of it makes sense.'

I explained about Beachy Head, and the mystery appointment at the pub. When I had finished, she contemplated her coffee for a long time before speaking.

'Harry, none of that means she didn't jump. It just means she didn't *intend* to when she went to the Head. She didn't go there to kill herself – but what if she went to meet someone at the pub, and something happened that . . . *changed* things?'

I shook my head vigorously. 'I just don't think she'd kill herself. No way.'

Sam turned away and stared into space. 'Verity was seeing a psychiatrist,' she said eventually.

That took a while to penetrate, because it was about the last thing I was expecting to hear. I think my mouth dropped open. I might even have drooled, I wouldn't have noticed.

'She . . . A psych – But I thought . . .'

Sam stared philosophically into her cup. '. . . that she was happy? I thought she was too. She *said* she was. But she said this was different. Wouldn't tell me anything else, just made me swear I wouldn't tell. Doesn't seem much point in secrets now, though, does there?'

'Do you know who?'

Sam shook her head. We stared at each other for a beat, then I got up and went into the sitting room to find Verity's Filofax.

A card was tucked inside the back pocket: 'Kate Fullerton, Dip. Hyp. Psych. PHTA, Psychotherapy and Hypnotherapy' – a phone number and a north London address, 'Strictest Confidence Assured'.

I rang the number.

eleven

Kate Fullerton lived and worked in a flat in a high, square housing block with white paint peeling to grey. The doorway was in an alcove, up three wide grey-stained marble steps. The doors were wood, darkly varnished, also peeling. A brushed-chrome box, bent at one edge, had ranks of buttons for the sixty-odd flats in the block. I pressed number thirty-two, then had to lean close to the speaker grille because the alcove was amplifying the din of the endless stream of cars. The sky was muddy blue, the streets glaring, and the fumes oppressive. Sam gazed out at the traffic, hugging a ridiculously small cardigan round her, though it wasn't cold.

I was glad she was there.

There were some rattles and a click from Kate Fullerton's intercom, then a voice said, 'Hello?' loud enough to make the speaker howl.

'Hi. It's Harry Waddell,' I yelled, convinced I would be inaudible against the traffic. 'I called yesterday.'

'Fifth floor. Turn right out of the lift. Number thirty-two.' Which was obvious, because I'd just rung the bell.

We went up in a cramped metal lift with a lino floor. It wobbled as it set off. Sam gave me a tight little smile. Her arms were still wrapped round herself. She shuffled impatiently when the lift stopped and the doors took several seconds to open. The carpet in the corridor was a threadbare beige, patterned with a darker brown lattice. Number thirty-two was round two narrow corners. The door was ajar. I looked at Sam, raised my eyebrows. It felt as bad as going for a job interview. Nervously I pushed the door a foot or so open, and peeped in. 'Hello?'

'Come through,' a voice called back.

I followed it into a large square room, with an electric fire in a mean black grate, and metal mullions on the windows. There were glass ornaments on the green-tiled mantelpiece, books on every wall. The room smelt of paperbacks and burnt air from the fire's bars. There was a loosely stuffed three-piece suite, covered in what looked like worn green corduroy. One of the two armchairs was almost hidden behind the door. In it sat Kate Fullerton.

She was older than I had expected, perhaps sixty, with a print dress and thick tights and an astonishingly clear young voice. Her face was young too, despite the lines and thinning skin. It was the eyes, I suppose: they were mild and brown, unblinking, inquisitive and calm at once. They smiled at me in a friendly way, and I felt as though I was being assessed.

'Harry,' she said. Sam came in behind me, and Kate Fullerton looked at me with one eyebrow raised.

'Yes. And, um, this is Sam Mandovini. Sam, Ms Fullerton.'

'Kate, please.' She smiled warmly.

'Sam's a friend of Verity's,' I said. I glanced at her. 'And mine,' I added. 'To be honest I was a little nervous about coming. Sam's my moral support.'

Kate Fullerton laughed. 'Moral support, eh? Perfectly under-standable. Why don't you both go into the kitchen and make yourselves a tea or coffee? Or there's herbals on the shelf above the kettle. I'll see you in a mo.'

We filed along the book-lined corridors of her flat to a tiny kitchen. Sam had to stand in the doorway while I filled the kettle because there wasn't room for us both. The mugs were smoked glass, with a painfully sharp seam down the handle. Sam had a ginseng and something or other, I had an instant coffee, which tasted thin, powdery and acid all at once. The glass was too hot to hold.

We trooped back in. Kate Fullerton had not moved. We sat next to each other on the sofa and looked at her: I don't know quite what I was expecting her to say, since it was I who had wanted to talk to her, not the other way round, but there you go.

'Ms Fullerton—'

At exactly the same time, she said, 'Perhaps you—'

We both paused to let the other continue. Then I nodded at her to go first.

'I was going to say, perhaps you should tell me exactly what happened to Verity. And, please, call me Kate.' She smiled reassuringly. Sam, next to me, hugged her arms and leaned back into the sofa.

So I told her, filling in the detail I had skipped on the phone. I missed out the encounter with Karel – I felt degraded by it and I didn't want anyone to know – but I told her everything else. I described to her the when and the where, and how Verity had fallen and what state she was in now. I told her about my visit to the pub. I told Kate about Verity's debts, even about her fashion collection.

'Ah, yes,' Kate murmured gently. '"Damaged Goods", wasn't it? She mentioned that. I thought it was a good idea.' I looked at Kate with new eyes. She didn't seem the type to go around wearing ripped plastic bags; she looked more comfortable in her green woollen tights. She raised an appraising eyebrow, and her eyes betrayed a moment's humour. 'Not personal taste, I assure you. It was part of the psychotherapeutic process. In lay terms, I was encouraging her to get things out of her system. Go on.'

'Nothing more to tell. The police say suicide, and there's no proof otherwise. Except it feels wrong.'

'In what way?'

She did not move, she just kept looking at me mildly – but I swear that in her head she was taking out a notebook and pencil, licking the point ready for a new page. I was being processed. It pissed me off. 'Look, I know Verity, all right? She wouldn't have gone anywhere near Beachy Head if you paid her. She was happy, for heaven's sake. I know she was seeing you, but she was happy. OK, she was broke – but that's just Verity. There has to be some other explanation. I *know* her.'

The frustration showed. Sam did her best to reassure me. 'Hey, Harry, it's all right. That's what we're here for, remember? Answers.' She put one hand over mine where it rested on my knee.

I took a deep breath. Kate Fullerton was watching me, her eyes sharp now, her expression still mild. Sam was right, of course. 'Sorry,' I conceded. 'It's all such a shock. I can't make it make sense. We came here to ask if you could help us explain it.'

Kate pursed her lips, ever so slightly, and settled deeper into her chair. A clock ticked in the silence, light and fast – a small square alarm clock with a big metal winder, resting among the glassware on the mantelpiece like a living thing among the dead. Kate rested her arms on her chair's high arms.

'I do understand, Harry. But there's little I can tell you about Verity's problems, I'm afraid. It would be quite improper for me to divulge anything she and I discussed in confidence.' She raised a hand to forestall my obvious reply. 'I know she's no longer in a state to tell you herself, and maybe she would have. But she didn't, and I have to respect that. If you were the police, I *might* consider telling you – provided there were sufficient grounds. But a friend who's trying to come to terms with what has happened? I'm sorry, Harry. If that's what's you want, I can't do it.'

I stared at her, trying to fathom her unresponsive brown eyes, all placid sympathy with no sign of the person behind them. The room smelt faintly of damp old building and the clock's tick was becoming oppressive in the quiet. It was like a waiting room. Each hurried little tick lasted an age.

Sam gave my hand another squeeze. 'Kate,' she said, 'you did agree to see us, though, didn't you? If you weren't going to tell us anything, then why bother?'

Kate gave me a wintry smile. 'I wanted to know what had happened, Sam. Verity stopped coming to see me a few weeks ago. She rang and cancelled on a few hours' notice. She hasn't come back. I am as concerned to understand what has happened as you are.' She looked back and forth between us and smiled again. This time her unblinking brown eyes seemed sorrowful. Kate Fullerton was baffling.

'So we're here for your benefit, are we?' I said curtly. 'You have no intention of helping us, you just want to close her file.'

I stood. Sam didn't. 'Harry, get a grip,' she said tiredly. She turned to Kate Fullerton, and said, 'There's a "but" somewhere, isn't there?'

Kate leaned forward. 'Yes, there is. Harry, please, do sit down. I didn't mean to upset you. I'll tell you what I can.'

Totally confused now, I sat down again.

'Thank you.' She straightened with the painful care I usually associated with people in their seventies or beyond. 'As I said, I

109

can't disclose confidential information about Verity. But I *can* tell you what I think about what you've told me. And to tell you the truth, I am puzzled too.'

That got my attention. And Sam's. This time Kate's responding smile was warm.

'I can tell you this,' she said, sitting perfectly still. 'The Verity I was coming to know was an optimistic person, but also very confused – else why would she have come to me? You both know her well enough: her personal life was disorganised, to say the least. She was very creative, she had huge energy, she had friends who cared for her, but she found it difficult to settle down and accept that as the primary part of her life. Sometimes she was quite self-destructive. Not suicidal – I agree with you there, Harry – but she didn't always behave in her own best interests. You both know all this.'

An image of Karel flickered through my thoughts. I tried my best to banish it. I wasn't quite sure how I felt. I had my own mental picture of Verity – well, several pictures, really – a sort of abstract composition of her on the riverbank one winter, of her hand on mine as she told me She Loved Me, No, Really (did she ever know how that felt?), of her hugging her knees on the grass in the park one Sunday. And Kate's words somehow sank straight into this picture and made it more real, more true, without changing it. And I felt so sad and so happy, because the bright snapshots in my mind were so perfect. And now they were all I had.

Kate continued, 'When Verity stopped coming to see me, she was only half-way through her treatment. There were issues she was only just beginning to address. Important issues. As I said, I can't tell you what they were. In fact, I don't know the details myself, because she stopped coming before we had worked through it. The question is, why did she stop coming? I can think of three reasons.

'First, she might have run out of money. I know she wasn't well-off, but I think that's unlikely to be the reason. I had already told her that we could come to an arrangement.

'Second, she was finding therapy very painful. She was reluctant to face whatever we were about to uncover. That does happen, quite frequently. In Verity's case . . .' Kate paused to consider the idea. 'Unlikely, but possible. If people are going to run they generally do it early, when they realise that it isn't going to be an easy process. But Verity was making progress. We were close to breakthrough. People do get nervous at that stage as well – and if they drop out of therapy late, they are likely to experience very low self-esteem, maybe even guilt.'

'When did she last see you?' Sam asked.

Kate picked up a tiny blue leather diary from the mantelpiece and flicked briefly through it. 'Three and a half weeks ago,' she said. 'On the third. She must have rung on the fifth to cancel her next session.'

It matched with what Sam and I had pieced together from Verity's Filofax in the car on the way over. She had had a regular diary appointment with a KF for months – and the last few had been crossed out. Verity had stopped coming to see Kate Fullerton almost three clear weeks before her fall. I must have seen her that same Wednesday evening for our regular date – and we'd met for a pub lunch the next Sunday. We'd had fun. We'd laughed and been happy. 'I saw her after that,' I said. 'She was fine. Actually, she was pretty high.' I looked at Sam for support.

She nodded. 'I think she was,' Sam said. 'High, I mean. Just completely happy and elated. She was amazing at work. Just so creative. Paris was going to do it for her. She was so together.'

Kate watched us for a beat. 'People on that kind of high are rarely as *together* as they seem,' she said. 'There's usually something else going on. She might have been in denial, avoiding her own guilt feelings, for example. I'd rather hoped that was the explanation, but I'm afraid it doesn't sound very likely.' She shook her head very slowly. 'The third possibility is altogether less happy.'

Less happy? Verity was in Eastbourne General. Less happy than what? Sam and I both shuffled uneasily.

'It is possible that Verity completed the therapeutic process on her own – unsupported,' Kate said. She sounded very final, as though that was that. I think we must both have looked bewildered. Kate steepled her fingers and tapped them against her teeth. Then she leaned forward. 'As I told you, I can't discuss the specifics. However, I can tell you a little about how psychotherapy works in general. It may help.' She sat bolt upright: it looked like a posture she was comfortable with. The lecture began.

'There are patterns in our behaviour, in all of us. Habits of speech, habits of thought. We are unaware of most of them. I don't just mean things like scratching your nose when you're embarrassed, I mean *subtle* things. Always choosing the same kind of lover, for example, or behaving aggressively when you're afraid of getting hurt. We all do these things, and they don't usually affect the quality of our lives. They're just who we are. But for most of us, there comes a time when depression hits out of the blue and we can't drag ourselves out of it, or when we feel unable to cope for some other reason. The patterns of behaviour start ruling our lives. That's where psychotherapy comes in. What I do is help people understand their own patterns, and how they came to play such a powerful part in their life. When they see what they're doing, and understand the events that led them there, the patterns lose their power.' Kate smiled. 'In a way, what I do is set people free.'

Free to do what? Jump off a cliff? I bridled inwardly. I've always found the idea of meddling with people's thoughts and emotions disturbing, and I'd assumed Verity would have felt the same. I had obviously been wrong – or else her need was so strong that it overcame her resistance. And she never told me, she preferred to tell a stranger.

'Occasionally, patterns of behaviour are linked to events in the client's past, events they have buried,' Kate continued, staring hard at me. I didn't like it. 'The client doesn't consciously remember what happened. They may have built all sorts of barriers around the memories to prevent them ever surfacing. Those repressed memories frequently generate problematic constructs – those destructive patterns of behaviour I was telling you about. My job is to tease them out. Different things work for different people and problems. In extreme cases, where the memory is too painful for the client to face, hypnotherapy is the only answer.'

'Is that what you were doing with—' Sam started to ask, before Kate interrupted her with a gesture and continued.

'I'm talking about psychotherapy in general, Sam. I'm not going to tell you what problems Verity did or didn't have, or how we worked on them. Verity's was a long-term case, she wasn't going to be cured overnight. That's all I shall say.

'Where was I? Yes, repressed memories. The long and short is, getting at what happened in the past and helping a client deal with it can be difficult and slow. And until it's done the person is vulnerable because they've opened up painful areas of their life, but have not yet worked through them. They may get powerful mood swings – be buoyant and energetic one minute, full of despair the next.'

She frowned.

'We hadn't got to the bottom of Verity's troubles. I had a pretty good idea where we were heading, though, and so did she. So I was worried when she rang to cancel. I warned her. I thought she might be stopping because we were getting close to something. She said it was because she had this show coming up.'

'She did,' Sam and I both said. Sam laid her hand on my knee.

'Yes . . .' Kate agreed. 'But our sessions had been difficult. I was worried. And, by the sound of it, I was worried about completely the wrong thing.' She sighed. She looked up at us both and her eyes were a little misty. To me, she seemed suddenly frail. Her shoulders sagged. She continued, 'Sometimes, when a client uncovers what they have been repressing, it causes them the most terrible pain. And they simply cannot cope. We have to work very hard and very fast to help them come to terms with it. But once you start searching for those buried memories, the process can continue by itself – with or without the psychotherapist's help. A face might spark it off, or a phrase, or an old photograph. Sometimes when they find the memories, when the pain starts, they don't know where to turn. They'll do anything to make it stop.'

She straightened herself again, and gave a dignified sniff; smiled at us, a little helplessly. 'I may be wrong – and I do assure you that there was never anything that I or anyone could have done – but it is possible that Verity found exactly what she had been looking for, and that when she found it, she just couldn't cope. I know it seems unlike her, but whatever she had buried, I suspect it was a powerful and painful experience. That is all I can tell you.'

Silence, except for the nervous patter of the clock on the mantelpiece.

I tried to imagine Verity in that much pain, pain so intense that she only wanted it to stop: dragging herself to Beachy Head, regardless of her prejudices – because who cared? She had wanted to end it all, and that had overwhelmed all normal thought and feeling. Verity leaping, just to be free of whatever demon was riding her. Verity, who hadn't come to see me, not even to say goodbye.

'What was it?' I grated. This was a hard question to ask. 'Her mother dying? Moving house? Something at school? A family thing – she was adopted, abused? What?' My heart was thumping in my ears. The truth was that I didn't really want to know. This felt all wrong, it was scaring me. But I had to ask. It was what we had come for.

Kate Fullerton's brown eyes were, once again, expressionless. 'Harry, even if I knew, I wouldn't tell you.' She stood and reached for my cup and Sam's.

'Could she have been seeing someone else?' I blurted. 'She cancelled her sessions with you, could she have changed to someone else?' It was a desperate question. I felt so close to . . . *something*. Verity, perhaps. I didn't want this to be the end.

Kate's smile combined kindness and ice. 'Very unlikely, I'm afraid, Harry. From what you've said it sounds to me like she was going it alone. I'm sorry, Harry. I really am.'

The sadness in her voice was genuine. It startled me to realise that she might be as rattled as Sam and I were.

She stood by the door, clearly waiting for us to leave. We filed out, Sam first, into the dark corridor lined with books and joyless prints. Sam opened the flat's front door. As I left, Kate called out, 'Harry?' I turned. 'She did care for you, you know. She talked about you a lot. There was nothing you could have done.'

And that, of course, hurt more than she could possibly have imagined.

Sam sensed it and grabbed my hand, swinging it a few times before releasing it. 'There's still the key, remember, Harry?' she said. The key she had found at the studio, a gentle reminder that there were still stones unturned, small puzzles to be solved. She stretched up and pecked me on the cheek. 'We'll get there, you'll see.'

I was not sure that I believed her, or that she believed it herself, but it helped, and that was the point. There were things to do still: leads to follow. What did that key fit, if it wasn't for anything at the studio? 'Verity's flat, then,' I said. 'Let's go.'

And as we walked back towards the car, my step felt a little lighter, and for a while the sun was less harsh in its bitter-blue sky.

twelve

Verity's flat had been wrecked.

I stood in the doorway and gaped. Sam was a few steps behind me. She bumped into me, and then she, too, stared. I could feel her breath on my neck; it was warm but it made me shiver.

'Oh . . .' she said softly.

Pictures had been ripped from the wall: they lay in puddles of shattered glass. The cupboards were all open, and their innards had been spilled into the room. Chairs were overturned. In places the carpet had been shredded and rolled back. The curtains had been torn down, leaving dark holes and dribbles of brick dust where the rail had ripped out of the wall. I could see the door to the kitchen, and beyond it was more of the same. Verity's precious white sofa had been slashed; folds of material hung from it, and I could see the hollow spaces and its wooden frame. It had been burned too: some of the curtains had been piled on it, and there was a dark smoke stain running neatly up its back. There were several crumpled beer cans on the floor. The place stank of burned plastic and piss. The stench seemed to be coming from a puddle of damp carpet just inside the door.

The black wooden stand that held the television and video was broken and on its side. The machines had gone.

I jumped over the puddle. Sam followed, treading carefully through the detritus. Glass crunched under my shoes and I looked down. The photo of Verity at the seaside with the lollipop. The glass had scratched her face. I headed down the corridor towards the bedroom. I heard Sam ringing the police.

The wardrobe had been gutted, the clothes and bed-linen had been torn and scattered. The drawers had all been yanked out of the chest and emptied on to the floor. The locked drawer had been forced open and thrown into a corner. There was a small pool of slips of paper, beer mats, matchbooks and plastic trinkets. Absently I took the key from the drawer and compared it to the one Sam had given me. They did not match. I put the key back into its hole, and picked my way out into the corridor.

They had even kicked in the wooden panel on the side of the bath.

There was nowhere to sit, and nothing we could do until the police came. We opened the windows, and went outside to wait. We sat side by side on the doorstep, dazzled by the sunlight and relieved to be breathing the dust and fumes of London, instead of the toxic air of the flat. The traffic washed past. Our knees were touching lightly, both of us glad of the contact. She lit a cigarette and offered it to me. I took a drag, with no thought to the fact that I don't smoke. It made me dizzy and sick – but I was feeling that way already, so what the hell?

Two police officers came. Both were sympathetic – no PC Bastards this time, thank goodness. One explored the flat, while the other took our statements outside. He was kind and supportive, and he tried gently to explain to us that there was almost nothing they could do. They would take some photographs, and they would take some of the beer cans to check for prints, but we shouldn't expect results. He was very sorry but these things happened. The neighbours below had heard nothing, but they had been away for part of the weekend. I suggested analysing the piss-soaked carpet for DNA, and got a lecture on the limits of police resources, and the vanishingly small chance of success. He continued his questions. I had no idea of the serial numbers for the TV and video, or even what make they were, so there was no real prospect that they could be recovered.

And I finally cracked. I was too frustrated to speak, so I shouted: 'You can't be serious! Verity's found at Beachy Head less than a week ago – and I do *not* believe it was suicide, whatever you lot say – and now you're trying to tell me this burglary's a *coincidence*? Come *on!*'

At the mention of Verity's fall, the policeman perked up. 'You mean the owner, do you, sir? Verity Hadley? Are you saying she's been involved in another incident?'

'Well, if you call falling off a two-hundred-foot cliff an incident—'

'Harry.' Sam put her hand on my arm. When she had my attention, she turned to the policeman. 'I'm sorry, Officer. This is a little difficult for us. Verity fell off Beachy Head on Wednesday last week.' I wanted to scream, *No* – and inside, I did. Sam went on, 'It was a terrible shock. We were both close to her. And now there's this . . .'

'Perfectly understandable, Miss, er . . . Mandovini.' The officer had to consult his notes for her name. 'If you'll give me the details, I'll make sure we cross-reference the files. Suicide, I assume?'

I was about to answer – angrily – but another squeeze from Sam forestalled me. 'We're not sure,' she said. 'That's what it looked like, and that's what the police recorded . . .' She looked to me for confirmation. I mumbled something. '. . . but Harry's not convinced. It seems odd to me too.'

The policeman's eyes flicked between us, then focused on me. 'May I ask what made you suspicious?' He seemed almost eager.

'Beachy Head's not her style,' I said lamely.

'Anything else, sir?'

'She'd arranged to meet someone nearby that afternoon. They didn't show up.'

'Who, sir?'

I shrugged. 'No idea. She didn't write their name down.'

The policeman's face settled back into blankness. 'I see.' He sounded disappointed. 'I'm afraid none of that really constitutes evidence, sir. Meeting people is hardly unusual, even if they don't turn up.' As if I needed telling: last Wednesday wasn't that long ago. 'And as to your opinion of Miss Hadley's style, sir, well, I'm afraid that's not much to go on either. Suicidal people *do* do *very* strange things, Mr Waddell, believe me.' He gave me the kind of look that made sure I was aware that he knew all about it.

'Well, what about the flat?' I snapped, exasperated.

'The burglary, do you mean, sir? Well, as I said, there's not much more we can do.'

'But surely that proves something's going on.'

The policeman folded up his notebook and crossed his arms. 'Sir, do you have any idea how many burglaries there are each day in London?' I didn't feel like another lecture, but it seemed I was in for one.

'Well, loads. But—'

'*Loads*,' he mimicked. 'In the last two days, I have personally attended six. And that's just *one* officer in just *one* station, if you see what I mean. Any flat that's left unattended is fair game, I'm afraid. And by the look of it, your lot here were just a bunch of hooligans out for a laugh. These weren't serious criminals. All they did was smash the place up. They nicked the easy stuff, of course – the telly and that – but for them this was just a night on the town. No offence, Mr Waddell, but Miss Hadley's flat was a prime target, what with her being away. We see it all the time. It's gangs. It's what they do.'

Well, *someone* had certainly done it, but I found it impossible to accept that it was a gang. It was too unfair, the coincidence too brutal. This was *personal* – at least, it was to me. But if it hadn't been a gang, then who? Who would hold her in such contempt that they would rip her flat to shreds when she could never return to it anyway? Did they care at all? Did they even know? That was when the answer hit me.

'Wait!' I yelped. 'I know who did it!'

The policeman looked at me attentively, pencil at the ready. I felt like bouncing up and down. I was so sure: that thin face, the sneer, the fag ash on Verity's calico sofa, the spite.

'Karel,' I said firmly. 'Karel ... Shit, what's the bastard's name? Karel ...'

'Novak?' Sam sounded startled. 'The little runt Verity was seeing? What makes you think he did it?'

I explained about my encounter a couple of days before. Knowing that Sam was listening made me go red. I wished I has been able to tell her earlier – the embarrassment of revealing it now was far worse.

The policeman earnestly took notes. 'And you know where we could find this Mr Novak, do you, sir?'

I was about to reply, probably something unhelpful about whose job was to track down criminals, when Sam stepped in: 'I do,' she said, 'but, honestly, I can't see it being him. He's a poisonous little worm, but he's too lazy for this kind of thing. He's a sponger, not a burglar. All that ripping and banging around ... And what's he going to do with a telly, for goodness' sake?'

I was torn. I was secretly pleased that she shared my opinion of him, but her scepticism was annoying – particularly because I half suspected she was right: trashing Verity's flat was taking malice a little far.

'Well, how come the door wasn't kicked in?' I asked petulantly. 'He's the only other person with keys.'

'Probably picked the lock, sir,' the policeman said helpfully. 'Kicking a door down makes a lot of noise.' He was staring around him distractedly. He'd lost interest. 'Well, we'll have a word with Mr Novak, sir, just to be sure. But gangs is more likely, I'm afraid.'

And with assurances that they would do everything they could, and yes, they would keep us informed, the police left.

'Down to us,' I said to Sam.

She shrugged. 'We'd better get going, then.' I nodded but didn't move. She added, 'Come on, Harry. It's not going to be any easier tomorrow.' She gave my arm a quick rub. I was frowning at my watch. I was trying to figure something out, but I couldn't find a place to start. I was caught in an endless loop of irrelevant thought – four thirty, best get going, four thirty, best get going ... 'Harry?' When, again, I didn't respond, she disappeared into the building.

I looked along the street. Hot red brick, and a grubby breeze that puffed grit and dust at me. The place was quiet. There were only a few parked cars and no people, as though some apocalypse had removed everyone, and left only the buildings, mouldering slowly in the wind and dust.

But there was no time for self-indulgence. There was some bastard's piss to clean up. Sam was waiting. Reluctantly I followed her upstairs.

She had already found the cleaning materials, and was zipping efficiently from place to place armed with some kind of spray, wearing Marigolds and an apron. There was something foamy on top of the carpet puddle. It already smelt a little better. She had set the table straight and the chairs were upright in a neat row against it.

I hopped over the foam pool and gaped around vaguely. Sam

stopped and appraised me, then bustled into the kitchen and came out with a plastic sack, dustpan and brush.

'Cans. Curtains. Glass.' She pointed with her spray canister. 'Anything that's broken. Those burnt cushions. There's newspaper for the glass over there.'

And she was off again. She didn't stop moving for a second. I pottered. I swept a bit of glass, stared at the wall for a while, emptied the dustpan, maybe picked up a crumpled beer-can, stared at the wall again. I can't even blame my misery: happy or sad, I'm just crap at cleaning. Still, I was trying. Sam worked around me as best she could. By the time my bag was full, the flat was looking better, small thanks to me.

'Coffee,' I said. She nodded.

I headed off towards the kitchen, but she caught me by the shoulder and twirled me back to face the living room. 'I'll make it. I'm not sure I trust you.'

She pressed past me. Her body was cool and firm, an odd counterpoint to the strange sensation of my shoulder being squeezed by a yellow rubber glove.

'If you're done with the glass and stuff, try to find a number for the insurance company,' she called.

I hadn't even thought of that. I scanned the room. The cupboards had been stripped, and the mounds of stuff on the floor had all been sorted and stacked. Sam had covered the table with orderly piles: CDs, instruction manuals, ornaments, mostly broken. No papers, though. I started going through the cupboards. They were all empty; the burglars had pulled everything on to the floor, and Sam had tidied most of it up.

She was clattering around in the kitchen while the kettle boiled. I leaned against the door, my chest against the jamb, the side of my face pressing against the door itself. While the kettle boiled, she was cleaning the kitchen surfaces.

'Sam?' She stopped and looked at me. 'I'm really grateful, Sam. This must be as bad for you as it is for me.'

She straightened and pursed her lips at me. 'Insurance,' she said sternly, and waggled a canister at me.

I headed reluctantly back towards the piles of paperwork. On one corner of the table was the answering-machine, its cable stretching dangerously across the room to the wall socket. The table it had been on was splintered and unstable and had been consigned to a corner, along with the support for the television, several ripped cushions and curtains. The machine's display showed four messages.

Vaguely I remembered that when I had come here to collect the zoetrope there had been only three, and I hadn't wanted to play them. Now they seemed more appealing: the alternative was to keep rummaging through the remains of Verity's life. I hit the button.

First message. 'Verity, dear, it's Erica.' An old woman's voice, deep and throaty – too many cigarettes, I thought. She didn't say anything else. There was a long silence, followed by a few rattles and then a click.

The next message was just a dialling tone.

The third was short as well: 'Where were you?' My own voice, muttering indistinctly.

Good question, Harry, and where were you?

Fourth message, the new one. 'Verity? It's Erica again. Erica McKelvie.' This time, the voice was nervous and unsure. 'I just wondered if you were all right, dear. It's pension day tomorrow. I didn't know whether you had gone away perhaps.' There was a long, uncertain pause. 'Do call, darling.' Another long silence, as though she wanted to say something more, and then a click.

'Harry, *insurance.*' Sam was standing watching me, Marigolds on hips.

I was avoiding it, of course, though I have no idea why. I think I was overwhelmed by the huge amount that needed doing – and now I had to add tracking down Erica McKelvie to the list.

The kettle clicked and Sam went back into the kitchen.

I stared round the room for inspiration. I started to call to Sam, 'Any idea where—' and then stopped, because I had caught sight of the answer. In the middle of the room was Verity's precious sofa, one end of it blackened and burned away. The foam from what remained of the cushions was tarry and molten. I muttered something under my breath.

'Any idea what?' Sam said. She was standing in the doorway balancing two mugs, the Marigolds finally removed. I ignored her.

The fire had burned a hole right through to the base of the sofa. I peered in. It was full of ash and blackened springs. Charred edges of paper hung from them. 'Shit!' I yelled, and kicked the side of the sofa angrily. The ashes settled a little, and black motes rose into the sunlight, filling the air with the reek of stale smoke.

'No insurance papers,' I snarled. 'In fact, no papers at all.' I booted the sofa again.

'Harry, sit,' Sam said firmly. She pushed a coffee-cup across the table towards me. I felt terribly weary. I sat.

'There's nothing left.' I mumbled. 'I'm going to have to chase down the whole damn lot, aren't I? I know there was a phone bill and a credit card. I'll have to ring and get duplicates. God knows what else there was.'

'You didn't find papers anywhere, then?' In answer, I pointed at the sofa. Her eyes widened. 'They burned the lot?'

'I've looked everywhere else. Oh, *shit* ... How the hell am I supposed to work out who her insurance company even *was*?'

Sam's eyes crinkled, her lips pressed together in sad sympathy.

'We,' she said gently. 'Not you, we. And don't worry, we'll work it out. Maybe she had them in her Filofax. Or the bank will tell us who she paid bills to. We'll get there.'

Her words solved nothing, but they helped. I wasn't alone, and that made all the difference. I put my hand over hers and squeezed. We sat silently amid the wreckage for a while. Occasionally I sipped my coffee – I have to admit, it was better than when I made it – but I put my hand back on hers afterwards.

She stood and announced it was time to get back to work. The Marigolds reappeared, and once again she was all business. Watching her bustle round Verity's flat, though, I could see the pain in her eyes. Her skin seemed flushed and fragile.

Nice bum, though.

She caught me looking at her, and cocked her head at me; then she threw me a flirtatious kiss.

And a duster.

When we drew up outside Sam's house it was late, somewhere past eight o'clock. We sat in the car, both unsure what to say. 'What a day,' was hardly going to cover it.

'OK. I'm going to ask you in for a drink,' she said. 'You won't take it the wrong way, will you? Only I damn well need one, and I don't fancy being alone.' In answer, I shut off the engine and climbed out. I hadn't been looking forward to staring at my own empty walls either.

Sam's flat was large, and simple to the point of austerity. The walls were white. The furniture was pale wood and cane, upholstered in rough, undyed canvas. The sitting room was dominated by a single abstract painting in vivid blues and yellows that somehow managed to suggest both the sea and a prison.

'Like it?' She handed me a strong gin and tonic. It was sharp and bitter, and the fumes drove through my head. It helped.

The painting must have been eight feet square. It wasn't in a style I recognised, but it was definitely an original; I could see the lumps in the oil paint. I squinted to make out the signature, but it was illegible. She looked at me, amused. 'Before you pronounce judgement, I'll tell you. It's one of mine.'

I was astonished. It was good. But now she wouldn't believe me when I told her. I did anyway, and she seemed to accept it.

I wasn't used to people who were secure enough to accept a compliment. I found it unnerving. I was baffled by Sam – but I liked her too. What was strange was not quite knowing *who* it was that I liked. She was still staring at the picture. 'I did it as a backdrop for my graduation collection,' she said. 'The clothes were crap, but everyone loved the painting. Ironic, really. I'd been working on the collection for the best part of three years. The painting only took me half an hour.'

She crossed the room to a sofa. I followed.

'I'd say you've got a whole new career there.' I meant it.

She snorted softly into her gin, drained it and half got up. She looked at me enquiringly. I knocked back what remained of my own drink and handed her the glass.

While she fixed the drinks, I looked at the painting. Aquamarines in soft-edged curves, barred rays of gold and fine black lines. It was beautiful. It spoke to me of order and regret. It made me think of trees – and of Verity, now lost to the implacable truth of her fall.

Sam came back in and slumped next to me. Her eyes were watery. Guilt shot through me again. I turned sideways on the sofa to face her, and gently stroked her knee.

'I . . . don't really know what to say,' I mumbled. 'I keep being selfish. Sorry.'

She looked at me and then away. Her lip trembled and she

sniffed fiercely. She took my hand and swung it back and forth aimlessly. Her eyes were brimming.

'And we will get there, you were right,' I added.

She leaned over and settled against my chest. I wrapped my arms round her. I could feel the sobs shaking her. I let her finish before I spoke again. 'I miss her, Sam.'

She straightened. Her face was marked by dried tears. Her lashes were matted and her eyes were reddened, and her hair was in a mess. She looked fragile and strong all at once – like her painting. I brushed away a lock of hair that was getting in her eyes. She leaned her face towards my hand – and I kept it there.

We looked at each other for a long while. Then she took my hand and led me to her bedroom.

It wasn't the best sex in the world, for either of us, and it didn't mean anything much – but who cared? We both needed it, we were both adults, we both did it – and I suppose we both got what we wanted from it. For a small while, during and after, I felt a little less alone. Sam seemed content enough to lie next to me. Don't ask me why we did it, because I don't know. I don't think Sam had planned it any more than I had. Maybe it was for comfort, maybe to forget. Whatever: it was urgent and basic. Neither of us was thinking. I'm sure we both knew there would be embarrassment afterwards, awkwardness and uncertainty. But, of course, we didn't let that stop us.

Afterwards we were both quiet, making no demands, expecting nothing. When we started to fidget, Sam mumbled something about another drink. I volunteered and wandered naked into the kitchen. There was a bottle of white wine in the fridge and I found a corkscrew in the drawer under the hob. There was something comfortable about finding things so easily in her kitchen, they were in familiar places. And, of course, it was secretly thrilling to be naked in someone else's flat. I felt airy, liberated. When I walked back through the sitting room, the feeling evaporated as I noticed it was dark outside, the room lights were on and the curtains open. Then I thought, What the hell? It's not my place anyway, who cares? And I padded back with the bottle and two glasses to the bedroom, free as you like.

While I was gone Sam had put on her dressing-gown and

switched on the television. Some cookery show was on, with two chefs-cum-drama-queens and a load of pointless celebrities, struggling to do something inventive with tomato sauce, half a courgette and a bar of chocolate. I handed Sam a glass and sat next to her, glad not to have to talk. She patted my leg absent-mindedly, then pulled her hand back on to her lap.

The wine had a cool perfume. Like the sex, it felt good: ordinary, undemanding, safe. I poured us both another glass.

When the bottle was finished I felt self-conscious. I was naked, she wasn't. The TV was boring. Neither of us was speaking.

'Look, it's getting late,' I said. 'I ought to . . .' She looked at me. I smiled weakly and muttered, 'Yeah. Er . . . thanks.'

It was awkward. I got dressed. She switched off the television and watched. She hovered by the door to the flat while I prowled round the living room collecting my things. At last I was ready, and I stood in front of her.

She didn't quite know what to do with her eyes. Neither did I – not least because her dressing-gown was gaping open. I remembered her small breasts, soft skin. Her bum had been as nice as I had thought.

'Well . . .' she said.

'Well . . .' I agreed.

I glanced at the door-latch, but did not reach for it. She put a hand on my chest and slipped a finger in between the buttons.

'Harry . . . Stay,' she murmured.

I looked at her. Her eyes were earnest, pleading.

'Stay,' she said again.

And I did.

thirteen

I hope I haven't shocked you. I never claimed to be celibate.

I had flings and one-night stands and not-quite-girlfriends, but nothing you might call even semi-permanent – and in between, I wondered what might have happened if that childhood kiss had been the beginning of something, and not its end. But you can't build your life on a fantasy, can you? The point is, my blood is as red as anyone's. Why *shouldn't* I sleep with Sam? This may be Verity's story, but it's not as though I had nothing else in my life.

I woke next to Sam, aglow after that strange, restless sleep of a night in bed with someone new. Sam woke a little later, and we made love again, slowly this time, and with more purpose and attention than we had the night before. We sat opposite each other at the breakfast table, me clutching a cooling mug of tea, neither of us knowing what to say, my thoughts whirling impossibly fast.

The shadows of the trees outside threw complex patterns across Sam's huge painting, flattened reminders of the street below, the sinews and bones of living shapes. I have always loved trees: their stillness, their strength, the lightness of their beams. Now, suddenly, I needed to capture that feeling on film. I made my apologies, gave Sam one last kiss – which I enjoyed enough to come back for another before I'd even reached the door – and headed for home. There, I scooped up my cameras, and headed for Battersea Park.

Perhaps I was trying to recapture the long-ago magic of when Verity and I kissed, or the lightness and comfort of my night with Sam. Or perhaps it was a memorial of sorts, a way of recording

Verity's passing. Perhaps it was just therapeutic. Whatever: it worked.

As I sank into the work I actually began to *feel* properly. For the first time in days, the numbness lifted. I became what I was doing, absorbed in each shot. Massive branches arching up into a hot sky. Crazed silhouettes of twigs and leaves, blurred by the sunlight bleeding through them. Vast, impassive trunks in ordered rows, one with a small boy crouching by its bole to touch a squirrel. The texture of flaking bark. I was in love with all of it. I laughed aloud, I cried. Everything was intense, the world was heightened, it was hard to bear. It was a kind of ecstasy.

And when I came home, I called Sam; and she came over, and did not leave until morning.

Perhaps I should tell you a little more about myself, about the bits of me you otherwise won't see.

I was born in north Oxford, thirty-four years ago. My dad, David Waddell, made precision instruments for a small local firm, mostly serving the university labs. He was a partner in the company; our family was doing the north Oxford thing, climbing the slippery ladder for all we were worth.

Mum is Carol. She spent three days a week as a medical secretary at the John Radcliffe Hospital, sorting out the private practice of a bushy-browed man she called the Prof: his eyebrows and his flapping white coat are all I can remember, I don't even know what his speciality was. The other days she spent at home. I'm not sure what she did with her time. I was at school mostly, and in my spare time, as I grew up, I would wander further and further afield; I was hardly there except for meals and bed.

A gang of us used to cycle down to Port Meadow, to ride the smooth-swept bumps that led down to the floodplain like a rollercoaster. Sometimes we'd fish for chub in the Cherwell or the Isis, or race our bikes (illegally) in a circuit round the courtyard of the Bodleian. We were a loose group and only a few of us would meet up on any particular day; the combinations were always changing. They were schoolfriends mostly, and a couple of neighbours.

We lived in a big house – but it can't have been big enough, because Mum and Dad were always talking about moving somewhere better. I was at a private school, New College Choir School, which was one of the very few acceptable schools to discuss at north Oxford dinner parties and was costing the family more than we could easily afford. It was a high-pressure environment, and I never quite managed to keep up. This was more out of attitude than inability: I was averagely good at most subjects. I was good at English and maths, top in art (except for pottery), and I was lousy at the sciences and French. I detested Latin and it detested me.

Our garden was large, and Dad had put a rope pulley from one side of it to the other. In summer we would set up the water sprinkler and dash through the spray, and the grass was slippery and cold and tickled our bare backs when we fell.

I loved Oxford, and the house and my friends. I loved my parents. I was an only child, but I truly do not believe that my parents spoiled me – well, maybe a bit, but I also remember being kept firmly in line: there were rules and lectures as well as treats. I was never starved of company. Unfashionable though it is, I have to confess that I grew up mostly happy.

Then, when I was twelve, Dad's firm went bust.

There must have been a day when he came home and it was all over, but I don't remember. There must have been agonising months while he looked for another job, and failed to find one. Bigger firms were taking over, German firms, Japanese firms. The craft had gone out of instrument-making, he grumbled, it was the big boys now, just like everything else. And the big boys weren't interested in the skills of a man who had left school at fourteen, served his apprenticeship at an old firm with grime on its tiny windows and an interior of dark wood benches and peeling varnish. Dad had worked with the same firm all his life and, in a way, his life ended when the firm's did. He lost weight. His temper became worse. He paced through the house. When he sat, he seemed to grind his way into the chair. Doors that were normally silent screeched when he opened – or slammed – them. He never recovered his peace.

Christmas came and went, joylessly.

At the time I didn't understand why we had to move, and Mum and Dad never chose to explain. Each day's post contained sheaves of house descriptions, photocopied images of squat bungalows, a few terse lines of measurements. Most of them were strewn on the outsize table in the dining room in complicated piles, interspersed with blank sheets covered with spidery calculations. They would occasionally bundle all these papers up and vanish in the car for hours; they would come back grim and hardly talking. Then, one day, some men came with a van and took away half of our furniture, and I never saw it again. The day after that there were packing-cases in the hall, and Mum and Dad began to fill them with what remained.

My most powerful memories are of the empty house. The wood floor in the hall echoed loudly as I staggered across it, my heavy suitcase clasped in both arms, uncomfortably high to avoid crashing against my knees. The place smelt different when it was empty, dry and light, as though it was waiting already for the dust to settle.

The suitcase went in Mum's car (Dad's car had been sold some time before), and we drove off – Dad had gone ahead with the removal men. We drove up the Woodstock Road, turned left at the roundabout, down into Wolvercote. Mum said nothing, all the way. She led me up the narrow path to a post-war two-storey semi. It was small, cream-painted, with ungenerous square windows. I lumped up the path, with my suitcase brushing the tops of the overgrown shrubs that hung over the paving. She unlocked the door, and we stood in the hallway like a couple of timid ghosts. She told me that this was where we were going to live.

It was the start of a new life, and a new me.

The local comp was tough for me. The children didn't have much fondness for boys from private schools. They called me Waddle; they used to make a line behind me, paddling along with their hands stuck out like penguins. Very funny. When they played football, they made a point of not inviting me – because, they said, I was too posh for a 'common' game. I ignored them, and only cried after school when I sneaked away to play in the woods on my own. But there was not much violence, and what little there was stopped after I hit back.

It was an accident as much as anything. It all happened at the measured, predetermined pace of a ballet. It was towards the end of my first term at the school, his name was Greg Winston, and I hated him. A small group of boys had backed me into a corner of the playground, needling me and shoving me. Greg swaggered through his cronies and swung a hefty, badly aimed kick at my crotch, flinging his arms out for balance. It was a lazy swipe, he was showing off, not trying to damage me – but I was scared, and I was already pressed as far back against the wall as I could go. As the heavy-booted foot rose up, I squeezed back another few millimetres by twisting away from the blow. That brought my shoulders round, and my hands were suddenly under the rising arc of his leg. I clamped them round his ankle and pushed outwards to deflect the strike. He was after points for style, not strength or accuracy: it was the sort of kick that sends the kicker tumbling if they don't connect and all I did was stop him connecting. As the leg rose, his own momentum lifted him. He jerked off the ground and fell from waist-height, flat on to the Tarmac.

His whole back hit the ground at once. There was a faint pneumatic squeak as the air smashed out of his lungs – the kind of noise you get in children's toys – then the wooden knock of the back of his head, then the clatter of his leathery boots, then silence. The other five or so boys looked down at their leader in confusion, perhaps waiting for him to show them his brilliant final move, which the fall was obviously leading up to, but he just lay there, his eyes bulging wide, and a barely audible sigh coming from him. His hands were lifted, twitching and waving, the fingers splayed.

I was not thinking a single conscious thought. Acting out of some ingrained (private) schoolboy idea of honour, I reached down, grasped one of his hands and pulled him to his feet in a single heave. (Actually, this was the only thing I did that was impressive because he was incredibly heavy. Of course, no one noticed it.) He stood, bent double, the breathless whine still trickling out of him. He grabbed one of his cronies' waistbands for support and, handover complete, I walked away.

My hands started shaking violently after about three paces. There was no sense of victory, just fear and unease. The fear was first: fear that I had done him some permanent harm. I would be found out and punished. Perhaps he would die, and I would end up on trial, innocently imprisoned, the jury deaf to my pleas. Then came the nausea, and the fascination of replaying the incident over and over, letting him crunch into the hard ground, again and again and again, detecting the subtle squelch of blood as his head struck, the sharp mechanical crack of ribs. It's horrible when you really think about an injury, and doubly so when you inflicted it: there's a wrongness about the idea of bodies bending and breaking and slicing open that makes me feel sick. I can work myself up into a state even about minor cuts if I really try – but this time there was no need because Greg's fall had been very nasty indeed. So I huddled in a corner of the playground and muttered to myself, and in front my eyes there he was, hitting the ground again and again and again, skull crumpling, backbone cracking, rib shards scything through his lungs and bowels.

Five minutes later he came up to me, unharmed. He put out a large rough hand and mumbled, 'Truce.' I took the hand, and we hardly spoke again for months. Some of his hangers-on tried following me around and being friendly. I played with them sometimes, kicked a ball around with them or went swimming, but even when I was with them I kept my distance. I preferred my own company.

At home, I felt like a stranger. The house had its own moods, mysterious rhythms – rages, sadnesses, the grim silences that swept through Mum and Dad. They performed the functions of their lives with blank eyes and bitten-in faces. I woke each morning, wondering what the house would make them say and do that day. Would they be full of brittle cheeriness and enthusiasm? Or would the house make them bitter, Mum hacking savagely at the bread over breakfast, Dad dry and bent and stalking restlessly from room to room? Sometimes the days were soft and sad: Dad would retreat peacefully to his shed to work on unspecified jobs that needed doing but never seemed to be done, and Mum would sit in a hard nylon-covered chair in the living room, staring at the electric fire. Sometimes I saw tears on her cheeks, but I never asked her about them. No one talked much.

Dad moved out soon after my thirteenth birthday, just before the summer term began. I hardly noticed. In truth, he was already long gone.

We ground on through May and June, Mum and I. Puberty, the move, my parents' separation, all reinforced my isolation. Mum didn't know how to cope with my moods, and neither did I. I was confused and unhappy. Looking back, I think Mum blamed herself – but it's just what happened, a combination of chance and the kind of boy I was. I played on my own a lot. I cycled along the canal to old haunts, sitting alone and taking a certain pleasure in loneliness. Some time that term I discovered Whiteham Woods. I would spend my weekends climbing trees, or imagine that I was a paratrooper behind enemy lines and stalk the gamekeepers. They must have known I was there, but they gave no hint. On one of those visits I discovered the treehouse. It was my secret and my refuge, mine alone.

Then came the summer holidays.

And then there was Verity.

fourteen

I waited in the garden by the apple tree.

I had thought of nothing but *her* all weekend. The time with Dad had drifted by, evaporating as easily as the clouds through two hot blue days. It had been one endless moment, a single mood made of leaflight and dry wood and anticipation and thrill and fear, all shot through with her warm smell and lips. It was unbearable – and I loved it. Finally the wait was over. I clambered from Dad's car and said my farewells, kissed Mum hello, dumped my bags and rushed outside. Verity knew when I was due back. I had been secretly hoping that she would be waiting for me. In fact, I had been secretly hoping all sorts of things, many of which I could hardly put a name to.

I waited in the garden by the apple tree, in the early evening.

She was having her tea, or Gabriel had taken her out for the day, she would be back at any moment. She had homework to do (*homework*, two weeks before starting at a new school?). Or she was ill, or Gabriel was ill, or she had moved house without telling me, she had known it all along. Why wasn't she waiting? Suddenly the days since we had kissed seemed an eternity. It had been enough time to alter everything. She had vanished – or, worse, she had changed her mind about me.

She was at the treehouse, waiting for me, that was it. I strolled completely uncasually to my bike (no running, I was determined to be cool) and set off, fast.

I waited on the same boards I had sat on after our kiss two days ago, stroking the planks where we had lain, summoning her out of the wood, touching her, bones and flesh and supple skin, not minding the splinters. The same leaves and branches arched through the same green light, carving shapes and substance from the air. The same whispers surrounded me whenever breezes shimmered through the tree's green vault. The soft sigh of the woods, untouched by time or thought. Or solitude.

She wasn't there.

The cameras were gone. The piles of earth they had stood on had been kicked flat, the stones and trigger-twigs scattered. Tangles of string littered the great tree's shade. I gathered them up and wadded them into my pockets. Then I cycled home slowly, meandering between the lane's broad banks, thinking nothing, riding each erratic curve.

I waited in the garden.

Cushioned in the long grass at the apple tree's foot was a half-inflated football. I picked it up, tossed it a few yards away, and followed. I slipped my toe beneath it and hoicked it up towards a three-pronged fork in one of the tree's stubby spars. It missed and dropped slackly to the ground. I collected it, slipped my toe beneath it once again.

When it was too dark to see the tree, I headed for the back door. I glanced up at her window. There was a light in it, slitted through the curtains, and a shadow moved inside.

There was no sound at all except the last screams of the swifts.

I woke late, and rose later. My bedroom was at the back of the house, and when I opened the curtains I saw Verity kicking idly on the tatty metal swing in her garden. She glanced up and I turned away guiltily, as though she had caught me snooping, embarrassed and thrilled that she had seen me in my pyjamas. I dressed hurriedly, but when I checked again at the window she had gone.

It was a bright day, but overcast. The sky was a white haze and sudden cold gusts stirred the hedges and the dusty ground. On the rim of the sky's bowl, heavier clouds passed us by.

I waited in the garden. I was trying to lodge the ball in the tree.

I couldn't bring myself to knock for her. It would have shown her my eagerness. It would have been humiliating. I would let it happen naturally, as everything else had done. It would happen. I just needed to be cool, patient. She couldn't have changed her mind. Not Verity.

After lunch I went to see Adam. I didn't dare ring, not after what his dad had done, so I hung around on the other side of the road, kicking a crumpled can along the gutter, one way then the other. Fanta. Sticky orange round its lip. I sat for a while on the low kerb, arms dangling outwards, my upper arms propped on my knees, squinting at nothing in particular. After an hour, I gave up.

I rode along the river towards Port Meadow. At the far end there was a slope covered in smooth hillocks, perfect for riding down and for bike jumps. I wanted to speed up the slow roll of time through the afternoon. The distant thunderclouds seemed heavy and immobile, the river so sluggish it barely stirred the reeds. I passed the ruined abbey and headed for the river lock. The meadow stretched beyond.

A bike I recognised leaned against the arm of one of the lock gates. Sitting on the narrow board that spanned it, legs dangling over the ten-foot drop to the water's outflow, was Adam. He didn't look at me. I dumped my bike on the verge and walked out along the gangway. I sat next to him, arms hung over the lower spar of the handrail, chin resting on the cold metal, staring along the towpath towards the meadow. Below our feet, the river frothed through gaps in the gate, creating a steady roar and sending thin bubbles whirling uncertainly out into the current.

'Not allowed to see you,' Adam said, not looking round. The side of his face was swollen and shiny. The skin around his eye and across the bridge of his nose was stained purple and black.

I looked away. A coot skittered between two clumps of river-grass, screeching as she went. 'Yeah,' I said, and sniffed companionably.

Adam sniffed too, and we watched the river together. Then he sighed wearily, and unwound himself from the rail post he was straddling. He clambered to his feet, wincing. Rather than climb round me, he walked off the gangway the wrong way, along the side of the lock to the other set of gates, and crossed there. I craned to follow his progress. He headed back down the lock for his bike. He was limping.

'Adam,' I pleaded. He ignored me. 'Adam!' He stopped, not looking at me, but his posture told me he was listening. I hauled myself upright and crossed to stand in front of him. He still did not look at me.

He was standing awkwardly, lopsided, with his head twisted to give his unswollen eye a better view. When the wind shoved us unexpectedly, he swayed and flinched. His jaw was puffed, and his lips were thick and too red on one side. There was a scratch running down his temple towards his good eye.

'Leave me alone,' he said.

'Have you seen Verity?'

'Not allowed to see you. Not allowed to talk.' He looked at me, then got on his bike and rode back towards home.

'Adam, what's going on?' I called after him.

Over his shoulder, he yelled, 'Fuck off, Harry,' and was gone.

I waited by the river.

I went and sat where he had, legs dangling above the water, watching the clumps of muddy foam from the lock spiral unevenly out between the pale banks, catching one by one on the river-grass and the dead branches and the weeds.

A few days later I knocked on Verity's door. Gabriel answered. His eyes were deep and glittering, his face solemn and untroubled.

'Is Verity in?'

'She's gone away for a while, Harry. She's staying with her aunt in Huntingdon. Sorry.'

'When's she back, then?'

'She'll be back in time for term, Harry. But she'll be very busy. She won't have time to play.'

I must have stood with my mouth open. I had no idea what to say. I had a thousand questions, and I asked none.

'She doesn't want to see you any more, Harry,' Gabriel said calmly. The words sliced through me. There was a small, bitter smile on his lips. 'I'm sorry, Harry,' he said.

He closed the door very gently in my face.

The next morning, my five cameras were in a torn cardboard box on the back doorstep. None had films in them, although we had bought or borrowed new film for almost all of them before we had even developed the first set of photos. A few days before, the cameras had seemed like instruments of infinite potential. Now they were a message, written in brute lumps of plastic and brushed chrome. Their single eyes were dulled and unseeing.

Later that day, as I came downstairs from reading a comic in my room, I saw Gabriel start his car and drive hastily away. In the back seat, next to a few bags and boxes, hunched a small figure. A yellow dress, dark brown hair in a bob, and for a fragment of a moment, two wide dark eyes. Then they were gone. When Gabriel drove the car back two hours later, he was alone.

I waited in the garden. I nudged my toe under the half-inflated football, and flicked it upwards towards the tree. It slapped against the underside of a branch and dropped heavily into the grass.

I picked it up and began again.

fifteen

'Harry, I'm worried about you.'
I shook my head vigorously, then had to hold on to the table for a moment or two to get my bearings before I could carry on. I must have been about three pints in and the evening had barely begun. Typical Adam. 'What's to worry? I'm just saying that whoever Verity was supposed to see in that pub must have had something to do with her falling.'

Adam opened his mouth to reply, then shut it again and settled for rocking his hand uncertainly from side to side.

He had been ringing me for days, worried that I wasn't as fine as I sounded – which, of course, I wasn't. Actually, I was confused: by what Kate Fullerton had told us, by the burglary, and also by Sam, although I didn't admit that to him. The burglary and the psychiatrist were enough for Adam to insist that we should meet. I'd agreed, reluctantly.

I had intended to spend the evening with Sam, going over Verity's Filofax for anything we might have missed; I suggested to her that she stay over anyway, and promised I'd be back sober and in good time. But good intentions and an evening with Adam were not exactly compatible. I'd already blown it, and the night was still young.

'She was seeing someone,' I insisted.

'Yeah, her boyfriend. That Slav bloke, Karel Whatshisname. Plus the psychiatrist. You told me.'

'No, not them, the person she was supposed to meet at the pub.'

I fished around in the plastic bag at my feet and slapped Verity's Filofax down facing Adam on one of the few dry patches on the table. I flicked through the diary section and smartly tapped the Birling Gap entry to drive home my point.

Adam rolled his eyes impatiently. 'Harry, I'll bet you any money it was Whatshisname. Or even if it wasn't, maybe she's got some frail little auntie, lives in Eastbourne.' We were on uncomfortable ground, and we both knew it. Adam really didn't see any mystery: when he looked at me, all he saw was a friend in distress.

His suggestion was no help at all. Verity had no relatives other than Gabriel. I thought guiltily of the calls from Erica McKelvie on her answerphone, and promised myself yet again that I would track her down. Tomorrow. Soon. Some time. Whoever she was, though, she surely wouldn't have arranged to meet Verity in Birling Gap, then left messages at Verity's as though nothing had happened.

'Well, if there isn't an auntie, then it had to be Whatshisname,' Adam said, as though it was self-evident.

I wagged a finger at him and gulped at my beer at the same time. 'This was someone new. Look.' I pushed the Filofax closer to him.

I marched him through the last few weeks of Verity's life, page by page, jabbing and barking in a rather more emphatic voice than I really wanted to use. Against every appointment in the diary, she had neatly written who she was seeing. Mostly she used initials: I was H; KF was the psychiatrist; K, I assumed, was her poisonous boyfriend, Karel. But over the last two months, there had been frequent meetings with no name attached, one or two a week, sometimes with a gap. There didn't seem to be a pattern, except that they were all in out-of-the-way places: a hotel in Dorking, a pub in Catford, another in Docklands; a couple were even in car parks and lay-bys. The only thing that connected them was that none had a name attached to them, just a time. There were also a few entries with just a time and no other information; Sam and I had wondered if these marked meetings at places Verity already knew.

It looked nothing like a life. There were very few fixed points. I was there, an H every second Wednesday, circled. There was also a note from the day before the fall, 'ring H', also circled, then question-marked, circled again. But she hadn't.

Adam listened patiently to my explanation. Then he shrugged and pursed his lips.

'Anyway, it's just not her style,' I yelled, over the din. A television had been switched on at the far end of the bar, adding a fuzzy rumble to the higher notes of chattering drinkers. 'Beachy Head's not her style.' I was getting nowhere with the mysterious meetings: time to play the trump card.

Adam frowned. 'But you said yourself. It's beautiful. Perfect spot.'

'But she didn't *know* that, did she? Not until she got there. So why would she go there in the first place?' I really thought that was the clincher. Adam didn't, though, and his argumentativeness was irritating.

I pinched the bridge of my nose for a moment, trying to squeeze some clarity into my thoughts and my tired eyes. The drinks weren't helping my concentration – not the three pints I'd already had, or the fourth, which was half empty in front of me now.

'What I mean,' I said slowly (and loudly), 'is that she had a big prejudice about that whole stretch of coast. If she talked about old people she'd make jokes about sending them to Eastbourne. She thought the whole coast was made up of retirement bungalows and screaming children.' I reached for my beer. 'It just isn't her style,' I said again – then corrected myself. 'Wasn't. Whatever.'

Adam slapped his thighs and stood. 'Food,' he said. 'We'll talk about it on the way.' He pointed at my drink. 'Down the hatch.' I obliged, and immediately regretted it.

It was around half past nine, and still light. It had clouded over, and the streets were grey, glowing, and quiet. Adam knew a wine bar nearby, and we strolled through the streets, me meandering, him walking more purposefully.

'Then there's the break-in,' I said. 'It all ties together. You're not going to tell me that's coincidence as well. I mean, come *on!*' I stopped dead and waved my arms expansively, forcing an oncoming pedestrian to veer into the gutter to avoid being hit. 'Oh, sorry. Very sorry.' The woman didn't look back.

Adam watched me expressionlessly. 'I thought you said that was this guy Karel. He knew the flat was empty, didn't he?'

I squinted at him. 'Actually, you've got a point there,' I conceded. I felt a little foolish, the way you do when you have become absorbed in something, then suddenly see yourself as others must.

Adam laughed and clapped me on the back. 'It doesn't matter, Harry. We'll work it out.' He pointed across the road towards the far end of the street. 'Nearly there.' I could see a cream-coloured awning with a few diners sitting at tables on the pavement.

We got a table, ordered more beer and a couple of steaks, then some wine.

'It's not just me, Ads,' I said. 'We both reckon there's something weird about this.'

'We? Who's we?'

'Sam and me. Verity's design partner. We both reckon—'

'I thought you were pissed off with her.'

'I was but then she came round. And ... well, stuff.'

'What stuff?' He frowned at me. Then a grin split his face. 'Harry, you're not screwing her?'

I couldn't help grinning. 'I demand my right to a lawyer.'

'Aha! That'll be me! You'd best tell me everything.' Adam slapped the table and roared. 'Harry, you crafty old bastard!'

'Well, I *like* her.' And as I said it, I discovered that it was true. Within limits, of course. Sam made me feel good and guilty at the same time. Since the fumblings of our first night, the sex had been fantastic. That wasn't the appeal, though – and neither was the fact that I liked her, if I'm honest. It was something far more basic: it was just knowing that someone was there.

But, nevertheless, it was a kind of betrayal. While Sam and I made love, Verity lay in ITU, with a tube down her throat. Verity deserved better – of me, in particular. I clung all the more fiercely to my determination to understand what had happened to her.

'You really think there's nothing to it, Ads?' I asked. 'Just life as normal, what happens if you're down?'

Adam sighed dramatically. 'Harry, how could I possibly know?'

It was a rebuke, if a gentle one. I had reminded him endlessly over the last few days that I knew Verity and he did not. I studied him blearily. He hadn't shaved that morning. The light, patchy stubble almost hid the way his jaw muscles tightened then released, over and over. And there was something in his eyes: they were remote, and perhaps a little sad. Had I been sober, I might have read the signs of his growing frustration, but I was drunk, and although I was aware that he was chiding me, I took his gentleness as encouragement.

'What *is* it between you and Verity?' I blurted.

Adam looked startled. 'What on earth are you talking about?'

'You always avoided her.'

Thinking about it (fuzzily), it seemed odd that Adam and I had never discussed it. As the years passed the subject had become taboo somehow, for no other reason than it had become pointless to discuss it with either of them. Long before any of us moved to London, they had become insignificant to each other. It had never seemed anything other than natural, but now, obsessed and inebriated, it seemed worth chewing over.

Adam looked at me expressionlessly for a long time before he spoke.

'Harry, you're upset, and you're tired,' he said carefully. 'And, to be completely candid, you're pissed.' He blew out sharply. 'Look, I really can't cope with this. I'm . . .' His eyes were shining. 'Um, I'm pretty fragile myself at the moment. So let's just get you home, yeah? Talk in the morning.'

I failed to ask him what the problem was. It wasn't that I didn't care, it was just that I was too busy being selfish. Adam waited for me say something. I didn't: I simply didn't think to.

'Yeah,' he muttered. 'Whatever.' He dumped his napkin on the table next to the half-full carafe, and stood. I sat back. He was right: I was drunk, very.

He went over to join the waitress, and bantered with her in a low voice as she prepared the bill. She laughed. I watched from a great distance, my thoughts swaddled in booze and indistinct memories that were just out of reach.

When he came back to say the taxi had arrived, he had to help me up.

Coping with the jolts and sudden swerves of the cab took all my attention. Adam sat neatly next to me gazing out of the window. We didn't talk much. It was me who broke the silence: about half-way home a thought drifted through my head. And when I studied the idea, I was puzzled. Then surprised. So surprised that, for a moment or two, I felt almost sober. The question blurted out of me, with no conscious intervention on my part. 'So how come you know where she lives, then?'

'Oh, for—' Adam snapped. Then, more calmly, 'What *is* this, Harry?'

'Nothing,' I protested. 'Just, you don't know her, right, 'sall nothing to do with you, you said – so how come you know her address? Picked me up there the other day.'

'You must have told me.'

'Didn't.'

'You must have. On the phone. When you rang me. How else would I know it?'

'Didn't.'

'I'm not going to argue, Harry.'

'Yeah, but how did you know?'

'You *told me*, Harry. You must have. Now *leave it*.'

'Well, I think it's weird,' I muttered.

Adam ignored me. I tried to focus my thoughts enough to make sense of the puzzle, but the effort blurred my vision. Drunkenness swept back over me, and I felt sick. I concentrated once again on keeping my head from rolling.

The taxi stopped at the end of my street, because there's a one-way system and it takes another five minutes and a couple of extra quid to get dropped at the door. 'Nightcap time,' I said to Adam, and lurched out of the cab.

Adam leaned forward to talk to the driver. 'Can you take me on to Clapham?'

'Nah, mate. Got another job, see?' the driver yelled cheerfully. 'That's six eighty, ta, guv.'

I reached into my pocket and had to stagger to stay upright. Adam shook his head and fished in his own pocket. He paid, and we set off towards my flat. He flipped out his mobile and ordered a taxi to collect him from my address.

'Thanks, Adam,' I said blearily. 'Not for the taxi,' I added, in case there was any confusion. 'Just thanks. You know. Being there and stuff. I know I'm being a bit – well, you know . . .' I banged him on the shoulder, an attempt at a gentle squeeze. He staggered, looked at his watch and sighed again. We stopped outside. I groped for my keys, then poked around for the lock.

'Hey!'

The yell came from somewhere behind us. I turned as quickly as I dared, which wasn't fast. By the time I had got all the way round, Karel Novak was mounting the kerb. He stopped a few paces short and waved his fists at me. 'You fucking shit bastard! I fucking kill you, maybe.'

His heavy accent didn't disguise his fury. But somehow his anger made him seem smaller. Maybe I just didn't care. Maybe I was drunk.

'You!' he yelled.

He lunged closer and pushed me in the chest. I tottered back until my ankles caught on the doorstep, and sat unceremoniously – and painfully.

'Fucking bastard fuck idiot, Harry, man!'

Really, it would have been funny if only I hadn't been so tired.

'You fucking tell police! You say, "Oh, yes, Novak, he bad guy, do stuff with flat of Verity." And police they come take me. *Lose* fucking girlfriend, *lose* fucking job next day. I complain and they say they send me back to Czech Land! Is lie, I have visa – but is no fucking good, man! And Karel do nothing!'

I buried my spinning head in my hands, feebly hoping that perhaps he would go away. A woman down the road opened her window and yelled at us to shut up. All three of us ignored her.

'This is Karel Whatsisface, is it?' Adam asked me coolly.

I tried to nod. Failed. I looked blearily up at Adam, who seemed as sharp as ever.

'Novak!' Karel screamed at him. 'Not Whatface, Novak. Karel Novak.' He thumped his chest in time to his name and jerked his head forwards aggressively.

Then he made a foolish mistake. He spat at Adam's shoes. Worse, his aim was bad. The spit smeared across Adam's trousers. Karel stood glaring at him.

Adam stared at his trousers. 'You dirty fucking snake . . .' he said wonderingly. Then he stepped forward, and buried his fist in Karel's stomach. Karel's eyes nearly popped out. He made a slow, retching noise and doubled over. Adam kicked his knee, and he slumped on to the pavement. I was still sitting propped against the door, struggling to follow what was going on: too much, too fast.

'There's a couple of things you might like to think about, Karel.' Adam spoke quietly, although he was breathing hard. 'First, watch your language. Second . . .' Adam paused just long enough to kick him '. . . do *not* break into other people's flats.'

'Not me,' Karel rasped. 'I not—'

'Bullshit the police if you want, Novak,' Adam snarled, 'but *don't – bullshit – us.*' The last three words were accompanied by kicks. Karel was past talking. He lay in a ball, gasping out little spasms of air. Adam stood back and took a deep breath. 'Now *fuck off.*'

He turned away from Karel, dragged me upright, took the key from me and shoved me inside ahead of him. I think I must have mumbled something, but I'm not sure. Adam just growled, 'Up.'

There were heavy breaths behind me on the stairs.

When we reached my flat, he helped himself to a whisky, without asking or offering, and slumped on the sofa. His hands were shaking, and his eyes were damp – whether from the whisky or for some other reason I didn't know. We sat and waited for his taxi.

It arrived and he left, without saying a word. I tottered to the window and leaned out unsteadily to watch him go. Through the branches of the trees that lined the street I saw him sweep outside and into the car before the front door had slammed behind him.

The empty pavement was glossy with heat and streetlights. The trees hung motionless, their leaves limp and yellow. There was no sign of Karel Novak. I wondered where he had gone. Then I wondered if Sam had stayed, or if she had lost patience with me and left. Then I wondered how I was going to get to my bedroom. Then I realised I was going to throw up. But I was too tired for that: I flopped back on to the sofa, and let the humid warmth wash over me – the flickering orange of streetlights on the ceiling, light glimpsed through a cage of leaves, a neon, pavement-hard echo of one soft summer, long ago.

sixteen

I was woken from a dream. Someone knocking.

I rolled over and grunted. Sam was next to me and I was in bed. I must have made my way to the bedroom some time during the night; I didn't remember it. She had stayed. Her skin was warm and smooth, and I had an instant erection. I peeled myself away from her while I could. The alarm clock said six twenty-five. I had no idea how long the knocking had been going on. I padded out of the bedroom, grabbing a towel; I didn't own a dressing-gown.

Birdsong drifted through the living-room windows, the cool air of a summer dawn. Amazingly, I didn't have a hangover – at least, not yet. Perhaps I was still drunk. I wasn't particularly alert, but I did feel fairly good, which was a change. No, I didn't just feel fairly good, I felt *good*. I could smell Sam on me.

The knocking was getting louder.

'OK, OK,' I muttered. I didn't want to call out because of the neighbours. But whoever was knocking had no inhibitions about that.

I had help opening the door: I did the first couple of inches, and whoever was on the other side did the rest, then strode briskly past me. I had an impression of jeans and a rolled top, a waft of soaped skin; I smelted that it was a woman before I saw her. She turned smartly round to face me.

'Well? Where is he?' she snapped.

You know how it is when something unexpected happens? You see the event or the person, but it doesn't filter through to the bits of your brain that make sense of the world. I was freewheeling. Of all the people it might have been (neighbours complaining about my car, the police, Sam's granny, the Spanish Inquisition) the last person I'd have expected was Sarah Yates.

I rubbed my face and tried to focus my thoughts. 'Um. Sarah. Hi. How—'

'*Where is he*, Harry?'

'You mean Adam? Where's Adam?' Daft question. It *would* be Adam, wouldn't it? She was his wife, after all.

I should tell you now that I'm not very good at mornings. It's a bit of a disability in a photographer, because dawn is the best light of the day. It's also a disadvantage when your best friend's wife comes barging in at six thirty demanding to know where said best friend is – and when you haven't a clue, because he should have been at home, and anyway you were looking forward to a lazy morning doing something altogether more pleasant. I heard a gentle snore from the bedroom. At least Sam hadn't woken yet. Maybe we could do the pleasant bit later.

I slowly came round to wondering why Sarah was asking me about Adam – in fact, why she was here at all. Obviously he hadn't gone home when he'd left me. But, surely, if anyone knew where he was, it would be her. I yawned and shook my head to clear it. Sarah was still staring at me, and I was staring fuzzily back at her. Eventually her frown dissolved.

'Oh, for— Wake *up*, Harry!' She glared at me as though I was self-evidently an idiot. 'Where's the kitchen?'

I pointed feebly.

She marched in and I heard her rummaging around. Then she poked her head out.

'Where's the coffee? Harry? *Harry?* The coffee?'

She said it very slowly the second time. She had clearly decided I wasn't awake yet, and she wasn't wrong. But I was blearily aware that my doziness wasn't going to save me from answering her for much longer, and I had no idea what to say. The coffee might buy me a bit more time. And, after all, Sam's thoughts on my coffee skills aside, it really wasn't as though I didn't know how to do it for myself. I elbowed in beside her and she stood back. I put on the kettle and rummaged for cups. I made myself as busy as I could. Sarah Yates stood and watched me, her brown eyes brooding. Any moment now she would run out of patience. Obviously she thought I knew where Adam was, which meant he must have told her I would know. What was I supposed to do? Lie for him? And what was the lie supposed to be?

I rarely saw Sarah, except for occasional dinner invitations, when she would feed me over-rich food from her cordon bleu chalet-girl days, and quiz me endlessly and chirpily about my work, my love-life, and what Adam and I got up to on our boys' nights out. She was gregarious, occasionally sexy, a little vague. But I felt uncomfortable in her company, and I had never been able to pin down why.

It had taken me years, but I'd finally decided that Adam and Sarah were perfect for each other. For Sarah there was Adam's charm, his powerful energy for work and play, his intelligence and the comfort of being with someone who knew exactly where he was going. For Adam there was Sarah's family wealth to support his political ambitions, her contacts, her manner. Sarah stayed contentedly, and busily, in Adam's shadow, the creator of the perfect dinner party, the chooser of Adam's ties and suits.

I mustn't sound too cynical. Of course, there was more to it than that. There was surely love, sex, respect, too. But neither of them was the type to talk about it. Even while he was trying hard to pretend he was still a bachelor out for a night with the lads, Adam had shone with something new from the moment he met her. Perhaps the best way I can put it is that they looked good together. They were confident, glossy, stable.

But she and I lived in different compartments of Adam's life. In truth, I was the last relic of Adam's past – perhaps the only person with whom he did not have to *be* anyone. Our time together was in a realm set aside from the rest of his life, and in it, we still shared our silences and our memories. I think that, in a way, Sarah was jealous of us – and perhaps she was right to be. But whatever the reason, the truth was that she and I rarely spoke. I hadn't seen her for over a year.

Over time, she had lost the fluffiness that had seemed to surround her when we first met, and gained a kind of simplicity. Her features were strong, her skin bronzed and clear, her eyes fiery and full of intelligence – and, now, anger. She stood with her legs neatly together and her arms crossed a little too tightly. Her posture and the brisk frown left no doubt about who was in charge; but for all the confidence of her stance I sensed insecurity in it also.

Perhaps that was just imagination, I can't tell. There was strength of purpose too; and over it all, the scratchy, impatient kind of fury that never comes out as cleanly as you'd like.

I made coffee and gestured for us both to go into the sitting room. Just like Sam, Sarah grimaced when she tasted it. In other circumstances I might have laughed. Just now, though, that didn't seem like a good idea.

It would have to be the truth, I decided. If Adam hadn't gone home, I had no idea where he was. How could I lie convincingly when I had no idea what was going on? In any case, Sarah looked as though even my best attempt at a lie wouldn't wash. But before I could tell her anything, she saved me the bother and, simultaneously, gave me one hell of a shock.

'It's that Hadley woman again, isn't it?' she said. 'Verity bloody Hadley.'

She snorted, a soft little laugh, and stood staring out into the street.

For a surreal moment, I had absolutely no idea what she meant. I knew what she *couldn't* mean, so my sleep-befuddled thoughts struggled to make some other sense of what she'd said. *It's that Hadley woman* . . . But Verity was – was . . . And, anyway, how the hell could Sarah know Verity? And was she really saying that *Adam*, that Verity and Adam, that . . . My thoughts stumbled to a halt.

'Verity's dead,' I said – then went instantly back into my funk. Because she wasn't dead, was she? She was . . .

Sarah looked at me, cool and assessing. Then her gaze slid back to the window. 'Shame,' she said. She didn't sound like she meant it.

'Yes it is, actually,' I snapped. 'She was my friend, and now she's in a coma. She's gone. Gone. Full stop. And it's more than a shame, it's, it's . . .'

What was it? A smile and broad white teeth, large eyes full of care and insecurity. A summer day long ago in a treehouse. Gone.

Sam defused the moment by padding out of the bedroom in the middle of a prodigious yawn. She'd put on one of my shirts, and nothing else. She glanced at Sarah without a sign of curiosity, yawned again, and drifted into the kitchen.

Sarah watched the performance disinterestedly, then turned to face me again. She sat opposite me, tight and composed, her face unreadable. 'You don't even know, do you, Harry?' I must have looked blank. Sam sloped out of the kitchen and slumped on to a chair, sipping coffee, still looking half asleep.

'Sam, Sarah. Sarah, Sam,' I muttered. 'Adam's wife.'

Sam yawned again. Sarah turned to look out of the window. Having ensured that they were definitely going to be the best of friends, I went back to Sarah.

'*What* don't I know, Sarah? And how do you know Verity?'

She swirled her coffee cup in both hands, put it down wearily. 'Well, you must be the last person in London to hear the news,' she said, lightly, bitterly. 'They're screwing each other, Harry. Adam and Verity Hadley are having an affair.'

Sarah frowned again, 'At least,' she added, 'they *were* ... But even Adam's not going to fuck a girl in a coma. So where is he, Harry? Where's my shit of a husband?'

seventeen

Sam and I walked along the riverbank. The silence between us seemed more natural in the open air than it had in the flat. Battersea Park was full of people walking, playing with children, clambering over the golden pagoda on the riverbank, all somehow distant from us, muted but companionable.

It was windy and cool. Crows tumbled in the air like dusty scraps, rising in eddies against the embankment wall, folding and dropping again to skim the river. The wind carried the scent of water and bruised leaves.

We held hands for a while, and then we didn't; I needed to clean my glasses with my handkerchief and when I had finished, Sam's hands were in her pockets. Sam leaned against the rail, with the wind tugging back her hair, and flicking the ends around her cheeks. I turned to face the river too, and smelt cool mud, and tried not to let the moment mean anything. I was somewhere else, though, and there was no point in hiding it. I couldn't let go of what Sarah had said. It was unreal.

Adam and Verity? Impossible – and impossible to ignore. *Adam and Verity, Adam and Verity.*

I picked up a leaf and released it into the wind. It flicked straight up towards the canopies of the trees, hovered uncertainly, then fluttered down and outwards towards the water. The wind caught it again and whipped it once more towards the embankment's high stone wall.

'Sorry, Sam,' I said quietly.

We both looked out to where the boats tipped and tugged at their moorings. Tiny clouds of thin grey spray rose where the water slapped at them. Sam moved closer, and rubbed her shoulder against mine. 'I'll go home,' she said gently. 'Get the bus.' There was no bitterness in her tone, just understanding.

I pressed back against her, until our thighs were touching also, and I slipped my hand round her waist. It was warm and soft, sheltered under her jacket from the wind.

'Unfinished business,' she said finally.

'Unfinished business,' I agreed.

We pushed ourselves up from the river rail, my arm still round her. She reached up and kissed me, quick and hard and hot. 'Call,' she whispered, into my half-open mouth.

As she walked away, I watched the play of muscles in her legs, the loose swing of her arms, the lick of her hair in the wind – and the soft sounds of play and laughter from the other people in the park who had shared the moment and who hadn't even known we were there.

'He's in a meeting. I'm sorry, Mr Waddell, but he just can't see you.'

I had tracked Adam down to the town hall. As usual, he was busy. Rita Patava's protests were becoming increasingly shrill. Of course, it was her job to make sure that Adam wasn't disturbed, but she knew me, I was his friend, and as far as I was concerned that meant I shouldn't have to put up with all this 'meeting' stuff.

'Rita, I need to see him.' I did my best to sound weary and patient. In fact, I was mostly pissed off. 'Just tell him I'm here, Rita, OK?'

She had been unhelpful on the phone too, which was why I had come in person. Even then, I'd had to con my way through the reception area. The guard was Malcolm, the same man who had watched Adam lead me out of the building in a daze a few days before. I walked straight over to him. He stood by a small rope cordon in front of the lifts, checking everyone's passes. 'Hi, Malcolm, any sign of Adam yet?' I'd said casually. 'Adam? Councillor Yates?' We had shaken our heads companionably, and sucked our teeth together at the poor organisation of Malcolm's favourite councillor, who couldn't even keep a diary engagement – but he had a heart of gold, didn't he?, oh, yes, absolutely – and

Malcolm had let me through on a nod. So now I just had Rita Patava to get through, and I wasn't having much success.

'Mr Waddell, there's no *point* telling him you're here,' she said tartly. 'He's busy, I told you.' She bent to flick through her diary, licking a sharp finger and adjusting her half-moon glasses on their cord. 'He does have a window this afternoon—'

I gave up on her and burst through the door into Adam's office.

Now, I've seen the movies. You burst in and they're not in a meeting at all, they're alone, poring over a few papers on a gleaming desk. As the guards scramble to catch up with you, he looks up calmly and waves at them to leave you both alone. That's how it goes, isn't it? Every time.

Adam really was in a meeting.

The room was full of cigarette smoke, biscuit crumbs and the milky stench of weak tea. Three faces looked at me blankly. I stared back, unsure what to do next. Rita fussed around me. She pulled me from the room, apologising to them.

I waited in Adam's outer office. Rita busied herself, although it was clear she had nothing much to do. Every few minutes she would look at me, smug and stern all at once, before sumptuously licking her finger and flicking through sheets of paper. She never moved any of them from their piles, just flicked through them, then glanced sideways at me again with lips pursed as though she was sipping acid. Needless to say, the conversation was a little thin. After half an hour or so, the door to Adam's office opened and the sound of goodbyes floated out in a smoky cloud, closely followed by two councillors. The door closed again. I looked across at Rita, my mouth half open to ask the question. She looked back, silently inviting me to try it. I didn't. More paper was flicked, the finger was licked so much that I imagined it slowly becoming as gummy and bitter as the back of a stamp. Perhaps one day when she put it to her tongue it would stick. I hoped so.

Another quarter of an hour later, the door opened again and Adam strode out. 'C'mon, Harry. Now or never.' He whisked past without looking at me. I got up and followed in his wake, leaving Rita behind me, her eyes widening and one finger pressed to her tongue, her jaw dropping with surprise.

We went to a meeting room on the floor below. We didn't speak as we walked. Adam slapped the door closed behind him and sat heavily in a chair opposite me. He glanced at his watch and glared. He looked tired. 'I get the strong impression you wanted to see me.'

'Yes. Look, I'm sorry about barging in—'

'Cut to the chase, Harry. I've got a hell of a day.'

If he wanted blunt, then blunt he would get. I was hardly in the mood for social niceties. 'Sarah came to see me this morning. Wanted to know where you were.'

He looked startled, then thoughtful. The fatigue lines in his face creased deeper and he blinked once, very slowly. He shoved his face in his hands, pushing his glasses up on to his forehead. 'I see,' he said. 'Oh, *fuck*.' He dragged his hands slackly back down his cheeks, accompanied by a low groan. He smiled, and I glimpsed a flash of the Adam I was accustomed to. 'Sorry. Knackered. OK. So, Sarah came round. Should have warned you. What did you tell her?'

I didn't bother answering. He studied the room bleakly – peeling grey wallpaper, school-style tables topped with brown Formica and set in a horseshoe, a trolley for an absent overhead projector, a whiteboard covered with dim traces of red and green marker, no windows.

'Oh, sod it, let's go for a coffee,' he muttered.

As we left the building, Malcolm the security guard gave me a thumbs-up and a conspiratorial grin.

We settled on the third coffee shop we passed. Adam had glanced inside the first two and shaken his head. One had people in it I recognised from the town hall. The third café was almost empty, and I could see why. We took a table against the back wall and hunched over cups of coffee. The place smelt of toast. I waited for Adam to speak.

'I didn't go home last night,' he said eventually.

I knew that. I waited for more.

'And, yes, I told Sarah I was with you. Should have warned you. Stupid of me.' He looked up at me for the first time. 'What *did* you tell her, Harry?'

Again, I didn't reply. He got the message, and nodded wearily. His face was saggy and drawn. His shoulders were humped and crumpled, his eyes had a defeated stare. He traced the curve of a dried coffee spill on the plastic table mat.

'Things with Sarah . . . They're not going well,' he mumbled. 'Haven't been for a while, to be honest.' He paused for a slurp of tea. 'We had a row when I rang and told her I was seeing you last night – *another* row . . . I just couldn't face going home. I walked out. Just for the night, understand, not for ever. Told her I'd be staying with you. But – well, I didn't.'

'She told me about you and Verity,' I said coldly.

Well, I wanted to sound cold: whether I did or not, I'm not sure. I doubt I managed to hide the hurt or the uncertainty.

'About me and Verity? Told you what?' Adam talked slowly and absently, as though he was past caring. And at that moment I knew Sarah had been telling the truth.

'That you were seeing each other. You bloody were, weren't you? How could—'

Adam raised a hand to stop me, then stared thoughtfully at his cup. He dipped a finger into his coffee and sucked it. Then he slumped forwards a little further and stared at the tablecloth. The silence stretched.

'Adam,' I growled.

He snapped forward, then immediately sank back morosely. 'Listen, *back off*, Harry! Oh . . . Shit, sorry. This is . . . Just give me a minute. Oh, *God* . . .' I thought there was a hint of tears at the corners of his eyes. He groaned. 'OK, confession time. Yes, Harry, I was seeing Verity.'

I had thought I would be speechless when – I had still hoped for 'if' – he admitted it. I was anything but: I was furious. 'You fucking bastard!' I snarled.

The one who was silent was Adam. Then he buried his face in his hands again and muttered, 'Fuck fuck fuck,' under his breath.

'You could at least have told me,' I added.

'Oh, *could* I?' he spat back. 'Want to think that through for a moment, Harry?'

I didn't want to think anything through, I just wanted it not to be true – but it was.

Adam shook his head. 'It's been so hard, Harry.' His voice was a sigh. 'Lying to you, all the pretence. Keeping secrets. Harry, I'm so sorry.'

'Not sorry enough to fucking tell me,' I muttered.

Adam pinched his nose. He spoke carefully. I had the impression that *he* was irritated with *me*, the bastard, but was trying to stifle it. 'I did try to tell you, Harry. I wanted to last time we saw each other. But you were so absorbed in your own troubles, you didn't have the slightest— Oh, forget it . . .' His hand strayed up to his forehead. He took a handful of hair, clenched it and twisted. When he sighed, it sounded as though someone had punched him. 'I should never have let it happen in the first place. It was only a bit of fun anyway. And I admit I should have told you. *We* should have told you.'

'*We*,' I echoed bitterly. But the anger in my voice was a lie: what I was feeling was more like . . . grief.

Adam met my gaze. His eyes were glassy, his face was sad and . . . puzzled, I think; as though my reaction bewildered him. 'You're supposed to be my *friend*,' I hissed.

'I am,' he said. I snorted mockingly. 'Listen, Harry,' he went on, 'I wish I could turn back the clock and not do it but I can't. I did it. And I can't make that OK for you. I can't even ask you to forgive, because how could you? I did it, we did it. It's over. I'm sorry.'

We.

Adam's betrayal was only part of the cold fury that was creeping over me. *We* did it, *we* lied, that was the real agony. And now Verity would never be able to explain or beg forgiveness, or comfort me through the pain of learning what she had done. I would not have the reassurance of her guilt, of her sadness at my hurt. There would be no attempt to deny the intolerable truth that was searing through me: that I had lost Verity long before she fell.

'Why, Adam?' I moaned. 'Just – why?' Tears were burning in my eyes, and in his.

'It was just fun, Harry. We both knew it wasn't going to last.' He gazed at me mildly.

I glowered back.

'OK, the truth. The truth is, Harry, we didn't want to hurt you.' He held up a weary hand to forestall any response. 'I know, it's the oldest cliché in the book, but it's the truth, Harry, I swear. We knew how you felt about her. If you knew we were . . . you know . . . it would have torn you apart. It didn't mean enough to risk that.'

I wanted to laugh. It was so bloody ironic. Adam nodded. He knew what I was thinking. 'And now here we are,' he murmured. 'And you *do* know. And look what it's doing to you. Harry, I'm sorry. I don't know what else to say.'

'Don't even try,' I grated.

He couldn't help himself, though. This was his opportunity for confession. I wished he would shut up – but I listened.

'I was so close to telling you, Harry, I swear. But it wasn't love or anything, it was completely casual. It was never going to last long. Verity swore there was no point coming clean.'

'So you kept quiet,' I said coldly.

He nodded again. 'Except Sarah found out, so we had to stop it anyway. She hired a private detective, can you believe that?' He laughed bitterly. 'We drew a line under it. Said our goodbyes, went our separate ways. I promised Sarah I'd be a good boy, but she still doesn't trust me. Well, you've found that out for yourself now.'

'When?' I tried to keep my voice steady – and almost succeeded.

'When what?'

'When did you finish it, Adam?'

'With Verity? Months ago. I was trying to get my marriage back together.'

'What, going out secretly at night and pretending you were with me?'

He spread his hands in surrender. 'Like I said before, it hasn't been working. It's been a nightmare. I've wanted so much to talk to you about it. Sarah's been obsessed.'

'I'd say that's understandable.'

'For fuck's sake, Harry!' he barked. 'If you're going to cut me dead, can you do us both a favour and get it over with? You're my friend. Did you *want* me to hurt you?' I started to protest but he cut me off. 'Don't bother denying it, Harry. Of course it would have hurt you. It's hurting you now. You know it, I know it.'

I could see him trying consciously to get a grip. I was trembling, a bizarre mixture of rage and fear. My heart was knocking, I felt weak and dizzy. For a moment I had thought he would hit me.

'It was months ago, Harry,' he said at last. He was talking hesitantly now. 'It was *over*. We saw each other for a couple of months, then Sarah found out and that was that.'

'When?' I asked again.

'Oh, for— How would *I* know? Four months ago? Thereabouts
... I suppose I saw her a few times in the month or two after.' He
waved his hands vaguely.

'Sarah thought you were still seeing her.'

Adam laughed bitterly.

'Not now,' I said. 'Before. Until – you know.'

His eyes were filmy and distant. 'Until she fell? Harry, that was
such a shock. It was only a few months after ... And we'd had such
fun. What *happened*?'

'Well, for one thing, you dumped her.'

Adam shot me a withering stare. 'Just forget it, Harry.'

'I'm just saying—'

'I *know* what you're saying, Harry, and it's rubbish. You have
no idea what you're talking about. It was a *fling*, that's all. It
was no big deal. We met up a few times afterwards, and she was
fine.'

He slapped the tabletop; our cups jumped, and clattered back
into their saucers. A waitress in a pink check pinafore looked round
and pursed her lips at us, before turning back to chat in Italian with
the man behind the counter.

Every word was another cut, slicing away any illusions I might
once have clung to – that I mattered to her, that I knew her better
than anyone; that I knew her at all. My thoughts, my memories, my
certainties shredded.

And if it hadn't been for Sarah, I'd never have found out. Verity
had been so careful, he wasn't even listed in her Filofax ...
Unless ...

Perhaps it was a moment of unworthy suspicion, but it was going
to take more reassurance than Adam had yet given me to restore
my faith in him. 'Was it you?'

'Was ... Harry, what are you on about?'

'Was it you? At Birling Gap?'

Adam laughed angrily. 'Oh, *wake up*, Harry!' I waited for more.
He peered at me speculatively. 'Good God, you don't think— Oh,
for Christ's sake, Harry, I was in Manchester, remember?'

I had forgotten. I'd barely registered what Adam was up to when
I rang him after Verity's fall: all that had mattered was that he'd
dropped everything to be with me, that he'd been there for me.

Yeah. Ha bloody ha.

'So, what about the other times? In her diary.'

'*Leave it*, Harry! Please. Look, *I don't know* who she'd been seeing. What about the psychiatrist woman you told me about? Or that bastard Karel? It could have been Gabriel for all I know – or Sarah, or the Pope. Harry, *I don't know*.' He stood abruptly and fished in his pocket. He slapped a couple of pound coins on the table. He caught himself before he left. 'Look, I'm upset, Harry. Sorry. But I've got to get back. We'll have to talk later.'

The two Italians stopped their chatter to watch us go. Immediately we were out of the door, I heard them start again.

As we walked back to the town hall, Adam grimaced and stopped. When I peered at him, he set off again, his voice cracking. 'I couldn't even tell you, Harry.'

Was that true? How would I have reacted? *Verity and Adam* ... Oh, I would have been hurt, so hurt, they were right. Maybe, even if she had told me, I would have turned her away.

And Adam. Stupid, callous, hurtful – and so obviously desperate to put this behind us. Our friendship was changed for ever, of course – if I could even think of it that way now. Certainly, I would find it hard ever to trust him again, no matter how hard he worked at it. As for forgiveness ... It would either come or it wouldn't: although I was humiliated and resentful, we had known each other over twenty years – and despite the strangeness between us now, he was still Adam and I was still Harry. I groped for an explanation of my own feelings, some *reason* why I was not intent on removing every trace of him from my life and thoughts. I clung to the first idea I found that seemed sufficiently harsh: he was useful to me. The real reason I buried as deep as I could. But it itched at the fringes of my thought, and I couldn't keep it away: without Adam, I would be utterly alone.

I rang his secretary later – of course – and, of course, she wouldn't tell me anything without Adam's permission. I needed to know for sure that he had been in Manchester that day: I could never recover my confidence in him on the strength of his word alone.

Rita Patava was less than pleased to hear from me. I can't say I blamed her, but it made a difficult process even harder.

'Mr Waddell, I am sure you will *appreciate* that there are issues of *principle* here.' She was enjoying this. She rolled her Rs, and made the most of her shrill Indian accent, phrasing her sentences in a manner that was *most proper*. She had a score to settle. 'You will realise, Mr Waddell, that a job such as mine involves certain *responsibilities*, there are *obligations*, there are *protocols* to be observed. The job must be done *corr-rrectly*, the *right* way. This is *most* important.'

What she meant was that *she* was 'most important' – and that I had broken her rules. I bit back on my annoyance: it wasn't going to help me. 'Rita, I do absolutely understand. And if—'

'What I am saying is that there is a proper *procedure*.'

'Yes. And—'

'There are *rules*.'

'Absolutely. Could—'

'We cannot simply do as we *wish*, Mr Waddell. As I am sure you appreciate.'

'Can I suggest—'

'That would be most improper.'

I gave up, and overrode her. 'Look, Rita. I'm sorry about this morning, but can we take the apology as read, and get on with it? You can't go through Adam's diary without his permission, fine. Is he there?'

There was a nettled silence, then muted shuffling noises, a knock, a door opening. I heard her voice, but not what she said, then Adam's gruff reply, a brief exchange. She picked up the phone again. She didn't sound happy. 'Mr Yates has consented to allow me to discuss his business arrangements with you, Mr Waddell. Why, I am not sure, but this is none of my affair. Please be brief. I have many things to do.'

The bad grace didn't matter, just the facts – and those she told me.

Adam had been in Manchester the day Verity fell, exactly as he had said, and exactly as I already knew. As we went back through the dates in the Filofax, relief flooded through me. There was another trip to Manchester, a meeting at the town hall, he was in court, on a fact-finding trip to Leeds ... His diary was blank for one or two of Verity's mystery dates, but Rita was able to tell me where he had been for almost all of them. I thanked her, and she made it clear that it was Adam I should thank. She kept her opinion of me to herself – sort of.

Adam called me about three minutes later. 'Satisfied, Harry?'

'No, Adam. Not satisfied at all.'

'But you do believe I wasn't there?'

'Yes.'

I resented it that he had been telling the truth. I wanted to hate him. I wanted a *new* betrayal that would make everything his fault, rather than merely the consequences of a squalid affair that I couldn't bear to think about.

'I know I can't expect you to trust me, Harry, but I will do what I can. I'll try my best to help you. And no more lies, I promise.'

As if a promise meant anything now.

eighteen

Verity's eyes were open and she stared. Not at me, not at Sam, not at anything.

The ventilator was gone, the heart monitor's endless beat had stopped. A thin plastic tube was taped to the side of her head below the bandages; it slid into one nostril. The swelling had reduced, and reds and blacks seeped across her face beneath the olive skin. A round plastic mount for a non-existent drip bulged out of her wrist, swathed in grey surgical tape. Beneath it, I knew, a needle sank deep into her, and the thought made me cringe.

But it was the eyes. I couldn't help but search them for a blink, for the flick of a glance, the subtlest movement in the iris or the lids, a narrowing so slight that you were never even aware; the person behind them, the life. I tried to smile at her empty face.

I crouched beside the bed, in the line of her not-really-sight, and spun the zoetrope for her. It flickered in the corner of my vision, vivid green, bright warm light, Verity turning round and round and round, screaming with delight – and as she was now, eyes lolled, drool trickling thickly from her mouth. I imagined her lost inside herself, tumbling in the dark, falling endlessly, grasping, finding only emptiness. I spun the zoetrope again and ached for it to help. Perhaps it would reach her, give her at least a memory to live with. If she was there at all.

Did she dream? If there were nightmares, who would comfort her?

'Hey, Verity,' I whispered. I brushed back a lock of hair that had escaped from the bandages, more for my own comfort than anything because it wasn't out of place. I leaned past the slowing zoetrope and kissed her temple. 'It's OK, gorgeous,' I said. 'It's all OK.'

I felt Sam's hand on my back. She brushed the lock I had just straightened.

'Hey, Babes,' she murmured, 'it's all right.'

Why do we say these things? Nothing was all right. The same slack face sagged towards us. The same dulled eyes kept watch on a point somewhere past my shoulder, loose in their sockets. But who else was there to keep her company in the dark?

Gabriel was in Oxford. Probably by now he was waiting in the corridors outside the neurology ward, waiting even though it would be hours before we arrived.

I crouched again, spoke to her gently. 'We're going to take you home, Verity.'

And when I smiled again, I cried.

Not home at all. We were taking her to another ward, to a hospital closer to Gabriel. If she had been conscious, she would have told me that her home was London now, and Gabriel had nothing to do with it. But she was comatose, and Gabriel was her next-of-kin. And lying there, her eyes blank and wide, she looked again like a little girl, lost and bewildered and afraid of the dark.

The porter snapped off the bed's wheel brake with an expert flick of his toe, and leaned against the metal headrail. The bed squeaked reluctantly, and rolled towards the door. We followed, carrying the clothes I had brought, and the zoetrope.

We cruised behind the ambulance at a sedate sixty miles an hour. It seemed cruel to abandon her. We had to be there. The air seemed somehow easier as we left Eastbourne behind.

It was a grey day, cool and bright and somehow quiet despite the roar of the motorway. It had rained that morning, but now the road was dry. The oncoming traffic was a glare of reflected metal. My old Renault snarled and bumped, and added an overtone of stale rubber to the unconvincing breeze from the fan.

On the back seat, the zoetrope jogged and jittered. Sam had turned to look at it, kneeling dangerously in her seat. 'Did you really make that when you were thirteen?'

She and I had settled for a vague truce based on the idea that we were both free agents, companions because it suited us now, and to hell with the future. There was no obligation, no meaning, we were two people sharing whatever they chose to share, for now. It was liberating. I reached over and patted her behind. She wriggled contentedly, and grunted. I left my hand there for a mile or so, then had to reclaim it to use the indicator.

'Did you?' She squirmed round to face forwards.

'Hmm? What? Oh. Did I make that when I was thirteen? No. I was thirteen when we took the photos, but I didn't make the zoetrope until I was ... oh, twenty-five, I suppose.'

'Why wait?'

'It didn't occur to me at the time. Verity and I had a few ups and downs while we were growing up.' I said it as lightly as I could, and grinned uneasily. 'Actually, when I was thirteen, I fancied the hell out of her ... Anyway, the treehouse gang broke up at pretty much at the same time as we took the photos. I ended up with the negatives, but we pretty much buried the whole photo thing for years.' I laughed, remembering. 'Then there was this party. We must have been in our twenties – and we got badly drunk and started reminiscing.'

Sam swivelled and sat sideways, facing me. 'Wasn't it odd, not talking about it all those years?'

Uncomfortable questions. Instinctively I prickled, then tried to relax. She wasn't prying, she just didn't know ...

'To be honest, Sam, I counted myself lucky that we were talking at all. She was so flighty – all the way through school, always. Say the wrong thing and she'd just vanish, wouldn't talk for months. Most of the time I was worried that she was about to cut me out completely.'

The zoetrope tapped. Sam listened, and thought. Cars washed past, sun-bright machines full of bright, busy people.

'I'm not really sure she liked it that much,' I added. 'The zoetrope.'

Sam gaped at me.

'Are you kidding? She loved it! She put it carefully away before every party, wouldn't let anyone touch it. We always wondered, you know – sneaked a peek when she was out of the room. Sometimes when she was pissed she'd just sit there holding it.'

That was too much for me. I didn't want to think about it; I didn't want to think at all. I put on the radio.

The news: a reassuring background mumble that the world was full of tragedies, that all of this was normal; it had happened before and would happen again, the endless miseries of the turning world.

But I couldn't exorcise my ghosts so easily. I imagined Verity, clutching the zoetrope, rocking back and forth maybe, gazing at somewhere far inside.

'I always thought she just put it out for me when I was there,' I said. The car's din made my voice high and insubstantial.

Sam rested her hand on my thigh, stroking lightly with her thumb, and had the wisdom not to reply.

It was ten past twelve. Two hours to Oxford. We swept along a brilliant grey stone stream, past cars, trees, buildings, past other people's lives, glimpsed for an instant. The zoetrope pattered restlessly against the seat. We reached the M25 – more a river than a stream, broad, flat, slow – and filtered on to it. The junctions came and went in slow counterpoint to the zoetrope's impatient beat.

'So, what about Adam?' she asked. I concentrated on the road. 'You said the treehouse gang broke up. That was you and Verity and Adam, yes? What about him?'

'I don't understand.'

'Where does he fit in?'

I was puzzled.

'Harry! He's been having an affair with her!'

I let that roll around my head for a while. I had told her about my confrontation with Adam, and she had been as confused as I was. Verity had always confided in Sam, yet she never mentioned Adam. Why? There was no obvious reason not to tell her, unlike me. And Adam wasn't mentioned anywhere in Verity's Filofax – there were no entries with an A next to them. The only explanation we could think of was that Adam had demanded absolute secrecy: plausible, but not Verity's style.

Sam fished a packet of mints from her bag and offered me one. I shook my head, then changed my mind and reached over. It was sharp and sweet, reassuringly real. Finally, I felt able to reply. 'We were all so different. We had this one brilliant summer, then it all just fell apart. I suppose we reverted to type. Verity went scatty, Adam went all reserved – when he wasn't acting it up for the crowd at school. I went . . . home. I just holed up and waited for it all to end.' I wound down the window. I needed air. 'To be honest, my school years are hard to remember.'

Actually, I didn't *want* to remember. Really, I'd had enough. Enough of mysteries and puzzles and secrets and ambulances. And grief and loss. And loneliness.

I grimaced an apology at Sam. She caressed my thigh. It was good to be reminded that not everyone had gone mad, that some people could still see the world clearly.

'But you stayed in touch with both of them?' she persisted.

'Sort of. No, I did. They were my friends. I was a bit of a loner, really, but if I belonged anywhere it was with Adam or Verity.'

'But not both of them together.' Flatly; a fact.

I shook my head, then waved a tense hand in the air, searching for something I could grasp.

'No,' I admitted finally. 'Not together.'

It was a question only an adult could have asked. As a child, the divisions between us had been as natural as all the other feuds and friendships of the playground. We'd spent a summer together, pursuing one mad project – Verity's project, not Adam's or mine. When the project was done and the summer was ended, there was nothing left to hold us together. With the photos taken, and with the social isolation of the holidays ended, Verity and Adam had little use for each other. Verity had got what she wanted, and Adam settled into life at school: he couldn't risk the mockery of his peers by spending time with a girl two years his junior. But while they drifted apart, Adam and I did not. We shared something. Occasionally, when he was not studying or swaggering with his older friends, we would sit after school and watch the river, or throw stones into a pool; just being there, saying nothing. We'd learned everything about each other that we needed to, months before, one day in Verity's garden when Adam's dad came calling.

And Verity, poor damaged Verity: why had I stayed close to her? I think that the answer then was the same as it has been in all the years since. It's a thing too painful to name. It has to do with hope.

Who could have foretold what we all became?

'How did they even meet, Sam?'

'Maybe they just bumped into each other, on the tube or something,' Sam offered. 'Don't get cross, Harry, but I suspect you think their affair's all wrong because you *want* it to be wrong.'

I'd thought of that, of course. In fact I'd thought of little else. I felt betrayed and bewildered. My two closest friends had lied to me, taken themselves away from me and made a new centre for themselves somewhere else. Verity's jump had shown me I didn't know her at all; and, worse, I knew now that Adam's life had been closed to me as well. That was less of a shock because he had always been private, but the betrayal was real enough. What had he thought on the nights when he and I went out, when he knew he would say goodbye to me and go to her? Or when he had seen her earlier in the day, was still warm from her, or sticky, or buzzing with her smell. *Adam and Verity, Verity and Adam.* Impossible, unbearable, wrong.

The ambulance turned off the M25 and curved towards the M40.

I longed for her to come back. She would explain it all, tell me the truth a different way: how I had misunderstood what Adam had said, how she would never do that, not to me – *Harry, it's not what you think. I'd never hurt you, Harry. I love you, Harry, you know that.*

Yeah.

'I miss her, Sam.'

She looked at me strangely. 'I know,' she said.

We slid along behind the ambulance, towards a new home for Verity, where new machines and starched new sheets waited. Where nurses in white would chirp and bustle around her. Where her father waited to tuck her in, and then to say goodbye.

By the time we'd found a parking space and walked back to the hospital, Verity had already been delivered to the ward. A nurse sat with Gabriel, going through the paperwork. She was quite young, perhaps twenty. Gabriel was hunched in a chair that was designed for leaning back and relaxing in. He was reciting Verity's life for the nurse – full name, age, medical history, known allergies (the nurse read out an entry labelled 'symptoms on admission', then realised how foolish it sounded for a patient in a coma, and moved on quickly, her ears turning pink). She charted Verity's history with neat ticks and circles and precise, backwards-sloping writing.

Gabriel nodded at us when we came in, then his eyes glazed again and he returned to his recitation. When it was over, she stood and thanked him, smiled at us with too much compassion, and was gone. Somewhere further down the ward, someone laughed, then there was silence again, except for the tap and creak of the nurses' rubber shoes against the lino.

I set down the bag of Verity's belongings, and introduced Sam to Gabriel. Odd, that they had never met.

Sam fiddled with the zoetrope. Gabriel raised his head, and his eyes showed a glimmer of his old stare. She risked a smile. He returned it weakly, and sank back into himself. 'Her eyes are open,' he croaked. 'Wasn't expecting that.'

'We should have warned you. Sorry. Yes, it's ...' I trailed off. There wasn't a word for it: lifeless eyes in a living person, eyes that used to follow you across a room, used to sparkle and laugh.

Gabriel put his hands on his knees and pressed himself upright. His eyes seemed almost as dead as Verity's. A purple vein throbbed on his temple, under skin as dry and fragile as old paper.

Verity had a room of her own, by some quirk of the NHS's mysterious workings. Perhaps they were concerned that other patients on the ward shouldn't see what brain damage could do, or perhaps it was out of respect for visitors. More likely it was luck, or a cock-up in the system. Either way, my immediate reaction was that she'd been fortunate, and that was instantly followed by despair. She would be alone, isolated from the comings and goings of the ward. The laughter of the nurses would always be somewhere else, in another room, in a corridor, not with her.

The room was nice enough. There was a standard metal bed, a standard bedside unit, standard plastic armchair, a window with a view of a large aluminium duct that leaked a thin trickle of steam. A plastic tube with earphones at the end was twined in with all the other tubes – oxygen, drips, nasal feeding tube.

She lay under a single clean sheet, which was slightly ripped. She was on her side, set neatly in position by the nurses, one hand reaching towards the rail along the side of the bed. Her empty gaze was fixed on a blank wall. Her new home.

Sam nudged past me, zoetrope still in hand, and squatted next to the bars on the bedside. 'Hey, doll,' she said. 'Guess who's here?' The eyes did not move. Nothing moved. 'Harry's here, I'm here, and your dad.' She had the happy inflections of a mother talking to a baby, so soft, so gentle. So hopeless. 'We've got all your things. And look.'

As I had earlier, she held up the zoetrope in Verity's line of sight and spun it. Two blank brown eyes, sagging in their sockets, did nothing at all, there was not a flicker. Her tongue moved briefly, pushing more spittle from her mouth, then it, too, dropped slackly back.

'D'you remember it?' Sam chirped. 'Remember the photos? It was your idea, wasn't it?' Another spin. Nothing. 'Hey, d'you . . . do you . . .' Sam let the zoetrope settle to the floor, and her hand drifted to her face, stroked her cheek ineffectually.

I put my arms round her, and she turned and crushed herself on to me, her body shaking with hard, slow sobs. I stared at Verity's slack face and tried to make it mean something, but there was nothing left. Nothing at all.

'Be four o'clock soon,' said Gabriel. Meaning, we were doing no good here. He was right.

Sam mopped at her face and sniffed a lot, while I turned back to Verity and held her unresponsive hand for a wordless minute. Then we trooped out, thanking the nurse in over-cheerful voices. She looked over her glasses at us, smiled efficiently, and bent back to her paperwork.

nineteen

I hadn't been back to Wolvercote for several months, and it didn't feel right. We parked, and stood uneasily while we said goodbye to Gabriel and watched him prowl the five or so yards to his own front door.

I had packed one bag for both of us; and I was feeling uneasy about it. How would Mum react? Sam had pointed out that it was only one night, so two bags would be daft; and arguing with her had seemed less appealing than brazening it out with Mum. Besides, this was my home too. The door opened when we were a few paces away from it – Mum must have been watching from the living room – and there she was, all nervous smiles, brushing down the front of her dress with hands that wouldn't stay still. She hugged me and pretty much ignored Sam until I broke away and introduced them. She shook hands uncertainly and invited us in. 'I've made up the spare bed,' she said over her shoulder, as she scuttled indoors. So she expected us to sleep separately. I pulled a face at Sam. She blew me a kiss. Relieved, I dumped the bag and headed after Mum towards the kitchen.

'So, how are you?' I called. That would keep me from questions for the next half-hour or so. I paused long enough to let Sam bump into me as she followed, and reached behind me with both arms to squeeze her. She pressed back, and held my hand as we filed into the kitchen.

Mum's habitual tale began. There was never enough money, but you found ways, cut down on what you wanted from life; she never saw enough of me, she understood and she didn't want to impose but surely a weekend now and then; Mr Winston was dead, Mrs

Winston was carrying on with old Mr Thompson, but of course that was hardly news, they'd been at it for ages. It was a stream of consciousness: there was rarely any need to interject. She moved around the kitchen, drying already dry mugs from the draining-board, pausing to elucidate some point of village politics, vaguely putting the mug back on the draining-board and fiddling with the stacks of glasses in a cupboard, picking up the same mug, polishing it some more. I glazed over, and Sam stared out bleakly at the wizened apple tree at the end of the garden.

I love Mum. How could I not? She has been the one constant element of my life. For three and a half decades she has been there, always the same. When she split with Dad there was talk of change, new opportunities, but it never came right for her. She took her nervousness with her into every new venture, her self-fulfilling conviction that it would all turn sour and that the fault would be hers. She also took her generosity, and her willingness to let others take credit, while she backed quietly away from the light. She would come home and cry – then tell me she was sorry, she was just being stupid, it would pass. I knew it wouldn't. It was just how life was for her. For me to leave home was the cruellest blow of all, but what could I do? She had kept herself busy, and therefore contented. When I came up to see her we had fun. We'd get drunk and gossip and laugh about things from years before, and she'd lecture me about the future, and women, and about how she was right to worry, it was only natural for a mother. She wanted, always, above all, to know that I was happy. Well, life's more complicated than that, isn't it? But, yes, I'd say, life is good for me, all of it good. And she'd pinch my cheek and her eyes would mist over, and she'd busy herself for ten minutes making a single cup of coffee. She wasn't without friends or support. She wasn't even without a son. But we both knew she was without something. Perhaps it was a future.

Sam, bless her, fitted straight in and made all the right noises. After ten minutes, it wasn't me prompting, 'And what did *he* say?' it was her; and ten minutes after that, Mum stopped ignoring her and the two of them began to talk. After half an hour, I was surplus to requirements. They had settled at the table, elbow to elbow, and were complaining about the inadequacies of men – including, I might add, me. When I protested, Sam told me, accompanied by a huge wink, that I might as well push off, they were only just getting started. I grumbled my way out of the room. Behind me, I heard Sam say something in a low voice, and the two of them erupted into coarse laughter.

I found my old football in the back of the shed at the garden's end, now a shapeless, deflated lump of sun-bleached plastic. It was on top of an ancient ripped-out kitchen unit, alongside a pair of broken shears and a bundle of sticks and twine. I peered inside the cupboard: age-blackened wrenches, a rusting saw – Dad's old tools, part of the past which Mum swore she no longer clung to, but which she couldn't bear to throw away. I carried the ball into the garden. There was no chance of toe-flipping it into the tree: the fork was covered in new growth, the old familiar shapes were gone. I slung it back into the undergrowth.

The path to Gabriel's door was lined with weeds and dry moss. Just as when we'd arrived at Mum's, the door opened before I got there. It must be something about villages: not enough to do.

Gabriel shuffled ahead of me along the hall towards the living room. There was a bottle of whisky by his chair, and a glass. He was hitting the hard stuff and it was barely five o'clock – although, to give him credit, the bottle was less than a third empty. He trudged to a sideboard and bent painfully to peer inside for a second glass. He scooped up the bottle, and poured as he walked, filling the tumbler to the brim and handing it to me. He headed back to his chair, bent at the hips, head bowed, his bushy frown directed at the age-stained floor boards.

I settled into the tattered chair opposite. The whisky fumes did their usual thing, acid vapour penetrating the back of my nose, my eyes starting. It tasted foul: this wasn't your single malt, this was the stuff they use to run generators in Africa. He contemplated me for a moment before raising his glass and an eyebrow, then downing a generous slug. If he'd drunk a third of a bottle at that rate, the whisky wasn't going to last more than an hour. From the look on his face, he intended me to help finish it off.

He waved his tumbler in a vague toast – 'Verity' – and sank his face into his drink again.

I couldn't reply. Verity *what*? Verity, goodbye? I didn't want to say that with cheap whisky and a sad old man in a dingy room.

Actually, I didn't want to say it at all. Verity, come back? Verity, why – why Adam? Why didn't you call me? What I heard in his toast wasn't goodbye, come back, or anything: it was self-pity. Somewhere behind those shrewd eyes, he had given up. Gabriel was mourning himself.

He attacked his glass with savage conviction, refilled it with a haphazard wave. He held out the bottle to me to top up my glass. When the bottle ran out, he found another – mercifully only half full. There were sounds in the silence between us. There was a clock, there were birds and a breeze outside, sometimes a car would whisper past; and there was us. I fancied I heard Sam and Mum laughing next door, but it was distant and then it faded.

Time passed, the clock ticked.

'What will you do?' I asked, at about six.

He sniffed. He pursed his lips and shook his head. Ten minutes later he answered, slowly and indistinctly, 'Nothing. Can't look after her, can I? She should have died.' He was breathing heavily, his lips pressed together, black eyes fixed on the floor and glistening. He fought the tears for a minute, then seemed to crumple. The tension left him, his shoulders folded, and another small piece of him seemed to vanish. It was unsettling.

What must it be like to lose a daughter? I don't have children, but I can imagine the loss. All that long history gone, all that potential, the hope, the certainty of a future. All vanished. I'm in my thirties, but Mum still treats me like a child. She seems to think she has the right to criticise, question, cut me down to size, and I let her. In a funny way, as well as being patronising and irritating as hell, it's proof that she loves me, and that she always did. It's a familiar old pattern, clinging to something that, in truth, evaporated with childhood. Mum needed the illusion, so I collaborated. Looking at Gabriel, I knew that it must have been the same with Verity and him. What must it be like to lose a child? You lose all the meaning of all the love you ever gave.

And what *do* you do?

He didn't answer, and I knew it was a crass question, casual conversation in the midst of a crisis. Verity needed constant medical attention. There were decisions he would have to make. If she got pneumonia should they treat it? If her lungs gave out should they put her on a ventilator? Decisions made in the absence of hope. He couldn't bring her home. He couldn't live at the hospital, and care for a girl whose mind had gone for ever. *What do you do?* It didn't matter to her where she was, the people who loved her didn't matter to her, even her own survival meant nothing. She hadn't died, but he had lost her anyway, as he had lost his wife all those years before. All the love he had ever given was wasted.

'You mustn't blame yourself, Gabriel,' I mumbled, because I thought it might help, because I was drunk, because I couldn't bear the silence – and because I meant it. He looked sharply at me. 'Seriously,' I went on. 'It's not your fault. It's not mine. It's ... It happens. You know.' My hands were waving expressively, always a bad sign. It hit me that maybe it would be a good plan to shut up. I ignored the bit of me that was doing the nagging, and continued, 'She was unhappy. Dunno why. She didn't tell me. Seeing a psychiatrist and stuff.' I spilled a little drink as I gestured, and rose unsteadily to fetch myself a refill. I had collapsed back into my own chair and taken a swig, before I noticed Gabriel's stare, and gradually realised that I was being more than a little insensitive. 'Oh ... Shit. Look, Gabriel, I didn't mean – you know ... She loved you. Honest.'

Not that *he* had ever shown much sign of loving *her*. I'd always thought of him more as watching Verity than as sharing his life with her. My memories were of him staring out of a window while she played in the garden. I remembered the dark light that flickered in his eyes as she kissed him goodbye in the mornings, the sharp, unmoving lines of his face, his tongue wetting his thin lips before he spoke.

She doesn't want to play with you, Harry. Not with you.

A child sees as normal things that would horrify an adult. I was used to Gabriel's ways and manner, used to him being taciturn, familiar with the strangely fearful jealousy with which he watched over his daughter. He had lost his wife: he and Verity were alone in the world; she was precious to him, and he was afraid.

'Gabriel, listen ... It's just the whisky,' I mumbled. 'I'm ... confused. Sorry. Look, she never even told me she was sad. She isn't normally. It's not you. Not anyone. No one's fault. Seriously.'

Gabriel flicked me the kind of look that kills plants. I shut up for a while. My head felt detached from the rest of me, it was shooting round the room in random directions, I didn't dare move. I was overcome by memories, and even those were making me feel queasy. Playing on the swing in Verity's garden. The day they moved in. Gabriel's face the day he told me Verity didn't want to see me any more. When she was older, waiting for her with him, where was she, who was she with, didn't she realise? The clock, dividing up the night into tiny parcels.

'What happened, Gabriel?' I blurted. 'What was it? One day we were fine and the next day she wouldn't see me any more. You drove off with her somewhere, I saw you. It was like she hated me suddenly. We were so nearly … It was all brilliant. Then – bang, she wouldn't even talk to me.'

I risked waving an arm again, and regretted it. So I stayed very still. I was scared by my own daring, and scared of what he might say. Twenty years, and only now had I found the courage to ask.

Gabriel didn't answer. He gazed at me for a while, sucking thoughtfully on a mouthful of whisky. Then he poured the last of the bottle into his own glass, downed it, and stalked out of the room.

It took me a while to grasp that he wasn't coming back. I stood uncertainly, with my own words still bouncing around my head, an echo of humiliation, and wove my way down the hall to the front door. I didn't call goodbye. There wasn't any point.

Back at Mum's, the rest of the evening passed in a haze. I didn't talk about what had just happened, I couldn't bear to. Instead I brooded – about Gabriel, about psychiatry, about She Doesn't Want to See You – and let Mum and Sam's exuberance wash over and past me.

We had supper at half past seven or so – and a couple of bottles of wine to sluice it down, heaven help me. (Mum and Sam were two or three bottles gone by the time I got back from Gabriel's, so maybe I didn't stand out as much as memory tells me I should have.) There was laughter, a lot of it, from Sam and Mum, mostly about men. There was me, silent and heavily drunk. Me announcing that I really needed to go to bed (it must have been all of nine o'clock), and Sam saying to Mum that she ought to go up to say goodnight, and Mum saying, 'Go on,' while I was still negotiating the first few stairs. I remember Sam helping me into bed and – how much later? – her talking to Mum on the landing and Mum saying something about it was fine whichever room Sam ended up in, and

Sam saying OK, not that Harry'd be up for anything anyway. There was a cackle of laughter, and then there was Sam, naked next to me.

She slipped under the duvet into the narrow bed, cold body, prickly skin, murmuring something. I rolled towards her, murmured something too, flopped a heavy arm over her and slept again. I remember her easing herself out from under me, whispering something about snoring and sharing the duvet, saying she'd see me in the morning. And I remember that she bent over and kissed my forehead before she left, and she whispered something to me briefly in the moonlight.

Whatever it was, it sounded nice. And I slept around the cooling empty shape where she had been.

twenty

She didn't want to see me any more.

She had driven away rather than even be near me for the remains of the holiday. She hated me, it was obvious. She had been playing with me all along, using me. And now her classroom would be next to mine, she would be in the playground at break, in the corridors, at the tables during lunch. The last few days of the summer holiday were a miserable blur. Then the day came.

I was dragged from bed by an alarm clock, for the first time in months – and then by my mother when I dozed off again. She was busy and anxious, rushing around with breakfast and bits of uniform, fussing at me when she saw my top button undone, yanking at my tie, tugging at my hair. In the end I yelled at her to stop it and sulked upstairs to get my books. When I came down, her eyes were smoky and she would not look at me. She gave me one last head-to-toe fuss-over and let me go, sniffing busily.

I have only realised as an adult – since Verity's fall, to be honest – that I was the centre of Mum's small world for all those years. What else did she have? There were old friends, of course: colleagues from the hospital used to visit for a while, but Mum's hospitality was now bereft of the frills and graces of north Oxford living. New friends came and went: girls from the pub where she worked after the Prof retired, even one or two of the regulars who propped up the bar. There was a trickle of strangers through our lives, but when each had gone, it was me who remained with Mum, listening through long evenings to the creaks and echoes of the house. The shadow of Dad was always there. Mum had moved the furniture, repainted the walls, scrubbed floors, but the imprint of him remained. His tools stayed in the shed, his camera in the loft. And I stayed too, because who else did Mum have? But, to my shame, I could hardly bear to be near her.

So, until the start of that autumn term, going back to school had always been a relief. Compared to home, school was easy and familiar: friends, gangs, flirts and feuds and grudges. Comfortable patterns, all of them.

But this term would be different. This term, Verity would be there.

In the two weeks between kissing her and the start of term, I went from longing to see her to dreading it. I had thought the kiss was real and the slap just a game. Now I knew better. Her laughter, I was sure, had been contempt. I was humiliated. She would be at the school gates with a crowd of friends, laughing, pointing, mocking me. (I knew that in reality she would be alone, that she knew no one in the village – but fear does strange things to your imagination.) I scuffed and slouched, delaying each step as long as I could. But the moment came, I couldn't avoid it.

And when I got to school, it wasn't Verity who betrayed me. It was Adam.

It was Oba who cast the first word. But they were all primed, with knowledge only Adam could have given them.

'Harry's in *lurve*,' Oba sneered.

The others giggled, so Oba giggled too. Adam stayed well back, prowling the fringes of the group, smiling and simultaneously managing to look like it was not his idea. But I knew, and it hurt. Encouraged by the laughter, Oba carried on. 'Oh, *Har*-ree,' he warbled. 'Do you *lurve* me, Harry?' He pretended to twirl a non-existent lock of long hair, and pouted. 'Do ya, Harry? Do ya, baby?'

The gang held no fear for me any more, not since I had knocked over Greg. The key was not to show pain.

I blew Oba a big fruity kiss and walked past, my neck burning. I heard laughter behind me, except from Oba, of course, who yelled something about how very funny it fuckin' wasn't, and ha fuckin' ha.

I waited for school to begin, alone. There was a lot of hunching around in groups in the playground and corridors, kids casually aligning with the circles of their choice, eyeing up other groups, shifting between them, the usual. The first-years had mostly gone in to claim desks and organise their new universe. They sat neatly, arranging the contents of their pencil-cases, casting nervous glances and smiles.

While the other year-two children gossiped in the corridors, renewing old friendships, one girl sat alone in the front of the classroom. I saw her through the window. Wounded brown eyes, small high breasts, pencil case unopened, pigeon-toed and self-contained. Her face was blank, her eyes wide and full of thought. I leaned against the window, shading my hand to see in. She didn't turn. I scurried away in an uneasy mixture of misery and relief.

I stared at my desk all morning. Ink stains seeped along the grain of the wood. Sharp letters, scratched with keys and compasses – 'So-And-So Is A Git, I Hate Maths . . . If I put a pencil along the groove where the desk hinged open, and tapped the desk leg, the pencil would roll all the way down the desk and into my lap. Again. Again. She had looked so vulnerable. She was alone. She would be picked on, teased, newcomers always were.

Poor Verity.

She doesn't want to see you, Harry.

Poor Harry.

I didn't see Adam again until morning break. He had changed too. No, that's unfair, he hadn't changed, but another part of him had come to the fore. He was confident and sure of himself. He had friends. They were mostly the bully gang that had once made my life a misery – and his. I knew them all: Wayne Smith, Dave Oliphant, Obafemi Olukojo (Oba, the school's only black kid – and huge, so no one picked on him, ever), Greg Winston, the leader. The gang was all right. I had fun with them occasionally. I had never enjoyed the collective bravado, or the teasing and bullying, but I had loved the madness of being spurred on to do something that you would never have dreamed of doing alone – and the crowing afterwards, the sharing.

Today I stood apart, against a wall, alone, and watched the playground's games. Adam split quietly away from the group. He came over and leaned against the wall next to me. 'Didn't mean it, Harry. Sorry.'

I didn't answer: why the hell should I?

'Want to come out after school?' he pressed. 'We're going down the canal.'

I looked along the playground's length. At the other end, groups of first and second years were playing, neatly divided up into boys and girls. The boys had a football and were kicking it against a wall, the girls were playing tag. And one pigeon-toed girl sat against a bench in the shelter of the school entrance, neat white socks and skinny bare legs, mouse hair, wise eyes looking nowhere. I looked at Adam. He glanced away, embarrassed, and idly kicked at the wall.

'Yeah, all right,' I said.

He nodded, and moved back to join the group. They had stolen a ball from the new boys and were kicking it around, shoving the youngsters out of the way.

Through a whirl of children, at the very far end of the playground, I saw her in glimpses: her bony knees, her solemn face, her reddened eyes. And I wanted the summer not to have happened, and I wanted to touch her all over again. I knew what Oba and the gang would say if I went over to her. I couldn't even shove myself upright from the wall where I leaned. She caught my eye and held it – and the yards between us stretched into miles.

Eventually the bell went, and lessons began again.

After school, I wandered into the playground looking for her. She wasn't there. A big arm draped itself over my shoulder and Greg leaned his full weight on to me. 'Coming, then?' He mock-punched my ribs.

Oba skipped backwards in front of us. 'Takin' our bikes. Jump the swing-bridge. Smoke some fags an' stuff.'

The swing-bridge idea appealed, but not the smoking. I'd always had this problem with Greg and Oba's gang. They did fun things and stupid things in equal measure, but if you didn't do it all you were mocked. Well, so be it. They had mocked me earlier and I had survived. In fact, from a few hours' distance, it seemed like a kind of acceptance ritual, as though they had been testing me after a summer of non-acquaintance. The teasing had been over in moments, and Greg's arm over my shoulder told me that nothing had been meant. Adam would be harder to forgive. He had betrayed me, and no amount of denial by him could alter the hurt they had all seen in my eyes.

In my memory, all this seems so petty. Somewhere, probably within weeks, Adam was forgiven and the event forgotten. In fact, Greg's gang brought us closer. We often sat for hours together after the others had moved on. We were both quieter than they were, more introspective. And both of us had nothing much to go home to. We sat out in the evenings, watching the days grow shorter and the stars appear, cold, bright and uncaring.

'Dad smacked Mum around again last night,' he'd say, and I would say nothing. (He never talked about his own bruises – so obvious from how he moved, and sometimes visible on his face. No one else talked about them either.) Or I would say, 'Mum's got that bastard Mark in tonight. I hate him.' And in his turn Adam would say nothing.

Verity slowly came out of herself, too. She made new friends. She played, laughed, became a new version of the mad Verity I had once known. But now I watched at a distance. If I came close when she was with her gang, she'd joke and flirt; they all would, all at once, calling out suggestions, giggling, pouting and blowing kisses. They did it to half the boys in the school, I was nothing special. If I tried to come closer or talk to her, they would all run off twittering.

Her clothes changed too. She wore her uniform as raggedly as the rest of them, tie undone and pleated grey skirt too short. Buttons gaped open down her blouse. Her hair grew long and tangled. She swanked in front of the boys, and they all stared at her with an anticipation she never fulfilled.

She played at the other girls' houses, never at home. Her garden was always empty, her house quiet. At night I would stand by the apple tree and stare over the tall hedge at the light in her window. I rarely even saw a shadow pass across it. I hugged the tree – pressed against its sharp, cold bark until my face went numb and my socks and trousers were drenched with dew or frost – and still nothing would stir.

Sometimes the serious Verity came to school, and she would sit on the bench by the entrance, knees tight together, toes and eyes pointing inwards. One day I went and sat next to her – and she let me. I didn't dare say a thing. When the bell rang, we got up wordlessly and went to our separate classes.

It became our custom. We would sit there while the others all had lunch, her gang and mine safely occupied. We said nothing for weeks. Eventually I found the courage for words.

'Why?' I asked.

The air was sharp and clear. Withered leaves gathered in drifts in the corners of the playground. She wrapped her arms and rocked forwards on the bench. Her bare knees were blotched with cold. She said nothing.

'What was it, though, Verity?' I urged. 'What did I do?'

She stood suddenly and strode away, her schoolbooks clutched across her chest.

But the next day she was back, and we sat again side by side. I noted the passing of each dry leaf.

After school she would change again. She rushed out of class with her friends, chattering and whirling and laughing. They gathered round her and I would half hear as she laid out some plan; then they would be gone.

I only spoke to her one other time on the bench, and that destroyed what little we now had.

As with everything else, it began with the treehouse.

Greg was bored with the swing-bridges. He was bored with the humps that led down to Port Meadow. He was bored with the old cement works. He was bored, and that meant we all were – because what Greg said went. We all sat on a low wall along one side of the playground after school, bored and cold and not saying much, because whenever one of us suggested something, Greg laid into them. 'Oh, that's a bloody *great* idea,' he'd snarl. Then, usually, he'd throw something at you.

When Jules Waters – younger than the rest of us, a hanger-on – suggested bike races down the ramps in the multi-storey car park in town, Oba chased him and threw him against a gatepost in an unenthusiastic way. That was the last suggestion anyone made. Until Adam spoke up. 'I know somewhere,' he said lazily. He wouldn't look at me.

Greg heaved himself off the top bar of the climbing-frame and stood in front of him, threatening, waiting.

Adam was unconcerned. 'Somewhere new,' he said. 'But only if you've got the guts.'

I tried to catch his eye, but the game was already lost.

'Better tell us, then, hadn't you?' growled Greg. He weighed his fist in front of Adam's face.

'Whiteham Woods,' Adam said.

'Ain't that fenced in?' Oba protested.

Adam shrugged. 'Told you you wouldn't have the guts.'

'What's in there, then?' Greg asked.

'Come and find out,' Adam said. And he grinned. He dared to look at me – and now the flush was no longer embarrassment: it was triumph.

Verity and her gang were by the school gates. I don't remember what they were doing, hopscotch or something. Oba saw them first, and swung his bike round in a skid – he'd been practising it for weeks.

'Going down the woods, girls. Whiteham Woods.' He leered at them. 'Nice and quiet, know what I mean? Wanna come along, have some fun – like, *real* fun?'

He ground his hips on the bike's crossbar and pursed his lips in mock-ecstasy. The gang laughed – except me. The girls jeered and giggled – except Verity. She looked at me, full of shock and hurt. There was a kind of horror on her face that I can't quite pin down, even now. It wasn't an accusation, it was ... I don't know. Loneliness, perhaps. I had wounded her, and there was nothing I could do about it.

Adam was behind me. 'Come on, Harry.' His voice was edged with excitement. I didn't move, so he spoke louder. The whole gang could hear. 'Come on, mate, forget her. She's not even good-looking, daft old slapper.'

The gang laughed, and Verity blushed. Her lips were trembling.

'Oh, Verity,' Adam called, his voice mocking, sing-song. 'Oh, little gi-irl. Show us your knickers, then. Go on.'

The gang joined in, getting louder as they realised they had hit on something. Even the girls were laughing. Encouraged, Adam sauntered over to her and made a grab for her skirt. Verity screamed something at him and ran away, her eyes squeezed shut against the tears. Both gangs jeered until she was gone. Oba wolf-whistled.

I didn't stop them. If I had tried, I would have become a target too, back at the bottom of the heap. I didn't want that: what else did I have except the gang? Verity had already rejected me, my friends from my old school had long since vanished. I needed a place to belong. The moment passed in a kind of fugue. It was the pecking order of the playground. Verity had clawed her way up over the term; now she had fallen again.

But I saw the hurt in her eyes as she ran. She thought I had led them to the treehouse. She knew that I had watched as they mocked her. The sounds around me faded. If I had been able to, I would have crawled away and wept. But the boys were on their bikes already, wheeling in wide circles, waiting.

I didn't dare go after her. And perhaps that was the greatest betrayal of them all.

So now, Verity, decades later – now that I am someone different, and now that it is too late – now I can say it.

I am sorry, Verity.

So sorry.

They loved the treehouse. Of course they did. They whooped and yelled, they dive-bombed each other. They hung from the edge of the platform and attacked each other with hammed-up karate kicks.

For the most part, I sat on the platform and looked straight out, past them, at the tattered brown curtain of leaves. As the boys clambered and swung and banged about, the leaves detached and spun down, light and lifeless, one by one; and another tiny patch of the cold autumn sky stared in at me. From time to time one of the boys would make me join in. They grabbed my foot, tried to pull me over the edge, they swung round the trunk to land on top of me. And I would wrestle my way out of their tumble and scramble back to my remote vantage. Their yells got louder as fun took over from caution. The warnings Adam and I hissed at them were ignored. Adam sat and watched, too, away from me, perched on one of the higher branches beyond the reach of the rope or a boisterous leap.

It was Oba's idea to see how many of them could get on to the swing. He hung twirling in open space, giggling maniacally, and one boy after another made the leap to catch the rope. Poor Jules Waters missed and landed badly, but no one cared. When four of them were on it, with Jules still out of action nursing a twisted ankle, they started to yell at me and Adam to jump. I ignored them, so they focused on Adam, who yielded with a grin. He swaggered down on to the platform and nudged me aside with his foot. He was moving slowly, relishing it. This was the moment when they all remembered that coming here had been his idea. He spat into his hands and rubbed them together. The rope was swinging and spinning, slow and heavy under the weight of bodies. I couldn't even see where he was going to find a place to hold on. They were yelling encouragement at him, telling him to hurry. He grinned even wider. There was a muffled complaint from Oba that some bastard was sitting on his face, and the mass of bodies rippled as he yanked himself into a better position under the pile – and Adam lost his chance to jump.

It was a mixture between a crack and a howl. The branch above them split and the rope swung sideways, the boys yelling now and kicking to get free. Then the branch gave way and dumped them four feet straight down. Some fell off, screaming and cackling. The others were pulled short with a jerk that ripped the branch from its socket. They spilled to the ground, and the foot-thick beam landed atop them, cushioned by its smaller spars and twigs. There was a hiss and a crackle, then silence. Then hysterical giggling as the boys wrestled their way out.

Adam was in fits. Even I broke out of my mood.

It *was* funny. On the ground, they were all leaping into the cushion made by the twigs, or taking turns to throw each other in, four boys each holding a leg or arm. Adam stood on the edge of the platform and yelled encouragement, until Oba lunged up to catch him. He missed, which made Adam laugh harder, and gave Oba an idea. He grabbed the fallen spar, and rammed the thick end into the underside of the treehouse like a battering ram. Adam giggled and clambered to the next level. I jumped down. Oba enlisted the others to help him, and they smashed the spar repeatedly into the underside of the deck. Eventually one plank came loose, then another. Then they dropped it, and Adam scrambled down and yanked at the loosened board. After a few tugs it came away in his hand, a few curling black nails showing beneath it. He launched it outwards across the hornbeam's vault. It took for ever. It seemed to glide. Then it lodged itself in the veil of branches.

The others whooped, and scrambled up to have a go themselves.

One by one they dragged and hauled at the boards until they came free. The game was to try to dislodge Adam's plank. When they succeeded, the next game was to try to lodge another in the tree. When all the planks were gone, it was who could throw one furthest. And that slowly became a mock-war: Wayne went to collect some of the planks and took it on himself to throw them back. A couple of the others took his side, and the air was soon thick with flying, nail-embedded planks.

From an adult perspective, this might seem crazy, but it was no different from the rest of what we did. The games we played were dangerous.

The game warden must have heard us from miles away. None of us noticed him arrive, though. When he yelled at us, we ignored him. When he yelled again, someone threw a plank at him. When he pointed his shotgun into the air and fired, we ran – at first terrified, then whooping with fear and exultation.

It was two weeks before I dared tell her. The last time I had spoken to her, she had walked away. So the days passed, and we sat next to each other on the bench in our usual silence.

'They smashed the treehouse, Verity,' I said eventually.

She stayed: she didn't reply, but she stayed.

'It wasn't me,' I pressed. 'I didn't show them. I didn't break it. I wouldn't, honest. It was—'

And at that moment, I made the connection. With the feeble and purely emotional logic of a thirteen-year-old, I was suddenly sure: it had to be the truth . . . I knew why she hadn't wanted to see me. I knew why Verity and Adam made a show of avoiding each other, and why Adam's teasing upset her. I saw again the look in Adam's eye the day we took the photographs, relived every flirtatious moment.

'You're seeing him, aren't you?' I blurted. 'You got off with Adam, didn't you? That weekend.'

And for the second – and last – time, Verity slapped me. This time it was hard. Then she hit me in the chest with both fists, over and over. Savagely. She said not a word, made not a sound. She threw her books at me. Then she ran away.

I sat very still, not physically injured, but swept by a numb ache to which I was already accustomed. If you live with hurt for long enough, you get used to it. It becomes a part of your life. You come to need it. I knelt by the bench and carefully gathered Verity's books together, scraps to offer her, to beg for conciliation – though I knew now that I had lost her for ever.

Across the playground, I could see the gang. Oba, Greg and Adam were watching me. And laughing.

I returned to the treehouse two days later, early one morning, before school. There was a frost on the fields, and the wood lay blackly beneath a pale, cold sky. The edges of dead leaves were traced in ice. Below the hornbeam, the fallen branch had been sawn into manageable chunks, the planks were ranged in neat piles. Where parts of the treehouse had survived the gang's assault, there were now white gashes in the tree's trunk, the black scars of nails. The leaves and twigs had been swept into heaps, and the clearing was bare and frozen, dark except where the frost had touched it.

I stood in the middle, where Verity had once leaped for joy, and gazed at the neatly stacked remnants of my wild, dead summer.

twenty-one

Sam brought me coffee and aspirin at eight. She shoved me over to one edge of the bed by wriggling her bottom until there was enough room for her to sit next to me, fully clothed. I was tousled and dazed, and still hiding all but my forehead under the duvet. I felt dreadful. My third hangover in two weeks. Not clever. But the only moral I could find in it was this: never, ever, let your closest friend fall off a cliff. Not under any circumstances.

Sam fitted comfortably against me, and put her arm round me when I slumped against her side. Her T-shirt was loose, and my nose just touched the skin of her waist. It was cool and clean, it smelt of laundry.

She had drawn the curtains and opened the window. The air carried the scent of dew and grass, and the distant chatter of birds, the burr of busy wings. I could hear Mum in the kitchen, directly below: cutlery tinkling in a drawer, plates being stacked, the cupboard door that had squealed for the last twenty years. Sporadic sounds, mostly silence. Life as normal.

'Morning.' I groaned.

Sam squeezed my shoulder and wriggled a bit. 'Morning,' she said cheerfully. 'How bad are we?' She sounded like a nurse.

I didn't answer. I was going to, but then I couldn't think of a word horrible enough, and while I was trying to think of one I drifted into a kind of limbo where I really wasn't thinking at all – which was a blessing. 'Sorry,' I croaked at last.

I felt her shrug. When her T-shirt settled back, its edge was teasing my lashes. It made my eyelids flutter. With a dramatic moan

I hauled myself upright and rubbed my face, which didn't help much. Matter-of-factly Sam handed me the painkillers and a glass of water. I slugged them down and nearly threw them straight back up. Eyes watering, I mumbled, 'Thanks.' Then, 'Bad. Very bad.'

'I'm not surprised.' She wasn't gloating. If anything her tone was sympathetic.

'Was I dreadful?'

'No, not really. Just drunk.' She dimpled and her eyes flashed. I hated to think what she might be remembering, so I closed my eyes and didn't think at all. 'You said Gabriel had you on the whisky.'

'Did I? Yeah. Whisky.'

I didn't remember anything I'd said. I suspect that my memory was at least fifty per cent dramatic reconstruction.

'And then wine with supper. Poor you,' Sam said. I groaned again. 'So are you up to going out?'

'Out?'

'To the woods, remember? Where the treehouse was.'

I groaned again and huddled back down against her. 'Do we have to?'

She curled over and round me with a satisfied 'mmm', and pressed her cheek on to the top of my head. 'Take your time,' she said.

We walked, with me hunched as though it was about to rain, hands in my pockets, eyes sliding over the road barely a yard ahead of my feet. Sam linked her right arm through my left. It was a strange and uncomfortable sensation and it put me off my rhythm. I kept rigidly upright, not giving against her at all; and after a minute or two when I self-consciously scratched my nose, she had to disengage. When I shoved my hand firmly back into my pocket, she didn't try again. We hardly spoke: she pointed out the weather, made comments about the size of the village, and I replied with grunts. Eventually we ducked on to the farm track, and down the hill (a slight slope, really, now that I saw it as an adult) to the wood's edge. We clambered over a bank, jumped a ditch, slipped through the barbed-wire fence beyond. We were scratched and stung, but in.

'Wow,' breathed Sam.

Whiteham Woods. Huge ancient trees, and bare dappled ground. Sunlight dancing in blotches, and birds, and the scent of warm earth.

I saw it differently. I saw dark narrow spaces. It stank of loam, heavy from the dew. There was moss on fallen boughs, fungus gripped and probed. Roots clutched at thin soil.

But, then, I did have something of a hangover.

Sam squeezed my hand. 'Which way?' I pointed, and we set off.

It took us an hour to find the hornbeam. There were familiar landmarks, a hollowed tree, a stream with just one crossing point, but I couldn't remember the way. The route had never been marked in my head, just in my habits. At the time I had known the way without thinking about it, just doing it. Now, thinking hard, navigating my memories, I found myself following false hunches. That tree had been at the centre of my childhood – and I didn't even know where it was.

When I found it, I wasn't even sure it was the right one, until Sam pointed to a few boards scattered below it, rotted and tinder dry. The tree had changed. There were new branches, and stumps where old branches had once been. Gradually, though, it took shape again in my mind, the way it had been, and I began to tell Sam about it. This was where the platform started, and it went all the way round to there. And you got to it up this branch, you couldn't do it now, of course, but you could then, easy. That's where the rope went. And here – you could reach all the way out to here if you swung hard enough. You landed with a hell of a thump though, nearly broke my ribs the first time I tried it . . .

Sam stood behind me, chin on my shoulder, and hugged me as I brought the past back to a thin kind of life.

'She's still here,' I said. 'Kind of.'

She turned me round and kissed me. Beneath the tree's arch, below the healed wood where once there had been a treehouse, we made love.

The ghosts didn't seem to mind.

Mum cried when we left. She stood in the doorway with a hankie pressed to her lips, although it was her eyes that were streaming. Sam craned round to keep eye-contact as long as possible. Then she turned to face forwards, and settled herself into the car's uncomfortable seat. She reached over to touch me, but stopped short and withdrew. I hated leaving Mum's. It made me tense.

'You're lucky, Harry.'

'Hmm? How?'

'Your mum. She really loves you.'

True – but to me that sometimes felt like a burden.

Sam looked at me quizzically. 'You should see mine some day,' she said. 'She's a dragon. Mum flogs horses and children to within an inch of their lives, thinks it's character-forming. She eats corgis for breakfast. Believe me, Harry, love's not so bad.'

The hangover had made me sorry for myself: I didn't need this as well. I concentrated on driving. Sam took the hint.

We ripped along the Oxford ring-road, which was dangerously crowded, and spilled out on to the M40, which was strangely empty. Sam found some music on the radio – golden oldies, they claimed, but the songs were all of five years old. Then, half an hour later, she switched it off sharply. '*How* many cameras did you say?'

'Huh?'

'At the treehouse. How many?'

'Oh . . . Eleven.'

The motorway flicked by. Wind thumped through the open window, the scent of the fields mixed with burnt fumes.

'Strange.'

'Hmmn?'

'Well, are you sure?'

'Well, I *was* there . . .'

'I'm not trying to be funny, Harry.'

'I know.' I stroked her knee. It felt good. 'Hmmm. Eleven. Definitely.'

Sam mouthed, 'Oh.' Two miles later, she turned towards me again. 'Look, are you really sure?'

I ticked them off on my fingers. Eleven.

She frowned. 'Well, it's not that many now.'

I must have looked confused. 'The zoetrope,' she explained. 'I mean, I didn't count exactly but there's definitely not eleven shots on it. More like six or seven.'

'Six or seven?' I gaped at her until she calmly pointed forwards. I had to veer sharply because I was straddling two lanes.

'Six or seven, trust me. Or ring the hospital.'

'I trust you.'

In my mind I spun the zoetrope again, held it to the light. It was too quick, too jerky: not enough pictures. Sam was right. She reckoned six or seven; I might have guessed eight – but she was right. Between three and five photos had been cut out of the circle.

Another mystery. I felt terrible. My eyes stung: the wind from the open window, perhaps; we were going fast. She put her hand on my thigh, and rode out the tears, her expression unreadable. Patience, it seemed, was one of Sam's virtues. 'Sam, I'm—'

'Don't.'

'But I *am*. It's not you, honest. Not really.'

'Not *really*? Great!' But her laugh was gentle, and her hand was still on my thigh. She leaned over and kissed me. 'We'll get there, Harry.'

I put the radio back on, and pressed harder on the accelerator. The wind became a buffeting roar. I gripped the steering-wheel tightly, and wondered what I was getting myself into.

twenty-two

'Harry?'

'Oh. Hi. Adam ...'

'How's things?'

'Er. Yeah. Fine. I was asleep.'

'At nine o'clock! You lucky so-and-so. I'm almost at work.'

'...'

'Anyway, I wanted to ring, see how you were. Been a few days.'

'Yeah.'

'Yeah ... Look, Harry, I know it's going to take more than the odd phone call to get me out of the doghouse but, forgiven or not, I'm worried about you.' A sharp intake of breath. 'And to be completely honest, I could do with a bit of TLC myself. This has been rough for me too, you know.'

I didn't answer.

'Harry? You can join in this conversation any time, you know ...' A sigh. 'Look, Harry, if there's one person in my life I'd never want to hurt, it's you. I need you, Harry. I – Oh, hang on ... Morning, Malcolm.'

I heard the security guard's muffled response.

'Sorry, Harry. Listen, I really want to talk. Could we meet for lunch maybe?'

'I'll call you, Adam.'

'OK, I'll keep lunchtime free.'

'Not lunch, Adam. Sometime.'

I heard him sigh again.

'OK. But just remember I'm here, OK? Please. And that I miss you. The last two days have been hell.'

''Bye, Adam.'

There was a long silence. Then he rang off. I crawled back to bed and stared at the ceiling.

Sam rolled over on to me, still half asleep. She trailed her fingers over my stomach, and then her hand drifted downwards.

'Mmmmm . . . Who was that?'

'Adam. Wants to meet.'

'Why?'

'No reason.'

Given what her hand was doing, Adam was the last thing on my mind.

'Why, though?'

'Dunno. Wants to stay friends.'

Sam was stroking slowly. I arched up, trying to strengthen the contact with her hand.

'So where was he calling from?'

'The office. Town hall.'

She brushed her lips against my neck. 'Now's your chance to go and see Sarah, then, isn't it?' she murmured. 'You can have the rest when you get back.'

And she kicked me out of bed.

Adam and Sarah lived just south of Clapham Common, in a large house on a wealthy, leafy street.

It was Sam who had insisted that I should see Sarah. Unfortunately, I knew she was right. I needed to know more about Adam and Verity's affair – and I refused to ask anything more from Adam. Also, as Sam pointed out, I was going to have to apologise for Adam's behaviour: he was, after all, still my friend . . . Sort of. I was dreading it. The apologies would be uncomfortable; the revelations about Verity could well be unbearable. The mission could only go ahead when Adam was not there, of course, and for the last few days I had been using this as a pathetically thin excuse for not going. Sam had been needling me more and more, and this morning's escalation of the rules of engagement to include sexual frustration was . . . Well, actually, it was rather fun. I was looking forward to getting her back to the negotiating table later.

First, though, there was the small matter of the moment I had been trying to avoid.

The air was sharp and clean, and the familiar faint roar of London traffic seemed more remote than usual. On the street itself, nothing moved. Adam's house (well, mostly Sarah's actually, she was the one with capital) was set back from the road. It was high, white and square, with steps leading up to the front door, flanked on both sides by a sunken well that let light into a lower-ground-floor-cum-basement. Through the windows I could see a terracotta tiled floor, and a pair of feet in socks and dark blue cargo pants, standing against a kitchen unit. I rang the bell and the feet turned and walked from view. Thirty seconds later Sarah opened the door and stared at me, her blue eyes full of calm hostility. Her hair shifted in a whisper of breeze.

One cheek was swollen and blue, her eye was puffed to a slit.

She said nothing, just turned and walked ahead of me along the darkened hall and down the stairs to the kitchen. I shut the door behind me as quietly as I could. Ahead of me, I heard crockery clattering.

The kitchen was huge and bright, despite being half below ground, because one wall was all window, giving on to a well-lit garden. The floor was an ocean of terracotta with a breakfast bar set in the middle of it like an island. Sarah was sitting at it on a stool. She held a cup of coffee neatly in her lap with both hands. She offered me nothing – not a drink, not a seat. Her bruised cheek distorted her frown. She didn't speak. Eventually I gave up waiting and sat at another of the stools, the worktop a reassuring barrier between us.

'I didn't know,' I said. 'About the affair. I had no idea.'

She jiggled her head at me – 'go on', 'who cares?' and 'heard it all before' rolled into one easy gesture.

'Seriously,' I persisted. 'What you told me. I never even guessed.'

She smiled bitterly. The skin of her bad cheek went hard and shiny. 'Why are you here, Harry?'

Good question. I wished I wasn't. I took a deep breath, conjured a vision of Sam's face if I bottled out, and went for it. 'I wanted to make sure you were OK. You seemed pretty upset when you . . . when, er . . .'

'Barged in? Yes, that must have been terribly disturbing for you. I'm so sorry.' It would have been nice if she'd sounded more like she meant it. She set down her coffee and rose, fiddling with some

195

drawers on the other side of the kitchen, doing nothing in particular. 'Adam wasn't best pleased either,' she muttered.

She must have sensed me gaping, because she snapped at me, 'I *fell*, Harry. On the stairs. I'm clumsy, apparently.' Her hair framed the bruise and almost hid it. She slumped against the worktop, and her head drooped. 'Sometimes I wonder if he hates me.' She spoke to the floor. A mocking smile. 'And then, other times, I wonder if I hate him.'

Occasionally I'm clever enough to let other people do the talking. Today I was clever. She went on, 'It's not just that Hadley woman. If it was just her I could forgive him. Maybe. But *again* and *again* and . . . And I'm tired of it. I'm sure she was nothing special, just his latest screw.'

'Actually, Sarah, that's the other reason I'm here.'

She stared at me blankly, then went on, as though I hadn't spoken, 'I don't think he even means to be cruel, you know. But he is. Emotionally, he's cruel. But you know, the thing is, after a while you just give up being hurt. You realise that actually what you are is not hurt any more but really, *really* angry.'

She looked around her, then walked over to an open shelf scattered with plants and designer crockery. She fetched down a thick handful of dinner plates – porcelain white with a thin rim of blue and gold. She held them out in front of her, then dropped the whole pile on to the floor. The shrill sound of the crash was over quickly, but she held the pose, hands open in front of her, gazing at me, dazed. She looked down at the shards at her feet. China splinters had scattered across the tiles. A pile of jagged-edged half-moon plates lay before her, toppled to one side. She lifted her foot and stamped down on them. Her sock slid sideways and she wobbled on one leg but kept her balance. The pile did not shatter: instead, the middle four plates squirted outwards, landing flat and sending a second wave of shards skating across the floor. Still wobbling, Sarah set down her stamping foot, with no regard for the fragments beneath it. I heard the bone-dry, high-pitched crunch of crushed ceramic as her foot settled. She wrinkled her face – half pain, half disgust, all control.

My heart was hammering.

'Why are you here, Harry?' Her voice was quiet.

You had to admire it. You had to be scared, too.

I spread my arms feebly. Then I did it again, because I still wasn't sure what to say. 'When did you last see Verity?' I blurted at last.

Sarah looked at me for a while, then save a soft laugh. 'Fuck off, Harry.'

'I'm serious,' I said. 'You knew they were seeing each other. You had her followed. Adam told me. Just followed? Or did you try to warn her off?'

Sarah walked slowly back to the breakfast bar, limping, shards tinkling and grinding as she trod on them. There were tiny smears of blood on the tiles where her feet had been. She picked up her coffee-cup and sat. Then she set it down again.

'It's not just the affairs,' she said thoughtfully. She delicately pressed one fingertip on to a knot in the wooden work surface, then on to another. 'It's not even the lying – well, he scarcely bothers with that, does he?' She tapped a couple more tiny knots, then drew her hand back to her coffee. 'It's the future. It's what happens next.'

I was confused, so I stuck to my guns. 'Sarah, did—'

'Did I go to see her?' She laughed. 'What the hell would that have accomplished?' She raised her hand limply, forefinger dropping over another knot in the wood. She squinted at it, so hard that she winced as her cheek pulled tight. Then she stood. More delicate crunching noises. 'I'd like you to go now, Harry.'

'Look, I need to know what happened, Sarah. I know it's hard for you to—'

'*Hard!*'

'But Verity was *my friend*. I didn't know about the affair. If I had, believe me, I'd have given anything to stop it. But it happened. Look, I . . . cared about Verity. A lot. And I'd just like to know what happened to her. You may be able to help.'

'Oh, I can. What happened to Verity Hadley? Easy-peasy. A poisonous little tart who got exactly what she deserved. Well, maybe not exactly. People who fuck other people's husbands in lay-bys deserve a lot worse than Beachy Head. And *bars*, too. It's so *tacky*. They couldn't even manage a decent hotel. But I shouldn't complain. He was using her, of course, and she must have been feeling miserable. That's a comfort. *Bitch*.'

She drained her coffee, then lightly dropped the cup on to the floor to join the plates. She bent and picked up one of the pieces, frowned at it, scraped its sharp edge across her palm. It left a white line. She did it again, harder, and beads of blood oozed out. She sniffed them, looked bemused. 'I'd like you to go now, Harry,' she said again, absently, still gazing at her palm.

What she read there, I have no idea. I didn't stay to ask. I stood uneasily, and led the way back up the stairs. On the doorstep, I turned, unsure what to say. Her cut hand was clenched white at her side. 'Do you think I should hate him, Harry?' She looked genuinely puzzled. So was I. I shrugged, and she nodded her understanding – although goodness knows what she understood. I made to go. I looked again at Sarah's cheek, and she touched it self-consciously. Suddenly her eyes filmed, and she covered her face.

I watched, helpless, as her shoulders shook. 'Sarah . . . Did you really fall?'

She looked up, curious, enquiring. Unreadable. She sniffed away the tears and straightened. 'Remember after our wedding, Harry? Your speech.' Her eyes creased. She half closed the door then slumped against it, her uninjured cheek pressed against the flat of the white-painted wood. 'You told me to look after him.' She laughed at that, sadly.

'Um. Look, Sarah—'

'Fuck off, Harry.' She sounded tired.

An aeroplane coming in to land moaned distantly. Another shone in the sky, white steel against the blue.

She began to close the door. I turned and started down the steps. 'Harry?' I stopped, looked back at her. 'Don't tell him you've seen me this time, Harry. Please.' Her face was a mask. There was more than just fear there. More than weariness. I saw something deeper, and far more shocking.

After everything, all he had done, she still loved him.

twenty-three

I was looking forward to getting back to Sam. I was on a promise, after all. But my encounter with Sarah hadn't left me feeling exactly frisky, so when Sam announced that she had other plans for me, I wasn't as frustrated as I might have been. She was dressed and ready for business.

'Done?' She quickly cleared away her coffee and newspaper.

'Done. Weird – scary, actually – but done.'

'Learn anything? Oh, never mind, you can tell me on the way.'

'The way where?'

'Unfinished business, remember?'

The unfinished business I'd had in mind had been in the bedroom. But she came over to me and pushed me gently through the front door.

'Karel Novak,' she said firmly.

Just as I had begun to get interested again.

Damn.

Karel Novak was the closest Sam and I had yet come to an argument.

I had only meant it idly when I said I should try to find him. My thoughts had been in a slow post-coital drift. Sam had answered equally idly that she had his details. I tried to ask, casually, what she was doing with his phone number. She must have felt me stiffen. 'He's sexy, Harry,' she said defensively. 'A girl's got to take her chances.'

'He doesn't do a thing for me,' I grumbled.

She rolled over on top of me and pressed her nose against mine.

'D'you want to find him or not?' she asked, grinding her hips against me. I felt myself rising in response.

'Mnngh . . .' I said, because her tongue was in my mouth. When she was finished, I added, 'I suppose so, yes.'

She rolled back to her bedside table and groped beneath it for her bag.

'Anyway, you already knew I had it.'

'I did?'

'Well, how else could I have given it to the police after the break-in?'

'Point,' I conceded. And added, trying to sound casual again, and failing, 'So when did he give it to you?'

She peeped over her shoulder at me, one eyebrow raised, lips twitching subtly at the corners. She had those wonderful lips that seem soft and alive, they moved with her every expression. Right now they were laughing at me. 'Harry Waddell, are you jealous?' She poked me in the side. She didn't pull the jab. Her nails were rock hard and they hurt. 'Harry Waddell, the great international man of mystery, seducer of women. Mr Commitment himself – oh, don't *worry*, Harry! You, jealous!'

I huffed a few times in a wounded sort of way. I couldn't win. If I said I was jealous, I sent her all the wrong signals. On the other hand, if I denied jealousy she'd know I was lying.

She gave up looking for the address book and sat on top of me, wriggling herself against me comfortably. She stroked my chest and neck with one hand and reached down behind her with the other to trace a finger along my thigh.

'Relax, Harry, he's just a flirt. He gave me the number ages ago. Fancied his chances. I was pissed. I must have taken down five boys' numbers that evening. Didn't phone any of them. But you never know when you might want to. And, like I said, Karel's sexy. He's a bastard, but he's sexy.'

Her finger reached a little higher. 'Now, *you*, on the other hand . . .'

Her hair and warm breath tickling my face. Her skin smelt of warm sheets and the faint perfume of our sweat. I ran my hands down her sides towards her hips, over her back and the crease of her buttocks. She crushed her mouth against mine.

I could her feel her smiling as we kissed.

But that had been then. No sex today, just unfinished business.

Karel Novak lived in a shabby house near Elephant and Castle. The road was shadowed by tall boarded-up warehouses. The house squatted between them, red brick underneath the grime. Large metal bins clustered opposite in a disused lorry bay. The rubbish overflowed on to the pavement – drifts of paper and half-eaten burgers, bent bike wheels, empty TV casings. A thick smell oozed from the pile and seeped along the street, loamy and warm, like dry yeast. The smell itself wasn't unpleasant, except when you knew where it came from.

With a nervous glance back at my car – the only one on the street, and an open invitation to whoever lurked behind the blanked-off windows – I rang the bell. Sam put her hands into her pockets and rested her chin on my shoulder while we waited. I fidgeted uncomfortably, and she pulled away, which made me feel even more uncomfortable: I hadn't meant her to.

A young man answered the door, wearing a green satin bathrobe, pink fluffy slippers and mascara. He looked us up and down, then pouted and waited for us to speak.

'Hi. Could we see Karel? Karel Novak.'

'Well, it was hardly going to be Karel *Vorderman*, darling, was it?' The man rolled his eyes. 'Not in a dump like this,' he added, in case we hadn't got the point. He looked at us some more, stroking the lapel of his dressing-gown between forefinger and thumb.

'Is he here, then?' I asked.

Which got me another looking-over, but no reply.

'Who is it, Josephine?' someone called.

Josephine?

Boots thumped on wood flooring, then the tatty blue mat in the hall. They belonged to a tall man in a white T-shirt and black leather trousers with high cheekbones and an unshaven chin. He peered at us over 'Josephine's' shoulder.

'Is Karel in?' I asked the newcomer.

'Upstairs. Second floor,' he said. 'Still in bed, the lazy bitch.'

Josephine was still in the doorway, eyeing us. 'I'm not surprised he's in bed,' he said. 'He can't work, can he? Not with a face like that.' He winced, pursed his lips like he was sucking a lime, nodded in satisfaction.

'Come on, Joe. Let the nice people in,' the other man said caustically.

'Do this, do that,' Joe snapped, without taking his eyes off us. 'You've no sense of timing, have you, Michael? That's your problem.'

'Oh, shut up, you old tart. Get out of their way.' Michael stomped back along the hall and yelled, 'Second floor,' over his shoulder. Joe tossed his head in the direction of the stairs and sashayed down the hall after Michael.

'Models,' Sam muttered to me. 'They're bad enough on their own, but get two of them together . . .'

It hadn't occurred to me that they might be models, but thinking about it, they had both been quite good-looking, in a gaunt sort of way. Mind you, Joe's mascara was doing him no favours.

We trudged upstairs, our shoes slipping on the ratty hessian carpet, worn smooth where it wasn't worn through. On the second-floor landing there was a shabby bathroom and one closed door. We knocked. A muffled voice yelled at us to fuck off in an impenetrable accent. I walked in.

Clothes were everywhere in rumpled pools; they lapped over magazines, speakers and wires from a stereo I couldn't immediately see, empty tobacco pouches, crisps packets. I couldn't tell if the carpet was patterned because I couldn't see any of it. A large mirror balanced on top of a long low dresser. Photos – all of Karel – were slipped into the frame by their corners. At the mirror's base, a scattering of toiletries stood like offerings at a shrine. The bed was a double mattress on the floor, its smutted covers spilling into the general chaos. A bony foot protruded from the end.

Karel was lying in bed with an overflowing ashtray next to him, a magazine balanced on his knees, a television droning at him from the corner, his hairy chest and taut belly exposed to the world. Smoke from his roll-up curled up into his eye and the lid flickered. He wasn't happy to see us.

'Hello, Karel,' I said evenly.

He dragged on the butt, then picked it out of his mouth and tapped the ash on to the covers, a good six inches away from the ashtray. He blew a thin cloud of smoke at us.

He didn't look good. There was a large purple bump on his forehead and his nose was swollen, smeared across his face. One eye was flushed and bloodshot. The hand that wasn't holding the cigarette was in a sling. Adam had really done a number on him. All in all, Karel deserved credit for taking our entrance so coolly.

I walked further into the room and propped myself against the dresser. Sam came in behind me. He eyed up Sam in much the same way Joe had looked at me downstairs. He twitched the corners of his mouth and wrapped his lips sensually round a new roll-up.

'Want to know why we're here?' I snapped.

He dragged his attention back to me. The eyelid was flicking again.

'You tell me soon, so why I bother asking? Or maybe beat up me again, yes? For fun, maybe. For make you laugh, yes?' He turned a page and began to read his magazine.

'Karel, we're not here to beat anyone up,' Sam said patiently. 'And if Harry seems edgy, you'd best forgive him. *He* didn't beat you up.'

'No, he watch and think is funny,' Karel said.

He'd hit a nerve. I loathe violence, whether I'm the victim or not. I rose to my own defence. 'Listen, Karel, I'm sorry he hit you, but it's done,' I spat. 'And it wasn't me, and there's nothing I can do about it. For your information, he had every right to be pissed off with you – plus *you* were attacking *us*. So live with it. We're not here to trade insults.'

He sniffed haughtily and began work on his next roll-up, a fiddly job with just one hand.

'What for, then?'

'What?'

'He means, what are we here for?' Sam said.

I began to lose the plot. I don't think I'd expected it to be easy, but this was as daft as those 'talks about talks' politicians love so much. We were getting nowhere. I put my hand to my head and tried to calm down. Deep breath.

'OK. We're here because we want to know what happened to Verity. We think you may be able to help us.' I held up a hand to prevent Karel's anticipated reply. 'I'm not going to talk about the burglary. I know what I think, and I'm not changing it, but what we want to know is when you last saw her.'

Sam slipped past me and sat on the end of Karel's bed. He raised an eyebrow and his eyes livened briefly. Sam ignored this, but spoke kindly none the less. 'Karel, Verity told me weeks ago that you'd split up. But when you met Harry at the flat, you told him you were her boyfriend. Now, if you were seeing her just before she fell, we really would like to know about it.'

Karel made a noncommittal gesture, half jiggle, half shrug; a trickle of tobacco spilled from the end of his cigarette. He lit up, hunching towards the flame, then blowing the smoke straight at me with a satisfied sigh. I breathed as shallowly as I could.

'She was our friend, Karel,' Sam urged. 'You liked her too, I know you did. We just want to understand. If you *were* seeing her, then maybe you can help us understand why she did it.'

'I make lie,' Karel said smugly, as if that explained everything, as if it was as natural for him as being honest. There was no hint of shame. 'I go to flat, want see Verity. Maybe patch up, maybe she give some money – hey, maybe we fuck.' He spread his one good hand. 'Is for weeks, no money, no fuck since Verity.' Again, as normal as going to the shops. 'She not there, I go in, I wait. Then *this* guy come.' He measured me with his eyes, and sneered. 'This guy is so important, he say I no right be there. I think, Hey, fuck off, this guy is little nobody bastard. So I say am boyfriend, he is nobody. Of sudden he is crying!'

He mimed a trembling lip and wide eyes, then laughed at me. That made him cough; he winced at a twinge in his ribs, and I felt slightly better – but only slightly. I fidgeted. I was furious. I was embarrassed. He had been jerking my strings for a laugh. If I wasn't such a wimp, I'd have hit him. Instead, I was letting him jerk the strings all over again. I was glad he still hurt from Adam's attack. I hoped it stayed that way for a long time.

'Were you seeing her or not?' Sam was as patient as ever.

He pursed his lips and ash dribbled on to his chest. He flicked it on to the covers, squinting against the smoke.

'Not.'

'Since when?' I growled.

'Since weeks. Who cares? Ask her.' Nodding at Sam.

'Verity told me you'd split four or five weeks ago,' Sam said.

Karel fixed his gaze on her, intently. She idly returned it.

Whatever was happening between him and Sam, I didn't like it. 'So you didn't arrange to see her last Wednesday?' I asked sharply.

'Naaaa,' he replied, still leering at Sam. She looked away, but she stroked the edge of the bed, lightly back and forth. 'Last Wednesday was shoot,' he continued. 'Test shoot for big commercial. Arrive back London, maybe one in morning. I get job, good money.' He slapped his chest importantly – and winced. Then he growled, 'Some bastard smash face up and break rib, and agency they say, "Hey, no. No work now for weeks." Lucky for me, Joseph say no rent.'

'You can prove that, can you?' I asked caustically. I refused to be made to feel guilty about the job he'd lost – if he really had. If it hadn't been for Adam, the bastard would have attacked me. Now he was eyeing up my ... My what? *Girlfriend?* Uncomfortable thought. Ignore it. Call it pride, or arrogance or something: Sam should have been looking at me, not at him.

'Ask agency. Ask photographer.' Karel shrugged. He laid out the kit for another cigarette, tobacco pouch, Rizlas. The tobacco tumbled on to the bedclothes, and he pinched up each strand carefully.

Sam held out her hand and looked expectantly at me. It took me a moment, but then I twigged and handed her Verity's Filofax.

'Verity was seeing someone,' she said. 'Here. The day she jumped. And here, a week before. And another, two days before that.'

He took the Filofax and studied it with the eye that wasn't full of smoke. Then he went through stabbing at each entry with a forefinger. 'This Wednesday was test shoot. This one, Bristol for party – ask Michael. This one, OK was here alone, so no proof, but not me. This one ... don't know.' He ran rapidly back through the weeks then stopped triumphantly on a page. 'Ha! Here. Says K. K is for Karel, yes? Restaurant, then film. I remember. I am K. Other person is no letter. Also, why I go ...' he flicked back to more recent times '... Granada Service, A4? I want Verity, she live Battersea.'

That was hard to argue with. Also, if he could prove where he was the day Verity jumped, then that was that. Except for one other thing. I tried to keep my voice casual, because if he sensed the venom he wouldn't reply. 'So why did you do it, then, Karel?' I asked. 'How much did you get for the TV and stuff? Why piss on the floor and rip things up?'

Strangely, Karel was unfazed. He replied as calmly as ever –

directly to Sam, of course. 'This is burglary, yes? I not touch. I take money sometimes. Like when this guy come –' he nodded towards me '– I take money for making him angry. But break in? Hard work, no point.'

'Of course you did it,' I snapped. 'The doors were unlocked – *unlocked*, understand? The house door *and* the one to her flat. Now, who do *you* know who had the keys?' I injected as much savagery into the sarcasm as I could. 'Well, there's Verity ... Couldn't have been her, she's in intensive bloody care. Oh, and there's *you*.'

He shook his head happily. At Sam.

'Not. Not have key.'

'You bloody do!' I shouted. 'You showed me.'

'Hey, Sam, you *like* this guy?' Karel opened his mouth in mock-shock. Sam's eyes widened subtly and she moved the faintest fraction towards him.

He grinned toothily round his cigarette. 'Friday, after Bastard Face say go from flat, I see this guy. In street, in car,' Karel said. To Sam. He nodded vigorously. 'He call over, hey, you got key? I say yes. He say, is nice flat? I say yes.' He beamed. 'Man say, hey, fifty quids for key.' He settled back with a satisfied sigh.

'You sold the key,' Sam said flatly.

Karel blew smoke at the ceiling. 'Fifty quids.' He grinned fruitily at Sam. He kissed two fingers, and blew across them in her direction. She slid a little further up the bed towards him. I might as well not have been there.

'So, what did he look like?' Her eyes were wide. Her face glowed with fascination. Her gaze was locked on him. 'What car was he in, did you notice?'

'Small guy,' Karel said airily. His roll-up had gone out with less than an inch left. He snapped his lighter at it – quickly, so as not to burn his nose. 'Yellow hair, smaller maybe even than Bastard Face. And thin, thin, thin. Car was small also. Old. Ford, maybe. Beige. Not cool.' He laughed.

'Is that it?' I growled. 'That's all you remember?'

Karel glanced at me, then turned back to Sam. 'Hey, Sam, you very sexy girl, you know. I tell you before, I very great lover. Great body, last long time. Do many times – all night, I think. Why you stay with this guy? You come with me. Hey, now maybe?' He eased the covers open beside him and favoured her with a wicked smile.

She rolled her lips together. 'I'd rather screw a slug,' she said sweetly.

Home – at Sam's – she grabbed me and nibbled my neck, and mumbled something about unfinished business. And I stood, wooden and unresponsive, wondering who I was supposed to be.

Her familiarity with Karel had left me uncomfortable. I knew that she'd been putting on an act, flirting with him to encourage him to talk to her. But jealousy wasn't the real reason for my discomfort: it was just the excuse. The truth was, I wanted to put some distance between myself and Sam, but I couldn't admit why, to myself or to her; there was only so much pain I could bear. Today I can talk about it – just barely; but back in the days immediately after Verity's fall, how could I have begun to explain to Sam that, even though what was sustaining me was her warmth and support, being with her also forced me to confront feelings I had successfully buried for decades? I needed Sam, but I also needed our relationship to have no meaning – and that was impossible, because even if this *was* only a casual fling, every touch and kiss was still an act of betrayal. I still felt I was being unfaithful.

Eventually Sam gave up trying to kiss me. She studied me from a few paces away; I studied the carpet, furiously. I had no idea what to say, and she seemed content to let my silence do the talking. After a while she nodded, as though I had finally made a point that made sense to her.

She began tidying her flat. Loudly. As though I was not there.

Later we sat opposite each other with cups of tea in front of us, unnoticed. I was tired. More than anything I wanted to go to bed. On my own. To sleep.

I tried to concentrate on my tea. I don't really like tea.

As I left, we kissed – uncomfortably – and Sam smiled at me. She pulled away from me and folded her arms. She stood with her legs neatly together, suddenly self-contained and rather fragile. She looked sad. It was another unwanted burden.

'Off you go, then,' she said quietly.

'Look, Sam—'

'Will I see you this evening?'

'I haven't ... I'll have to see ...'

''Bye, then.' She blew me a kiss, and turned away.

The drive back to my own flat was miserable. I could see what I was doing, and I wasn't proud of it. For a mile or so, I tried to justify it as an understandable insecurity about Sam and Karel, but that was so obviously unlikely that I found I couldn't even pretend.

Betrayal: Adam seeing Verity; Karel selling the key to her flat (why? who to?); Gabriel's face at Verity's childhood window ... Me sleeping with Sam while Verity stared at an empty wall – the biggest betrayal of them all.

Then I was home. I scooped up the post in the hallway, and trudged upstairs to my flat, opening the first letter as I went. It was a mortgage statement. Another: credit-card offer from some obscure bank. Another: this one was a duplicate of Verity's phone bill, one of the documents that had been burned in the break-in and I'd had to track down the supplier and request copies.

And Verity's phone bill held a surprise for me. Because the last person Verity had ever called from her flat had been Adam.

twenty-four

You find the years have passed. You find that you have found a way.

For me, rejection became a part of life; for Verity, rebellion did. The rest of our school years were spent in the same ritual dance – she initiating, drawing us together, the gathering intimacy, then withdrawal. So eventually I found a distance from her, close enough for warmth, not so close that it hurt, and I stayed there: good old dependable Harry, around when he's needed, but always knowing when to make himself scarce.

'Coming out tonight, Harry?'

Someone pressed behind me and put their hands over my eyes. Sweet cool breath against my neck, Wrigley's and woodscent. She released me. She looked up at me – though only slightly, because she had grown far more than I in the last two years. Her smile was white-toothed, soft-lipped; her eyes large and alive, her skirt too short, her breath a little too rapid. Grey school jumper, slack-knotted tie, nylon shirt, soft warm breasts. The skin on her knees was mottled with the cold, red and olive. She stood close and lifted her face towards me.

'We're going down the Cavern. Coming?'

The Cavern was a nightclub – we called them discos back in the dark days of the early eighties. I wasn't the hippest of fifteen-year-olds. I preferred the dim light of the darkroom to the disco. She tutted at my obvious reluctance. 'Oh, come on, Harry, it's brilliant, you'll love it. See you outside Central Library at ten. We'll wait till quarter past.'

She skipped away from me, blew a kiss, twirled towards a group of sixth-formers on the far side of the playground, all of them boys. 'Be there, Harry,' she sang over her shoulder.

The boys widened their circle to accommodate her, their postures shifting enough to show interest, not enough to be uncool. She swung on the nearest boy's arm as she talked to them, and they all crushed a little closer.

'Hey Verity! Show us your knickers, girl!' Oba yelled from the climbing frame. She glanced over her shoulder and flicked two fingers at him. One of the boys she was with ran a few steps towards the gang, threatening, and they clattered from the climbing frame in all directions. Verity grabbed his arm and pulled him closer to her, hips swaying towards her newest knight.

She was fourteen.

It was freezing. I hugged my arms for warmth. The clock in the entrance hall said twenty-five past one. Five minutes to lessons, but I had a study period. The lights in the classrooms were warm and bright. A few of the more serious-minded children were already inside, making sure of good desks, propping books open, setting pens and rubbers in line. I headed round the back, towards the darkroom, wondering if she would notice me going.

Of course I would go, I would be there at ten. But, then, she knew that. It was part of the ritual.

I was there at nine fifty, in my best (dull) finery, my ears burning from the cold cycle ride to get there, and from the row I'd had with Mum to be allowed out. Waiting on the frozen concrete benches opposite Central Library, hugging my numb hands between my knees, I didn't have a coat – what the hell do you do with an anorak at a disco?

I was there at ten thirty, when she turned up with her best mate Gail, plus two other girls from her class and a couple of rough-looking blokes, shaven-headed, in their early twenties. The girls clung together, giggling. They wobbled unsteadily across the road.

'Harry!' Verity yelled raucously, and fell about laughing. Doubled over, she beckoned for me to come over. I felt painfully self-conscious. They were dressed to the nines, I was wearing the corduroy 'best' trousers Mum had bought me.

'Looking good, Harry,' Gail said, when they had calmed down enough – and they both wailed hysterically again.

I stood, mute and unsure, until Verity hugged me sloppily. I almost toppled as she slumped on me. I caught the sharp smell of cider. The two rough-necks prowled uneasily about the periphery, their eyes scanning the shadows, necks craned.

We poured into the club past two unconvinced-looking bouncers. One of them muttered, 'Fuckin' kiddies' night.' Verity was clinging to me, giggling. Sound and smoke and light poured out.

It was early, and the disco was almost empty. Red and green light pulsed rhythmically on the tiny dance-floor. The bright lights and deep shadows made it seem far larger than it was. Two girls in white leather trousers were dancing unenthusiastically to 'Tainted Love'. They were using a rhythm that had nothing to do with the music, curling around each other at a distance, arms rising for a few swaying beats, then falling again, each instep tapped against the other in turn. A handful of much older men cruised the room's perimeter.

We grabbed an alcove. Verity did the introductions. She couldn't remember the two men's names, and none of us heard what she was saying anyway. We were under-age, so Verity persuaded one of the men to get the drinks. He was clearly not best pleased that he had to include me in the round. The other sat on one end of the curved bench, his eyes flicking around the room. The drinks arrived, and we sipped and sat looking at the two girls gyrating, wrapped in angry sound. The lager was watery, and dry-ice fumes burned my nose and tongue.

Verity tugged at my arm. She mouthed something at me: I couldn't hear her, but I knew what she meant. Reluctantly I let her lead me on to the dance-floor. I shifted uneasily from side to side, dazed by sound, and Verity danced for both of us. Gail brought one of the men out to dance with her, and with three couples on the floor it seemed a little less strange. Verity grabbed both my hands and swung them from side to side, singing the words of whatever the song was, pulling me along with her, smiling into my face. I sang back – kind of – still moving awkwardly, but moving, at least, following her lead.

I don't remember the songs, only their effect. It's so easy to stereotype a period: the early eighties, that would be disco, or ska, or New Romantic, or reggae, but actually it was all of those, and loads of other stuff too – Bucks Fizz, Chas and Dave, Abba, the

Boomtown Rats, 'Remember You're a Womble' – but in recollection, the music all compresses to a single feeling, a time and a place. I remember endless discos from my teenage years. I patrolled the edges of countless rooms, afraid to stay still in case it showed that I was alone, watching the strange rituals of the dance, unsure even how to begin. Verity was trying to pull me into a world where she was someone else. I allowed myself to be pulled.

We danced. And soon enough, as the floor filled, a ginger-haired boy began to dance around us. She opened our circle of two to admit him, and then we were three. And then they were two. I returned to the smoky alcove, now the sole custodian of slopped drinks, purses and coats.

A slow track came on, and the groups and singles filtered away to their tables, leaving pairs of strangers eyeing each other uncertainly. Some slipped into a clinch, others not. Gail clamped her man firmly to her and went straight for the snog. The other man who had been with Verity and Gail had disappeared. Her other two friends were at another table, talking to a group of three men. Verity shrugged and smiled at Ginger, and he gave her a philosophical grimace. She came and flopped next to me. I smiled at her, and she clutched my arm and smiled back.

She drained her second Malibu. I went to buy her another and amazingly, the barman served me without a word. When I got back, Ginger was leaning over her, talking. I nudged him aside to pass the drink, and he stood back, fidgeting. As I sat next to her, Verity tweaked her eyebrows at him and grinned. He grinned back, and disappeared into the thickening crowd. She shuffled closer to me and leaned across to chink her glass, inaudibly, against mine on the table. I chinked back, pushing closer to her in turn, and swigged.

People swayed in silhouette, hair fringed with slowly cycling colour: red, green, blue, yellow, red. The dry-ice machine roared, clouds of smoke rolled out across the floor, swirling round the dancers' feet.

Later, I sat with my second water-flavoured pint and watched them kiss. They were perched on a brass rail that ringed part of the dance-floor, craning towards each other, necks extended, bodies not yet touching. She groped for his hand and planted it on her waist. Without unlocking their lips, he manoeuvred round to stand in front of her and squashed himself against her, his thigh between hers, her throat arched up to meet his mouth. His hands running down her sides, stroking up, her skirt riding higher. Lights pulsing, music pumping, each thick beat harder and more forceful than the one before.

Later, she came over for her coat, trailing him behind her on a fingertip. She mouthed, 'See ya, gorgeous,' wrinkled her nose confidently, and winked. They drifted together towards the exit.

I waited, so that I wouldn't see them again outside. The music was a chant: *Go, Harry, leave, Harry, go, Harry, now – go now, Harry, leave, Harry, now, now, now.* I left.

The air was sharp and still. The concrete buildings shone in the orange streetlight. I walked towards the bike racks. My ears were ringing in a suddenly silent world.

Two in the morning.

They were there, on a low wall by the bikes. She was on his lap, one arm round his neck, the other hand drifting over his chest, with her fingers poking through the gaps in his shirt. One of his hands was on her waist, the other was up her skirt. Her eyes were closed, his open. He saw me, and hitched his hand higher on her thigh. She moaned through his mouth, urged herself towards him. His gaze moved away from me, unconcerned.

I bent to unlock my bike.

'Harry!'

She unwound herself from Ginger, straightened her skirt and tottered over to me. 'You going, Harry?'

I could barely hear her. My head still sang in time to the music – *Go, Harry, go, Harry, now, go now.* I nodded and bent back to the rusted lock. The key snagged in it. I jerked it savagely.

She stood, uncertain, tight to herself and shivering. I put my leg over the bike and flicked the pedal into position.

'Thanks for coming,' she muttered, not looking at me.

I hefted my weight on to the pedal.

'Hug,' she blurted suddenly, and held out her arms.

Stiffly, we hugged, her yielding towards me, me astride my bike. She tilted up her face and reached for my mouth. I pulled back, turning it into a kind of peck.

Not too close, Harry.

Never too close.

213

'I love you, Harry,' she said drowsily. Drunkenly. 'You're a good mate.' She nestled her cheek on my collarbone.

'Verity? Come home?'

With a slow effort, she straightened and took a step back. She sniffed hard, and her gaze seemed to clear. 'Wassa time?'

'Two.'

'Be along in a mo.' She nodded sagely.

She staggered back to Ginger and sat astride him again, sank her head towards him, closing her eyes. I watched for long enough to know that she wasn't coming.

I cycled home in the cold moonlight, the wheels of my bike humming on the silent streets. In north Oxford, I ducked left on a whim and followed the canal. I could barely make out the path, a dark gravel strip between the dark water and the darker verge.

Home, I manoeuvred my bike through the narrow gate and round the side of the house, quietly cursing the shrubbery and my still-ringing ears. I caught a movement and looked up. Lit by the moon through a window, Gabriel's face was flat shapes and dark gashes. He let the curtain drop, and the windows became as lifeless and blank as they had been when I arrived. Verity's curtains were open, the room still in darkness. Somewhere in there was her bed, her clothes, mirrors, hairbrushes and perfume.

Still looking up, my face offered to the moon, I tripped over a tussock and fell flat on the grass. It was wet, it tickled my face, it was embarrassing.

And I wished she had been there with me. To laugh.

twenty-five

One afternoon a week, Adam played squash.

I walked along the viewing gallery. The air smelt of sweat and hot rubber. The whipcrack of ball and racquet echoed off the walls. Adam was playing on the last court of five, on his own, hitting the ball in an easy rhythm from backhand to forehand, and back again. I watched him for several minutes before a particularly wild slice dropped the ball limply at the front of the court. He scooped it up, and as he turned he saw me. 'Harry! How are you? Come on down.'

When I opened the door to the court, he was playing again. He deftly caught the ball on his racquet.

'Fancy a game?' He jerked his head towards where his kit-bag was tucked away. There was a second racquet, with a towel and his glasses on top of it. I shook my head. 'Mind if I carry on?'

He settled back into his rhythm, step–lean–hit–return, step–lean––hit–return . . . A steady beat of pneumatic impacts.

'Glad to see you, actually . . .' *thwack* '. . . been thinking of you . . .' *thwack* '. . . this isn't social, I take it?'

I had to time my reply to his strokes. Between smash and bounce, I said, 'There's something I need to ask you.'

'Yes?' He grunted each time he hit the ball. His face was slick with sweat and his shirt was sticking to him.

'About Verity.'

'Well, *that*'s a surprise.'

'Oh, fuck's sake, Adam . . .'

'All right, Harry. Chill. I care too, remember.'

Chill – whack. I care – whack.

'Actually, that's why I want to talk to you.'

The ball bounced past him and rolled slackly to a halt near the back wall. He stared at me, breathing hard, his eyes wide.

'Shoot,' he said cautiously.

I stayed against the wall, but it was a struggle not to pace up and down or wave my hands around.

'You stopped seeing her months ago, yes? Cut her dead. Your words.'

'I wish you'd— Oh, forget it. Yes. Yes, I did.'

I was back in the movies. I asked it casually, the confidently dropped bombshell. 'So why was she still ringing you?'

Only Adam didn't stick to the script. He should have been defensive, or shocked, he should have broken down. But all he did was nod, equally casually. 'She rang all the time.'

I was nonplussed. 'But you said . . .'

'I didn't say *anything*. I told you when I finished with her, that's all.'

I started to get angry. Back on script. 'You lied, Adam!' Well, not angry as such: more crabby. Still, I can dream, can't I?

Adam put his racquet down carefully. He started doing sit-ups.

'Where's . . .' *oof* '. . . this . . .' *oof* . . . coming from, chum?'

'What I want, *chum*, is the truth.' I handed him the letter I had received that morning.

Verity's phone bill, updated to the day she fell. There were calls to several numbers I recognised: me, Sam, the studio and Adam, at home and on his mobile. Well, fine, I had thought, I may not like it, but they *were* seeing each other. Then I had looked at the dates. The calls continued right through the three-month period of the bill; there was at least one a week, often many more. The last call – the one that had caught my attention – was on the morning of the day she fell and had lasted nearly forty minutes. Adam was the last person Verity had ever called.

He stopped doing sit-ups and studied the bill, squinting without his glasses. Then he handed it back to me, and sat examining his squash racquet. 'Oh, God . . .' He rubbed his face.

'Adam, you *lied*! *Again*!' I couldn't quite believe how cool he was being.

He shook his head behind his hands, then dragged his gaze up to meet mine. 'Yes, I did, Harry. I lied. Again. I lied. Oh, fuck fitness, I'll buy you lunch.' He stood, wincing at the effort.

I waited for him in the club lobby, sipping a revolting espresso, and wondering what he would tell me this time that I could possibly believe.

'The thing is . . .' Adam said, between mouthfuls of steak '. . . I love Sarah. That's the thing to remember. I mean, I really do *love* her.'

I shoved a couple of herby sausages around my plate, in a soup of gravy and mash.

He watched me, chewing. 'I didn't know what to do, Harry,' he said. 'She just kept calling. And I had finished with her, months ago. It was supposed to be fun, just fun.' He waved his fork about, as though he could describe something with it. Then he was still, suddenly, downcast. 'You've no idea, Harry. She was ringing my mobile five, six times a day. Rang Rita at the office endlessly. Then she threatened me. Said she'd tell Sarah it was still going on.' He sniffed reflectively. 'I told her it was definitely over, she could say what she wanted.'

Adam gave up on his steak, and took a slug of wine. He finished the glass in two swigs, and poured himself more. He offered me a refill and I shook my head – I was getting wiser, belatedly.

'Anyway. She went ahead and did it. She made sure Sarah knew. Started ringing me at home when she knew I wasn't there. Wouldn't leave a name or a message. Sarah guessed who it was, of course.'

His glass was empty again. He cupped and swirled it. A meniscus of wine spread around the inside, thinner and thinner. He sucked at his lips pensively. 'Well,' he muttered to himself, 'there you go.'

I'd hardly said a word since the squash court. I wasn't about to start now.

Adam prodded his steak unenthusiastically. My bangers and mash were cold. He waved at the waitress for another bottle of wine, looking at me speculatively, but I wasn't going there, not again. He ordered a bottle anyway, and set about another full glass.

'But excuses don't matter, do they?' he continued. 'The point is, I lied. It was easier to say I wasn't speaking to Verity than it was to explain why I still *was*. She was getting so . . . *intense*.'

He looked at me earnestly, his eyes magnified through his glasses, his pupils wide. They were slightly misty, raw from the wine. Whatever he read in my face, it disappointed him. He dropped his head into his hands and rubbed savagely, before hauling himself upright again with a huge effort.

He filled my glass, and drained his own. I made a mental note just to leave the glass alone: if it was already full, he couldn't top it up. The waitress collected my untouched sausages and what remained of his steak. She put dessert menus in front of us, and we ignored them. Adam drew a pattern on the tablecloth over and over with a butter-knife, which she had forgotten to clear. 'I need your help, Harry,' he said. 'I don't deserve it. I don't even know how to ask for it any more.'

'Oh, *do* you?' I said – more gently than I had intended. I knew I shouldn't, but I felt sorry for him, damn him. He did need me, I could see it in him: not so much to talk, but to sit and watch a sunset, or the traffic streaming along the Oxford ring-road, or the foam swirling in the river, at once caught and adrift. And for all his deceits, I needed him too.

'Sarah wants to leave me,' he said bleakly. He glanced at me, then dropped his eyes to the tablecloth again. The butter-knife traced an endless loop, round and round and round. 'Those phone calls . . . Verity really went for it. She was ringing Sarah all the time. Screaming at her, all sorts of stuff – pretty damned explicit, some of it. Scary, too.'

He stared out of the window, blankly, before dragging his attention back. His eyes were watery. 'We'd agreed it was just a fling, Harry. I swear. But when I ended it, she clung on.' He paused. 'And now Sarah's hardly talking to me. And when she does, she just screams at me. Throws things. A couple of nights ago she locked me out and I had to go and find a hotel.' He pinched the bridge of his nose, squeezed his eyes shut.

The waitress walked over. She opened her mouth to ask if we wanted dessert. I caught her eye in time, and mouthed, 'Bill, please.' When she came back with it, Adam didn't even notice. He traced a finger round the base of his glass, lips pursed. 'She scares me, you know. She's not in control any more. She's sobbing one minute, violent the next. You should have seen our last row. She actually threw a knife at me, can you believe that?'

He chuckled sorrowfully. He rolled up his sleeve and showed me a line of bruises on his forearm.

'We're eating off plastic these days,' he muttered. 'She's smashed all the crockery. But the worst is, after the knife I hit her back. I just couldn't make her listen, and she wasn't stopping, and . . . I *hit* her, Harry.'

I opened my mouth to tell him I understood, that I had seen first hand what Sarah was capable of – but I caught myself in time: I had promised her. Let others do the betraying: I would be true to my word.

Adam saw straight through me. He laughed softly. 'I do know you went to see her, Harry. She told me. Actually, you're her latest weapon.' His face contorted as he imitated her. '*Harry*'s got the decency to apologise, Harry's a *gentleman*, I bet *Harry*'s not screwing other women . . .' He laughed bitterly.

More betrayal, then: from Sarah this time. But, then, hadn't I betrayed Adam by going to see her in the first place? And hadn't that been because Adam had lied to me? None of us were angels.

'Yeah.' Adam sniffed. 'Enough said. Forget it. Still, don't go and see her again, Harry. Please. Things are fragile enough without other people sticking their oar in.'

He reached for the bill, waving away my offer to split it, and we left.

We shared the silence, sitting on a bench in the park and watching the world. A group of boys were playing a loose game of cricket, still in their school uniforms, ties loosened and shirt buttons undone.

'I'm scared, Harry.' Adam laughed self-consciously. 'She could kill me, Harry. I mean it.' Adam's tone was reflective: sad. 'If she doesn't do it with the knife, she'll do it in the divorce courts. She's going to rip me to shreds.'

I thought of her foot crunching down on shattered crockery. Her finger pressing every knot of wood on the tabletop. Her distant, nervous eyes. Her voice: *You realise that you're really, really angry . . .*

The boys gave up playing cricket and began to toss the ball to each other. The aim was to throw it so hard and low that the other boy couldn't possibly catch it. The game was leisurely, brutal, slow and savage.

'What do you want, Adam?' I asked, gently. The truth is, I don't find it easy to stay angry for very long. I felt sorry for him.

'I want her back, Harry.' He said it heavily. 'I want the way we were. The real Sarah. The one who doesn't throw knives.' He raised a hand to stop my obvious thought. 'I know. My fault for screwing Verity.'

Screwing. An ugly word. But, then, why should the truth be pretty?

'True,' I said.

'Yeah, true. And I shouldn't have lied.' He blinked hard, and sighed. 'I need you, Harry. I need *this*.' He was waving his hand vaguely between us. 'The way we used to be. No questions, no lies, no mysteries. I fucked up, Harry. I admit it. But I still need you.'

It's hard to hate a person you've known for twenty years. Filmy eyes, puffy face, serious mouth, jaw set. I had never seen so much of Adam before. A single mistake had shot cracks through everything that mattered to him. And I wondered: *Could I?* Could I just put it all behind us, start again?

He searched my eyes, knitted his eyebrows. 'Never again, Harry,' he said. 'No more lies, no more fuck-ups. I swear.' He sniffed another rich lungful, the scent of trees and grass. 'And, Harry?' He squatted in front of me and peered earnestly into my eyes. 'Thanks.'

We got a taxi to the Ship, a pub by Wandsworth Bridge, and bagged an outside table. The view was a grey-painted derrick and a stretch of stagnant mud, but neither of us cared. The wind was blowing onshore, bringing the clammy scent of ooze. The wooden all-in-one table and bench rocked on the uneven paving, and spilled our drinks. The sky was big and clear and the blue was softening into evening.

'Aren't you supposed to be at work?' I slurred.

'Fuck 'em.' Adam raised his glass and grinned. I grabbed at mine to prevent it spilling when he set his down.

A woman walked past, carrying drinks to another table. He swivelled to watch.

'Hmmm. There you are, *much* more interesting than work. Which reminds me. You were saying in the taxi. Sam Someone. Give.'

'She's Verity's partner,' I said defensively. 'I like her.'

'Ye-e-e-s?'

I tried for a shrug and my elbow slipped off the table. Adam spluttered into his pint.

'Well, *I* don't know, do I?' I grumbled.

Adam wagged a finger at me while he swallowed. 'But you do like her.'

'Suppose so.'

'Well, then.'

He seemed to think he'd proved something; and once my slow thoughts had caught up with the conversation I realised that, in a way, he had. If I liked her, then I liked her. Nothing more, nothing less. We were all busy doing exactly what we want to do, the trick was just to let it happen.

He was looking at me, his expression somewhere between amusement and sorrow. 'Are we friends again, Harry?'

I thought about it for a beat or two. Then I nodded fuzzily. 'Sort of.' I buried my face in my pint.

We sat relishing the low sunshine, the leggy women in short skirts at a neighbouring tables, the distant buzz of traffic, the barges trudging up the river.

'What do I do, Harry? What can I do?' Adam said wretchedly.

'I think you should get out of there.' Adam looked puzzled. 'She's dangerous,' I pointed out.

A barge's horn blared out across the river, then the boat emerged from the bridge's arches, shoving a hump of foaming water ahead of it. The growl of its motor was eerily close across the flat water.

Adam gazed at it as he spoke. 'Do you know what she did last Monday, Harry? She cut out the crotch of every pair of trousers in my wardrobe. She didn't even tell me. I only found out the next morning when I went to put some on. When I confronted her, she didn't say anything, she just went and got the scissors and started on my shirts. I got out, sharpish. I thought she'd stab me with the bloody things if I stayed.'

'Stay at mine,' I offered, hoping he would refuse. I wasn't remotely ready for him to do that. In fact, I was still uncertain how far we could rebuild our friendship, but Adam was in desperate circumstances. I would have made the same offer to anyone in trouble – at least, that's what I told myself.

Adam hunched helplessly, watching the shifting pattern of oily water where the barge had been. 'If I leave her, it's all over. She'll change the locks, hire thugs to keep me away, take out an exclusion order. Seriously, Harry. She'll run me down in the car or something. All I can do is stay there, prove that I love her by sticking with her. Maybe she'll come round.'

'Or maybe she'll kill you.'

He laughed bitterly. 'Yeah. Maybe.'

Another barge. Its wake rippled outwards and licked at the grey mud at the base of the river wall.

'It wasn't Karel who broke in, Ads,' I said eventually.

'Huh?'

'Verity's flat. Karel didn't do it. He sold the key to someone.'

Adam snorted out half a mouthful of beer. '*Sold* it?'

I told him about my visit to Karel, and the man in the beige Ford.

'Any idea who?' he asked. 'Doesn't sound much like a burglar, though, does it, buying a key? What's the point? They'd just break in, surely. Sounds more like one of those private-eye types. They've got a thing about brown cars. I ought to know, Sarah hired enough of the buggers.' He rolled his eyes up to the sky, and banged his head softly on the edge of the table, one, two, three. 'What am I doing, Harry? She's killing me, I swear.' He slumped pathetically, his head on the table.

And while I watched him, a thought crawled slowly across my befuddled brain – something to do with hiring private eyes, and Sarah's casual pleasure when I told her of Verity's fall, and *you realise you're really angry* . . .

My mouth slackened, and my eyes glazed. Belatedly, because my brain and body weren't as well connected as they should have been, I jerked bolt upright. Suddenly, though, I felt very sober indeed. 'Adam?'

He looked up at me, straightened himself uncertainly. 'What?'

I picked my way through the words carefully. 'Where was Sarah the day Verity fell?'

He stared at me. His mouth drooped slowly into an ill-concealed gape. 'She – where—' He blinked hard. 'She was – I don't – You're not thinking—' His eyes widened. 'I have no idea where she was,' he said faintly.

I pictured Sarah as I had last seen her – eyes calm, voice tightly controlled, crushing shards of china underfoot, smears of blood across her perfect terracotta floor.

Adam, mouth open, must have been having similar visions. 'Oh, fuck,' he said. 'Harry, what are we going to do?'

I gazed back at him. I had no answers at all.

twenty-six

Time passes.
Even when each second is an intolerable thud of despera-
tion, tension, anticipation, even then time passes.
Adam had promised he would talk with Sarah the next morning:
we agreed that we couldn't gauge what to do next until we knew
her reaction. Adam swore that, although he had kept in touch with
Verity, the last time he had spoken to her was two weeks before she
fell. That meant the calls Verity had made to his house had to have
been to Sarah – and some of them had lasted half an hour or longer.
What had they said to each other? What had Sarah threatened?
Where had she been that day? If Sarah frightened Adam, I didn't
want to think what she might have been capable of doing to Verity.

I waited. Adam didn't call.

I saw Sam, but not often and not for long. We met, shared coffee,
then went our ways. One night, two days after seeing Adam, we
made love – or tried to: I couldn't forget myself enough even to kiss
her properly, let alone keep an erection. After ten agonising
minutes, we flopped apart awkwardly and stared at the ceiling.
Shortly after, I kissed her cheek absently, then left.

Time passes, whether you want it to or not. And hopes and fears
eat at you. You imagine things. Doubts itch at your mind. You long
for something to happen.

And on the third day, something did. My mother rang and told
me that, the day before, Gabriel had killed himself.

There was no reply from Adam. Rita thought he must be in court;
his chambers thought he must be at the town hall. His mobile went

unanswered. I didn't have the energy to worry about him, I was too panicked and frustrated.

Gabriel had killed himself. Shock is a confusing state. I was bewildered. Gabriel, dead. Suicide.

I rang Sam. I think I cried on the phone. I just wanted it all to stop. I wanted the world to go away, I wanted nothing to happen, I wanted peace. I also wanted someone there. Sam came over, I didn't even have to ask. She made coffee, persuaded me to sit down and stop pacing the flat. She covered my hand with hers, and said, 'Tell me.'

So I told her. She said nothing, just watched me patiently.

I even told her about my half-confrontation with Gabriel, the disturbing suspicions it had left me with: childhood trauma . . . a pale face watching, half hidden behind a curtain . . . Verity, nervous, 'Why should I trust you?' And it was only then, hearing myself talk, with the thoughts and horrors tumbling out of me, and with Sam staring wisely at me over her coffee, that I began to see a new shape in the jumbled scraps of what I knew.

There would never be proof, not now. Verity could never tell. I jumped up and started pacing again, ignoring Sam. Because, proof or not, it all connected, it made sense, and to contemplate it was agony.

'I need to see someone,' I snapped. 'Sorry.'

'Harry?' Sam's expression was somewhere between patience and confusion. As I left, I shook my head at her. I didn't want to explain myself. I was thinking about proof.

I came to my senses before I had even reached Kate Fullerton's address. I rang Sam on her mobile to apologise. There was no answer. I mumbled my apology – unconvincingly, I suspect – explained where I was going and why, and rang off.

I pressed the bell outside Kate's flat. After twenty seconds with no answer, I pressed it again, a long, sustained buzz. Her voice answered tinnily.

'It's Harry Waddell,' I called, fighting the traffic roar. 'Verity Hadley's friend. I need to see you.'

There was a long pause before she answered. 'Harry, I've got clients all day.'

'It's urgent.'

Another pause. Then, curtly, 'Wait in the hall.' The door-release buzzed harshly, and I pushed in.

When I reached her floor, her door was locked. I waited five minutes before impatience got the better of me, and I knocked. There was no reply, so I knocked again. The door ripped open almost immediately. Kate's eyes were like razors. 'Either you wait there without knocking, Harry, or I refuse to talk to you at all. *Grow up.*' She hissed the words, then snapped the door closed again. I watched it until I was certain it wasn't going to open, then I slumped down and squatted against a wall to wait.

It was twenty minutes before a gathering buzz of conversation roused me. The door opened, and a man ushered himself out, calling, 'Thanks,' back into the flat in a disconcertingly cheerful tone. He winked at me as he passed. Kate favoured me with a sour glare, and led the way to the sitting room.

'You've got five minutes, Harry,' she said sternly. 'My next client is due.'

I plunged straight in. 'Gabriel's dead. Verity's father. Killed himself.'

Kate raised an eyebrow.

I nodded eagerly. 'I saw him the other day. Told him Verity had been seeing you, about having traumas as a child. And he went so quiet. It was scary, really it was. And now he's killed himself and—'

I was aware that I was gabbling, and I didn't care. It was all so horrifying, so obviously *true*.

Gabriel had been abusing her . . . Maybe . . . Perhaps. Probably. It was a notion, not a certainty – talking to Kate was the only way I would ever find out. But, as I babbled on, it all seemed to gel. As I spoke, my questions were replaced by certainties. It all made such perfect sense.

'Harry, *calm*! Sit down.'

I did so, fidgeting. Kate sighed heavily. She let the silence grow, then continued in a low voice that I found rather intimidating. 'Do you have *any* idea how ridiculous this little fantasy of yours is, Harry? And how destructive? I'm surprised that young lady you were with let you go so far off the rails. She seemed quite sensible.'

'Sam. Didn't tell her,' I muttered sullenly. I felt like a schoolboy again, but I still thought I was right – at least, until she spoke again.

Her face was white, her jaw set tight. Belatedly, I saw that she wasn't playing the schoolmistress, she was genuinely angry. 'I'm about to break one of the most cardinal rules of my profession now, Harry. I'm going to break client confidentiality. Thanks to your . . .' she struggled to find a word with enough venom, then spat it at me '. . . *absurd* concoctions, I suspect telling you more is the only way to limit the damage. So I'll tell you.'

She hunched forwards in her chair. Her eyes were like dark dewy marble, strangely mild, but her stare was piercing. 'We explored the possibility that Verity was abused, Harry. We were still exploring it. Verity was a fragile soul, and her love-life left a lot to be desired. As I said last time, she was self-destructive. And, yes, those can, rarely, be signs of an abusive past. We had only just started on the hypnotherapy and regression work, but it was immediately obvious that if she had been abused, her father most certainly had nothing to do with it. She trusted him absolutely. She ran to him if she needed comfort. He went to extraordinary lengths to make sure she was happy and secure after her mum died. I'm not saying he was perfect. I think he was probably over-protective, but that's understandable. He smacked her if she stepped out of line, but this was twenty years ago, and people did smack their children. There were no dominance games going on, though. There was no hint that he was getting any gratification out of it.

'Children can construct extraordinarily vicious fantasies about their parents, Harry. Verity was no exception. She certainly resented the control he exerted over her, but there was no fear or guilt in it. I never detected the slightest sign that Verity dreaded punishment particularly, or felt dirtied by him in any way. Punishment for her was the usual mixture of outrage and inconvenience.'

Kate shot me one last stare. 'There's no sign that Gabriel abused Verity, Harry. And the reason that there's no sign is because he didn't.'

I bit my lip, picked at my fingers, shifted uneasily. There was no uncertainty in Kate's tone, no room for doubt.

'And before you start feeling sorry for yourself, or claiming that he killed himself because you mentioned childhood traumas,' she said tartly, 'give the poor man some credit. I'm sure he was furious with you, but that wouldn't make him kill himself, not after he'd survived his wife's death and Verity's fall. He was a man with great purpose – and that purpose was Verity. I'd bet any amount that what killed Gabriel was, effectively, grief. He loved her, Harry. She was everything.'

The doorbell rang. She stood, and waited for me to do likewise. 'Time's up, Harry.'

She didn't bother picking up the door-phone to find out who it was, just pressed the release button. The machine buzzed, then clicked.

She studied me, lips pursed. 'I'm going to give you some advice, Harry – although I doubt you'll take it.'

She gathered her thoughts for a few moments before continuing. 'You want a reason for Verity's fall that you can live with. You don't care if it's outlandish, implausible, downright impossible, as long as it doesn't involve *you*. She knew you loved her, Harry. And I think she really wanted to respond to that, but she had no idea how to. I was as surprised as you to learn that she had tried to kill herself, but it's no surprise at all to me to know that she was in pain – and I don't think that surprises you either.'

She opened the front door for me. As I passed, she put a hand on my arm. 'This *does* involve you, Harry. It involves everyone she cared for and everyone she loved. So my advice is, *accept it*. Accept that she was who she was. Accept what you feel. Make your peace – and move on.'

Further down the corridor, I heard the lift doors open. A man shuffled past me self-consciously, muttering, 'Good afternoon,' as though it was embarrassing to admit that it might be. He disappeared towards Kate's kitchen.

She gazed at me a few moments longer, a watery, bleak stare. 'Move on, Harry.' Then she closed the door on me.

Two days later, we went to Gabriel's funeral, Sam and I.

I'd rung and grovelled and assured her that, however confused I might be, she was still important to me, and I was sorry. She was reluctant, but she came.

I tried Adam as well. No reply. Rita had no idea where he was, and sounded annoyed about it: he had already missed several important meetings. Given his various misdemeanours, I couldn't be bothered to get too worked up about this: all I felt was irritation and a faint worry.

On the way up, I told Sam about my visit to Kate – not the bit about Verity's hopes and fears, just the bits about Gabriel. Sam was miles away, though, cloud-spotting, perhaps, or hypnotised by the blur of trees and traffic. She was remote, I couldn't reach her. I wasn't sure how hard I wanted to try.

'I could've told you about Gabriel,' she said colourlessly. 'Those two clung to each other like limpets. If she was down, guess where she ran?'

It was true, of course. Verity had always spent weekends with Gabriel whenever life in London was tough, and I knew it. I had known it even while I was convincing myself that Gabriel had done terrible things to her. Verity had loved and trusted Gabriel absolutely. They shared something no one else could ever have touched.

I know now what made me accuse Gabriel. I'm not proud of it, but I do at least understand. He was her protector, I was not. She trusted him, she ran to him, not me. *She doesn't want to see you, Harry.*

I reached over and stroked Sam's leg, wanting reassurance, the comfort of a familiar touch. She didn't respond.

We laid earth on his grave. There were eleven of us: Mum, Sam, me, the vicar, and a handful of villagers who had turned out to make up the numbers.

It was quiet. Even the breeze moved delicately, as though it might disturb us. Between us and the road, invisible in the greenery, a blackbird sang fitfully. Otherwise there was just the priest and the crisp damp sounds of the earth.

Mum clutched a twist of handkerchief to mop her damp mascara; her legs were prim and plump below the hem of an unflattering black dress. Sam stood at a little distance until I reached for her. Cautiously, we held hands.

The earth clattered hollowly on to the coffin. I imagined how the sound of the earth falling would be from inside, echoing in the tiny space, percussive taps and scrapes pulsing through his dead ribs and fingers. There was no pain from those arthritic knuckles now. It seemed to me that he would look like a painting, perfect and expressionless and utterly remote. The black glitter would be gone from his eyes, of course, replaced by a film of ooze from the canal –

he had been found face down, snagged in weeds and used condoms, the water seeping in and out of his mouth like dead breath.

Once the earth was thrown, we left. We had brought two overnight bags so we could stay with Mum but, without even discussing it, we made our apologies, clambered into the car and clattered towards home.

We didn't get far. As we circled Oxford on the ring-road, I muttered an apology to Sam, and turned inwards towards the city. Towards Verity.

Saliva trickled from the corner of her mouth. Her gaze aimed blankly at the zoetrope, and at a clutch of bright daffodils beyond it on the bedside table – I had paid a fortune on my credit card to have them delivered. I crouched beside them now, squarely in her eye-line, and looked at her. She looked at nothing.

Who was going to take responsibility for her now? Me? Not possible. Nurses had to turn her every four hours, day and night. They had to scrape the shit from her sheets, empty her catheter bag, feed the tube that snaked into her nose and down into her stomach. They talked bright nothings to her each morning, opened the nylon curtains that never quite met. Verity had company: what need did she have of family or friends – or love? Fallen, she didn't need Gabriel, and she didn't need me.

For a moment I felt empty. Then I looked at her, and I remembered what emptiness really was.

Gabriel, dead.

Sam leaned in the doorway and watched me; and when my shoulders started shaking, she said, 'Come on, time out.' We went to the visitors' room. As we walked along the corridor, a nurse looked up, smiled, then whisked into Verity's room. I heard the bright tone, but I couldn't make out the words.

The back of my nose filled with salty liquid. I sniffed and swallowed, and blinked as savagely as I could, which seemed to help.

Sam stroked my back.

I tried to say, 'It's just . . .'

She answered, 'Ssssh.'

There was a print on the wall to my left: three narcissi, garishly splayed from a red blob of a pot. Next to it, and low enough for children to look at, was a poster of a stegosaurus, ripped and scrabbled at by crayons and small grubby fingers.

'I don't know what to do,' I said.

Sam had no answers. Instead, she lifted her free hand and rubbed it over my shoulders. 'Sssh,' she said again.

She left me and padded off in search of tissues.

The car. On the way back to London.

'I counted the pictures.'

I drove.

'The zoetrope,' she said. 'Seven.'

'There were eleven cameras. Definitely.'

'Seven pictures now, though.'

'Any idea what's missing?'

'They're all just Verity, twizzling round. It's pretty jerky.'

'It would be. It was jerky even when there were eleven.'

I recalled the strange jolts in the picture that I'd half noticed when I was spinning the zoetrope for Verity in her hospital room, but it wasn't much help: at the time, I had been trying hard *not* to look. I tried to picture the zoetrope's pictures as they had been, shot by shot: scuffed knees, and her grubby cheeks bunched up in a huge grin; her dress about to fly up; her hair lifting behind her, arms up and to the sides. The pictures were all of the same thing – that had been the whole point – so why cut out four photos? What could be different about them? Verity would still be spinning there whether there were eleven pictures of her or just seven . . .

I banged my palm against my forehead and yelled, 'Doh!'

Sam looked at me, puzzled, and slid her hand away from my leg.

'The tree!' I explained. 'Where did the tree go? Shit – what an idiot!'

I felt so stupid. I should have noticed instantly, weeks ago.

'Why get rid of a tree, though?' Sam asked the question as if I might know.

'Maybe she wanted the photos for something else.'

She sniffed philosophically. 'Or maybe she didn't like the look of it.'

'Maybe we'll never know.'

Light drizzle spattered the windscreen, out of a bright grey sky. I flicked on the wipers. They left muddy arcs across the glass, so I switched them off again and let the tiny drops dry in the wind. The sky ahead was darker.

'Thanks, Sam,' I said, much later.

She chuckled. 'What for? Telling you some pictures were missing?'

'For putting up with me. Giving me another chance.'

'Are you feeling all right?' Her eyes were creased with amusement – and suspicion.

I had no idea if I was feeling all right. I had no way to judge what was normal any more. Hour by hour I was swooping from elation to despair, confusion to certainty, and I could trust none of it. One moment I was full of purpose, the next I was paralysed and contemplating the void.

'Sam, I truly don't know,' I said eventually.

Sam thought about that for a long time before replying. Her voice was soft and sad. 'Yeah. Well. Let me know when you do.'

The journey passed in a kind of peaceful sorrow. For me, that was progress. Then we turned on to my street – and Sarah Yates was waiting on my doorstep.

twenty-seven

She had been 'clumsy' again. The left side of her face was swollen and reddish-purple. Her nose was swollen too, and a butterfly stain was spreading across both of her eyes. She squinted at us, and flinched as she stood. She wore a jumper and a pair of jeans that were ripped on the left thigh. Her hands waved around in front of her as though she was trying to shape words with them, but nothing came.

'I didn't know where else to go,' she said unsteadily. One hand touched her puffed-up cheekbone, then fell back to her side.

I pushed open the door and stood back to let her in. Tension tugged at my neck and jaw. I was tired. I wished the world would leave me in peace.

Sam offered her some water – and, diplomatically, made the task of finding a glass and filling it last for about ten minutes. Sarah and I spent all that time in silence. I couldn't find a way to start. Sarah stroked her face endlessly, outlining each new bulge and bruise. She started at sounds from the kitchen, even at things she caught in the corner of her eye – a photograph, a doorframe. Then, when Sam came back with water, Sarah spoke – to her.

'It's over,' she said. 'He, he . . .' Her hand trembled up towards her mouth, then settled round her other hand on the glass. I could see her knuckles going white. I was convinced the glass was about to fracture.

'Where is he, Sarah?' I asked coldly.

Her eyes searched mine, then she turned back to Sam. 'I was scared of him,' she whispered. 'I had to make it stop.' Her lips twitched, forming a stream of half-words. Her eyes were wide and wild.

'*Where's Adam, Sarah?*' I was having trouble staying calm. I struggled to keep my voice low; the intensity, I couldn't prevent.

'He's – I—'

'Harry!' Sam's warning was a growl.

Sarah hunched over her knees and rocked slowly. Her eyes never left mine. They were wide and deep and terrified, and they showed no sign of rational thought at all. 'I *had* to end it,' she whined. 'I had to.' She said it as simply as a child.

End it *how*? Had Adam confronted her as he'd promised? What had happened? I heard Adam's voice – *She's killing me, Harry, I swear.* It was just a turn of phrase, not something anyone would really do . . . Surely? But I had seen her, seen the shards flying, the blood on the floor from her ripped feet, so calm, so full of hate. And it wasn't going to go away. I was going to have to confront it myself.

'What have you done, Sarah?'

This was horrible. Images flooded through me: Adam stabbed and gasping, or his eyes bulging inside a plastic bag wrapped tight at the neck; Sarah at home among her shattered glass and crockery, while private eyes followed Verity, reported her every move; Sarah's hatred; Verity, falling into oblivion . . . Sarah's reaction, so cold. *Oh. What a shame.*

'Oh, Sarah, no . . .' My voice was a whisper, but I could feel each tendon in my neck, and my blood hissed in my ears.

Sarah was frozen, her gaze locked on me. And, looking at her wounded face, I slumped, my tension replaced by miserable certainty. 'Oh, God. It was you . . .' I swallowed a sob, momentarily exhausted. 'Wasn't it Sarah? *Wasn't it?*'

My heart was thumping. Sarah cowered in her seat, hid behind her hands, and shrieked, '*Stop! Stop it!*' She curled up, whimpering.

'*Harry!*' Sam. She threw me a contemptuous glance and sat on the arm of the chair. 'Hey, hey,' she soothed. She stroked Sarah's hair. 'It's OK. You're safe. He's upset, that's all.'

I was drained and unsure of myself. I felt as strange, as dangerous, as Sarah had been the day I went to see her. I'm not good at anger. Frostiness, fine; remoteness, hostility, no problem. Anger? Not really me at all. Now the fury was gone, and its memory disturbed me. Looking at Sarah, I couldn't get Verity out of my head – the bruises, the vulnerability. All I could see was Verity.

'There, see?' Sam said, frowning at me.

Sarah breathed in slowly and faced me. Then she flung away her glass convulsively. It landed intact on the carpet and splashed water on to the wall.

'He's been stealing from me,' Sarah said. She looked desperately at Sam and then at me.

'Oh, for fuck's sake,' I muttered.

Sarah wrenched herself away from Sam and lunged towards me. '*He's been stealing from me!*' she shrieked. Then she stopped dead, and folded back into her chair, each successive sob making her whole body bounce. Sam grimaced at me.

'A hundred and eighty thousand pounds.' Her voice was still congested with tears. She waved her tissue futilely. 'I thought it was only sixty, but it's everything. Granny's estate, everything. How was I supposed to know? Michael deals with all that. And Adam.'

Michael: accountant, broker, brother? Maybe all three. Who cared?

'What happened?' Sam asked.

Sarah shrugged angrily. 'I owned shares, now I don't. Michael sold them. Adam showed me. Signed instruction letters, everything. Money to be paid into a joint account I've never even heard of . . . That *bastard*!' She howled inarticulately. Then, suddenly, she was perfectly still again. She even laughed lightly. 'Of course, that account's closed now. God knows where the money's gone.'

Both of them were looking at me – as though the ball was somehow in my court. If it was, I had no idea how it had got there, or what I was supposed to do with it. 'What do you want, Sarah?' I snapped.

She looked at me like a deer in a gun-sight. Sam glared, her fury with me barely concealed. She had such an immediate affinity with Sarah: I hated it.

'Look, Sarah,' I said bluntly – but, I hoped, more calmly, 'you won't tell us where Adam is. You were talking to Verity on the phone right up to the day she fell – we *know* that. You hated her, we all know that. What are we *supposed* to think, Sarah?'

Instead of answers, I got another dose of the same – *two* shocked expressions, Sam and Sarah both looking at me as though I came from another planet. And I lost it.

'Oh, for God's sake! *Wake up*, the pair of you!' I roared. 'Verity's in hospital! She's a zombie, she might as well be dead. *And there's no fucking reason for her to be there*! And that's *it*, isn't it? She's gone, for good!' I was furious and, in a way, it felt good. '*And you know all about it, Sarah, don't you?*'

The silence swelled.

'*Where's Adam, Sarah?*'

Sarah's glance flicked between Sam and me. She stood, painfully and slowly. 'I shouldn't have come,' she muttered. She made for the door. When she reached it, she turned. 'Oh, and since you asked, Harry, the day your precious little tart Verity tried to kill herself, I was with my parents in Wales. Adam was away, *again*, and I needed some TLC. Also, for your information, I've never met the bitch *or* talked to her on the phone – and I never had the slightest desire to do so. Goodbye, Harry. If *you*'re ever in desperate need, I hope *you* find someone you can count on.'

She limped away, fighting the contortions of her face with each step.

We both listened to her slow progress down the stairs and out of the building.

Sam looked at me with absolute contempt. 'That went well, Harry, don't you think?' she said acidly.

You don't want to know how I looked at her.

In answer, Sam strode into my bedroom. I followed, feeling a little sick. She packed a few things into a plastic bag, slung it over her shoulder and squeezed past me.

'Um . . . Sam?'

I stayed in the doorway, and even though I kept my voice pretty level, I did not sound remotely casual or calm.

She smiled a small smile, and pecked me on the cheek. 'Call me when you've grown up, Harry.'

After the front door closed, I stared around the room we had – occasionally – shared. My room. There was a pair of her knickers on the floor by the bed, and she must have left the box of tampons in the toilet. Somehow I didn't think they'd be enough to lure her back.

I poured myself a drink, put on some music – I don't remember what, but I put it on very, very loud. I sat through a beautiful cool summer evening, watching the light change; sipping and staring, raging at the savage injustice of life. And feeling very empty indeed.

twenty-eight

Towards evening, the walls of my flat became too small for my misery. I trudged to Battersea Park, and walked along promenades of trees with my camera in hand.

Heavy clouds were massing above me, although the sun was still shining. I caught glimpses of a purple-grey sky through the leaves. Heat beat up at me from the Tarmac paths. It was hard to breathe. Rain would have been a relief, even thunder, but none came.

In fact, anything would have been a relief. I had hoped the trees might spark some feeling back into me, but they were drab and textureless. The living arches that had so often inspired me were meaningless shapes against the clouds. The leaves were limp in the heat. A grey-muzzled dog plodded listlessly across the grass towards some shade.

There was nothing for me here – no inspiration, no answers. Verity was gone. She wasn't a puzzle I could solve, she had simply gone. Now there were just memories, a parade of regrets among the stiffly upright trees.

The park ended, and my meanderings took me through heat-deserted streets. The pavement crunched greasily under my shoes.

I was depressed – of course. It must have been building for some time and now, finally, the tide had overwhelmed me. The world looked physically dark to me, it was a black and alien place. If the business of those around me on the streets had a purpose, it was hidden from me.

And then her door was in front of me, her familiar windows above me, the plants on the sills now dried to ragged sticks. Her name was still on the slip next to her bell – *Verity Hadley, Ring twice but* do not *ask for Rosie*, and a little yellow and gold daisy, hand-drawn with a smile and pinprick eyes.

And, finally, I knew what I needed to do. I had an appointment here. This was the place. Here, Verity and I could perhaps be together again, at least for a while.

I wrestled my mobile out of an overtight pocket, and called Sam. While it rang, I rummaged for Verity's keys. Answering-machine. My voice sounded lifeless and flat; I didn't care.

'Sam, it's Harry. Don't delete this. Please, it's important. I want to apologise. There's nothing I can say. I understand what you think about me, and you're right . . .' I found the right key and fumbled it into the lock. 'But, listen, it's all making sense now. I've ended up at Verity's place. I went for a walk and . . . I just got here somehow. And that makes sense. I mean, she's gone, isn't she? So to hell with it. To hell with it all. I wreck everything I touch, and it's all because of me and Verity, and it's taken me all this time to work it out. So what's the point?' I laughed hollowly, headed up the stairs. My voice was too dulled to echo. 'Anyway . . . I suppose I rang to say sorry. Really. I know it doesn't change anything but—'

Then I dropped the phone.

Because the door to Verity's flat was ajar. And there were sounds on the far side of it.

I leaned cautiously towards the open gap. There were soft scrapes and clunks – cupboards, drawers, perhaps. Floorboards creaked, shoes whispered on carpet in a flat that should have been empty. The sounds were brisk, the pace was even. Whoever was in there was busy. I waited, breathing as shallowly as I could manage.

The sounds faded. Probably the interloper had moved down the corridor towards the bedroom. What choice did I have? This was my moment. I wished it hadn't come.

I swept open the door and stepped in. There was the brush of the wood on the carpet, but no creaking hinges or floorboards. I was in.

There are moments that make a photograph in your head. I saw everything in a glance: it was the processing that took time. The flat had been trashed – again. What had been left of the curtains had been torn into strips and lumped in a pile. The sofa had been shredded. In places, the carpet had been completely ripped away; green humps of underlay were scattered through the room.

Floorboards had been pulled up, leaving gashes in the floor, full of joists and insulation and wiring. Cupboards had been flung open, and their contents – which Sam and I had put back so neatly – had been slung into piles. Shelves had been ripped out. Plants had been uprooted from their pots.

And the interloper had not left the room. He was there, squatting near the door to the kitchen, sifting through a slippery pile of paper. His shirt was stained with sweat, his hair was damp and tangled. His tie was loosened and thrown over one shoulder. Behind his thin-rim designer glasses, his eyes were wide and alert. He was looking at me intensely.

'Thank God you're here,' he said, in a rush.

There are no prizes for guessing who it was, I'm afraid; still, I was shocked as hell.

Adam picked up the sheet of paper he had dropped when I appeared, and frowned at it. 'Look at this. I've cracked it. I swear.' He beckoned excitedly.

'What are you doing, Adam?'

'It's all here, Harry!' He slapped the piece of paper with the back of his hand. It looked ordinary – an invoice or a letter, maybe.

As Adam dusted himself down, I picked my way across the room. His eyes were dark and manic. His nostrils were flared and he was breathing heavily. Sweat glossed his face, a milky drop hung from his nose. The air had a salt tang. I hopped over the last curl of rolled-back underlay, negotiated a hole in the floorboards, and took the paper from him.

He gazed at me and smiled. Then he smashed his fist into the side of my head.

The blow lifted me off the ground, and threw me sideways. As I fell, my head and one shoulder snapped down painfully on to the bare floor. I didn't get up, because Adam didn't give me the chance. He kicked me hard in the face. He grunted a little, but his expression remained calm – at least, it did until the moment of impact: after that, I have no idea what he looked like.

Did you know that noses are crunchy? They are when they're kicked. You get a kind of gritty collapse for the first fraction of the strike, as the cartilage crumples, then a dull thump as boot hits bone. There's a bending sensation, then a snap as the fragile bits give way; then a lurch as the main bone breaks – it sort of grinds off sideways, like rubble. Then the impact spreads across your face, heat and pressure through your cheekbones, and your ears start to ring. But it's the rubbly part that stays with you: it's like rolling logs across gravel.

You notice these things. Time slows to treacle – and, later, you play out the memory over and over again.

Adam moved round behind me, and swung his foot savagely at my ribs a couple of times.

There ought to have been pain.

He moved further up my body. His boot connected with the back of my neck, just where it meets the skull – and my already crumbling world shattered into brilliant shards.

twenty-nine

I came to. I didn't groan, or do any of the dramatic stuff you see in films. I just was awake, all of a sudden.

I was on what little remained of Verity's calico sofa, lying on exposed springs. A sharp end dug into my ribs, adding to a list of jabs and thumpings that I couldn't begin to catalogue. Apparently Adam hadn't stopped hitting me just because I was unconscious.

Oddly, none of my injuries hurt too badly; that came later. I was extremely uncomfortable, though: I wriggled, and discovered why. My arms had been pinioned behind me, like a swan's wings, and tied at the elbows. The difference was, a swan's wings were designed to do that and my arms weren't.

As my sight and hearing cleared, I realised Adam was still there. He had started on another box, its innards spilled across what was left of the floor. He muttered to himself as he rummaged under the floorboards for stray papers. Then he noticed I was watching. He stopped what he was doing and looked at me. His eyes were expectant, interested. 'Hey, Harry,' he said brightly.

He came over and kicked me in the balls. Mercifully, my position on the sofa meant he couldn't connect really hard – but it was still hard enough. I retched, and gagged for breath between spasms. 'You're something of a problem, Harry,' he said reflectively. Then he turned back to the papers he had been scanning. He talked to me without looking. 'See, Harry, it's here somewhere. It has to be. If it was at the office, you and Sam would have found it. And there's nothing at Gabriel's, I took his place apart yesterday.' He glanced up at me, and winked. 'Thanks for the messages about him. Very considerate. It let me search the place uninterrupted. Nothing there, though, so it's got to be here, and that cack-handed idiot I hired just missed it.'

He straightened and shook his head mournfully before bending back to his work. 'Can you imagine? Buying the key when he was supposed to be faking a break-in . . . Stupid or what?' He shoved his hands under an edge of floorboard and yanked savagely upwards, yelling, 'Fuck it!'

The board came half loose, and his hands slipped and gashed on the nails. He frowned at his wounds, brows clenched, and his lips bulged forward, like a village idiot trying to make sense of why his hand was bleeding. The pain from his kick had subsided just enough for me to be able to grind out a few words between gasps. 'Adam, what – what are you – What the hell's going on?'

My head wasn't just spinning from the beating he'd given me. For a start, there was the fact that he was obviously alive and healthy, which meant all my suspicions about Sarah had been wrong. I didn't have time to feel guilty about that, though: I was too busy trying to make sense of Adam, in the grip of some strange mania, tearing apart Verity's flat.

'Adam?'

He glanced up at me, then continued, talking to his own ripped palm. 'I've got to believe her, you see – haven't I, Harry? She said she had proof, and she did. She had those tapes . . . Now, *that* was *me* being stupid: I should've watched my mouth while we were talking. But she only ever showed me the copies.'

He chuckled, then bent back to the floorboard, tugging more gently until it screeched and gave way.

'Clever little Verity, eh, Harry? I got the copies, of course. And the tape-player. Sorry I couldn't give it back to you.'

My ears were ringing. Sounds were remote. Even Adam's voice was distant, as though I was listening to someone else listening to him, not hearing him myself. It felt strange – but it was nowhere near as strange as what he was saying.

'You found my walkman?'

It was surreal. Why attack me, then suddenly talk to me about my lost tape-recorder? What was he doing here?

Adam grinned. 'Got the tapes, too – but not the originals. She was right, you know. Those tapes could finish me. But they were just copies. The originals' – he hauled on another board –

'are somewhere' – he jerked it free savagely – '*here* . . .' He peered hopefully into the hole, then turned away and picked his way across the room. He squatted next to the sofa, sharing my view of the destruction. 'There's a whole box of stuff, not just the tapes. She told me. Just before . . . well, *you* know . . . *Evidence*, she called it.' He spat the word out. 'But, surprise surprise, she wouldn't say where.'

He looked at me expectantly. My head was spinning, each breath was still half choking me. I needed to throw up.

And beyond my obvious physical troubles there was a nauseating series of emotions – confusion, horror, uncertainty. Because, horribly, it was all beginning to make sense.

'Verity,' I gasped. 'You – did you—'

He tapped a finger on his lips to silence me. 'And then there's you, Harry,' he said. 'You're evidence too. See, politics, the law, they're tricky, Harry. They're tricky games. Reputation's the key. Got to be squeaky.' He cordially slapped my cheek twice, and left his hand there. It was slippery with his own blood. 'So it's good you came. Because I need your help.'

He slid his hand down my cheek until he had my neck in his grip. He squeezed – experimentally, thoughtfully, pinching on the point just below each ear with a regular beat. My jaw creaked. The pain was excruciating.

'Adam, did you—'

He squeezed harder, cutting off my words. But the *thought* was impossible to stop. *Evidence* . . . That gleam in his eyes.

'We need to work out what I've missed, Harry.' He said it so gently.

He let go of my throat and strode across the room, his gaze flicking around wildly. I watched him, through the pain. My jaw felt as though it had been popped out of its socket. I couldn't move it properly, every attempt was agony. But I had to talk to him. I had to *know*. I had to hear him say it.

Adam was heaving on another floorboard, grunting ferally, getting nowhere.

I struggled to speak. 'It was you, Adam, wasn't it?' My words were slow and uncontrolled. 'She . . . The affair . . . She was going to go public. Blackmail.'

Adam gave up on the floorboard and stared at me.

'The affair?' he said incredulously. 'The *affair*?' He laughed loudly. He bent back to tug at the floorboard, his breath rasping. 'There *wasn't* an affair, Harry – *oufff* – you idiot – *oufff*— You really think I'd – *oufff* – sleep with—' He straightened again, and chuckled. 'Get real, Harry. I just had to think of an explanation when Sarah caught me with her. An affair with Verity Hadley? Not if you paid me.'

'But you said—'

'There *was* no affair, Harry. I just told you.'

I struggled to reply, but he raised a hand to stop me. I fell silent, now utterly confused. He studied me, scratching his head and frowning.

'Did you know, I even thought about killing you? It's true,' he said softly. 'If it hadn't been for you . . .' A shrug. 'Ah, well. Life, eh? I kept thinking maybe I could just shove you under a bus, no one would ever know. And that day at Beachy Head, you were a pretty tempting target. I kept hoping you'd just drop it but, no, Harry the ace detective just had to keep unearthing the most ridiculous excuses to be suspicious.'

His voice was reflective. We could almost have been friends.

He came over again, and hunkered down next to me. I stiffened, anticipating another attack, but he just squatted and stared at me.

'Why did she have to rake it all up again, Harry?' he said eventually. 'It was twenty bloody years ago. I tell you, that psychiatrist has got a lot to answer for. It was all ancient history, no one cared – but go see a psychiatrist, call it a repressed memory, and all of a sudden it's OK to dig everything up again. All of a sudden it's personal, and it's *now*. And there's Verity bloody Hadley swearing she's going to make me suffer, have her pound of flesh.'

I was completely lost, struggling to catch up. There just hadn't been enough time to make sense of the incoherent scraps he was tossing at me. I was also terrified. I was tied up, beaten, and I was listening to a man who had just been discussing the benefits of killing me.

And then there was Verity. The one thing that had filtered through was that it had been Adam. He had thrown her off the cliff. It was him she'd arranged to meet. And the tapes, some kind of a threat to him – but not because of their affair, because that was all a lie: it was because of something that had happened twenty years ago.

She doesn't want to see you, Harry. Not any more.

And, slowly, the truth crept in. The horror.

Adam watched me put it together, and chuckled warmly. 'Hey, Harry, d'you remember what she used to be like at school? She was such a slapper. And you, chasing after her all the time like an abandoned puppy. You had no idea what she was really like. Truth be told, I felt sorry for you.'

He swung his foot. I tensed and closed my eyes – but it was the sofa he kicked, savagely. It was small reassurance. Adam was over the edge. I was in trouble.

With a snarl, he leaped across the room and attacked an already empty cupboard. He ripped off the doors, heaved and stamped at the low shelf that lidded the space. It half cracked, half gave. Plaster tumbled from the edges in a soft, hurried shower. He kicked the shelf loose and flung it away.

'WHERE ARE THEY?' His words were only just short of a scream.

I struggled to focus. He must mean the tapes. The *evidence*.

I tested my jaw. It hurt. But I had to keep him talking, to keep at bay the inarticulate savage in front of me now.

'What was it, Ads? Twenty years ago. What happened?'

But I knew. Memories whirled about me. Gabriel closing the door on me all those years ago; Verity at school, so small and afraid; Adam, bruised and bitter. I knew all right. And even through my fear, the pity of it, the horror, crept into my soul.

'Adam—'

I couldn't have known, Verity, how could I have known? Oh, Verity, I—

'She was using you, Harry,' Adam snapped. He was looking at me, his eyes glittering. 'She used everybody. She knew what she was doing.' He perked up suddenly. 'Hey, that was some beating I got, wasn't it? When I stole that money.' His smile was twisted. His eyes darted round the room. 'And there was Verity, batting her eyelids and pouting and showing a bit of leg whenever she needed to.' He grinned, and it contorted his face into something more like a sneer. 'She was asking for it, Harry. You'd have done it too, believe me. And a bit of a struggle – well, it's all part of the fun, isn't it?'

He ripped at another board, grunting as his back arched to take the strain. He worked one end free, and yanked the board savagely back and forth until it gave. He threw it convulsively towards the open door. He stood motionless, frowning into the hole he'd made, chewing at the inside of his cheeks. He made to move on – then stopped, looking suddenly crumpled.

'I didn't mean to hurt her, Harry,' he said slowly. 'I was ... angry. Or jealous, maybe. Something. I don't remember. I was fourteen. It was twenty years ago.'

He unleashed a wordless howl and kicked the exposed floor joist hard enough to make the whole room shudder. Then he made his way carefully back to the pile of papers he had been hunched over when I arrived. Most of the sheets were charred at the edges: he must have salvaged them from the remains of the sofa. He rummaged through them. Each sheet got a rapid glance, then he tore it in half and tossed it aside.

Words ground out of him, savagely, with each rip. 'So here we are, Harry.' *Rip. Rip.*

He looked at me contemplatively, then left the pile and came over, leaned towards me. Glazed eyes, acid breath. 'I did my best, Harry. I told you to leave it.' He kicked disconsolately at a rolled-over corner of carpet underlay. 'But there's Verity's little box of tricks somewhere. Her *proof.*' He shook his head and laughed at himself. 'She was supposed to tell me where she'd hidden it *before* she went over the cliff. She put up quite a struggle. She's stronger than she looks. I couldn't control her – she just slipped.'

'Adam—'

He rested his arm across my neck. And began to lean. 'And then,' he murmured, 'there's you.'

He watched me intently as he spoke. My eyes bulged. He stared at me for a long few seconds, as my lungs heaved and my back arched and bucked. He released me. He stood and rubbed his forehead absently. It left a sooty smear.

Then he hit me, hard. Dazed, I saw him bound away towards the kitchen.

He hopped through the detritus to the kitchen.

'So now it's you or me, Harry, isn't it?' he called over his shoulder. 'Just like old times at the treehouse.'

He emerged from the kitchen with a knife. A sharp one.

'So here's the deal. You're depressed about Verity. You come to her flat again, looking for answers. You turn the place upside-down –' he spread his arms to indicate the chaos around us '– but there's nothing.'

He set the knife down carefully – then hit me again, on the jaw. While I lolled helplessly, he picked up the knife, bent over me, and sawed me free of whatever he had tied me with. 'Now, don't go getting any ideas,' he warned.

He flipped me over, thumped me on the cheekbone brutally hard, and while I was dazed, he sliced a strip of calico from the front of the sofa, and retied my wrists in front of me. He backed away warily, his eyes alert, his body tense and dripping sweat. He looked like an animal about to pounce. The knife drifted through the air in front of him as though it was alive.

'No ideas at all,' he repeated softly. Then he laughed. 'You do amaze me, Harry. Did you really think that Sarah had been chasing after me with one of *these*?' The chuckles subsided. He watched me carefully, for far too long. 'I'm sorry, Harry,' he murmured. 'Truly.'

I hunched and wriggled until I could drop my legs over the edge of the sofa and sit. It was painful. The exposed springs of the sofa dug into me. My ribs were screaming, my neck was agony. The world was blurred, and splinters of light jagged through my eyes. Finally, I perched on the edge of the sofa, still bound at wrists and ankles, trying to focus on Adam – and, more importantly, on what he had just said, and the knife he was waving.

'I'll miss you, Harry,' he said.

He stepped closer, holding the knife high in front of his face.

And instead of terror, suddenly, it all seemed absurd. I was sick of it all. I was beyond pain and beyond terror. I'd had enough – not of life, I had no desire at all to die, but of the complexity and negotiation, and second-guessing, and being manipulated, of taking others into account all the time.

And so I said, 'Fuck off, Ads.' Thickly. Wearily. Finally.

He fingered his knife.

He seemed about to speak; he closed his mouth and rubbed his temple with the heel of his free hand.

He stepped closer, and set the edge of the knife against my neck. His face was next to mine, his eyes blank, his breathing sharp and shallow. Then he blinked, and focused. He looked at me. And there were tears in his eyes. 'Sorry, Harry,' he whispered.

I didn't close my eyes, I kept staring at him. He pressed on the knife. There was a gritty feeling as it bit and slid, then a warm trickle.

And then he stopped. He threw away the knife in an uncoordinated jerk. It landed somewhere near the door. I stayed very still. He sat next to me on the sofa. 'I don't want you dead, Harry,' he whispered. His voice was thick with exhaustion, and defeat.

He looked at me – and, behind the tears, I saw the same eyes I had seen twenty years before as his father beat him and dragged him away. Adam was terrified, and in pain, and driven by forces that were utterly beyond any control. I looked at him, and saw a small boy, bewildered and battered, sullen and bitter but full of hope for tomorrow. There was no hatred in him, just despair.

'What will you do?' I asked. My head was swimming.

'Plan B.' He shrugged. 'Get out of here. Start again somewhere.'

He hauled himself to his feet, and plodded over to retrieve the knife. I watched him, confused but unmoving. He cut the cloth strips that held my hands and feet. Released, my arms seemed to be trying to float. I tried to rub them, and I found I couldn't move them well enough to manage it. They flopped from side to side like sacks of dough.

'I'll have to tell the police, Ads. You know that.'

'I know.' He blew out his cheeks. 'Can you give me five minutes?'

'I'm not sure.' My voice was clotted and indistinct. My throat felt as though it was clotted with blood.

I was not sure he deserved a head start. If he had wanted to vanish, he could have done it the moment Verity first accosted him.

Adam nodded his understanding, and gazed round the room. 'There's nothing here, is there, Harry? No box with all Verity's clues.'

I squinted at the mess through puffy eyes. 'I think you'd have found it, Ads,' I agreed.

Adam made his way to the telephone, and cut the cord to the handset with the knife. He came back and stood next to me, staring at the door, avoiding my eyes. He chewed his lip.

'She called your name, Harry. Not on the cliffs, at the treehouse.

Screamed it, over and over.' Finally, he met my gaze. 'I'm sorry, Harry,' he whispered. His eyes were red and wounded.

He smashed his fist into the side of my head.

thirty

When I came to, Sam was there.

'Adam,' I croaked. Except my voice didn't work. Each syllable felt like I was trying to force a spiked ball through my windpipe.

'Hi,' she said gently. The word ripped through me. Currents crazed over my belly and arms, lightning tore at my eyeballs. Sam reached and stroked the hair from my forehead.

I passed out.

A lifetime later, I woke again, my eyes pressed closed. 'Adam,' I gasped – a single convulsion, not audible.

Clothing rustled, a chair creaked. 'It's all right, Harry, you're safe,' she said. Her voice was slow and blurred. My nerves screeched as sound brushed over them.

I sank away from sensation, into the velvet pool inside me.

You don't feel good after being beaten half to death. I had three broken ribs, a broken nose, a cracked cheekbone, splintered eye socket, fractured pelvis, and so many deep bruises that it was easier to count the patches between rather the injuries themselves. My cheek and lips were gashed and stitched. One eye was covered in thick bandages and hurt like hell. One arm was strapped, and the other felt like it should be. I was disoriented. My head pounded. My throat was half crushed. My jaw muscles wouldn't work properly: they were numb and unresponsive. When my lips touched, I couldn't feel them: they tingled and felt ten times larger than they could possibly have been. There was a sparkle in the room, the walls were over-bright and they seemed to be moving subtly, as though they were not solid but smoke, held improbably together.

I woke. The curtains were still closed, but there was a flickering strip-light in the room, unbearable green, throbbing.

Sam was there. She sat beside me, held my hand in both of hers and stroked it. She was talking and she was crying. I closed my eyes against the glare, and squeezed her hand. She squeezed back and stopped talking. I heard her sob. Later, there was silence. I opened my eyes. She was there, still holding me, just looking. The light was out, and a warmer glow spread over her from the corridor beyond. She smiled and her eyes glistened. She leaned forwards with her hair brushing my face, and kissed me.

'Adam,' I said. This time, I heard myself speak.

It was morning, grey and early. The nurse was scraping back the curtains. 'Oh! Good *morning*, Harry!' she said merrily, and bustled from the room.

I lay back and watched the dawn crawl across the ceiling. My teeth ached, my cheek throbbed. I couldn't open my eyes properly. My whole body was an immense sprawl of pain. The crisp fibres of the sheets tore at my fingertips, ripped at the roots of my hair.

Sam scuttled in. She looked anxious and uncertain. Her eyes were red and gritty. She saw me and smiled. 'Hey, you,' she said. She sat by the bed and took my hand. I closed my eyes and enjoyed the feel of knowing she was there. 'I thought I'd lost you,' she said. She lifted my hand and kissed it. Pain jolted through me, though I could barely even flinch. She started. 'Oh. Sorry.' She set my hand back down, still folded in hers.

I opened my eyes and glanced at her. Mercifully I didn't have to turn my head, she was just within squinting range. I tried to open my mouth and couldn't: my cheeks were too swollen, and the pressure seared my skin.

She saw and spoke for me. 'Adam.' She nodded. 'We know. He's gone. No sign at all. Bank accounts cleaned out, lock, stock and proverbial. Car abandoned in a gravel-pit, house sold, it's a total mess. The police are on to it, they've notified the airports and the ferry ports. Nothing.'

Something must have shown in my face. 'It's been over a week, Harry. Sorry, but there's no chance, not now.'

She looked at me for a very long time. Then she said gently, 'I thought you weren't coming back, Harry.' She squeezed my hand and a tear dripped on to it. I tried to squeeze back.

I slept.

Sam had saved me – but for all the wrong reasons.

She had got home about ten minutes after I left my phone message. She thought it was a grand farewell – that I had gone to Verity's flat to kill myself. From her perspective, I can see the logic: I had been remote, confused. My moods were swinging unpredictably. I was consumed by losing Verity, I *wanted* there to be a mystery in it. I was sad and desperate and Sam had cut me off.

Ironic, isn't it? Because I'd had no intention whatsoever of killing myself. It hadn't even occurred to me. I was just feeling profoundly sorry for myself, finally ready for grief, perhaps, and maybe that was why my apology to Sam had been truly sincere – at last. Who said growing up had to be easy? I'm glad she misunderstood and came running, though, because I didn't want to die.

She had tried to ring me back – but by then my mobile was half way down the stairs and I had never rung off, so she was stuck at her end with an open but useless line. She rang the police from a phone box, and drove to Verity's flat at lethal speed. She got there moments before the police and found me. The ambulance arrived shortly afterwards.

Of Adam, there was no sign.

They were treating my injuries as attempted murder, which seemed ridiculous to me – and Verity's too, of course, now that it was too late. The detectives explained to me, in charmingly methodical words, that they were also keen to talk with Adam about Serious Crimes in Which He Was Suspected of Substantial Involvement. Then there were the more petty charges: breaking and entering, fraud for some trivial misdemeanour at the council, which I couldn't follow. He was also 'suspected' of grievous assault on Sarah. There were various conspiracy charges for him to answer – and a private detective working under the arches in Hackney had been arrested on suspicion of illegally entering Verity's flat on Adam's instructions.

Sarah's godfather, Michael Antrim, was on bail, charged with false dealing and accounting. Strangely, though, the theft of over two hundred thousand pounds from Sarah (the damage was worse than she had thought) was considered entirely legal: the police were sorry but there was nothing they could do. Likewise, apparently, it was Sarah's responsibility that Adam had taken out a second mortgage of three hundred thousand on the house and defaulted on every payment after the third: that money, too, had vanished, and all the police could say was that there might be another fraud charge to add to the list.

But they would have to catch him first. He had close to half a million pounds in cash, and several very good reasons for making himself scarce. He could be anywhere, the police said helpfully. Interpol had been informed. After initial optimism and knowing nods, the police were now doing a good line in shrugs.

I stayed with Sam while I recovered – in her bed: she slept on the sofa ('Unfinished business,' she said brightly, when I complained that I was now feeling well enough for a little company – and shut the door on me).

One morning, three weeks after the attack, I announced that I was half-way well, and we went to Verity's flat. There were things to do. Verity's landlord was insisting that it was Verity's responsibility to repair the damage to the flat. Sam had weathered countless arguments on the subject, and we'd finally decided that the only sensible way forward was to salvage what we could of Verity's belongings, then leave the landlord to it, let him protest until he was hoarse. He was a belligerent, unpleasant man, preoccupied only with money. The need to let the place again would soon override any further posturing about who was responsible; and in any case, his building insurance would cover it.

The door had been boarded up and an apologetic police officer with a jemmy had to force it open, one last time. They had thoughtfully tidied the debris into a few large mounds. The furniture had been straightened: chairs and tables now stood back on their legs, a couple of stools from the kitchen had been placed neatly against the wall in the living room. What remained of the sofa had been removed. We wandered round the flat as though it was a museum. It smelt strange – not dusty but unlived-in. The photos that had been on the wall now lay in ranks along the dining-table, glass shards over dead black and white eyes; a row of children with their tongues out, one grinning for no reason. My dried blood was smeared darkly on the floor.

Sam wandered into the kitchen to gaze at the gutted cupboards and neat piles of crockery. I stayed in the ravaged remains of the living room.

The drinks table Verity loved and everyone else hated had been set upright, a tiny round top, a twined metal stem and three unstable feet at the bottom. The answering-machine had been returned to its usual precarious perch atop it – the one piece of rearrangement that the police had got right, pointlessly ornamental in a chaotic waste. They had even placed the phone's severed handset neatly in place. The machine's message light was flashing five, and idly I hit the play button. The machine clunked, spooled some tape, clunked again, paused, clunked (just how many clunks does it take to play a tape? Clearly the machine's manufacturers had decided to be generous, just to be safe).

It began to play – voices familiar from the day after the break-in: 'Verity, dear, it's Erica . . .' *clunk*; me, muttering, 'Where were you?' *clunk*; someone who had rung off without leaving a message, *clunk*; Erica again . . . and the last message, a new one, but an old voice, frail and distant.

'Verity? Darling, it's Erica. Erica McKelvie at number twelve. Darling, it's been *weeks*. I've been so worried. There's a charming man across the road who's collecting my pension – Sylvia's son, lovely man – and Vera's been going to the library for me, but if you can't find the time to help any more, *could* you ring and tell me, darling? Please? It's embarrassing, asking people.' There was a pause, and a rattle as the receiver went down – almost. Then she spoke again, in an even more martyred tone: 'And you'll want your things back. They're exactly where you left them, I haven't touched them. But if I shan't be seeing you . . .'

Then, with no goodbye, there was a click. The machine clunked a few times, and was silent.

I looked up. Sam was in the doorway to the kitchen, staring at

the machine. We gazed at each other. Then, without a word, we left
to find Erica McKelvie who lived at number twelve.

Erica was hard work. She wanted to make sure we knew how
difficult life was at her age, with her arthritis troubling her and
most of her friends dead. I didn't doubt it was difficult – but
surely it wasn't necessary to remind us of it every third sentence?
Eventually, we dispensed with the explanations and introductions,
and even with the endless commiserations about the terrible
problem of her legs.

She fetched the box Verity had left with her. She held it on her
lap and continued her monologue. We eyed the box and fidgeted
uncomfortably.

'She was such a darling,' Erica croaked. 'Came twice a week.
Pension, shopping, nothing was too much trouble. And such *fun*.
She was an energetic young thing.' She looked at us conspiratorially. Her eyes were filmy, and I saw that behind Erica's selfishness
lay desperate loneliness. 'Do you know?' Erica whispered loudly.
'Some of the things she told me quite made me blush. And I
thought *I'd* lived the high life!' She laughed throatily, and slapped
the top of the box with the slow deliberation her gnarled fingers
demanded.

It was a miniature treasure chest, less than a foot long, perhaps
six inches deep and the same high, with a domed veneer lid, and a
brass hasp with a tiny keyhole. Breaking it open would be easy.
Sam, however, had different ideas. She groped around in her bag,
still paying full attention to Erica – who didn't seem to care if we
listened, just as long as we were there – and pulled out a bunch of
keys, mine, which she still had so that she could look after my flat.

'Poor Verity, how terrible,' Erica burbled, as though Verity's fall
was a piece of gossip. She was relishing the horror. 'She was so
charming. A cheery soul, yes. Thoughtful. Helpful. Always did my
pension and the shopping. Never a bad word. I'm sure Sylvia's boy
– I think it's Martin, I never can remember, charming man – I'm
sure he doesn't *mind* doing it. But, yes, yes, I'll miss her, definitely.'

Sam was swinging the bunch of keys distractingly in the corner
of my eyeline. It was deliberate: she wanted me to look. I was
puzzled – and then, suddenly, I saw. She was dangling the bunch

from a single key: it was tiny, brass, and hollow-centred – the kind of key you might use to lock a drawer . . .

We took the box to Sam's, and sat with it on the table between us, until Sam shoved the keys over to me, and waited.

The key fitted.

It was a sewing-box – cotton reels and little cards with needles threaded through them, shreds of cloth, strips of foam, pinking shears. The inside was sectioned into small compartments, but stuff flowed between them without restraint; there was no pattern to it.

Sam obviously knew more about sewing-boxes than I did, because at that point I'd have given up. She slid her fingertips down the inside edges, and gradually pulled the whole thing upwards. It was a tray, set inside the box. Cotton reels spilled over, then the whole thing came free.

Beneath, in the bottom of the box, there were two audio cassettes and a manila envelope. Inside the envelope were four photographs mounted in a row on a thin strip of card, and a cheque. I stared at the photos. Sam picked up the cheque. 'Cash. Twenty thousand pounds.' She whistled.

'Who's it from?' I asked. The photos were absorbing me. Verity, the tree . . .

'Can't make out the signature. The account's Wandsworth Offshore Enterprises.'

'It'll be Adam's,' I said dully. 'His little stash. He must have tried to buy her off. So she kept the cheque as proof.'

Sam leaned over my shoulder to kiss me, and I groaned as one of my ribs grated. 'Oh. Sorry.' She kissed my neck instead. 'What about the photos?'

'The zoetrope.'

Verity in mid-air, caught from the side and behind, her hair flying, her legs kicked up, and beyond her the huge trunk of the hornbeam. My memory filled in the missing angles. She was screaming happily, her dress was bunched; skinny gold legs, her teeth glowing white in the failing light. Four photos.

'Eight, nine, ten, eleven,' Sam said.

And, at last, I knew why she had cut them out. It wasn't the tree, it was what hid behind it. In one shot, a crouched back and legs were visible. In the other three shots, on the other side of the tree, there was a face. It peeped out alertly at her. Glasses, thickish lips, wide blue eyes, a certain slyness that had seemed quite natural at the time. The face suggested nothing: it was as frozen as a cat staring at a bird. The gaze was beady and expectant.

She was asking for it, Harry. You'd have done it too.

No, Adam. No, I wouldn't.

'I think I'd like to lie down now,' I mumbled. I put the tapes and photos back in the box, and locked it.

Sam held me as I lay. She stroked my hair and said nothing.

thirty-one

Regret.

Is there a moment in a life, a single point around which everything turns? A glance, or a word, a person, a landscape, a proposition? Was there a moment when it all could have changed, when the outcome could have been different, our world transformed?

You can never know. Because what's done is done. What's lost is lost.

It was perhaps a month before she fell.

Jim's had had the usual crowd. There had been three men at the bar with cement-blunt fingers curled round their pints, there had been a couple of pinstriped idiots trying to drown the overloud music with their laughter. And there had been me, and Verity.

It was early summer, slightly chilly. The door to the street was open, admitting the bright grey light of early evening. Not many cars passed; when one did, you could hear the thump of its stereo even over the music. The air smelt of grass and traffic.

We had our usual small round table, its uneven top slopped with condensation and beer. Verity was scraping the puddles around with a beer mat, marshalling them and blotting them up. It was my fourth pint. Verity was on her third tequila but had two glasses of Pils waiting in the queue. We weren't far off the swift-piss-then-off-to-a-restaurant phase, but it looked like tonight we might not get that far.

I was miserable. The night before, a girl had tried to seduce me, a girl I didn't fancy. And after three and a half pints with Verity, it seemed to me that this was the story of my life.

'It's never exactly right, is it, Verity?' I mumbled. I grabbed my pint and created another spillage for Verity to mop up. 'They fancy *you*, so you don't fancy *them*, or you fancy *them* . . .'

'Oh, come on, Harry, it could be worse.' She stroked the back of my not-drinking hand where it lay between puddles on the table.

Above the pub's benches there were etched windows; above those, the glass was leaded and stained. The glass leaves of a vine wove their way round the edge of the ceiling, sharp green against watery yellow. As the twilight became paler, the colours faded.

The song changed. Verity stood without asking and bought another round. I raised my glass to her, and handed her a fresh beer mat from the neighbouring table to chase any new spills.

'I'm serious,' I said, after my first gulp. She knocked back half of one of her Pils chasers, then nursed her new tequila.

She was lovely. Her eyes were wide and attentive, her skin brown, delicately stretched over her cheeks. I could see a faint crease of tiredness beneath her eyes, but her smile was as wide, her teeth as bright as ever. She glowed. She always had.

'Thanks, Verity,' I said, 'for being there.'

'Hey,' she said, and spread her arms. 'How could I miss a date with a hunk like you?'

I sniggered for her, but I felt a lurch of emptiness. 'Seriously . . .'

'I *am* serious,' Verity said, nettled. She stroked my hand again. 'You're the biz, Harry. *Anyone* would have you.'

Her breasts were small under the sheer silk of her blouse, upturned, sharp-pointed. Lower, near her waistband, in the gap between two buttons, the blouse gaped a few millimetres, and I could see the sunken shadow of her belly button.

Time passed.

I stood to get another round. Somewhere, in the last ten minutes, the idea of finding a restaurant had begun to recede: it was already nine thirty, so what was the point? 'Yeah,' I said, wagging my finger again. 'But I want someone to *love* me.' I headed for the bar.

I stood next to the three silent wise men and ordered a Kronenbourg, a tequila and – I looked at Verity over my shoulder: best to forget the Pils. Jim nodded, then disappeared to talk to someone else who had just walked in. Rounds in Jim's took time. On the frosted panes beneath the tree motif, the glass was turning rosy. There were old black and white photos on the walls: long-gone people standing, gaunt, in stiff rows outside vanished buildings. 'There you go, mate, Kronenbourg, tequila.' I shoved a fiver at him. It was hard to make out the pictures in the twilight. I carried the drinks back.

I scraped at the puddles with a beer mat of my own, then gave up and turned it end to end to end between my forefinger and thumb.

'It'll happen,' she said.

'What will?'

'Love. You'll see.'

'Yeah.' I laughed bitterly. I drew rays of liquid outwards from the pool.

The pinstripes left. Another song.

'Yeah,' she said. 'It will.' She reached over, and stilled my hand from fiddling. She gripped it and shook it until I looked at her. Her eyes were glossy pools. '*I* love you, Harry.' She bit her lip softly. She looked strangely fragile.

I held my breath. I could feel each ridge of her fingers. Her thumb brushed against the back of my hand, softly, persistently. I knew the perfume I would smell if I raised it to my face – woodscent and leaves and olives – smooth skin and the finest hairs, gold and faint and all but invisible, to brush against my lips. She squeezed. I stared at the table. My back ached from holding myself still.

Because I couldn't move, not ever. I was frozen, suspended between hope and nothingness. The words she so often said but never really meant, because she *couldn't* mean them, because she never had. *Be home soon, Harry. Not with you, Harry.* I was adrift in memories, the endless game, Verity drawing me in, Verity dancing away. The misery.

Not *you*, Harry. Never you.

She searched my face, then dropped her eyes to the table. And after a while she stopped stroking my hand and she just held it. 'I love you, Harry,' she said again, softly, simply. 'Really.'

Her voice, so scared. And me, so still. So cold and so alone.

'I do, Harry,' she said.

Her eyes were wide and afraid. Her blouse was falling slightly away. Her skin . . .

I was transfixed, terrified.

'Um, yeah . . .' she said.

She squeezed my hand again, then pulled hers back to her drink.

We sat. After a while, she sniffed, then fussed and busied herself over her bag, made a show of looking at her watch. 'Yeah . . .' she said again. Her voice was uncertain and fragile. She hovered, and patted my hand again, unconvincingly. And she gathered her things, sniffing hard. And she left.

I stayed: one hand curled round a forgotten pint, the other frozen where she had touched it.

The thin smell of the city drifted in from the open door. I watched as rising shadows sucked the light from the stained-glass leaves, and the old staring pictures on the walls faded into the dark. Jim began drying glasses and straightening the copper slop trays on the bar. He glanced at his watch, and at me. Then he pursed his lips sorrowfully, and rang the bell for time.

thirty-two

Time passes – and you find you can never forget, that everything that's past will stay with you always. Verity will always be there in her hospital bed, and she will always be there in my memories. Nothing will change; nothing can.

I knew that I would keep visiting her until both of us grew old. Her face would sag a little further every year, her perfect skin would loosen and crease. And one day, she would finally be gone, or I would be. But until then, she was part of me, just as she always had been.

But there had to be a first time. A time when I told her that I knew, that finally I understood. I would keep seeing her until old age made it impossible – but still, I had to say goodbye.

It took me months. I knew it would be hard, and there was no hurry – so the time slid by. Eventually Sam shoved me into her car and drove me there herself. We said nothing on the journey, and when we got there, we sat silently for minutes. Then she said, 'I'll park, see you in there. Go on.'

Autumn had come early. The trees were nipped by a cold mist. A few muffled people drifted along the streets like uncertain ghosts. The brick front of the hospital radiated cold as I approached.

Verity hadn't changed, of course. Her eyes were fixed on the door, and when I walked in, they stayed fixed on it. Her gaze didn't follow me as I edged round her bed.

The sheet below her chin was damp with drool. Her mouth drooped and the flesh sagged off her face like half-set plaster. A bag filled with something thick and beige fed the tube into her nose. Another tube emerged from her gown at waist-level, and led to a catheter bag slung from a bed rail. Her knees were bent comfortably. Her hands lay lightly near her head. She didn't blink.

'Hey, gorgeous,' I said softly. 'I haven't been for a while, sorry. Still, you know why.' I laughed quietly at myself. 'Well, no. You don't, do you?'

I sat for a while, until I could trust my voice. I tried not to let her hear me sniffing.

'Ah, yeah. Yeah, so ...'

And I paused again.

On the far side of her bed was the zoetrope. The two cut ends were crudely stapled together. I was amazed I hadn't spotted it earlier but, then, perhaps we only see what we look for. I wondered if I should spin it for her – one last time, perhaps – or whether I should take it away. It was no use to her.

I spun it: a broken, partial Verity, spinning in the air.

But it's just *stuff*, isn't it? It's a ring of card on a melamine bedside table in a hospital in Oxford, next to a vegetative patient staring at a wall. I decided to leave it: let it travel with her wherever she goes. I sometimes imagine her in a home, as healed as she will ever be – perhaps *sitting* staring, instead of lying, or being wheeled around to stare at different walls occasionally, trolleyed from place to place, with all her tubes. Verity gradually growing old, always silent, always not really there – and a strange circle of photos by her bed. Perhaps the nurses spin it for her every night, but none of them knows what it is, or that the girl in the picture is the same girl who sits beside it gaping at nothing. The girl in leaflight and faded yellow. The girl in the middle of the air.

I leaned forward and rested my hand over hers. It was limp, unresisting, and a little too warm.

'Adam told me, Verity,' I whispered. 'He told me everything.'

I tried to imagine that she could hear me – that, even after so many years, the words might be some comfort, she would understand that she didn't need to be alone any more.

'Verity, he said you screamed—' And I had to stop, my throat heaving too much for me to speak, blinking sharply and failing to squeeze away the tears. 'Ah ... Screamed ... For me. Said you were screaming for me. I would've – Verity, if I'd—'

My body was shaking. Her limp hand jiggled under mine.

I never heard you, Verity. Not in twenty years of listening.

You never told me, and I never knew.

'She showed your collection, Verity,' I said at last. 'Sam did. In London. We missed Paris. Anyway, Sam said it was good therapy for her. She suddenly came over all grim, and just went for it. She didn't even put her own stuff in. She did it right for you, Verity. The plastic bags, the scars and bruises, they all looked half starved.' I laughed aloud and, strangely, it felt good. 'Tell you what, though, gorgeous: it bombed. Not a single review. Sam thought that was really funny. I mean, all these critics ponce around trying to make out that fashion's deadly serious – and then someone *does* something serious and they don't even spot it.'

I didn't tell her the next bit, the bit about me and Sam. Perhaps I didn't know what to say. We were close. Sometimes we were lovers, and I liked that, and I think she did too. But I didn't know what I wanted.

And Sam wouldn't wait much longer. After the fiasco of Verity's collection in London, her career had taken off. She said she had Verity to thank, because when 'Damaged Goods' sank without a trace, she'd realised that fashion was bullshit. She stopped taking it seriously, started playing the game. And she's a good game-player, Sam.

'I don't know what to do, Verity,' I muttered.

I was proud of Sam; I liked her. But I wasn't sure that there was any more to it than that – and did there have to be more anyway? You can't banish ghosts that easily.

But that was what Sam had brought me here to do.

My lips brushed Verity's ear, and the sharp stubble where the surgeon had cut away part of her skull. I breathed in – and smelt nothing but skin scrubbed raw by sterile soap.

'I've come to say goodbye, Verity.' I whispered. 'Sort of goodbye, anyway. I'll miss you.'

I leaned over her and kissed her lips, for the first time in twenty years.

I reached over her and spun the zoetrope. It ticked round, too far away for me to see the detail: the lonely girl who moved in next door, in mid-leap, screaming, the girl I would never see again.

I said, at long last, 'I'll keep coming to see you. I promise I won't forget you. Never.'

I stroked her hair, bent again to kissed her unresisting face.

And I searched for something in her expression, some flicker of where she had gone. But her eyes were locked on the door, and whatever lay beyond.